ONE PILL MAKES YOU SMALL...

Hecate turned to her pulsing green globe. "Take them! Take them all! *Do what I tell you!*"

Instead, the overhead beams fixed on her. There was a cliff's-edge moment of silence, then the Cepheid was on the move, homing in.

Hecate tried to fly from the globe but it enveloped her, then zoomed off among the terraced flow-forms of instrumentation. Floyt, Alacrity, and Paloma Sudan watched it go, none of them saying a word.

Suddenly the whole system blazed to life again—above, around, and even underfoot, as sections of the floor shone. Then Hecate's instrumentality began to *ungrow*.

"It's folding in on itself!" Alacrity roared. "It's rabbit-holing, to go someplace else!"

Floyt looked stricken. "Alacrity, *it* may be able to do that, but that's just one of those tricks I never learned!"

By Brian Daley
Published by Ballantine Books:

THE DOOMFARERS OF CORAMONDE
THE STARFOLLOWERS OF CORAMONDE

A TAPESTRY OF MAGICS

HAN SOLO AND THE LOST LEGACY
HAN SOLO AT STAR'S END
HAN SOLO'S REVENGE

TRON

REQUIEM FOR A RULER OF WORLDS
JINX ON A TERRAN INHERITANCE
FALL OF THE WHITE SHIP AVATAR

FALL

of the

WHITE SHIP AVATAR

A Hobart Floyt–Alacrity Fitzhugh Adventure

Brian Daley

A Del Rey Book

BALLANTINE BOOKS • NEW YORK

This tenth, as the first, for
Judy-Lynn Del Rey

My thanks to L. Neil Smith, Vivian Waters, and Suezy Kim
for their counsel.

CONTENTS

CHAPTER 1

IT'S ALWAYS DARKEST BEFORE THE BLACKOUT

FLOYT SIGHED. "WE'RE JUST GOING TO HAVE TO GIVE UP wine, women, and song, Alacrity."

"I vote we start with song."

As he and Alacrity Fitzhugh made their way to the customs counter in the odd, crane-mating dance of lunar walking, Floyt persisted. "But we're not going to get very far with so little money, you do realize that, don't you?"

"We sure as *scheisse* can't turn back," Alacrity pointed out. Off to one side, the crew chief of the Terra–Luna shuttle *Mindframe* was turning over Floyt's Webley revolver and Alacrity's big energy handgun to a customs inspector.

"Name?" asked the senior inspector, looking Alacrity square in the eye. His nameplate said he was Inspector Grissom.

You oughta remember! Alacrity thought at him silently. *You got a big enough bribe out of me last time we blew through here!*

Floyt, standing behind Alacrity, tried to maintain a certain aloofness and not look worried, guilty, or pursued. He was 175 centimeters tall and a shade more, compact and bearded and more than twenty centimeters under Alacrity's height.

The shuttle crew was passed through without so much

1

as a perfunctory check, but the two weapons still lay on
the counter. If the Lunie customs folks didn't recognize
Alacrity, they'd doubtless recall the Captain's Sidearm,
his pistol. The crewchief and his mates were happy; the
squeeze Alacrity'd paid them for helping Floyt and himself escape Earth was more than healthy, and tendered in
flawless novaseed gemstones. The two partners in adversity weren't simply in reduced circumstances; they
were just about broke.

"I said, 'Name?'" Grissom repeated tightly.

"Dr. Attila Von Cribdeath," Alacrity snapped.

"Professor Manglewords MaLarkey," Floyt supplied,
deadpan, trying to stay in form with Alacrity, but de-
spairing. The formerly sedate, law-abiding Earther
hadn't nearly as much experience fibbing as his young
friend, or in fraud, unlawful flight to avoid prosecution,
and impersonating an innocent party, but the last few
months had been an accelerated course of study.

The customs inspector gave them a gimlet stare.
"Let's just see your documentation, please." Customs
officers were watching, as were two guards who were
rocking back and forth and swinging their nunchaka nonchalantly.

Floyt tried not to feel panic. It wasn't the tightest spot
his young companion had gotten him into. Still, as a
former Earthservice functionary, Floyt dreaded and
feared bureaucracy. More, it couldn't be much longer
before their hasty escape from Terra was noticed. A
message to the Lunar authorities calling for their detention was a disaster not to be contemplated.

"Yeah, y'see, we're applying as undocumented per-
sons," Alacrity announced.

Which was ridiculous right on the face of it and had
the guards hooking their thumbs over their pistols, since
Alacrity and Floyt had just come up from Earth, where
every action—and particularly travel—was attended by
endless red tape.

Except that, in their case, it was true. They'd landed
on Terra under fire in an outlawed spacecraft, stayed

long enough to help bring down the Earthservice government and shake the foundations of worlds human and nonhuman across known space, then taken flight with very little forethought.

"Well,"—Inspector Grissom grinned—"this looks like it's going to take a little paperwork, eh?"

When Alacrity nodded emphatically, the man gave the other customs officials the eye. They made sure no one else was around to interrupt. The two guards wandered off so as not to take notice of what was about to happen. They'd get their cut later.

God bless Lunar flexibility, Floyt implored. Grissom turned out to be very understanding that Dr. Von Cribdeath and Prof. MaLarkey came from a place with no formal travel documentation, a world Alacrity specified as Sweet Baby's Arms, which might or might not exist. The fact that Alacrity was dressed in the outfit of a breakabout—a working interstellar spacer—and Floyt wore an ancient-style Terran tuxedo, white tie with black tails, didn't seem to shake the inspector's faith in them one whit.

Until, that is, Alacrity, leaning across the counter and speaking privily, could produce only a few dozen ovals and a handful of Spican ducats, plus small-denomination odds and ends.

Customs inspector Grissom then frowned. "Are you being cute, boys?"

"*Uh*-uh! We can get you more," Floyt heard Alacrity murmur as the other officials pressed closer.

"Good," Grissom said. "You can wait right here in the holding pen while somebody fetches it on down." A woman inspector had her finger close to a call-button, ready to summon back the guards. Floyt's gut suddenly tightened. He knew Alacrity would do just about anything to avoid being dragged back to Earth, but Floyt wasn't sure he was really up to dodging, dashing, and fighting his way through Lunar customs, and was painfully aware that Alacrity rarely consulted him on such matters before throwing the first punch.

"Well, it's not exactly like that," Alacrity admitted, and Floyt saw him casually glance to the inspector who held the guns. Floyt found his heart beating very fast. The man was some distance away and, moreover, had the two pistols. Alacrity's had been called a "dinosaur gun," while Floyt's Webley was loaded with Chicago Popcorn, dum-dums notched all the way down to the case mouths.

"But it'll really be worth your while," Alacrity maintained. "Believe me, it will; you know me. Look, we'll go get it for you, be back inside an hour, and you can hang onto our guns."

Grissom considered that for a moment. The reproduction Webley and the Captain's Sidearm—passed down from Alacrity's father—were plainly valuable, but the inspector had several coworkers and a couple of guards to satisfy, and maybe a superior or two to grease.

Alacrity saw him thinking it through and about to discard it. He turned to Floyt. "Ho, gimme your Inheritor's belt."

Floyt hesitated for a moment, then unclasped the Inheritor's belt from around his middle. It was a heavy ring of red-gold plaques. He and Alacrity had chanced across light-years to claim it and the inheritance it represented, becoming friends in the doing, through hardship, misery, and intermittent glory, after starting out as near enemies. The belt meant a lot to Floyt and had a much higher value than its intrinsic worth, if the two could get to the right spot to use it, since it gave Floyt the prerogative of asking favors of other Inheritors.

But it was useless if they were detained at customs and dragged back to Earth. Floyt set it on the counter, the plaques chiming.

They saw from Grissom's face that it was nearly a deal, but it was quite a chance that the Inspector was taking. "Tell you what, men: one of you stays, the other goes and gets the rest of the money. That's all I can do for you."

How long can it be before the Terrans raise the howl?
Alacrity agonized. They were on borrowed time already.

Earthservice had dragooned him into shepherding
Floyt across interstellar space, costing him months of
irreplaceable time, just as he was about to embark on the
mission that centered his life. To achieve his purpose
was worth any risk to him; to be chanceried on Earth
would be ruin, worse than death. Without seeming to, he
took a fix on the customs man with the handguns, getting
ready to move.

"Umm, does anyone have something I can read while
I'm waiting?" Floyt solicited, setting himself between
Alacrity and the guns to forestall any rash moves.

"I'll stay," he added to the gangly Alacrity, whose
mouth was slack. "After all, you have a few details to
look after. *But don't dawdle.*"

Alacrity understood what he meant: *keep going and
don't look back.* Floyt was saying farewell.

Just then a comset birred. One of the inspectors
leaned to a hush-speaker while Grissom got ready to take
an identity affidavit from Alacrity and issue him a temporary visa.

"Chief? Word from upstairs," the comset-answerer
said. "They got a twix from Terra, an all-points for two
guys named Alacrity Fitzhugh and Hobart Floyt."

The inspector with the guns held Alacrity's on them.
Another grabbed the Webley and leveled it. The woman
with her finger by the summoner waited for word to
touch it.

"I'll stay," Floyt told Grissom again. "And the pistols
and the belt . . . they're yours."

Alacrity wanted to scram the idea, at the same time
feeling a desperate hope, the opening of a bolthole. The
purpose he'd set himself in life was so much more crucial
than any Grail that he compressed his breath to a silence, face burning with shame, but praying and hoping
he'd be free to go.

"Which one're you? Damon or Pythias?" Grissom

asked Floyt with a facial twist. The place was silent for an attenuated, white-hot moment.

Then Grissom turned to an underling. "Tell upstairs we got nobody by those names offa *Mindframe*. Just a coupla undocumenteds from Sweet Baby's Arms off one of the O'Neill runs, filling out affidavits."

As that was relayed, Grissom smirked at the dumbfounded duo. "You're *them*, huh? The ones who broke the news about that Camarilla thing and shittubed the Earthservice? And got the Spicans and Srillans cleaning house too?"

Alacrity cleared his throat. "That'd be us," he owned up, with nothing to lose.

"Mm-hmmm." Grissom nodded. "Y'don't either of you look like the covers of those books about you."

Floyt coughed on the back of his hand. "Those are really just a very embarrassing mistake, those books." He smiled.

"I'm not surprised," Grissom drawled, motioning to his assistants and handing Floyt's belt back to him. Thunderstruck, Floyt and Alacrity accepted their weapons.

"Y'know, I never did like Earthservice, or those Spican bankers either," Grissom went on. He shoved the little handful of cash back across the counter at them. "And with things freeing up on Terra, Luna's looking way up there in the pilot's chair these days. So let's just say this one's on the Moon, all right?"

Five minutes later, Floyt and Alacrity were standing once again in the vast rotunda called Billingsgate Circus, a honky-tonk commotion of dives, drug dens, casinos, and the rest that went with starportside life. The kaleidoscope of holosigns and lightshapes reminded Floyt of a trove of garish costume jewelry.

The place was four times as busy as the last time they'd been there, even more clogged with robobarrowboys, even more choked with thronging out-systemers.

Nearby sauntered a young hetero couple from

Ashram, that unfailingly pacific world. They flaunted the distressing "Shock-Trauma" look, complete with synthetic lacerations and compound fractures, sucking chest wounds and other horrible injuries. Instead of pain, the boy and girl showed hostile condescension. A little farther along came a young woman in silver lace domino, dressed in a wandering boa of rolled, silver-taupe fabric bound with intricately knotted silver twine, giving off a delightful fragrance they could smell from ten paces. Her lovely haunch bore the membership brand of the very militant Professional Chessplayers' Guild.

Alacrity and Floyt had temporary visas in their chosen aliases and permits for the guns. Alacrity wore his in a hip holster on a reddish-brown leather Sam Browne belt that also carried pouches and cases of various sizes and shapes; Floyt carried the Webley in a shoulder holster under his tail coat. They'd tucked the Inheritor's belt into Alacrity's warbag; a token from the late Director Weir might attract attention.

Alacrity drew out the shoulder straps of his warbag, adjusted them, converting it into a backpack, and made sure his umbrella was secure. "Listen, Ho, about what happened back there—"

"*Fap*; if we start trying to figure out who's done more for whom at this point, we'll only drive ourselves rammy." Floyt gazed around Billingsgate Circus as if he'd put it out of his mind, but he was actually feeling pretty damn good about himself. "What now?"

"What I'd really like to do is start panhandling, but the Lunie cops're nobody to cross."

Floyt looked about. "Do you think they're after us? They and whom else?"

Alacrity shook his head. "I doubt Luna's been alerted, since Grissom cut our leashes, but we can figure on Langstretch operatives being on the prowl. And if there aren't a lot of Camarilla *members* looking to get even with us, then beer is rainwater and we should all go live in the gutters."

Floyt fingered his neat, graying, close-cropped beard.

"Do you think we can make it across Billingsgate Circus, much less out to the Sockwallet lashup? Um, you *were* thinking of asking the Foragers for sanctuary, weren't you?"

Alacrity's worried look made way for a quick grin. "Oh, you're fast today. Yeah."

"Don't some of those robohucksters over there sell clothes, as I recall?" Floyt asked. "And last time we were through here, there were vending machines that dispensed disguises, weren't there?"

Alacrity was shaking his head, his silver-in-gray banner of hair rippling. "Those're cheap dressup for people who are fooling around on the side or playing masquerade or kids out for some grabass. No, a little finesse, here. First, we tour the transport system."

They set off, not such an odd duo in the hodgepodge of Billingsgate Circus.

On the way, the two passed a data kiosk with a rack of current best-sellers on display. Conspicuous among these were *Hobart Floyt and Alacrity Fitzhugh in the Castle of the Death Addicts* and *Hobart Floyt and Alacrity Fitzhugh Challenge the Amazon Slave Women of the Supernova*. Since the title characters as portrayed in the ad loops resembled astoundingly rugged and handsome male models much more than they did the real items, the books' popularity had been a minor problem thus far. Floyt had read them and found his fictionalized adventures much more enjoyable and happy-go-lucky and less pestiferous and terrifying than the authentic versions.

A major part of their remaining funds got them two five-hour transit passes, and Alacrity snagged a guidemap. For the next twenty minutes they alternated between riding the tubeways, ascending and descending by carrier chute, and kangaroo-shuffling along pedestrian tracks.

Alacrity kept surveillance on the people and other beings around them, following a convoluted route, doubling back twice. Floyt monitored faces too, trying to pick out any tails.

In a coin-operated vicebooth near Plasm Dealers' Row, Floyt shrugged out of his tux jacket and removed his vest, white tie, and wing collar, all of which went into Alacrity's warbag. Floyt drew on a disposable smock bought from a vending machine along the way; all his other clothes were back on Earth. They left through a different door, and couldn't see anyone following, though that was no guarantee; with decent communications and even middling organization, it would be possible to follow them with never the same tail in view more than once—or for very long. Similarly, they'd examined themselves for a bug or homer, though they lacked the equipment for a proper sweep.

They grabbed an empty tubeway capsule out in the direction of Hubble City. Alacrity leaned his head back for a moment, closing his eyes. "You've been a real pal, not asking a lot of questions about where we go from Luna, Ho."

"Been a goddamn *prince*!"

They both laughed tiredly. "Anyway, I'll fill you in as soon as we're someplace secure," Alacrity promised. "It was nothing I could talk about on Earth because—well, you had the picture."

True enough. Their spectacular return to Terra had Citizen Ash, Earth's executioner, dismembering Earth-service almost singlehandedly and making the Alpha-bureaucrats tell all they knew about the Camarilla that had kept the planet in isolation for two hundred years. The atmosphere of intrigue and counterintrigue, upheaval and unrest that flared on Earth and across human space made it an unsafe time for confidences about future plans. Especially for Alacrity, pursued from childhood by Langstretch operatives and others, and particularly for confidences to Floyt, who was at the eye of the storm and—until a few hours before—destined for years of security debriefings and testimony before courts, boards of inquiry, grand juries, and all that.

"I'd just assumed you're going to lay claim to the White Ship, no?"

"Huh! You don't just show up in the Spican system and casually deal yourself in on something like the White Ship, Citizen Floyt. But I swear, she's gonna be mine."

Floyt looked at him dubiously. "You're not going to clomp around up on deck all night on a whalebone peg-leg, are you? And nail gold doubloons to the mast?"

"What? Sometimes I wish we had a language in common, Hobart." Alacrity opened his wide, oblique eyes and looked around the capsule uncomfortably. It wouldn't be so hard to wire the whole mass-transit system for covert monitoring. "I'll explain everything a little later."

Floyt nodded, leaning back, adjusting the shoulder holster so that the Webly rode more comfortably, studying the layout of the capsule for potential fields of fire.

Despite the joking, Floyt was still mulling what Alacrity had said regarding the White Ship inboard *Mindframe*. Alacrity had admitted to being more than just a shiftless breakabout; his grandparents were prime movers behind the building of the White Ship. For nearly thirty years the stupendous starship had been under construction and reconstruction, her sole mission being to uncover the secrets of the long-vanished, all-powerful Precursors.

The White Ship was a lightning rod of intergovernmental conflict, corporate bloodletting, and a near war or two. Who controlled the secrets of the Precursors stood to control the galaxy, or perhaps all of Creation.

Small wonder that a lot of people were eager to cancel Alacrity's postage and that "Alacrity Fitzhugh" wasn't the name given him at birth, but one of many aliases he'd picked up being raised by various breakabouts and serving as one himself.

The whole business of Floyt's inheritance and the destruction of the Camarilla moved Alacrity squarely into the public eye and splashed his name across the light-years. Then there were Sintilla and her books about Alacrity and Floyt. From what little Floyt knew, Langstretch Detective Network had a standing high-figure contract on the life of the man sitting there in the capsule with him. And Floyt had already seen how very effective Langstretch personnel could be.

He resettled himself and thought about his own decision, to put Terra behind him and venture out among the stars. Earthservice had originally had to *kick* him off the planet, force him to go claim his inheritance from Weir. But somewhere along the way some new, inner Floyt had emerged. Unable to go back to his pigeonhole as a nameless functionary third class, he'd thrown in his lot with Alacrity.

Floyt realized that he was tapping his lips, which were numb, and it came to him that they'd been that way for a while.

"Alacrity? It's no great matter, I know, but I've been noticing a certain, um, lack of sensation lately, in my fingertips, my lips—"

"Peripheral neuropathy," Alacrity said. "I've got problems with it, too. Look, we've been stungunned, gassed, actijotted, and whatever the hell else these last few weeks. All those zap-naps are murder on your nervous system. No immediate crisis, but we'll get it treated the first chance that comes our way."

He was silent for a moment, then added, "And we can get those friggin' actijots dug out of us at the same time."

It had been weeks since Floyt had spared any thought for the minute control devices implanted in the two back on Blackguard. One of the advantages of constant peril and turmoil, he'd come to see, was a certain preoccupation with the immediate.

The capsule viewscreen, which was showing the route's surface scenery relayed from a string of above-ground pickups, brought the ruins of This End Up City—"Upsie"—into view. It was history's first box-town, collapsed now and deserted for more than a century.

Soon after, the abandoned catapult head of Luna's original and smallest mass driver came into sight.

The capsule began to slow and Alacrity again blinked

open his great eyes, their irises glowing an unearthly, radiant yellow, striated with red and black.

"*Malákas!* I hope the Sockwallet Outfit's still here."

So did Floyt, thinking hopefully of a chilled mug of Old Geyserfroth beer, or a Gunga Din gin and tonic. He almost asked Alacrity why he hadn't made a few inquiries about the Sockwallets at Lunaport, then realized that was no way to keep a destination secret.

Alacrity opened his holster's thumbbreak. If there were Forager guards on the platform, he'd be expected to hand it over. If not, he might need it.

Floyt stood when Alacrity did, finding his balance with only a bit of difficulty. He made sure his smock was open, the Webley's butt accessible. The capsule came to a smooth halt at the abandoned catapult head's subsurface station.

The pair froze, looking for the loitering guttersnipes —Third Breath updates of Dickens's street urchins— who were the very canny Forager sentinels.

Instead, the platform put Floyt in mind of the sewers of ancient Paris, stories of the long-gone Casbah, and pictures he'd seen of hobo jungles. Someone was making music with sonic withe, synthesizer, and tin whistle; shabbily dressed children were doing an odd, flapping-scarecrow dance in the light gravity.

With darting glances Alacrity took in everything. He passed over the few foodsellers and their meager stocks; the end-of-the-line sex rentals who could no longer cut it in Lunaport; the fences with nothing worth buying; and the begging terminal cases. He registered the hawkeyed gang kids and lounging strongarm types, weighing dangers and options.

The squalid smell of the place nearly rocked Floyt back on his heels as he caught sight of the vacant-eyed faces, recalling a similar place light-years away where the stench had been different and yet quite emphatically the same.

"Boxtown," Alacrity muttered as they stood at the open capsule doors. "The Sockwallets are gone, and the down-and-outers've moved in and turned the place into a boxtown."

"Do we get off or pass?" Floyt preferred the latter. The capsule doors were about to close again.

"There's nothing for us in Hubble City. Stick close, and for Shaitan's sake keep an eye on my backpack. Everything we've got's in it, and I'm a sitting pigeon for pickpockets and cutpurses."

"Sitting duck," Floyt corrected automatically, taking up his station behind Alacrity and a hair to the left. They stepped out of the capsule. In that arrangement, one Alacrity had taught him, Floyt's right hand and arm were blocked from view and he could reach for the Webley with a certain amount of concealment. The capsule's doors closed and it slid away silently except for a rushing turbulence in the air.

Four of the healthier-looking idlers, three men and a woman, casually moved to take a better look at the new arrivals, obstructing the way. Floyt waited for a signal, sweat starting in his mustache, but Alacrity gave none.

As they closed on the strongarm group, Alacrity simply stopped, resettling his pack a bit, and put his hand on the grip of the Captain's Sidearm. Floyt kept watch on what was going on to the sides and behind them.

The music stopped and the dancers edged toward cover. The banter and goofing died away too as people took prudent steps to avoid possible lines of fire. Quite a few hungry, fearful glances were turned their way and Floyt compelled himself to glower in return.

The muscle were watching Alacrity. He sneered at them in some language Floyt hadn't heard before, tugging at his own clothes and pack, and gesturing to Floyt. The challenge wasn't too hard to figure out, given Alacrity's previous attitude in that kind of crisis. The two companions were more prosperous looking than most boxtown visitors, but they were armed and knew the ropes. Alacrity's question, in slum *patois*, conceding that pack and clothes had some value, had to be: *But are they worth your lives?*

Floyt drew the Webley, letting the lanyard ring at its base swing and clink, putting a hard squint on his face, keeping watch on their rear and flanks for a sneak attack. There was a profound silence on the platform.

In the midst of it, Floyt thumbed back the revolver's hammer, a sound that hung in the air. Not many hours before he'd been in the somewhat ensnaring lap of luxury, Hero of the Terran Weal, seemingly Earthbound for life. In retrospect, that fate had certain points to recommend it.

The muscle began to spread out to either side, to outflank them. Alacrity yanked out the Captain's Sidearm. It was a big, matte-black weapon with a basket handshield to protect the firer from blast and backlash.

"*Ah!* Now just go back and sit where you were, or we start hosing!"

Floyt brought the revolver up into the clear. The muscle looked at one another. Floyt had seen Alacrity kill their kind in another boxtown, not so long before. Then Floyt hadn't been obliged to fire; now it looked different. An altogether inappropriate time, but he found himself wrestling with his doubts.

The eyeing and silent debate among the muscle ended. They started a retreat to the main corridor that led up into the boxtown proper, seeming to surrender the field.

"Uh-uh!" Alacrity hollered, waving the energy pistol's muzzle, which was wide enough to fire walnuts. "*You* stay *here*. Get back where you were, or you'll all four of you get a *real* hot bath!"

They didn't like it, but they obeyed, eyes on his.

"Sit all the way down, pants on the pavement. And sit on your hands while you're at it!" Alacrity snarled, and they did. Guns held at waist level, Alacrity and Floyt backed into the corridor.

Floyt glanced back over his shoulder every few paces —or, more accurately, skips—until Alacrity advised, "Don't bother. You'll only trip their predator instincts.

Besides, they won't try anything else, at least for a while."

"What if they have guns?"

"Anybody in boxtown with a gun or the price of a gun wouldn't stay long."

Floyt forced himself to keep looking ahead. When he began taking in the scene, shock made him forget about the muscle.

The last time he and Alacrity had been through there, when it was a Forager lashup, it was clean, well maintained, and neat. Now it was seedy, walls covered with graffiti and smears of filth. Dirt and debris were everywhere, and the place smelled like a latrine. None of the make-do shelters resorted to by boxtowners cluttered the corridor yet; Floyt concluded that the rambling lashup hadn't reached capacity.

Much of the lighting and power systemry had been scavenged, leaving the place in semidarkness. Recalling how proudly the Foragers had kept house in their temporary settlement, Floyt found himself deeply offended.

The main airlock was open, unsecured, something the Foragers would never have permitted, being meticulous in preventing danger to their lashup from air leaks. The inner surface of the inner hatch still showed the effects of a bolt fired from the Captain's Sidearm, weeks before.

"Are you sure it's safe laying up here?" Floyt asked.

Alacrity's long eyebrows lifted. "The Sockwallet Outfit didn't leave too long ago, from the looks of things. There should still be room. It's a question of taking what we want. If we can, it's ours. Very Darwinian, boxtowns."

The lock had been stripped of all its insignia and emblems. Waiting there was another gang of bystanders, less menacing than the platform muscle.

"You looking for something?" a slender, swarthy little man asked. He had a suppurating wound on his neck, a healing energy-gun wound, Floyt thought.

"A flop," Alacrity bit out. "We lockered here with the Foragers, so we've got a claim."

The man was shaking his head disdainfully. "You don't stay nowhere unless we say so. We're the town council of New Upsie, and I'm the legal mayor, see? It's gonna cost you, bigboy."

Floyt was so outraged over what had been done to the lashup that his natural caution evaporated; he was fiercely glad when Alacrity's gun appeared again. Floyt raised the Webley.

"It's gonna cost *you* if you don't get out of our way, kumquat." Alacrity bristled. "Make up your mind; it doesn't bother me stepping on muttshit, but I hate to waste time."

The man glared at him. "Better think what you're doing, Stretch." But the rest of the New Upsie town council was already moving aside, Floyt covering them. The swarthy mayor saw he was alone and slouched aside.

Alacrity called out, "If we get any more trouble from you, or if you look at us cross-eyed, I'm gonna push you out a lock, read me?"

Floyt followed Alacrity into the onetime lashup proper. When they'd gone, the mayor of New Upsie turned to his council, snapping his fingers. "Who's got a commo token? C'mon, c'mon! I gotta call somebody in Lunaport!"

One of them surrendered a token unwillingly. "Look, we don't want any scuffle with the cops, or—"

The mayor cuffed his ear. "I don't deal with cops! Just stay away from those two highbeams, but keep track of 'em. I'll be right back."

The big gathering-area dome that Floyt recalled with such fondness, where the Sockwallets had thrown the best party he'd ever been to and changed all his attitudes about non-Earthers, was the worst shock yet. The central pylon, assemblage of trinkets, mementoes and keepsakes, accreted record of the long history of the Sockwallets, was gone, naturally, with the Foragers. But the place had been stripped by boxtowners scrounging for materials to sell, trade, or use in their own makeshift subdivisions. Even the Foragers' sacrosanct hatches weren't safe; some had been removed completely, while others were cored of usable systemry or saleable parts.

Floyt had expected that; what he hadn't expected was senseless defacement, mindless vandalism. Worse, there was a long crack near the base of the dome, where some uncaring squatter had removed an environmental unit by main force. The clear material of the dome had held, the crack sloppily patched. The sight made Floyt's hair stand up. So dangerous.

"Will it hold?" Floyt wondered anxiously.

"I guess so. Hope so." Alacrity looked to the sunlight heating the lunar landscape only meters away. "Piss fire and save the matches! Now I *know* we can't hang around here for long. Come on; I want to check something."

There were only a few dilapidated shelters in the dome; it was too open to intrusion and weakened to boot. Too, it looked like the abandoned lashup hadn't filled to anything like capacity yet. The few makeshift doghouse dwellings, mostly packing crates and slapped-together coops, were scattered around the base of the dome. It occurred to Floyt to wonder if a Pleistocene cave had smelled any worse. People in rags and castoffs peered at the twosome, unblinking and resigned.

Armed and healthy and well fed, Alacrity and Floyt had little to fear, but were on guard anyway as the bolder and more desperate ones approached, palms extended, begging for money, food, anything.

Alacrity had his long, sturdy breakabout-model umbrella out, his "brolly," a Viceroy Imperial. As the first of the rabble got to him—a fleshy man with a snarled beard, layers of dirt on him, wild bloodshot eyes, and a thick reek—Alacrity came *en guarde*.

"Stay back!" Alacrity had removed the brolly's ferrule cap, exposing its wicked point. The man disregarded him, coming closer, pawing for him, trying to get close enough to force alms from him or just make a grab for whatever Alacrity had to be stolen.

Alacrity jabbed him hard with the spike, making blood flow. The man screeched, clenching his bleeding forearm. Alacrity thwacked him on the head with the brolly. "I warned you!"

The other boxtowners fell back, Floyt following them with the Webley. Alacrity swung right and left, driving them even faster. The man he'd stuck was on his knees, moaning theatrically, cradling his head. "You've killed me! Give me money or I'll report you, you murderer!"

He was quick enough to scuttle away when Alacrity took a step in his direction, though. Alacrity waved the brolly. "If anybody even steps in my way again, so help me, I'll stick 'em full of holes like an ocarina!"

Alacrity checked his proteus, the do-all cyberinstrument on his wrist, for the time. Then he and Floyt crossed to the lock on the far side of the dome and skid-hopped into boxtown.

CHAPTER 2

"...AND CAULDRON BUBBLE..."

"DARWINISM" WAS THE OPERANT WORD IN BOXTOWN,
all right: a person could have just as much space, comfort, food, and status in New Upsie as they could wrench
free and hang onto.

Alacrity and Floyt walked down a trash-cluttered passageway in a salvaged hull portion from an old *Virago*-
class Solar Pact warship. The Sockwallets had refitted it
as living quarters for couples and severals.

But now it was a smokey, dimly lit maze of gerry-built
lay-ups, minuscule sleeping niches and nooks not much
bigger than so many sarcophagi. Among the human dis-
cards in residence there was a total inertia, an absence of
hope or thought. The adults had heads hung in misery, or
stared off at nothing with lost eyes; children were torpid,
too weak to go gang-jamming or looking for some minor
score.

"Not crowded yet," Alacrity observed. "The Sockwallets couldn't've left too long ago. Air circulators are
still working, sort of; utilities haven't been completely
stripped away. I figure, not more than a week or so."

There were sounds of construction, people improvising shelter in compartments, holds, and even storage
lockers, using pulpboard, mineralsheet paneling, and
whatever else came to hand.

Prime real estate was close to the air duct outlets and

19

had access to plumbing. "There'll be a lot of arguments over water rights," Alacrity predicted as the two made their way, hop-scuffing through the *Virago*'s lock into a long pressure-quonset that was being subdivided. "People get killed over stuff like that in a sealed-environment boxtown."

"But how much longer can this place support life?" Floyt wondered. The basic utilities and air system, stripped and vandalized as they were, with no Foragers to run or maintain them—the thought of that had him looking around uncomfortably. "It could become a deathtrap at any moment."

Alacrity nodded, picking his way around a coughing old man who spat blood into a soiled rag. Floyt gave thanks that his immunizations were up to date.

Alacrity said, "If they're dumb enough to let that happen, they'll either have to scramble for a new lay-up or hammer out some kind of system to keep things running. That's when a sealed boxtown usually goes through a shakedown and organizes, at least half-assed, even if it takes a few turf wars. Anyway, I think we're safe for a bit."

"*Huh?* Alacrity, we can't stay here!"

"Don't pop an aneurism; I'm with you. But we've got to take a second, here, and figure out what to do next. Besides, there's something I have to see." He led the way toward the end of the quonset. A group of box-towners stood there, looking apprehensive rather than mean. Floyt could see a few knives and a bo stave among them, and one tall, equine woman cradled a thing that looked like a crossbow built from metal scraps. On the floor lay a discarded vacsuit they'd been repairing; patching materials and spare parts lay all around.

"Just the local protection committee," Alacrity said out of the corner of his mouth. "They're not part of the extortion gangs."

No one impeded their way. Beyond the quonset, a kid who looked fifteen or so lazed on a mound of carpet that had been ripped up from some lashup deck. He looked

better fed and bolder than most, and wore a colorful
paisely jumpsuit and a skullcap sewn with shimmerettes.
He gave them a lackadaisical grin and held his hand out
to block their way, palm up, rubbing his fingertips. "I'm
in need, burghers, and you look like you've got it to
spare."

"No," Alacrity said tersely, about to shove the hand
aside. Floyt knew his friend was generous to the needy
but absolutely refused to give to the able-bodied.

The kid snatched his hand out of the way and shoved
himself to his feet with old-hand-Lunie grace. "Think
again; it could be worth it. I know things. I see things,
and I hear even better than I see."

Alacrity pointed to his right boot with his brolly.
"Then d'you see *this*? Know where it's going in another
second if you don't lose yourself real fast?"

The kid moved aside with fending motions of his
hands. "I'll be here if you change your mind. I'm Quirk;
I give good advice."

Alacrity threw a growl at Quirk as the duo went on.
Alacrity was headed, as best Floyt could surmise from
his recollection of the place, to where Simoleanna
Coup's quarters had been. Sim, a winsome, feisty young
Forager woman equally at ease in streetfighter's clothes
or sequined evening gown, was very taken with Alacrity,
and vice versa, during the brief stopover months before.

In that extreme end of the vacated warren, where no
squatters had yet staked claim, the pillaging had gone on
in earnest. The only light was from the occasional port-
hole or skylight, the harsh sunbeams cutting through the
stale gloom.

The boxtowners had been through like locusts, strip-
ping away furnishings and anything else that wasn't
welded down. There was more of the nitwit vandalizing:
a mural marked with urine; elaborate wainscoting pried
loose and pulverized. When the underclass got a chance
to work off its frustration, savage emotions broke loose,
and there were bloodstains to prove it.

Alacrity wasn't surprised to find that all the air ducts

in that section had been shut down to bolster circulation in the occupied areas. "The fights over air will be worse than the ones over plumbing?" Floyt inquired, and Alacrity nodded.

"But why didn't the Sockwallets sell off all this property before they left?" Floyt asked. "All this material— the lashup itself?"

"The real estate's public land, I guess." Alacrity was squinting at the walls as he went along. "Foragers can't just dismantle a lashup and drag it along with them, and people know that. So why pay for something that's going to be available for free when it's abandoned? When somebody with resources wants the buildings, they just come for them, and I wouldn't want to be living here then, pal."

"But surely somebody could find some good use for the place."

"The Lunies already did: they're letting all the trash pile up in one place. You heard Inspector Grissom; Luna's booming and that means a shortage of space. A big new boxtown eases the strain. You evict the riffraff, they come here, and you rerent your property for three times what you were getting. Yeah, I bet New Upsie's a real popular idea."

"Not around here. Listen, what are you hunting for?"

Alacrity had stopped by a hatchway. "Forager cues."

With the light spill from a nearby viewbleb to search by, Alacrity scanned the bulkhead by Sim's door, past pathetic scrawlings and retarded vileness left there by the looters. He went past something, then came back, bending close. There were simple code-runes, hidden in among the other clutter.

"What do they say, Alacrity?"

Alacrity chuckled, reaching out to pat Floyt's shoulder. "Everything's fine. They *heard*!"

"Heard what? Come, come now! I don't hold out on *you*, do I?"

Alacrity turned to him with a sober look. "No, that's true, you don't. Sorry, Ho."

Floyt suddenly wanted to bite his own tongue. He fought the impulse to make a clean breast of the White Ship matter; boxtown was no place for it and, more importantly, he couldn't face the idea of devastating his friend.

"The Sockwallets heard about us, and the Camarilla, and how the conspirators are being sniffed out," Alacrity was saying. "Sim says they're satisfied with the revenge."

"To be honest with you, I'd almost forgotten about that."

Two Camarilla assassins had made their way into the lashup to get Floyt and Alacrity, only to be killed themselves. But the sanctity of the lashup was violated and a number of Sockwallets injured. Gunny Readyknob and the other Foragers stressed that Alacrity and Floyt were obligated to let the Sockwallets know to whom they owed revenge.

"I'm glad they saw it that way," Floyt admitted. One less thing to worry about. "Do the cues say anything else?"

Alacrity was bent to them again. "They're headed for Gaeltacht to start a new lashup. We're welcome anytime, as adopted Sockwallets, for an hour or forever."

"That makes me feel good," Floyt began as they started back the way they'd come. "But I'm not sure staying here is such a good idea, even if you do know your way around boxtowns."

"I'll go along with that," Alacrity declared. "We've drawn too much attention to ourselves. And anyway, the main thing I had in mind was finding those cues."

"Fine."

"There's something else, Ho. You're right about not holding things back."

"Forget I said that," Floyt said quickly, conscience squirming. "I had no right to, you see, because—"

"What I want to say is, you've got a right to know what's coming. Y'see, I have to make my way to a planet called Windfall, because I'm old enough now to vote the one share of stock in the White Ship that my folks left me. And that means I can finally get into a meeting of the Board of Interested Parties of the White Ship."

"And that's good?"

"It's step number one of getting control of the Ship. So, our next move is finding a way to get to Windfall. I figure we'll make the rounds, get ourselves a couple of berths as able-bodied breakabouts in a ship bound out that way."

"And then on to Spica, where the White Ship is, right?"

"Yessir. On Windfall there's this guy, Lord Marcus Perlez. He was my father's, oh, godfather, I guess you could say, or mentor. Anyway, he's got my share in trust. With some luck, maybe he'll help us get to Spica."

"That would be wonderful."

"So now you know most of what I do. Tell you the rest as we go."

Floyt writhed inwardly, but as he had in *Mindframe*, he held back when he might have blurted the truth. Alacrity's whole life was focused on becoming Master of the White Ship, on recovering his family's heritage. It was what kept him going and saved him from the terminal despair that claimed his father. *How do I tell him that I know, know for* sure, *that it will never be—that he'll fail?* the question pounded in Floyt's head.

He couldn't. So he said, "Alacrity, you may be able to land a billet as a breakabout-able, but there's not much chance of my doing it."

"I was worried about that too, even though you picked up a lot while we were shipping in the *Pihoquiaq* and *Astraea Imprimatur*. But I took a look at some of the shipping newsblurbs at Lunaport. Didn't you notice how busy the place was?"

"I wasn't really paying much attention."

"Luna's economy's going straight up, and there're more ships making port all the time. And when there're fortunes being made right and left, that means people are jumping ship, salivating for their share. I'm betting there'll be a couple of berths for us, bound offworld and in the right direction."

"So be it," Floyt seconded. "Even if we end up shoehorned into the cuddy of another *Monitor*-class."

Alacrity slapped his back. "We'll blow up that bridge when we come to it!"

Floyt laughed, and postponed the truthtelling, unwilling to mar the good feelings of the moment, to rob Alacrity of soaring hope. They wended back through the warren. There weren't as many people around as there had been; Alacrity became guarded and watchful. He tucked his brolly into carrying loops on his pack and pulled the Captain's Sidearm.

Floyt drew the Webley.

"If you shoot, be real careful," Alacrity muttered.

"I remember, I remember," Floyt said nervously, recalling the Foragers' draconian rules against using firearms inside the lashup. For all their ingenious work, it was still a makeshift place. One shot in the wrong spot and a seal or hatch or dome might go, and perhaps kill every soul in it. "Where do we go from here?"

"There're a few different routes to the entrance, but there's only one way out."

When they neared the pressure-quonset they found Quirk, the young beggar, still on the pile of plundered carpeting. Now, though, he sat tailor fashion, wrists resting on his knees, watching for their approach.

"Another showed up in boxtown, another outsider," Quirk informed them with a yawn.

"Looking for us?" Floyt demanded as they stopped short. Alacrity swung his gaze this way and that.

"Who else?"

"Where is he? Did he say anything?" Floyt asked.

Quirk was silent, giving Floyt a languid smile, making the fingertip-rubbing gesture again. "Play 'im, pay 'im," Alacrity said. "This isn't begging; it's a business expense."

Floyt gave Quirk a one-oval piece, then hesitated,

wondering if he should dicker. Alacrity made an impatient, boiling sound and snatched another coin out of his friend's palm, slapping it onto the kid's.

"Is he coming this way?" Alacrity narrowed his eyes at the boy; the alley runner nodded and pointed to a passageway.

"You're sure it's only one? He's alone?" Quirk nodded as if Alacrity were a halfwit. "So what's our best route back to the main airlock?"

Quirk explained quickly, showing that he knew every turn and cranny in New Upsie. All the two had to do was cross through a lesser dome, use the length of water conduit that had been fitted out as a passageway for a shortcut, and make their way through a prefab hangar that the Sockwallets had turned into a rec center.

"Good, good." Alacrity nodded. "And which hatch do we take?"

But when Quirk turned to indicate, Alacrity grabbed him in a choke hold, dragged him down from his perch, and put the muzzle of his pistol to the kid's head.

"You're so sure it's safe, you little pustule, you go first." Quirk fought for a moment then relaxed, knowing he couldn't break free. Floyt was still gaping. Alacrity half carried, half frog-hopped the kid to the hatch he'd pointed out, not difficult in the low gravity.

"Okay, Ho; stand to one side and hit the control. I'm going to shove Mr. Information, here, through first."

Quirk began struggling wildly again, even though it was hopeless. "All right, leave it closed," Alacrity grated. "Secure it if you can do it without making noise!" He slammed Quirk on the floor in a heap and knelt on him, clamping the boy's wrists together with one big, knob-knuckled hand.

The Captain's Sidearm had a long, heavy rib running from its muzzle to the base of its handshield, a deflector for defense against edged or blunt weapons in hand-to-hand combat. Alacrity did something to the pistol one-handed; a glittering pistol-bayonet sprang forth from the deflector. Alacrity put the point against the base of the kid's right eye, with the weight of his shoulder hovering over it.

"Last chance, alley runner. How many are there?"

"Three, with guns," the kid said woodenly. "Two in a crossfire on the other side of that hatch, the other keeping watch on the back route, to the far side of the main dome."

Alacrity yanked Quirk to his feet, bayonet at his throat. "And how much did they pay you?"

"Hundred lunars."

Alacrity was impressed. "In advance?"

"Ten in advance, the rest later. I figure ten's better'n nothing."

Alacrity shook Quirk angrily, flopping him around easily. "You gullible asswipe! Can't you see they were going to shoot you, too?"

He looked around, then lugged Quirk off in the direction of a looted machine shop they'd passed. Floyt caught up as Alacrity bounce-shuffled Quirk along. "That hatch has a manual lock, Alacrity, but it would've been louder than Marley's ghost, and I couldn't figure out how it worked." He was almost whispering.

Alacrity was used enough to Floyt's obscure Terran references to understand what he meant about noise. He nodded again. "That's okay; cover our backs." Floyt did, skate-hopping sideways, bringing up the rear with the Webley pointed back the way they'd come.

Alacrity came to the machine shop, which he recalled from their previous visit. There were storage lockers built into the wall. He opened one and jammed Quirk inside, then slammed it shut and made sure it latched securely.

Floyt was surprised the boy hadn't put up more of a struggle until Alacrity said through the locker door's little vent grating, "We should kill you and you know you have it coming. If either of us gets hurt, the other's gonna come back here and shoot a few more holes in this locker door. In the meantime, think about what a screwup you are."

Back in the passageway, Floyt said, "How did you know? That he was lying, I mean?"

Alacrity smiled evily. "He's satisfied with just two ovals, especially when he sees you've got more right there in your hand?"

"Too eager, hm?"

"Let it be a lesson to 'im. He'll be older and wiser by the time his gangmates locate him. *If*. Look, how much do you recall about the layout of this dump?"

"Enough to know we haven't got too many options. How long do we have before those triggermen come after us?"

"Not long. I think if we can go through that aeroponics shed—remember, the one made out of the booster tank? We can outflank them."

The aeroponics shed had been stripped of all but its bulkiest fixtures. As the two skimmed carefully through the echoing darkness, Floyt found himself whispering, "There's just one thing, Alacrity."

"What's that?"

"What if they lied to Quirk, too? What if there're more of them and they aren't all waiting back there where they told him they'd be?"

The sudden tension of that thought might have been the edge that had Alacrity alert enough to hear movement. Or it may have been that the other ambushers overheard Floyt's remark and opted to move before their prey became spooked, even though the pair was still some distance away. In any case, Alacrity caught the sounds and threw himself and Floyt behind a holding reservoir.

A second later the shed was lit, its air cooked by sniper volleys. The assassins were using scatterbeams and pulsed lasers; there was little Floyt and Alacrity could do except keep their heads down, sweating from the heat and from fear.

"All right, Firing Studs!" someone yelled. "Come out now and we take you alive. Elsewise, we do it the hard way!" Floyt made to take a quick peek, but Alacrity pulled him back.

"Your choice, Fitzhugh; Floyt!" The firing began again. The two ducked molten globs from structural members that had been hit, and intense heatwaves. The massive reservoir provided adequate cover for the moment, but Alacrity feared for bulkhead and seal integrity, especially now that there were no fearless Sockwallets dedicated to protecting their lashup at all costs.

One shooter's angle of fire changed. "They're trying for position," Alacrity murmured grimly, perspiration beading his face and dripping from his nose.

Without leaving cover, Floyt angled his gun barrel up and fired away, ricocheting off the heavy-gauge metal ceiling, sending spanging composite fragments whining through the shed. It was a horrible risk, but it worked; the assassins' fire halted and the advance was stopped for the time being.

Alacrity gathered his nerve and edged his pistol around a corner to let fly, risking having his hand burned off or the Captain's Sidearm blown up. The monster handgun's blast pounded their ears; by design, it gave off light and muzzle blast like a cannon, for shock effect.

There was a lot of scuffling as somebody hustled for cover. Alacrity fired twice more. Floyt took the insane chance of popping up and squeezing off unaimed shots, the Webley jumping in his hand.

Whoever the assailants were, they were busy staying low. Floyt emptied the revolver's cylinder, hot propellant and bullet shavings spraying from the chambers, as Alacrity pulled him back the way they'd come. Alacrity kept up the fire, unleashing the furious blare of the Captain's Sidearm around the shed pell-mell, making the air broiling hot, keeping the attackers' heads down.

Until one of them gets desperate enough to rush us, Floyt fretted, working on the hatch. He got it open as Alacrity hosed the energy gun back and forth, alley-broom style, raising the temperature to blistering, backing along after Floyt. Alacrity jumped to cover on one side of the hatchway as Floyt shouldered it shut from the other, shots roiling and spattering from it as it swung to.

"No lock, fug-all." Floyt panted. "It's been stripped."

Alacrity backed away from the hatch, muzzle trained on it. "We can't stick around. Go to the next hatch and reload; I'll cover."

Floyt skimmed off in that direction. Alacrity checked his weapon. The charge indicator still read three-quarters full. Alacrity hoped he was getting a true reading; a fizzle now would be very embarrassing and harmful to his career goals. He backed and side-hopped, face streaming, to rejoin Floyt.

Floyt was at the next hatch along their route of retreat, nearly set. He had his top-breaking pistol open, holding it by its downturned barrel, reloading two bullets at a time. He had his tongue sticking from the corner of his mouth in concentration, but he worked quickly and calmly.

He's changed a lot, Alacrity thought again as he took a crouched firing position on the other side of the hatch.

"What now?" Floyt asked, closing the revolver. "If we go back, I bet we'll find the other ambushers have that route blocked, too."

"I'm stumped," Alacrity admitted. "They sure got everything covered in a hurry."

"Yes, it seems they're thorough."

"Uh-huh. You want to know what I don't get? That part about 'Firing Studs.' *Firing Studs?* New one on me."

Floyt had his slug pistol cocked and ready. "Oh, that; that's one of Sintilla's expressions. People end up calling us that in *Castle of the Death Addicts*."

"Wha—? *Fancula*, doesn't anybody have anything better to do than read those damn books?" He hunkered around to peer through the lock, into the next stretch of passageway they'd have to negotiate.

"It sounds as if someone decided to read up on his quarry," Floyt judged.

"Stop the clock!" Alacrity was looking at him pop-eyed. "They read the book; what if they believe all that pasture decor that Tilla made up about us?"

"Well, then they're probably a little apprehensive just at the moment. In the book we are truly remarkable fellows. Part of it takes place here in the lashup, as a matter of fact. It developed that you knew the secrets of the subsurface shuttle system of the Lunar Ancients."

Hissing and scorching sounded at the hatch behind them, covering fire for a rush by the opposition.

Raul Plantos, Langstretch Field Operative Class Two, was the one who'd just come through the aeroponics shed after Floyt and Alacrity, the one who'd offered terms of surrender to make it easy for him to braise them.

He was leery of his two targets; he was familiar with their astounding dash to Terra in a privateer starship, their final planetfall in a superstealth spaceboat, and their key roles in bringing down the Camarilla. In some fashion no one seemed to quite understand, the two hapless vagabonds had defied certain death and beat the odds, not just once, but repeatedly.

Plantos had read of their exploits in those absurd books, determined to know his prey as well as possible. He dismissed just about all of it as sheer fantasy, but was troubled by occasional doubts. How could the pair have survived what they had, out on their own in the Third Breath, if they didn't have hidden resources? That seemed as unlikely as the *Amazon Slave Women of the Supernova*. He knew he had them cornered, but Plantos still felt misgivings.

Footshuffles and hop-sounds came his way from behind. He whirled, fearing the targets had managed some flank attack, but it was only the last of his strike force, for a total of five. They moved loudly and were less professional than he preferred, but there was no help for that now.

Plantos, a deceptively lean man with a protruding Adam's apple and sleepy eyes, motioned with his scatterbeam assault weapon; the manhunters took cover to await orders. He cursed the need for haste that had required his obtaining local help. But the boxtown mayor's tip came out of the blue, and there was no telling when Fitzhugh would drop from sight again, leaving an absolute-zero trail, as he had in the past.

The standing bounty on Fitzhugh, already generous enough to let a field op retire in rare style, had been increased. That meant Fitzhugh and, inevitably, his sidekick Floyt, must be nulled with dispatch, before someone beat Plantos to it.

"Get ready," he said in a low voice. "They must be in there somewhere."

"We found the kid, Quirk," one of the latecomers said. "He's crammed into a locker. Him, we can adjust later."

"Come," Plantos said, rising. He advanced with the scatterbeam's skeletal stock clamped firmly to his right hip. His dearest wish was that his mission partner were there to help; a human juggernaut could be a liability at some times, and frightening, but a welcome companion at others.

But his mission partner wasn't there, so Plantos directed the assault with professional calm and skill, letting the local hirelings take most of the risks.

Counterfire didn't come when and where he expected it, which was disturbing. The targets had been driven into a dead end, an old land-dozer hull the Sockwallets used as a warehouse. There wasn't even access to the Lunar surface, not that that would do the quarry any good.

Plantos, bringing up the rear, found himself staring down a short passageway and through an open hatch into the warehouse. It as empty except for odd bits of trash, with no cover to be seen but for a low life-support service unit with its access panel hanging open. If the targets had gone to ground inside it, they were as good as dead. There were a few little viewblebs in the place, through which harsh sunlight flooded.

The locals were wary but eager as weasels, itching to have it over with and collect the head bounty. One threw himself down in a good firing position, leaning against the circular plug-hatch that was swung back, flat against the bulkhead. A second hireling got to the other side of the hatchway for a crossfire and still there was no sign of opposition. Plantos ordered up the remaining two gunmen, establishing commanding fields of fire. There was no sign of Floyt or Fitzhugh in any direction, including up.

Then he himself advanced to weigh the situation. After some tentative ducking in and out, a laser marksman and a scatterbeam gunner were inside, seeing no prey.

Plantos crouched in the hatchway, taking a better look at the service unit. The open panel had a symbol qwikgraffed on its inner side, a trefoil with a human eye beneath it. The blood in his veins seemed to stop.

"My god! The damned transport system! The secret transport system!" That explained some of Fitzhugh's and Floyt's unlikely triumphs. Plantos still didn't believe in Lunar Ancients, but apparently those books had some truth in them after all.

Plantos leapt through the hatch, plucking at his belt for the stun grenades he couldn't use earlier when he was in the same compartment with Alacrity and Floyt. He had no idea where the bolthole led, but knew that if he didn't act fast, the quarry would escape. His men crowded after, ready to fire at the first sign of a target.

Two gunmen took up firing positions inside the hatchway; the others and Plantos closed in on the service unit with infantry-style rushes. Plantos invoked an icy calm; he maneuvered to his right, scatterbeam leveled. At his command, his men advanced on the open access plate. He prayed that the targets were still within range of a dropped grenade; the thought of chasing armed enemies down through some underground maze made his skin crawl.

"Suppression fire." Plantos got ready to open up.

They would riddle the service unit and inspect for sub-surface escape shafts afterward.

All at once a tremendous gunbolt crashed across the warehouse to blast out one of the viewblebs. There was an eternal instant as an ocean of air, drawn irresistibly to vacuum, mobilized itself, during which Plantos whirled and saw Alacrity standing in the half-closed hatchway, the Captain's Sidearm held cup-in-saucer style. Though the hunter-killer team couldn't see him, Floyt was struggling from hiding too, shoving himself from the cramped hiding place that had been left when the hatch, like a number of others, was gutted for salvage.

The hatch was moving as the lashup's tremendous mountain of air surged into motion. Alacrity was putting another shot into the shattered viewbleb to be sure; a spectral wind-howl had begun.

Most of the assassins were too startled to move, but one began bringing his pulsed-laser alley broom around. Floyt fired the Webley again and again as the wind tore at him, throwing the man into convulsions of pain, the air whiplashing them all in a monumental surge.

Plantos was yelling, drowned out by the howling air-leak, and Alacrity dropped the Captain's Sidearm to grab Floyt, who was in danger of being whisked into the warehouse. Alacrity dragged his friend to one side, reaching for purchase with hands and feet, the light gravity working against him as the hatch was swung shut by the vast atmospheric flow. It nearly sucked them through, and the hatch came close to chopping off half of Alacrity's left foot.

The hatch whammed shut with such force that Alacrity feared it would split up the middle and give way. A few feeble alarms began, tribute to the Foragers' endlessly cautious engineering.

There were some few screams and impacts from the ruptured warehouse, but they grew fainter as the atmosphere bled away.

Floyt only had to wave the Webley around once or twice and that was it; the boxtowners kept an emphatic distance. They were scavengers, with no taste for gunplay and firefights.

When Alacrity showed up at last, in the repaired vacsuit he'd rented from the local protection committee, he looked several shades paler than usual. The ruptured viewbleb wasn't very big, so Floyt didn't want to think about what the assassins' remains looked like strewn across the airless lunar landscape.

"One of them was Langstretch," Alacrity said, throwing down carry-pouches and proteuses and an armload of guns. Searching quickly, they found that only the Langstretch man had much cash, but he was pretty well heeled.

"We don't have time to fence the guns," Alacrity admitted, "so I propose we give 'em to the protection committee, where they'll do some good."

Floyt fingered through the money solemnly. "It isn't enough to get us very far on our way to Windfall, though, is it?"

"No. This is." Alacrity held up a spacecraft code-key, smiling triumphantly. "That skinny guy who had all the money—Plantos, his name was—he was a Field Op Two. We needed a break, and it came to us the strangest way I ever saw: Plantos."

Floyt held up one hand. "Wait; slow down. You're saying to me that we have ourselves a *starship*?"

Alacrity was rubbing the end of the code-key on the tip of his nose, beaming. "Provided there's enough money here to pay the right bribes. The ship's called, um—" He double-checked—"The *Lightning Whelk*. And she's ours if we move sprightly. I say again: let's houdini the hell outta here."

Floyt was grinning. "What's the weather like on Windfall?"

Alacrity looked thoughtful, seating a new charge in the Captain's Sidearm. "It's nice there, Ho. It's always nice on Windfall."

CHAPTER 3

DARK MATTER

"NOT VERY WELL EQUIPPED, WAS HE?" FLOYT AN-
nounced after he and Alacrity had made their inspection
of the *Lightning Whelk*.

"I mean, for a Langstretch man? I don't see much of
the paraphernalia that Victoria carried."

"Me either," Alacrity said, feeding the last of the
mathematical models into the computer guidance suite.
The pliability of Lunar port officials increased when Alacrity flashed the sheaf of money he'd recovered from
Plantos's leg pouch. It had cost most of the op's cash,
but Alacrity and Floyt received priority clearance and
made immediate lift-off.

"But she's a Field Op One and he was only a Two,"
Alacrity added. He glanced around a cockpit/bridge that
was roomy enough for one but cramped for two. It
wasn't set up for two, but the rest of the *Lightning
Whelk* was, Plantos's permanent living arrangements
augmented by temporary provisions for a second person.
Or thing. A quick look at those accommodations gave
Floyt an uneasy feeling.

"Still, a starship," he said. "We must be pretty high
up on their shopping list, Alacrity."

A starship, but a small one resembling, from the outside, her namesake, a contoured, torch-shaped snailshell
hulk some thirty meters high when sitting on her tapered

36

tail with berthing stabilizers deployed. She was old, much overhauled and patched, *dangerous* when it came right down to it. But Alacrity fell for her wholly and without reservation, swelled in ecstacy by winners-keepers ownership.

"Umm," Floyt mulled. "With no cargo, she's only slightly worse than *Pihoquiaq* was." He saw from the look on Alacrity's face what he was about to say, and chimed in, so that they said it at the same time, "But still, a *starship*!"

Floyt eased down into the standby's jumpseat. "Nobody from Luna was interested in us, Alacrity? Nobody following?"

Alacrity was punching up various scope images, checking all the detectors. "Nope. What're you worried about, the Golem?"

That was Alacrity's name for Plantos's absent partner or hireling or whoever it was. The name seemed to fill the bill; the Golem's makeshift bunk was outsize, long enough for someone a meter or so taller than Alacrity and with three or four times his cross section. It was braced and reinforced to support enormous weight.

"Maybe Plantos was just keeping a couple of old reactor containment vessels in there, or something." Alacrity smirked. "Anyway, whoever it is, we left 'im behind. In another little while we can forget about him for good, because we'll be in Hawking. Good old sinful Luna. Buddha smile on everybody who can be bought and *stays* bought."

"Good to *us*, anyway." Floyt shifted the cuptray he was carrying, setting it on a flat area of the console.

"What's that you got there?"

"Breakers, have you forgotten so soon?"

"*Managgia*! It's been so long since we were on a regular Hawking jump, I didn't even think of blastoff cocktails."

Floyt nodded, handing out the drinks, two big, chilled hurricane glasses filled with some frozen concoction. Alacrity was right; except for their original departure from Luna inboard the freighter *Bruja*, their headlong comings and goings were usually in escape or as captives or bilge-class deadheaders. It was nice to have time for the amenities again.

Floyt turned the rimed glass in his hand and got to something that had concerned him. "Alacrity, see here. I know this Perlez fellow, your father's mentor, is supposed to help you, and I'm not trying to play Miraculo the Mindreader, but something about this situation is just eating you up."

Alacrity sampled the drink. "Not bad. Frozen, uh, banana daquiri? Except it doesn't really taste like bananas."

Floyt leaned his head against a power panel. "They're something called fidberries, from some planet named Anybody's Guess. The potables report is pretty bleak; a few hundred milliliters of perfumey-smelling vodka left and a half case of that defanged beer with neothanol in it. Plus an inhaler of updust, and of course that swill the whole ship reeks of."

Floyt held up a bottle whose label read "Old Four Smokes Wallop." "Some kind of drugged liquor, or nostrum, or whatever."

Unstoppered, it was the source of the stomach-turning odor that permeated the *Whelk*; the Golem's bunk in particular smelled of it.

Alacrity took a whiff of the Old Four Smokes Wallop and made an awful face. "Ug, I'd rather be sober! Pour it out, will you?"

Floyt restoppered the bottle. "No argument."

"So like that oldtime Earther said, we have to survive on food and water?"

"And not an awful lot of food," Floyt said. "We're going to be eating protein paste on crackers after a while, I should think."

The computers began running the transitional sequence. Alacrity sipped again. Floyt looked to the forward viewpane; this would be the first time he'd ever actually watched while a starship went superluminal.

"I'm not really that worried," Alacrity blurted. "At least, no more than usual. It's just—everything's riding on this. I'm sure I can trust Lord Marcus—except, aside from you, I don't trust anybody, really."

The Breakers cut in and the *Lightning Whelk*'s Hawking Effect generator seemed to vibrate the vessel like a banjo string. Floyt drew a quick, deep breath as he felt again that peculiar impression of velocity without movement. Then there was the profound over-the-top sensation. The Hawking generator put the *Whelk* beyond normal limitations and the outboard screens went blank.

Alacrity raised his glass and clinked with Floyt. "Breakers!"

There was nothing to see out the forward viewpane, but Floyt's brain insisted on imposing images. Or, if you listened to certain scientific popularizers, as-yet-undiscovered forces and influences were transferring information directly to his mind in some enigmatic way.

"No music," he realized suddenly. "I meant to find 'The Planets' and put on 'Venus, Bringer of Joy.'"

"Trite as hell, but it's a favorite of mine, too," Alacrity confessed. "That and 'Brainwire.' Oh, well, too late now. Tell you what I *did* find while I was poking around the data banks and memory files: whoever Plantos was, he liked current events. He left us with the latest news packets, bought on Luna about four hours ago."

"Where? Let's screen them!"

The fastest that news could travel between the stars was the speed of a starship, so news traveled slowly, filtering through the Third Breath over a period of weeks or months. No one really had any coherent idea of all that the human race was doing, especially out where the frontiers were ballooning. So people were always hungry to hear news and tales of strange new doings and places. Literature, drama, history, and the rest had taken a decided backseat; the traveler's journal and explorer's diary commanded *Homo sapiens*' attention as never before. People who could observe, survive, and come back to convey what they'd seen were icons of the Third

Breath of Humanity, which was the species' current
great leap outward after the end of the dark age that
followed the collapse of the Second Breath. The illusion
of "true" adventure was the appeal of Sintilla's shame-
less fabrications.

Once Floyt, who'd grown up on preterist Earth,
hadn't given the matter much thought. Now he was as
greedy for information as anyone else abroad in the
Third Breath.

Alacrity activated two infoscreens and a holographic
projector, adjusting for quick scan. The news flashed in a
dazzling mosaic, headline blurbs with in-depth stories
available on access request. They glanced from display
to display, barely keeping up with the highlight-dollops.

Researchers on New Saigon claimed an astounding
breakthrough that confirmed the existence of psi powers
and made them subject to rational study and control. The
new discipline was called Psience, its attendant mecha-
nisms, psenses.

"How many times have I heard *that* chestnut in one
shape or another?" Alacrity snorted. "The sucker quo-
tient never goes down . . ."

The new official religion of the Trilateral Dominion
was a kind of massage therapy.

Due to genetic drift and loss of gene diversity in many
human colonies isolated since the end of the Second
Breath, plasm-trading looked to become one of the great
growth industries and most competitive businesses of the
Third Breath. Piracy and strongarm commercial violence
were becoming more and more common.

A war had broken out between the New Hanseatic
League and the Bamboo Confederation over contractual
obligations and alleged treaty violations. It revolved
around disagreements arising from incompatible time-
computation systems; delegations of temporal arbitrators
were trying to hammer out a compromise by getting a
mutually agreeable reckoning system in place. The an-
nouncer reminded the audience of the tragic Calendar
Wars, which had started in much the same way.

Rumors from Amalgamated Science Networks, Inc., had it that a true "psychocopier," allowing detailed and orderly mental writing, was in prototype phase.

"Only about thirteen hundred years too late for poor old Boswell, who always wanted one," Floyt remarked dryly.

Truth-in-advertising laws in the Spican Union now required that all clergy, professional councilors, clairvoyants, and lonely hearts agencies refer to those who engaged their services as "customers."

And so it went. There were stories about the Camarilla, of course, and the uproar Alacrity and Floyt and their allies started, but not much new. Floyt was shocked to realize that he was already rather blasé about the whole thing. He and Alacrity scanned avidly, though, to see if the *Astraea Imprimatur* had been found, if the outlaw Janusz and Victoria Roper, the former Langstretch op, both of whom had led the fight against the Camarilla, had been captured. Most of all, Alacrity hunted the displays for word on Heart, the Nonpareil, the woman he loved, who'd stayed with *Astraea Imprimatur* on her escape, to aid Victoria and the injured Janusz in finding sanctuary. Heart's parting with Alacrity was bitter.

There was no reference to any of that though; the companions tried to convince each other it was a good sign. Then one split-second image as Alacrity was fast-forwarding made them both gasp.

"Alacrity, go back!"

"I saw it, I saw it! Sports news; why didn't I think of it?"

Then it was before them again on the holoimager: *Celeste Aïda*, the gorgeous racing staryacht of Captain Softcoygne Dincrist, the Nonpareil's father.

The last time Alacrity and Floyt had seen the ship, *Celeste Aïda* swept past them rather than blowing *Astraea Imprimatur* to component forces, not because Dincrist couldn't do it, or didn't want to because his daughter was inboard, but because he was, though behind, a strong contender in the very prestigious Regatta for the Purple.

The newsspew showed Dincrist standing proudly before his ship, accepting the first-place trophy, a racing starship carved from a single, enormous fire-drop.

"*Zhopa s ruchkoi,* that bastard," Alacrity breathed. "We should've killed him when we had the chance."

There were scenes from the race as a commentating talking head went on about Dincrist's brilliant performance, particularly during the solar sailing leg of the dangerous race.

"I hate to give him this," Alacrity grudged, "but either he's an awfully good racing skipper or he had one inboard with him, ghosting."

The shot switched back to Dincrist, surrounded by wealthy, powerful Regatta Club members whose friendship he'd been courting for so long. He was taller than Alacrity, deeply tanned, white-haired, and fit. His gleaming smile was frozen in place.

Floyt recalled the contempt in which club members held newspeople. The fact that a press opportunity was being tolerated showed that Dincrist, as winner, had impressive new influence among the august and mighty members.

Alacrity wondered if the irony was eating at Dincrist's liver—being compelled to give up the vengeance he wanted so badly in order to win the trophy, the only thing he wanted more.

"When will *Celeste Aïda* take to the stars again, Captain?" a fawning interviewer asked.

Dincrist chuckled regretfully. "My first love is sailing the stars, of course, but unfortunately I have weighty responsibilities to my family and to my business and financial affairs."

Another newsghoul, one who didn't sound so friendly, elbowed the first aside. She was young, barely postadolescent, and wore a fetching strawberry-color coat of dermal frosting over bare skin.

"Salome Price, for the Uncensored Network! Captain

Dincrist, aren't you referring to the meeting of the Board of Interested Parties of the White Ship? Haven't there been persistent rumors that you'll face opposition at the upcoming meeting and perhaps a drive to unseat you from the board? Isn't it even said that much of that opposition will come from members of your own family and from your daughter, the so-called Nonpareil, in particular?"

Dincrist glared at Salome Price furiously, then his eyes flicked around the crowd and into the pickups. For a moment Alacrity felt like he was eye to eye with Dincrist again and about to throw some hands and feet.

Floyt was certain Dincrist was wondering if he could get away with swatting the female newsghoul in front of all those people and recording devices, and concluding only with great reluctance that he couldn't.

The smile froze back into place. "Those are vicious and unfounded lies, as I suspect you know, foisted off by malicious people on the gullible and foolish, my dear. As proof of that, my business associates and family—and most particularly my daughter—will be backing me all the way at the meeting."

His mouth smiled wider; his eyes were chilling. "Backing me *all* the way."

Alacrity came halfway out of the big pilot's seat to bark at the projection, "Liar! Dincrist, you *limbic case!*" He turned to Floyt. "You don't think he found her somehow, do you?" Alacrity replayed the interview, but there was nothing more to learn from it.

"Something's happened to her." Alacrity was staring numbly at the spot in the air where the projection had vaporized. "Ho, we've got to find her." He was keypadding up new astrogational data from the computers, not sure where he wanted to go or what he would do there.

"Alacrity, we don't even know where to start. Look, she *must* be all right, otherwise Dincrist wouldn't have promised that she would attend the meeting, isn't that logical? *That's* where we have to go, Alacrity." Floyt was fond of Heart too and owed her a lot; she'd risked her life to save him as well as Alacrity.

"I don't know; if he's hurt her I'll tear his head off, and shit into it." But he stopped the dataflow and left the *Lightning Whelk* on course.

"I guess you're right, Ho. And to get into the board meeting I have to claim my share from Marcus. Right, we go to Windfall, as planned."

Floyt had found himself enjoying traveling with Alacrity in the *Bruja* and *Pihoquiaq*. Misery and peril, interspersed with some matchless good times, had gotten the two used to one another: Alacrity knew that Floyt disapproved of hearing the punchline of a joke repeated; Floyt had learned that breakabouts, like ancient submariners, should *not* have the habit of whistling or humming. The trip in the *Whelk* was something Floyt greeted as a welcome chance to rest, collect his thoughts, and increase his readiness to venture through the Third Breath.

But now Floyt dreaded the voyage, fearing it would be like sharing a cage with an angry tiger. Floyt had another preoccupation aside from the one for Heart's safety though, a gnawing apprehension about the shadowy occupant of that giant, reinforced bunk.

Alacrity backed up the recording and projected the scene again.

"Backing me *all* the way." Dincrist beamed smugly.

The Lunar port supervisor sweated a bit before repeating his lie. He glanced aside to make sure the guards in the outer office were keeping an eye on the situation; they were watchful and stonefaced, intimidated.

"All I can tell you is, they had the proper documents and they had the code-key for the *Lightning Whelk*," the supervisor said again. "So they had every right to receive clearance and lift-off, sir."

The man-mountain on the other side of the desk didn't move or speak. The night-black eyes bored into the official, who thought, *Hell, would even gunfire stop this ogre?*

His ID gave his name as Gentry Standing Bear. He was from the largely Amerind planet called Four Smokes and had an unsurpassed history in mayhem, crime, combat, bounty hunting, and frequently insane excess of all kinds. The sullen goliath had left a trail of carnage across the Third Breath, gouging eyes from gene-engineered champ gladiators, smashing in the ribs of giant, neutered Spican death-guards, tearing tongues from huge Sumo wrestlers on Fukuoka. The two liters of Old Four Smokes Wallop he'd drunk had him in an evil temper.

The port official and even the tough guards betrayed the fear he aroused in just about anyone he met. Gentry Standing Bear was too big for most doorways, networked with scars, calluses, puckered blasterburns. He had thick, horn-hard fingernails, gargantuan fists. The lumps under the skin of his chest were shotgun pellets he'd never bothered having removed. The end of his nose had been bitten off, with it not mattering to him enough to have it repaired. His gaze made it clear that he enjoyed violence, and no preamble required.

"Honestly," the supervisor said, licking his lips. "Look, maybe I can find out something for you—their flight plan, or something."

He damned himself for accepting the very considerable bribe—just about everything the two had, he'd assured himself—for letting Floyt and Alacrity board the *Whelk* and depart despite inadequate documentation. The vessel had arrived on someone else's shift, and if the supervisor had known this creature was part of her compliment, he'd have told the Earther and the breakabout to go suck vacuum.

Standing Bear offhandedly considered caving in the supervisor's face and, if necessary, wringing the guards' necks. But there were more important things to do. He held out a photoflat blowup of a newsshot of Floyt and Fitzhugh, one of the few ever taken.

"That's them, that's them!" the supervisor babbled. He reached for his commo button, grateful to have something to do, staring in fascination at the enormous hand with its alpine knuckles.

But the walking catastrophe turned to go without any word. For trying to take Floyt and Fitzhugh while he, Standing Bear, was following up a lead on another case on the opposite side of Luna, the fool Plantos deserved what he'd gotten. Not that the two targets should've been any problem. But Plantos went into an unfamiliar place without correct preparation, backed by a few local sods, and so had gotten what he deserved. More, Plantos tried to cut Gentry Standing Bear out of the hunt, and so received nothing as bad as what Standing Bear would've done to him.

If Standing Bear's contacts at Langstretch were angry about the death of Plantos and the theft of the starship, they weren't likely to demonstrate it to Standing Bear. The losses meant nothing much to him, unless Langstretch irritated him with complaints, which would be unprecedented. His services—when he deigned to sell them to the detective agency—were too valuable; more important, his anger was to be avoided.

Which left only the need to contact Langstretch for a new means of transportation and new leads—for someone who would look after details, as Plantos had.

Because Gentry Standing Bear cared only for the hunt and the kill.

CHAPTER 4

WE DON'T KNOW, BUT WE BEEN TOLD

THE WEATHER WASN'T *ALWAYS* NICE ON WINDFALL, BUT the planet was axially, geologically, and orbitally stable, with a placid climatic sameness over most of its surface, and so Alacrity's statement wasn't too far off the mark. Its ecology had been in place, with little change, for a long time in a rather benign environment, and so lacked adaptability; humans did rather well there.

Windfall was settled and peaceful, a languid timocracy with polite but very strict law enforcement for anyone below the top echelons, to make sure things stayed orderly.

"Which means no guns," Alacrity said regretfully, locking away his own and Floyt's pistols, the pouches and cases on the Sam Browne knocking and creaking.

"I'm less worried about that than about how good a forger you are," Floyt said, adjusting his throat ruffles fussily. "Are you sure you know what you're doing? If we end up in jail, there's no one to extricate us this time."

Alacrity was wearing his trusty old ice-blue, silver-trimmed dress skinsuit. He'd altered the *Lightning Whelk*'s ownership records so that she appeared to belong to him and that he and Floyt, in turn, were citizens of Sweet Baby's Arms, the Lunar documents supporting that.

47

The Third Breath saw contact among many disparate cultures, and documentation was often hit-or-miss; stealing or laying hands on a starship was difficult under most circumstances, but palming it off as one's own was less a problem if one knew the scams.

"We're fine for now. We probably won't be here more than a few hours," Alacrity answered. "The odds against this crate being on the Rat-'Stat by now are long, at least here. The bulletin would've had to be right on our tail, in a faster ship."

The Rat-'Stat was the list of wants, warrants, stolen ships, fugitives, and similar items of interest circulated among law enforcement organizations, Langstretch ops and stringers, bounty hunters, skip-tracers, informers, stoolies, and such. It was nothing if not cumbersome, and rather inefficient, given how out-of-touch many worlds were.

"But *you're* on the Rat-'Stat," Floyt pointed out, still adjusting an ill-fitting outfit borrowed from the late Plantos. Since the *Whelk* offered no autovalet services, Alacrity had showed Floyt how to arrange the suit under his mattress for a very passable prison press. Floyt had shown apprehension on discovering the Golem's huge clothes; Alacrity dismissed them, happy to have a bunk with room to spare, even if it did still smell of Old Four Smokes Wallop.

"Sure I am, but everybody thinks we're on Earth, m'friend. Not only that, a lot of folks think we look like those illustrations on Tilla's books: body builders with perfect hair and eye makeup. Anyway, who could recognize us from the Camarilla hearings? We were behind closed doors just about all the time, besides which Spica and Earth and the Camarilla probably don't mean much to these people. But still, you can wait here in the *Whelk* if you'd rather."

"I'd as soon open my wrists."

Windfall's starport was small and looked more like a campus or park. The customs people were polite but very thorough in searching the two for contraband. Two-day tourist visas were approved without delay.

Floyt scanned the applicable rules, restrictions, and penalties. For a bucolic sort of place, Windfall seemed oddly obsessed with long terms at hard labor. He and Alacrity converted the last of their cash into local currency and walked out under the red-gold light of Cornucopia, Windfall's primary.

Alacrity stopped to make a quick call to Lord Marcus Perlez, with Floyt looking on from the side in the little public commo studio. Floyt was relieved to see the cost of the call was low.

The call went through and the projector showed them a life-size image of a woman standing by a commo terminal configured to look like a *nostalgie de le juquebox* pedestal.

"Thermostat alert," Alacrity murmured. "Meltdown imminent!" Floyt clucked angrily and knuckled him in the back.

But she *was* special to look at, a toothsome size nine who was all legs and lush curves, tawny skin, and eerily transluscent blue eyes. She was barefoot, wearing an ensemble of burgundy-color glowtulle: wimple, loin bunting, forearm plaits, and thigh-high gaiters. Between her breasts hung a huge, faceted Lillith's eye on a fine silver chain.

They devoured her with their stares; she gave them a look of resigned good humor. "What do you wish, please?"

Before Alacrity could pounce on the line, Floyt nudged him again. "To talk to Lord Marcus Perlez," Alacrity supplied. "Tell him Lazlo Twill wants to catch up on old times."

She put them on hold and her image disappeared from the tiny public studio. Floyt realized his mouth was open and shut it. "Lazlo Twill?"

"I'll explain later."

"If you don't, I'll start *calling* you that."

A second later a lean, oldish man appeared on the

screen. He had stringy, sinewy lines to his face, a ram's-horn handlebar mustache, and great, full sideburns. His smile showed what looked like too many teeth, like chalk tombstones. "Well, well, Lazlo Twill."

Alacrity was holding up his hand, the commo link being insecure. "Nice to see you again, Lord Marcus."

Perlez's eyes narrowed as he nodded slowly. "It's been awhile, m'boy; that it has. I've thought of you often. How soon can you get yourself over here?" The image gave Floyt a canny glance.

Alacrity promised to jump into a hire-flier and get right over to Lord Marcus's estate, Ends Well. Floyt was disappointed that the man didn't offer to send transportation for them; a cab ride might well break them.

"It's better this way," Alacrity told him as they left the studio. "I'd just as soon not hang around here any longer than we have to, and this way nobody sees some chauffeur picking us up and makes the connection."

Several robofliers were waiting nearby, just as there were outside customs. Alacrity ignored them and, leading Floyt at a trot, hopped into one that was just discharging passengers at the terminal.

The cab registered their destination and required payment before it would move. Floyt fed it nearly all of what they had left.

Edenic cityscape and scenic countryside were hard to tell apart for a while when the cab got out over the wilds —or what passed for wilds on Windfall. Every so often they saw police cruisers among the traffic, even though most vehicles were remote controlled and there weren't many chances to break a law.

Well controlled, Floyt saw, thinking of Terra with a rebelliousness he'd somehow picked up since throwing in with Alacrity.

After an hour of modest-speed flying, the cab descended toward an estate that stretched across most of four low river valleys. Part of it was landscaped like an exquisite vivarium around the soaring manor house, but a lot of the place was scarcely prettified at all, a wilderness by Windfall standards.

"Lord Marcus's got more money than some *planets*," Alacrity commented, "but for some reason he likes his modest little sanctuary here."

The manor house reminded Floyt of a gigantic, burnished samovar set among outbuildings, stables, garages, and solaria. It was bigger by far than Old Raffles, the chateau where he and Alacrity stayed on Blackguard. Alacrity stared down at it with furrowed brow; he'd been preoccupied during the flight. Floyt tried not to puzzle over what his friend was thinking, regarding it as a kind of prying.

When the hire-flier touched down someone was waiting to meet them. Floyt's abrupt prayer was answered by the glint of burgundy glowtulle. The woman who'd taken their call watched them, Cornucopia's rays striking breathtaking highlights from her, her lips playing between smile and not-smile.

Floyt waited for Alacrity's inevitable response: hardwired glans–penis override to frontal lobes. But when she swayed over to meet them as they emerged, Alacrity slid out straightfaced, reserved, waiting for Floyt to come after. She smelled the way Paradise was supposed to.

Either he's really worrying about Heart, Floyt concluded, *or this meeting with Perlez is serious business indeed. Or else he's ill. Maybe all three.*

She gave them an engaging smile and didn't look offended when only Floyt returned it. Alacrity was staring at Perlez's vaulted artwork of a manor house, thinking things that were impossible to guess.

"Greetings and welcome, honored guests," the woman said. "I am Lord Marcus's special secretary, Tomasina. He's waiting for you in the kitchen, if you'd be kind enough to follow me."

The cab rose and sped back for the city before the three had gone half the distance to a pair of ten-meter-high green squeezewood doors set with blue ivory scroll-work, the main entrance.

The doors opened for Tomasina in silent, stately fashion. The wood was a half-meter thickness of facade; behind it was another meter or so of armor-grade alloy.

The house was done in Omnimedia Arcade Polyglot, an oddly luminous and happy-go-lucky motif for such an enormous, polished cathedral of a place. Ends Well was quite cheery, not only because of the neon brightness of its decor, but also owing to the many windows and skylights and because all the woodwork was very light, blond or white. Some kind of stately music in three-quarter time was playing over the sound system; Floyt had a vague impression that it was a military *polonaise* from old Earth, but his knowledge of the subject was shakey. *But the music's in keeping with the rest*, he told himself, looking around. *What we have here is a summer palace*.

He sighed. *We seem fated to veer between mansions and skid row. If we ever end up in normal surroundings I'm not sure I'll know how to act anymore*.

Ends Well featured old-fashioned stairs and hallways, no whisk-platform transport system or chuteshafts. Alacrity, looking around, couldn't tell if it had changed; he'd been there only briefly, as a child. An awful lot had happened to him since; several lifetimes' worth.

The companions took in the splendor with only a fraction of their attention, the rest devoted to Tomasina's smooth, finely muscled behind, which orbited through divine figure eights as she led the way. Floyt was reassured in that Alacrity had reemerged from his distraction enough to oggle. Alacrity did not, however, as might otherwise have been the case, offer to lick Tomasina's skin until his tongue wore down.

They came at length to the central kitchen, high up in the summit of Ends Well, a room only slightly smaller than a concert hall, with sky and sunlight all around. It was equipped with every variety of food processor and cooking tackle Alacrity could think of, along with a lot he didn't recognize, in glittering maxtech surfaces and brushed metal. There were banks of readout projectors and indicators in glowing colors.

But in one corner sat a modest little work area consisting of heating unit, sink, preservation locker, and countertop—archaic, simple, and uncomplicated. There Lord Marcus Perlez puttered, chopping and dicing, humming to himself, keeping one eye on a wok, his apron covering a very expensive housesuit. The place smelled nearly as mouth-watering as Tomasina.

A woman was standing by, attentive to him. She was Tomasina's duplicate, right down to the attire, the fragrance, and the darkly lustrous Lillith's eye at her bosom.

Lord Marcus turned as he heard their footsteps, gave them a cheerful, harried wave and a grin, bushy eyebrows fluttering, then went back to his cooking. Tomasina's double gave them a quick smile.

"Sorry, sorry; can't let this stuff get away from you, y'know, or it's ruined, just ruined," Marcus told them over his shoulder, waving a wooden spatula. "Take yourselves some seats! Here; keep me company. Too early for a drink?"

"It's late afternoon for us," Floyt replied as he and Alacrity sat on high, heavy old stools upholstered with bluish leather.

"We'll have what you're having," Alacrity added. "And thanks. You're looking well, sir."

Perlez took a moment from his cooking to wipe his hand on his apron and give Alacrity a quick, firm wrist-clasp. But there was something distracted about it, and Floyt could see that the old man and Alacrity were both thinking of less pleasant times.

"Good to see you, m'lad," Perlez said, winking, one bushy eyebrow lowering. He was gruffly compassionate, giving Alacrity's wrist a last squeeze. "Glad you made it."

He turned to Floyt. "You too, you too!" He had time for a rushed Terran-style handshake, then he was back to his chefery. "Callisto, if you'd be so kind as to do the honors, my pet?"

Callisto turned out to be the woman next to him and, what with the advanced systemry in the kitchen, she had five drinks ready with amazing speed, depth charges in frosted beer mugs, the liquor some thick stuff as dark as the Lillith's eyes. Floyt studied, with some trepidation, the shot glass standing on the bottom of his mug, but clinked glasses with the rest.

As Tomasina busied herself setting out sopmat coasters, Lord Marcus said, "My dears, these good gents and I have a few things we should discuss in private, so I'm afraid you must busy yourselves elsewhere. That's presuming you don't prefer to retire, too, sir?"

That last was to Floyt. Alacrity said, "No, I want him to hear this."

Tomasina smiled beautifully. "We have work to do anyway, thank you, sir. I'll be taking lunch and working on the staff roster in the greenhouse if you require any service."

"I'll be going through the household accounts," Callisto announced. Floyt, studying her closely, saw that her eyes were an even lighter shade of the eerie, miraculous blue than Tomasina's.

Lord Marcus let out a yipe, skipping aside and nearly falling as his right shin was struck. Floyt gaped down at what had buffeted him, a wooly brown thing about the size of a Welsh corgi with layered giltfix on its horns and a dog collar set with ranks of gleaming, pea-size lava pearls around its solid little neck.

Marcus had managed not to spill his drink, and now he set it aside, then stooped to pick up the dwarf bison that was still butting his leg. "How d'you like my little *bonsai*?" He scratched the thing's shaggy back; it squirmed, tail flicking.

"This is Larrup, old North American buffalo, bred from pure stock from Adam's Apple."

Floyt could only stare. The last American bison had died in the Second Breath, and he'd never expected to see a live one much less a gene-engineered miniature. Alacrity took a quick glance at Larrup and went back to studying Lord Marcus.

Marcus handed Larrup into Callisto's lovely arms; she and Tomasina took their drinks and left together while Floyt stared at the identical derrieres wistfully, as Alacrity and Marcus exchanged calculating looks.

"Clones?" Floyt asked in a low whisper, riveted on the callipygian grace.

"Nah!" Lord Marcus yelled, worrying the food with his spatula once more. "Any dimwit could have some clones run up, and what would that reveal to him or her about human nature and the Universe?"

Floyt was at a loss to tell. Perlez brandished the spatula at him—"Nothing!"—and resumed cooking. "No, I recruit my treasures based on an ideal of my own. How many such is our human race blessed with, out of all the planets we've populated? And of those, how many will consent to join my household? And then there's always the temptation to compromise my standards."

"They look the same as when I was a kid," Alacrity piped up suddenly.

"Yes; well. There's been a certain amount of turnover since then," Perlez admitted, and an uncomfortable silence flourished abruptly, except for the feverish cooking.

"I feared the worst when I heard the latest news, boy," he said to Alacrity all at once. "I thought you might've gone and gotten yourself hurt or tossed into the lockup somewhere, Jordy."

Jordy, Floyt registered. He'd known from the first that Alacrity Fitzhugh was an alias. He'd always felt it impolite to ask, and Alacrity never offered to clarify. It was still a shock to hear. *Jordy*.

"Oh, I got by all right," Alacrity was saying. "Had some help at the right time. Lord Marcus, this is my friend, Citizen Hobart Floyt, of Terra."

Perlez spared Floyt a cordial half bow and a wave of

the spatula. Floyt waved in answer and took another cautious sip of his depth charge.

"Rather thought that's who you are," Perlez called to Floyt over his shoulder, bending over his wok again. "You two laddybucks raised some fuss, eh? Get ready now; here's something you'll like."

Then he was handing them plates heaped with food, taking one for himself. The three sat there eating off a counter. They garnished with a bit of teriyaki sauce and dug in. The food was so good that for a moment Floyt almost lost track of what was being said.

"All the arrangements are made, Jordan," Perlez was saying, "or should I call you Alacrity? I'll transfer the voting share to you whenever you like."

"Alacrity's fine," Alacrity said, eating with great concentration. "And thanks."

Lord Marcus savored his own cooking a lot, even though he didn't look like he had to watch his weight. "Have you thought about what you're going to *do* with that share?" he asked, still apparently intent on his meal.

Alacrity looked up at him. "Haven't thought about much else, Lord M. I'm taking back the White Ship."

Perlez's chopsticks opened and a bit of beansprout dropped onto his chin.

"Taking her back," Alacrity vowed, "and I'm using her the way my family meant her to be used. And when I find out the secrets of the Precursors, I'll use *them* the way my family wanted, not the way the Board of Interested Parties or the Betterment League or the Progress Cartel or the Spican government thinks it ought to be done. The White Ship isn't for easy money or quick power. There's got to be something higher than that, something more worthy, or what's the point of it all?"

Perlez had cleaned up the spillage. "Well, that's a virtuous idea, boyo. But how?"

"I'm not sure yet, but I know I will. I didn't, until a little while ago, after I fell in with Hobart, here," Alacrity explained. Floyt cringed inwardly, knowing Alacrity was thinking of the causality harp.

"I'm not trying to be mysterious," Alacrity went on. "I'll explain the whole thing to you later."

Floyt was watching Perlez's face. The old man said, "Ever run into a man named Dincrist?"

Floyt looked back to his food and Alacrity showed no response.

"It is my conclusion that you have," Perlez continued, "because the word is that he'd very much like to get his hands on you. There's also mention of a gentleman named Baron Mason, an extremely influential and formidable man who's become an Interested Party of late. What's this all about, Jo—Alacrity?"

Alacrity thought for a moment. If he couldn't trust Lord Marcus Perlez, things were about as bad as they could get anyway.

"Dincrist has his own plan to take control of the Ship board. But all the details of that fell into the hands of . . . somebody I know." He held up his fist, showing his proteus. "I managed to get a copy and I've studied it all the way here from Luna. I think that same takeover idea can be used by somebody else. Me. Or *us*, if you want. It all involves leverage on the board."

Floyt watched, speculating on how far Alacrity would go in not mentioning Heart by name if the talk came down to cases. Perlez napkinned his mouth and mustache and stuck out his hand. Alacrity gripped his wrist and Lord Marcus reciprocated.

"As for Baron Mason," Alacrity thought it fair to add, "Ho and me had a kind of run-in with him, on a place called Blackguard. As a matter of fact—"

Alacrity dug another proteus out of his pocket, an ordinary-looking but powerful model. "I took this from Mason in the Grand Guignol Compound there."

Floyt recalled that vividly, surprised it had slipped his mind. Evidently Alacrity had simply been carrying it around in his warbag all that time since.

"This one is full of encrypted stuff I haven't been able to crack," he said. "But maybe if we could borrow some of your equipment, Ho and I could pump it dry."

Perlez was nodding thoughtfully, looking the thing over. "That sounds splendid. But the first thing we'll have to do is get your name on that share. And I want you in on a council of war with Vinzix. He's a minor shareholder, even though he's got a lot more of them than you. He and I rather see things the same way. He's from Darwin's Star."

Alacrity's frowned. "A Dar, huh? I'm not real fond of 'em. Bunch of snotty, high-handed liars."

Perlez stopped eating again. "So? I've heard a bit about what you've been doing and where you've been seen from time to time. I'd have thought you'd learned by now that you can't always be choosy about your allies, or judge them beforehand."

Alacrity toyed with his food for a second, then slumped his shoulders. "You're right as you can be. When can I meet Vinzix?"

"Any time you like. He's here at Ends Well just at the moment, as a houseguest. What I propose is that you and Hobart go freshen up while I fill him in. He and I were planning on playing a round or two of rovers this afternoon; if you two would care to come along, we could all discuss strategy. Er, do either of you play?"

Alacrity shook his head. "Never had the time. Besides, it's a rich folks' game. But it'd be nice to stretch our legs; we've been cooped up in a little padded trash-can for—anyway, for way too long."

Floyt, bewildered, inquired, "What's 'rovers'?"

CHAPTER 5

BAND OF ANGELS,
COMIN' AFTER US

ROVERS WASN'T THE GAME IT HAD BEEN BACK IN MEDI-
eval Terra, but when he was reminded of its origins,
Floyt the history buff recognized it at once. The Ancients had played it, a sort of forerunner to golf.

Millennia before, archers would go afield over a
prearranged course, firing arrows from a given point to a
particular target, the shots selected for their difficulty
and the challenge they presented. From there they'd fire
to the next, and so on over the course.

Rovers has changed a lot, observed Floyt, watching
the approach of Lord Marcus Perlez and the Darwin's
Star autochthon, Vinzix. *For one thing, I don't remember anything about the Ancients having robot cad-
dies.*

Or at least that was what it appeared to be, floating
along behind Perlez, a chunky thing that was mostly
torso, riding a compact hoverunit. It looked like a cross
between a mirrored chiffonier and one of Lord Marcus's
prized jukeboxes.

Marcus had on the traditional get-up: A sporty kilt
with an orange-and-green plaid that seemed to be made
of light-bulb filament, complete with a sporran covered
with some sunset-coral fur. A jaunty purple tam-o'-
shanter sat low on his brow. He also wore blinding argyle

socks, cleated shoes with tassels on them, and a shirt of rather rakish see-through beige cobweb.

Vinzix was a different matter. Alacrity looked the humanoid over, trying to keep an open mind about Dars.

Vinzix was a whisker or two shorter than Alacrity. The native of Darwin's Star was startlingly humanlike, with the look of some impossibly Olympian ideal, like all of them. His splendid bronze skin fairly shot the light of Cornucopia back into their eyes; his shoulders were wide, wider than a human's could've been for his height, and if they weren't articulated exactly like a *Homo sapien*'s, they were no less impressive: muscular bundles, striated and vascular. Vinzix's torso was short, narrowing almost absurdly to a tiny waist, but his legs and arms were long and well defined. He had too many fingers with too many joints, the way Floyt saw it, including some kind of little extra bottomside thumb. He smelled like polishing fluid.

Vinzix's face was like something that belonged among the long-vaporized images of Mount Rushmore, except that the forehead was eerily high and the eyes unnervingly back-set and unblinking. There was also the fact that the Dar's mouth appeared to run halfway around his head.

Vinzix wore only a winding of stuff that looked like woven bugle-beads and a kind of baldric that held a pouch at his hip.

Three women walked along behind Vinzix and Lord Marcus, barefoot on the soft-carpet turf of the First Castway, wearing the revealing glowtulle livery of Ends Well. Floyt almost waved and called greetings to Tomasina and Callisto, but it came to him that neither was necessarily present; such were Lord Marcus's staff. One of the three women held the *bansai* buffalo, Larrup.

Lord Marcus Perlez waved at the two happily as he and Vinzix approached, but the humanoid made no greeting. Alacrity wasn't surprised; Dars were notoriously condescending creatures who seemed to work at being arrogant and offensive. Alacrity speculated on how long Marcus had known him and how well the nobleman understood the Dar's language.

"Yes, yes, yes, ideal weather, eh?" Perlez said heartily as he and Vinzix joined Alacrity and Floyt on the first release point. The little robo floating along behind swiveled its head at Vinzix and hiss-popped a translation in the language of the natives of Darwin's Star. Vinzix listened impassively.

That explains a lot, Alacrity thought; the little machine was programmed as translator. Alacrity spotted where the linguistic junk probably went. The head wasn't very anthropomorphic, running more to receptors and pickups than smiles; it looked like it had directional sound. Its several arm appendages were folded up close to its torso. It was giving Vinzix a running, low-volume translation.

"Yes, the weather's fine, quite," Floyt said amicably, adjusting the floppy *petasos* sunhat he'd borrowed; the afternoon had gotten warmer. Alacrity nodded.

Vinzix hiss-popped something to the robot, which it dutifully translated. "Yes, it's a suitable day."

Alacrity knew enough about the Dar's language to know that the robocaddie was running a very sophisticated translation program, possibly something the Union of Species had worked up. Vinzix's reply, from the little Alacrity could get, was layered with sarcasms, insults, and threats—the sort Dars always used in dealing with other species.

"Nice robo," Alacrity said to Lord Marcus.

"Yes. Albrecht is a wonderful little fellow, the latest thing," Marcus answered absently, shading his eyes with his hand and studying the first castway. "With a special protocol augmentation module that the dealer recommended. I'm afraid neither Vinzix nor I are very good at the other's tongue."

Floyt said "Oh?" pleasantly. Alacrity hid his smirk by looking downrange, too. To the women Marcus said, "Well, my treasures, run along now." He gave Larrup's head an absentminded tousel; the trio of beauties headed back for Ends Well.

The first castway was a long shot, through an avenue of immense gaff trees festooned with garrote vines, under a yellow-green corridor of leaf canopy. The target was a holoprojection, what appeared to be an animal the size of a moose, many-legged and decked with a fantastic rack of antlers. It pawed the ground and caracoled but stayed in one spot, some one hundred meters and more downrange, in what looked to be a shaft of sunlight.

"My good friend Vinzix, will you please do me the honor of taking the first release?" Lord Marcus invited.

The automaton translated. Alacrity didn't catch any of the harsh or provocative inflections a Dar would routinely use to show contempt. *Real discreet program, all right.*

Vinzix grunted something that had at least one revilement Alacrity recognized, but Albrecht the caddy translated it as "That's most kind of you, sir."

The humanoid pulled on a pair of heavy, instrumented gauntlets that reminded Floyt of buzzball gloves he'd seen on Epiphany, except that these were nearly elbow length. Vinzix hissed something quick to the robo as he took up his stance on the release point, feet planted directly beneath his shoulders, side-on to the pawing holotarget.

In the meantime, Albrecht unfolded and extended two of his arms. The ends were equipped with odd fittings Floyt didn't recognize, and began to glow and tonesound. A bright nexus blossomed between the metallic palm-gadgets, gathering light and energy around it. It pulsed and whirled like a miniature sun, throwing off swirls of radiant spindrift.

Albrecht held it out to Vinzix, who took it in one armored palm. Floyt wondered if the energy ball had any substance, heft, or mass, or if it were just a balanced skein of forces.

Vinzix cupped it in both hands like a cricketeer and made a kind of prancing approach to the foul line. With a powerful windup that gathered all the fibrous muscles of his back and left arm, he released the energy globe at the target. As he did, his right foot crossed the foul line.

The light projectile flamed and spun away downrange, looping and curving a bit; Floyt had no idea how Vinzix could've judged what it was going to do, or calculated his aim.

The whirling sunball just missed a thick limb, then looped in to hit the pawing target holobeast on the withers, high up.

There was a spectacular outburst of light and sparks along with a crash of sound from somewhere, and the target was gone.

Alacrity saw that Vinzix was aware he'd crossed the foul line, but contrary to sportsmanship and form, the Dar ignored it when he should've reshot or conceded a point. Marcus saw it, too, and that the humanoid wasn't being a gentleman. The old man shrugged it off.

"My turn, I think," Lord Marcus said as Vinzix stepped out of the way with an upturned nose. "Alacrity, young friend, now what would you suggest for this shot? A novaglobe like my opponent's?"

"I'm the wrong one to ask, Marcus. By the way, are you playing evens?"

"Well, no; that is to say, it *is* my home ground, after all, even though it's a new course," Marcus said. "I spotted Vinzix two extra bolos and a dartspread. Only sporting."

Alacrity nodded, thinking, *I wonder what you'd say if you knew Vinzix thinks sportsmanship isn't worth voiding his scent sac on?*

"Very well, then," decided Lord Marcus, rubbing his encased palms together. "I think we'll have the blazing twirlspear. Might as well open up with my best, eh? Albrecht, if you will?"

Albrecht used one of the arms he'd used to make the novaglobe and a third, equally strange-looking one. Floyt couldn't help shrinking back from the process, worried about what might happen if all that tame energy somehow got out of hand.

Albrecht's palms, pressed together, sprang apart; between them a blazing rod of blue light grew. Small electrical arcs writhed and spat along it. Floyt let out an involuntary yip, boggled by the thought of what the technology involved might possibly cost.

Marcus took the spear of light, balancing it on his palm, squinting at his target, the holobeast having reappeared. He made his approach to the foul line, very like a javelin thrower, and released.

The spear twirled and crackled as it blazed away downrange. It didn't fly quite true, vibrating and waffling a bit in ways that weren't like a real spear at all, but more like it was alive.

Yes; this has to be a very, very expensive playground, Floyt concluded.

Lord Marcus had gauged his release against the timing of the hololoop, the rearing and pawing of the target. He'd gotten that right, but not the path of flight. The spear clipped through a hanging garrote vine, blowing it aside in a fierce discharge, deflected by it, missing the target. The energy spear struck a tree root to the left of the image and yielded the rest of its charge there.

Well, it's not all light effects. Floyt determined, gazing at the smoldering ends of the vine.

"Shall we proceed?" Marcus said. Albrecht translated for Vinzix, who strode off downrange, ignoring the humans.

Alacrity and Floyt trailed the two players. There were no easy routes through the undergrowth and trees between the casting point and the target. Except for Albrecht, who floated above, they were all obliged to bushwhack their way along. Lord Marcus seemed to enjoy it; Floyt and Alacrity simply put up with it—they were getting very good at that sort of thing. Vinzix muscled his way through, sometimes leaping over or wriggling around the more substantial obstacles. There was apparently some point to the added hardship, but it eluded Floyt. Eventually Lord Marcus beckoned them onto a narrow path like a game trail.

When the bush thinned a bit, Marcus said to Alacrity, "Oh, before I forget..." He passed over an intricately woven gilt document bearing ribbons and stamps. Alacrity took it and examined it closely.

"Exactly one voting share in the White Ship, made out in your name," Marcus said. "I've already registered the formal transfer, although how much good that will do you I can't really say, Jordan."

Alacrity opened an inside pocket to tuck it away. "More than you know; it'll get me into the next board meeting. That's all I need."

"Ah, yes," Marcus said, armored hands clasped behind his back. "Don't take this the wrong way, m'lad, but you really have two choices, the way I see it. Vinzix and I are cooperating on our *own* plan regarding the White Ship, you see. You can confide in me and let me help you—and I wish to, believe me—or you'll have to pretty much go it alone, although I'll do what I can for you, of course."

Alacrity wore the withdrawn expression Floyt knew so well. Albrecht was keeping up a running translation for Vinzix, who watched Alacrity closely.

"And don't get *me* wrong, Marcus," Alacrity said at last as they came up the rise to the target area with its scorched tree roots and vanished holobeast. The next castway lay just beyond, and from where they were they could see the target.

"I'm grateful to you," Alacrity went on, "but it's just not that simple. I have an obligation to—someone, to make sure the information I've got isn't used the wrong way." He was thinking of Heart and how much more she would hate him if she thought he'd used the data he'd stolen from her father to profit some outside party; as it was, she had little enough sympathy for his personal quest for mastery of the White Ship.

"Wouldn't you say you owe some debt or obligation for the help you've been rendered here?" Albrecht translated, after hearing out Vinzix's rasping, hissing remark. Alacrity was sure the gist of it was closer to fighting words.

"Son, you have to trust someone sometime," Lord Marcus said softly.

He's right there, Alacrity admitted to himself. *I trusted Ho, and it got me the only friend I have.*

"All right, Marcus. Um, lemme see, here..." He stepped back, shielding himself with his body as he worked on his proteus and studied the data he'd seized from Dincrist at the start of the Regatta for the Purple. When he turned back, the proteus was inert again.

Alacrity said, "Here's one for openers. There's a very sizable block of voting shares that's been inactive for a long, long time. Nobody's supposed to know who owns it, of course, under board procedures, but it's some woman named Loebelia Curry."

"Loebelia...*Loebelia Curry*?" Lord Marcus exploded. "Hecate! Hecate!"

Alacrity looked baffled. "Are you saying this Loebelia Curry was Hecate? The one my parents were always talking about?"

Floyt was looking at them blankly. "Who's Hecate?"

Lord Marcus was belly-laughing. Albrecht was translating to the impatient-looking Vinzix. Alacrity told his friend, "Hecate was—well, was one of the great eccentrics and—an adventurer, I guess you could call her. I wasn't even sure she was real."

He looked to Lord Marcus Perlez. "It looks like you're right about a partnership. I knew one thing and you knew another and now we've got something going here."

"We have indeed, we have indeed," Marcus said. "What else did you find out?"

Alacrity cocked his head at the old man. "Don't you think we ought to reach some kind of deal before we go into details? Make sure we have an understanding?"

Marcus was nodding, Albrecht still translating, and Vinzix regarding the humans with detachment. "I suppose that's fair enough," Marcus said. "I'll tell you what: we can take a shortcut back to Ends Well at the finish of the next castway and put it all down in legalese. And in the meantime I'll tell you a bit about what *we've* found out."

"Suits me. But what about Hecate?"

"Oh, she was very much a part of things in the old days. I never knew she had a large voting block, though."

"Can we find her? Is she still alive?"

Marcus thought it over. "I don't think she's been heard from in years, but I have a very comprehensive Whereabouts listing. We'll check when we get back to Ends Well."

The next castway was uphill, over thick jungle growth, the target a hopping, flashing animated figure resembling a big green imp. It rose and ducked behind the crest of the hill, circling a bit, appearing at random, so that the cast had to be made with sharp reflexes and a certain amount of precognition.

Albrecht went into his fireworks act once more, giving each contestant a missile from the allotted quota. Vinzix, after one false start, hurled a thing like an incandescent boomerang, his follow-through all grace and power. The boomerang-lightshape spun and flashed, catching the imp target from behind, obliterating it in a shower of sparks.

Lord Marcus chose an arcing, radiant bolo, casting with good form like a gaucho, but missing. In its caperings, the imp brushed past an overhanging frond that swayed aside, proving that the meshed energy fields of the target holos exerted gross physical force.

"Difficult 'way, this," he muttered, grinding the big white teeth. Vinzix seemed pleased, though it was hard to read him. For his next cast, Marcus elected to use his dart-spread, to be certain. The lightning sheaf fanned out, like a fall of meteors; the imp again boiled away into nothingness.

"That's what comes of lack of practice," Marcus said

as they advanced on the undergrowth again. "I just don't have time to keep up on my game. Sometimes I wonder why I had this silly blooming thing built."

Floyt was puzzling over that a bit, too, wishing Lord Marcus had installed a skyseat ride between release points, for nonplayers at least, as long as he was going to all the expense.

"Lord Marcus," Floyt said abruptly, "I'd like to ask you a question: who d'you think the Precursors were? Why did they disappear, and all the rest of it?"

Lord Marcus Perlez, squinting at the target area, gave a crusty grin, tugging at his tam-o'-shanter. "Let me just put my convictions to you this way, Mr. Floyt: if ever the intelligent life forms of this galaxy get to confront the Precursors before some higher power, I believe we shall be able to have them adjudged guilty of pet abandonment."

Floyt meditated upon that as the four reentered the forest. All around were strange plants, stranger sounds. It was hot, difficult, pointless inconvenience, which was pretty much Alacrity's definition of most sports.

Floyt wasn't quite sure how he became separated from the others, but given the jungle landscaping, it was no surprise. He could see the top of the target hill, and so pressed on that way.

Alacrity thought everybody was following his lead as he pushed and beat his way along. It took him a while to realize that nobody was behind him. He had a traumatized feeling there in the stillness and called out, but the undergrowth drank up all the sound.

He was edgy, forging on with his hackles up. He stopped calling out and moved furtively, stopping every four paces to look around. He came to open ground near the top of the hill but instinctively stayed in the cover of the forest.

At the top of the hill, where the target imp had been, Alacrity saw the hunched figure of Floyt, recognizing Plantos's jacket and the big *petasos* hat. Alacrity still couldn't put his finger on what was wrong, but decided he'd better give Floyt a whistle and summon him to cover until Vinzix and Marcus appeared.

Just then a spinning curvature of energy, another of Albrecht's missiles, came slicing up from the jungle and struck the reclining figure, crashing around it in a thousand tiny sunflares as it collapsed in on itself with an outpouring of energy discharge and smoke.

CHAPTER 6

LOGGERHEADS

ALACRITY BARELY KEPT HIMSELF FROM YELLING OUT; the warning wouldn't do Floyt any good now. Unable to absorb the fact of Floyt's death, he froze, waiting for the next firebolt to appear, with his name on it.

Fiddleheads of smoke and vapor wafted up from where Floyt had been crouched; there wasn't even a sign of remains. Maybe Albrecht had boosted the power. In any case, Lord Marcus and Vinzix were good with their chosen weapons and smart enough to know that they'd have to nail Alacrity at once.

That thought got him moving again, quietly circling away from where the boomerang had seemed to come, trying to look every which way at once. Something clambered up his leg. He slapped at it, and the little creepy-crawlie fell away. Then he cursed himself for making noise and resolved to let the next pest creep where it would; a sting would be a better risk than giving away his position.

He found a fallen branch and hefted it. It was fragile for a club and gave him little confidence. He backed and slunked along, not daring to rise, running through his options. *Going back to Ends Well just gets me killed sooner.*

He looked around at the trees, alarmed that they might have surveillance remotes, but he saw no detectors or security drones. *Which way's town? Where's the nearest habitation?* And then he recalled that Ends Well lorded over several river valleys.

Just at that moment, something grabbed his ankle.

Alacrity spun, resisting the urge to cry out, raising the club, heart about to beat its way out of his chest. Floyt had a hand up to ward off the blow; he said nothing, but motioned, *Sh-hh!* very quietly.

His coat, borrowed from Plantos's locker, and his *petasos* hat were gone. *Of course, blown to smithereens.* Alacrity understood all at once. *A decoy. And this is the guy Earthservice kept passing over for promotion!*

Floyt drew Alacrity a little farther downslope next to him and mouthed *Let's get out of here!*

Alacrity nodded enthusiastically, miming *But which way?*

Floyt gazed around, confused, and shrugged. At that moment they caught an exchange between Marcus and Vinzix, mediated by Albrecht, in slightly raised voices. They had a glimpse of the robo floating over a tangle of vines a few dozen meters away, uphill and to their right.

Marcus, in the target clearing, had found out that Floyt wasn't dead. He held up in gauntleted fingers a few shreds of cloth.

"Nobody was around, so I was playing with some of the target equipment," Floyt explained into Alacrity's ear in a whisper. "The imp reappeared, and I found out that those meshed force fields would support my hat—like the imp was wearing it. I was just passing time, experimenting. Then I tried my—Plantos's—mantle on him for size. Then I heard a sound and stepped off to one side to see what's going on. And all at once I've got Zeus Almighty displeased with me!"

Lord Marcus tossed the char aside angrily, beckoning Albrecht. Vinzix emerged at the edge of the undergrowth, carrying a lightshape boomerang.

As Albrecht summoned up a new weapon for Lord Marcus from thin air, Marcus and Vinzix made some rapid, soft-spoken exchange intertranslated by the robo,

the two of them peering this way and that. Floyt and
Alacrity hunkered to the ground, watching.

Albrecht manipulated another nexus, layering energy
warp and woof around it, to give Marcus a weapon like a
long double helix of bright plasma, a DNA lightning bolt.
Marcus balanced it in his gauntleted hands, scanning the
undergrowth, then went up over the top of the hill. Vinzix disappeared back into the treeline. Albrecht seemed
to debate for a moment, then floated off after Vinzix.
Alacrity was tentatively relieved, fairly certain that Albrecht had no special detection or hunting capabilities—
witness the fact that he wasn't all over Alacrity and
Floyt already. Likely, Albrecht could keep efficient track
of only those people wearing player's gauntlets.

The would-be killers would play out the drama very
carefully, Alacrity knew. *The Windfall cops are sticklers.
It's gonna have to look like a sporting accident for those
two to get away with murder.*

But Marcus and Vinzix had a good shot at it; all
they'd have to do, if they got Alacrity and Floyt, would
be to move the remains up to the target area. If the
killers phonied up the evidence right, there was every
chance the police would buy the story that way, of two
ignorant offworlders stumbling into the line of fire. That
would eliminate Alacrity as a problem, leaving them his
proteus and all its information, if they could crack it.
Still, the assassination attempt seemed rushed, and he
wondered why.

Vinzix and Marcus had no other choice now; attempted murder was a high dive on Windfall. Alacrity
still couldn't figure out why they hadn't waited though—
strung him along a bit more, or even gotten Floyt and
himself offworld somewhere, where murder was easier.

Alacrity touched Floyt's shoulder and pointed; they
moved off downhill and to the right. With no idea what
the hunters' plan was, their best bet was to try to disen-
gage, slowly and cautiously exfiltrating the area, then
make their way to some nearby human outpost.

Alacrity figured that when Lord Marcus and Vinzix

found their prey had eluded them, they'd try to get a jump in the matter of accusations, perhaps accuse the duo of attempted fraud or extortion or something that would similarly torque the jaws of the Windfall police. And Marcus had a houseful of identical concubines to back his testimony.

We'll dip that nacho when we come to it. Alacrity thrust the worry from his mind. *The thing now is to keep from getting sent to Holotarget Heaven.*

On the plus side, Alacrity knew that Marcus and Vinzix must be awfully edgy; they'd gambled on a quick kill and lost. They apparently couldn't carry more than one thunderbolt at a time, and Albrecht couldn't be with both of them at once. If one of them missed or used up his shot, it might take some time before the robo could rearm him; that had to give the old man and the humanoid some upstanding neckhair.

Alacrity lifted his head, craning for a view. Marcus Perlez might be hard to see, but Vinzix, with the gleaming Albrecht hovering near, should be easy to spot. Alacrity caught a silvery glitter farther downslope, almost directly along the path he and Floyt had been following. Vinzix must have been telepathic, a very good hunter, or astoundingly lucky.

Just then there was a crash from over the hill, in Marcus's direction. Floyt and Alacrity hit the dirt and froze.

Marcus called out, "Albrecht! Albrecht! Come here to me!" from a spot close to the top of the rise. Then, "Vinzix, stay where you are and be alert! I thought I saw them, but it was only a duffroller. They're somewhere close though! I can feel it!"

The two friends could hear a running translation coming from the near distance. Alacrity was trying to make up his mind whether now was the time to jump Marcus, before he could rearm. But Marcus was out in the open, and maybe Vinzix would be more than happy to kill all three humans. Then again, another chance might not come along . . .

He heard a sudden thrashing behind him. Alacrity turned, prepared to see Vinzix charging his way, only to see Floyt thrashing and wrestling with Albrecht, trying to drag the robo down. Albrecht's course between Vinzix and Marcus had brought him directly to them; Floyt had seized the chance without hesitating. Disabling Albrecht would leave Vinzix the only one armed, and that with only one bolt, improving the outlook a lot.

The problem was, Albrecht was no drone tea wagon. He spun and bucked, impossible to bring down, emitting bleats of distress. It gave Alacrity an instant's pause, seeing Floyt's daring and fast reaction. *I'd like to know how many other quiet little functionary third classes like him there are; you scratch some Earther's surface and all of a sudden you're dealing with a pit dog!* Even before he'd finished the thought, he'd thrown himself into battle.

The two found out right away that while he wasn't made for hand-to-hand combat, Albrecht was definitely put together with durability in mind. His hoverthruster blared full power, unable to lift him with the added weight clinging to him, but keeping him from being grounded. He slewed and slid and twirled around as they wrenched and grappled at him haphazardly.

Alacrity's club splintered over Albrecht's gleaming cranial turret without making a dent. Floyt's efforts to lever an arm out and wring it off got three of his fingers lacerated and several nails loosened, and almost got his *own* shoulder dislocated.

Luckily, Albrecht's defenses didn't include use of the roverbolts, or they'd have been parboiled. As it was, the machine tried to throw them off, pumping his arms in and out, rocking back and forth on his thrusters like a metronome.

Floyt lost his grip with one hand, clinging stoically with the other, half boots scraping and digging for purchase. Alacrity couldn't quite get a leglock on Albrecht's shiny, rounded torso and was fighting with one of the many arms. He didn't think that he and Floyt had more than another few seconds before Albrecht broke free, and was worrying hard about Vinzix's blazing boomerang, too.

Gripping the arm, Alacrity was yanked up close to the robot's head. All Albrecht's important machinery was well protected, naturally, including his pickups and detectors. About the only thing open to attack was the receptor for his programming augmentation. It abruptly came to Alacrity what it was he was staring at; he abandoned all thought of doing Albrecht harm.

Albrecht broke free of Floyt's grasp and grappled clumsily with Alacrity, while Alacrity concentrated on the receptor. One mechanical appendage opened Alacrity's forehead. Another came down hard across his collarbone, nearly stunning him. He locked his teeth and held on, trying to work while blood ran into his eyes.

Floyt was up again, circling to reenter the bizarre dustup, just as Albrecht pried Alacrity loose and shoved him backward, flailing. Alacrity landed in Floyt's arms, bearing them both to the ground, as the robo lifted free and floated away quickly in Lord Marcus's direction.

Marcus, hearing Albrecht's alarm stridences, was shouting for Vinzix and heading in the two companions' direction. Albrecht, homing on Marcus, was uttering loud translations in Vinzix's language.

Alacrity grabbed Floyt and the pair crawled, knee-walked, and tumbled for cover. In the denser undergrowth, they moved in a half crouch, ducking around trees and snagging themselves on vines, losing all sense of direction.

They stopped to get their bearings and catch their breath. Alacrity tucked something into his pocket, but Floyt was too winded and too concerned about being burnt to charcoal to ask what. Alacrity peeped around a lolling, paravaned leviathan tree.

Marcus was bellowing, not far off. "Vinzix! Over this way!" Albrecht translated at high decibels.

Floyt was all for running. But Alacrity stopped him, tugging him into a niche further up in the folds of the enormous roots. To Floyt's mind that was a sure way of getting cornered, and yet Alacrity was insistent. They silently found a crouching place, peering down on a nearby clearing. Vinzix bounded into it from one side, looking all around, the boomerang held ready.

Lord Marcus entered from the other side, the pulsing sheaf of a dart-spread in his gauntleted fist, arm reared back for a release. The two onlookers felt a lot of tiny things crawling around on the bark and in the humus beneath them, but kept absolutely still.

Floyt waited for Marcus or Vinzix to spot their prey, or Albrecht, who trailed along after Marcus, to detect them somehow. Floyt had heard about "the smell of fear" and always thought it a literary convention until he started traveling with Alacrity. Now, once again, he smelled it pouring from himself, from every pore, a thick reek that he was *sure* those below would catch, an acid stench that made him even more frightened.

"Where have they gone?" Marcus called to the Dar. Albrecht rasped the translation, which sounded rather short and curt.

Vinzix's head swung to Marcus, the pointy-toothed mouth opening to hiss something fierce in answer.

Albrecht piped to Marcus, "Stub-toothed groveler! Cease thy pulings, or I shall burn out *thy* sphincter as well as theirs!"

Alacrity grinned in triumph.

"Wh-what?" stuttered Marcus, disbelieving. "How's that again?"

Vinzix sounded like ice on a hot skillet. Albrecht rendered it as rage. "Address me with proper reverence, despised sublife! Use the respect you owe a noble of Darwin's Star, pallid vermin! I ought to smite you and give you over to the Pain Guild!"

Floyt couldn't grasp exactly what was going on until he stole a quick glance at Alacrity, who was holding up the protocol augmentation module he'd snatched from Albrecht's translating gear.

Floyt saw it all: *Why, they're getting literal transla-*

tions now! For the first time, Albrecht's not greasing the wheels!

"Now, just a moment, Vinzix, old man," fumbled Marcus as dutiful Albrecht kept up the translation. "Are you threatening me? I'll remind you that you're my partner, my *junior* partner; let's have no more of that talk! We've got more serious things to—"

"Partner?" Albrecht screamed as Vinzix hopped from foot to foot. "Junior? You dare speak so to one of the Master Species? Compulsive defiler of public comfort stations!"

Alacrity looked to Floyt with raised eyebrows and a nod of satisfaction. He'd *said* the Dars were the abrasive sort.

Lord Marcus's face was going magenta, eyes bulging. He shook his sheaf of Jovian darts. "Of all the impertinent, misbegotten heathen upstarts!"

"Aii!" Vinzix's nasal flaps were rolling up and down and his pupils appeared to be spinning in tight circles. Albrecht conscientiously did his best to put across the exact flavor of the Dar's spirited retort.

"You contemptible little subcreature! I have aberrant sex with your deity! I treat the gametes of your aunties as I would soil samples!"

"You, you *what*?" Marcus demanded, outraged but confused.

"And I laugh at your mother's ungainliness and place noxious elements in the fetish nooks of your elected representatives!"

Marcus stuttered and burbled a bit, trying to catch his breath, before supplying the capable Albrecht with more work: "You pompous, anchovy-brained scum! One more word and I'll teach you who's master here, you pelvis-faced castrato! And, and what's more, *you cheat at rovers!*"

That last proved too much to bear. With a gurgling sound, Vinzix launched himself at Marcus, ready to release his boomerang in a fast, aggressive windup.

Marcus stumbled back, coming up against the bole of the leviathan tree from which Floyt and Alacrity watched.

Marcus turned to the hovering robocaddy. "Albrecht! Emergency override Caliban! Target—"

But before Marcus could rattle off the rest, Vinzix jumped him. *Damn voice commands are so slow,* Alacrity reflected.

Vinzix moved fast as an adder, but somehow Marcus blocked the boomerang lightshape by bringing up his dart-spread to ward it off. It turned out to be an unwise tactic. The two energy bolts met in the middle of the meter and a half or so that separated the two disgruntled sportsbeings. There was a synergistic outsurge of energy, a sphere that engulfed them both, though Marcus took the worst of it.

The detonation shook the clearing, knocking Albrecht thrusters-over-cranial dome, even as he was readying new bolts. Marcus collapsed, body smoking a bit, quite dead. Vinzix was thrown to the ground and lay unmoving.

When Alacrity and Floyt had blinked back their vision, they saw the caddy circling the clearing aimlessly with a double helix pulsing in one hand and a flat disc glowing and humming dangerously in the other.

They looked at each other. Alacrity motioned that they should try to sneak down. Floyt concurred, deeming it imprudent simply to sit in the tree waiting for autumn.

They crept down cautiously and quietly as they could, but as Floyt was about to lend Alacrity a hand down, Albrecht made a loud, peremptory beep directly behind him. The two companions let out a shriek, Alacrity lost his grip, and Floyt ended up catching him. The pair froze, Alacrity in Floyt's arms, Floyt's knees quaking, as Albrecht studied them, energy bolts ready. Floyt shut his eyes, resigned to death.

"Further instructions needed," Albrecht said in a strange, neutral voice of his own. "Emergency override Caliban running."

Floyt dropped Alacrity, who yelped, then swallowed and said, "Clarify, Albrecht!" in a shaky voice.

The robocaddy didn't appear to recall his violent encounter with them of only a few minutes before. While Alacrity scrambled to his feet, Albrecht drew nearer. Floyt could feel the eddy currents from the rover bolts making the hair rise on his arms and head, stirring his beard.

"Caliban override in place," Albrecht clarified. "Weapons response ready, but Marcus-User disabled." Albrecht shook his weapons. "Target confirmation required."

Without hesitation, Floyt and Alacrity instantly pointed to Vinzix.

Albrecht released his lightning. Vinzix's body went up in fire and smithereens with such a blast that the humans were partly deafened. Albrecht took up position by Marcus's corpse as Floyt and Alacrity dropped hands away from their ringing ears.

"Do we hide the evidence or just run?" Floyt yelled, finding it difficult to hear himself.

"I like the idea of just running," Alacrity voted loudly. He was calculating times and distances. "We go back and have Tomasina call another cab, or even better, tell her Marcus wants her to take us to the starport herself. Tell her he and Vinzix are playing out the game together. I'm betting she's not in on the plot; murder's a serious deal here, so the fewer people involved, the better. We can be in Hawking by the time they find the remains."

Floyt drew a deep breath and moved his jaw around. A little more hearing returned. "That makes sense to me, but what shall we do in regard to *him*?"

He meant Albrecht, who was still on station in a hover. "He might have recorded everything—but no, Marcus wouldn't have wanted him to do that, would he? Albrecht, clarify, please, like a good fellow?"

"Recording mode not running," Albrecht chimed in. "Special accesses open. Standard restrictions suspended. Disinformation programs running."

"Well, that would appear to say it all," Floyt observed sourly. "Only what in the world does it mean?"

Alacrity combed sticks and moss and dirt and leaves out of his long mane of hair with his fingers. "Sez everything's status quo until someone tells him differently, I think. So there'll be no indication that anything out of the ordinary is going on, because Caliban's conducting a little business. That right, Albrecht?"

"Affirmative, subject to amending instructions from Marcus-User."

So Marcus tooled up his own skulduggery program, but he wasn't as good at it as he thought, Floyt realized. "Albrecht, see here, can *you* play rovers? Make the releases and so forth?"

Albrecht fixed him with glassy optical pickups. Floyt saw himself twinned in fisheye miniature. "Of course, sir. Does this indicate that the game's not over?"

"No, the game's not over. I want you to finish it; go to the next release point and carry on! But take your time; you're playing for two, don't forget. And when you've finished, go back to the first release point and wait for us. Confirm?"

"Confirmed, sir." Albrecht spun on his thrusters, Floyt's command ringing in his presets, and glided off to play the rest of the course. If anyone in Ends Well was monitoring the game, there was a chance they'd think all was as it should be. At least Albrecht was happy.

Floyt, coming to accept that he would live awhile longer, belabored himself, *You still haven't told Alacrity the truth. You'll have to soon!*

"Nope, the game's not over," Alacrity said with a laugh.

They straightened their clothes and cleaned themselves up as best they could as they made their way back to Ends Well. Floyt mulled over the various appalling revenges concubines had inflicted throughout history and tried hard to put together bright, convincing alibis.

Then they came around a big, flourishing clump of

spit-burrs and saw what was going on at Ends Well.
"Now what, Alacrity?"

Alacrity smiled wolfishly. "It's like I've told you:
there's hardly ever a down-market in accomplices."

Two long, luxurious touring motorcarriages and a
shuttletruck had been pulled up by the tall main doors.
Soldier-ant lines of Lord Marcus's adored, interchange-
able bacchantes were dumping armloads of stuff into
them. Some cargo was wardrobe bags and personal luggage, but the truck was taking on expensive pieces of
systemry and a few artworks. There were at least a
dozen look-alike women in the looting relay, all in the
burgundy glowtulle harem getups. Now, though, many
wore rings, bracelets, or other plunder.

One, clutching Larrup the minibuffalo, was directing
matters from the front steps. To her livery she'd added a
magnificent bib of Satan's tears trimmed with diamond-
droplet pendants.

"Hello, Tomasina." Floyt smiled amiably as the
women paused in their work to watch the two men war-
ily.

She patted Larrup, who bumped his tiny, blunted
horns against her. "Very good guess, sir. Or was it?"

Floyt blushed. "I, ah, happened to notice your dimples earlier. Briefly." It seemed more decorous not to
mention their location.

Tomasina smiled slowly. "Yes, We're not truly identical, are we?"

"Look, don't let us interrupt the clearance sale," Alacrity bade. Some of the women looked to one another,
then resumed.

"Now, what happened out there?" another harem
member—Callisto, Floyt thought she was—wanted to
know. She'd gotten herself a scintillating garter of white
wavestones and blood-red ardors from Lord Marcus's
trove. "Telemetry says the old perv is dead, but not
how."

"Him and Vinzix discovered their partnership was
based on mutual ignorance," Alacrity explained vaguely.

"How much time do we have before the cops come calling?"

Tomasina shook her wimpled head. "Marcus left the Caliban program running. It's set for times when he didn't want interruptions or the law. So, no alarms, no security monitoring, no nothing. The AI's and systemry will pretend to the outside world that nothing's wrong, no matter what, even using his own voice-image simulacrum. I'd say we have hours, possibly days, before anybody gets nosy."

Possibly-Callisto slipped an arm through Tomasina's. "But by then we'll just be a memory on Windfall. There's a passenger packet heading out-system."

Alacrity indicated the swag. "Even this might not be enough to buy you all interstellar tickets."

"I told you," Tomasina answered, "Caliban's running, but Marcus wasn't around long enough to give follow-up orders. That's the first time that ever happened; now *we* have access to most of the system, otherwise Marcus's deadman programs would be running and we'd all be dead, too, by now."

Floyt, still unsettled by the violence of the rovers game, shuddered. Callisto—Floyt was about certain it was she—said, "But as it is, the reservations are confirmed and the tickets were billed to Marcus's account, on his personal coded order. And as far as customs is concerned, he's ordered us to precede him on a business trip. We've got ourselves some *very* hefty bank drafts and power of attorney over some of his secret accounts, too. Not a clean sweep, but not bad either."

I wonder how long they've been planning it, Marcus's precious odalisques? Floyt wondered. Not that he could blame them. "Speaking of trips, Alacrity, it's time we were going."

"Waitaminute, waitaminute," Alacrity said with a calm-down gesture. "Tomasina, if you really have access to Marcus's data files, there's something I need to know from them."

"Not top-secret stuff, but most of it," she told him.

"Help yourself, but move fast if you want a lift to the starport."

Over Floyt's protests, Alacrity dragged him inside to a systems terminal. "Remember Marcus talking about that woman, Hecate? We need a line on where to find her, and whatever else there is."

Floyt reluctantly began accessing and searching. Alacrity disappeared, promising to return quickly. Ends Well's equipment was unfamiliar to Floyt, but he'd had a lot of experience in learning new systems lately. He was soon transferring info from Marcus's files to his proteus, scanning it as he went, fascinated in spite of his agonizing fear that he would hear the convoy gunning away without him.

Alacrity returned with an appropriated shoulder bag. "I raided the clinic stores and the autodocs," he told Floyt. "We can get rid of that peripheral neuropathy while we're in jump. Uh, that is, presuming we have a destination?"

Floyt shut down the terminal and clapped his proteus back on his wrist. "That we have. The story gets curiouser and curiouser, Alacrity."

"When was it otherwise?"

Outside, several of the women now wore different attire, conservative traveling clothes, and were getting behind the controls of the three vehicles, warming them up. Their russet hair, freed from the wimples, was fashioned in close caps of tight ringlets.

"The rest of us can change on the drive," Tomasina was saying. Last cases and pouches were tossed aboard and the former harem piled in. The truck was fairly filled with plunder and luggage, and the second touring carriage with exconcubines beginning to disrobe, windows and windshield adjusting to a dark tint. Laughter and the clinking of champagne glasses came from inside. Alacrity sighed.

Callisto and Tomasina were at the open passenger door of the lead carriage as another woman settled in to drive.

"Hurry up or you'll miss the wake," Tomasina called.

But as they trudged that way tiredly, hands reached out of the door of the second carriage and seized Alacrity by the shoulder bag. There was a lot of giggling, whooping, and wolf-whistling from within as he was dragged aboard, not struggling very hard. A few garters and loin buntings were lofted out the door, and just before it closed and latched Floyt heard another champagne cork pop.

"We're not exactly fair maidens; we'll take any edge we can get," Callisto told Floyt as he reached the lead carriage. "But that doesn't mean we don't know how to treat the gallant rescuer."

"Especially after a steady diet of Lord Marcus," Tomasina added. "I'm sure if you knocked, they'd let you in."

Floyt felt his face getting warm. "No, um—too crowded."

Tomasina gestured to the open passenger door and Callisto slid her arm around Tomasina's waist. They smiled at him appraisingly.

"Smaller gatherings still allow for some interesting permutations," Tomasina suggested.

If this was some other stringer, or contract killer, or field op—if it was anybody but this monster, Case Coordinator Deighton seethed, *I'd give 'em some hurts and run 'em out of the complex. Maybe even terminate 'em.*

But it simply wasn't anybody else; it was Gentry Standing Bear, one of a kind, smelling of Old Four Smokes Wallop, smoldering and bleary-eyed, too massive even for the outsize, reinforced chair across the desk from Deighton, making the chair groan and squeak beneath him.

Deighton's office there in the midst of the regional Langstretch Agency headquarters was supposedly equipped to handle trouble, even from somebody like Standing Bear—except that there was nobody else like Standing Bear—but Deighton by no means wished to

test that. There were astounding stories about the
amount of punishment Standing Bear could absorb.

Besides, Langstretch needed Standing Bear more now
than ever. Floyt and Fitzhugh's unnerving victory over
Plantos and his team had made a lot of people in Langstretch and elsewhere very apprehensive; their astounding success against Lord Marcus Perlez and Vinzix had
sent shock waves into many quarters and caused a
goodly number of crisis-action briefings.

"What've you got for me?" Standing Bear asked, low
and guttural.

Deighton found himself avoiding the devastated man-
iac mask of a face, then steeled himself to control that
and met Standing Bear eye to eye. Deighton, a tall man
carrying 130 kilos—twenty more than when he was a
field op, but they hadn't slowed him down very much, he
liked to think—had dozens of confirmed kills. He'd
done more interrogations than he could count. He was
used to being the intimidating one; that was not the case
in this instance, though.

Deighton got a hold of himself. "We don't know
where they went when they left Ends Well, but we're
certain that sooner or later they'll show up for the meeting of the Board of Interested Parties."

Incredible, Deighton reflected, how Perlez and Vinzix
bollixed the kill. And all because Perlez panicked and
rushed the job.

From what Langstretch could reconstruct from the
Ends Well systems and other sources, Perlez was very
worried about a proteus Fitzhugh had stolen from Baron
Mason. For some reason Perlez feared that the proteus
might reveal that he was one of the Interested Parties
who'd commissioned Langstretch to kill or capture Fitzhugh when Fitzhugh was still a kid.

Perlez was also afraid of what hideous things Fitzhugh would do to him if he found out that Perlez had
been instrumental in breaking his parents and even in
getting them hooked on undertow.

Perlez had been content to play Fitzhugh and Floyt

along until he was sure they had Baron Mason's proteus. Then he'd plunged ahead with that half-ass rovers murder scheme, with the unstable Darwin's Star native as an accomplice, no less.

Perhaps Fitzhugh's survival success lay not so much in aptitude as in the matter of inept opponents. Except now he and Floyt were top priority, and Gentry Standing Bear had a personal stake in the case.

"We have good coverage in the Spican system," Deighton went on, "but we're sending you there just in case—"

Standing Bear was on his feet before Deighton saw him start to move, fist crashing down, splitting the hard Promethea strandwood of the desk. Deighton almost went for a defense foot-trigger, but held off, breathing Old Four Smokes Wallop fumes.

"Pull them back," Standing Bear said in a shockingly level, controlled voice. "They can clean up after me; I don't care. The kill's mine."

"We have to be certain this time—" Deighton started.

"Keep your people out of my way or lose them. Makes no difference to me," the horrible face said evenly.

Deighton was about to object but decided to listen. He'd broken scores, hundreds of men and women in one way or another, and yet when it came right down to it he was scared by this man. Standing Bear made him feel, for the first time, like a little, fat, slow old man. Standing Bear had once carried out a termination contract on a wealthy power broker out in the Bamboo Confederation, right in her own office, her very well defended office that wasn't so different from Deighton's.

"You get me to Spica in your fastest ship," Standing Bear decreed. "To Eden, for starters, then maybe Nirvana. I'll need money, too."

Standing Bear untensed a little, distracted by thoughts for his mission requirements. Deighton relaxed the slightest bit, trying to breathe slowly.

"When it's done, you'll give me a bonus," Standing

Bear's huge hand retreated and Deighton gazed at the split strandwood. "Because I'm going to be *very* thorough."

Deighton swallowed hard and nerved himself for the fight of his life, should standing Bear lose control in the next few seconds. "I see no problem with a *good* bonus. But listen, you've gotta understand, this is beyond my control—there are certain requirements on this assignment now, new ones— Standing B—no, *wait!*"

Standing Bear, enormous hands resting lightly on either of Deighton's shoulders, fingers close to a neck so fragile to that overwhelming strength, decided to grant a few seconds' reprieve. Deighton's life depended on whether or not the goliath cared for the new requirements.

CHAPTER 7

ANOTHER THINK COMING

"NOT A BAD PLANET, IF ONE'S TASTE RUNS TO THE DEAD-end and obscure," Floyt allowed, peering down at Lebensraum. In many ways it resembled Earth, though it was smaller with much less surface water and more modest polar caps. It had less desert and more vegetation. "But the question is, why would a woman like Hecate want obscurity?"

He gestured to the cockpit data mosaic of screens and projections. "I mean, the woman spent decades courting celebrity and glory. Why would she elect to drop from sight? And then reappear after all this time *not* to reclaim her stock in the White Ship, but to establish a hokey little sideshow?"

Alacrity was staring at Lebensraum, too, chin on fist. "When we find her, you can ask."

They'd worried those questions all through the trip. Hecate—Loebelia Curry—was a renowned figure of the early Third Breath: explorer and adventurer, dauntless seeker of Precursor secrets, a prime motivator of the White Ship project.

Recordings showed her to be one of the great beauties of her day, a full-lipped siren with mounds of rich black hair framing her face and shoulders and direct, dark eyes that locked the viewer's. She'd hunted, tamed wild animals, fought in at least one war, and amassed a huge fortune through assorted businesses and investments. People rioted for tickets to her personal appearances. A life of passionate free-spiritedness didn't keep her from being recognized as a leading authority on Precursor matters.

She'd spent considerable time on Lebensraum, becoming a local legend some twenty years before, then dropped out of sight. By various accounts she'd died or left the planet or vanished into the vast Lebensraum wilderness.

"If we find her," Floyt said.

"We'll find her. Destiny and all that. How do I know? The causality harp told me so."

Partly due to Alacrity's high spirits at having such a strong lead on his Quest, but mostly because of the medicine Alacrity appropriated at Ends Well, Floyt didn't differ with him, though the Earther knew that Alacrity was wrong about the causality harp's affirmation of his destiny as Master of the White Ship.

There was a large container of stuff called neurogeneomicin. In small doses it was just the ticket to help counter their peripheral neuropathy. In larger doses it was highly addictive, the drug of choice among abuser medical personnel who could lay hands on it, and the addiction that led Alacrity's parents to tragedy. Among junkies its name was undertow.

Alacrity spent the odd contemplative moment looking at it, an incredible three liters, wondering what Marcus was doing with so much—a clear blivet full of it. But he kept his own and Floyt's dosages scrupulously to the prescribed microlevels.

In the presence of so much of the stuff that had contributed to the death of Alacrity's failed, despondent father—enough to O.D. a hardened addict hundreds of times over—Floyt held back his terrible news. Surely soon, with the therapy finished, there'd be some way to dispose of the stuff or render it unusable.

"No argument, Alacrity. We'll find her. But that information in Marcus's Whereabouts file was almost six months old. What if we pay the Lebensraum Company's landing fees only to find out that Hecate's gone on to better things?"

The Lebensraum Company was the chartered corporation—mining mostly; precious gems and metals—that controlled the planet under the lackadaisacal Bali Hai Republic, which held sway over five local starsystems. According to files, the company wasn't very cordial to visitors, though under Bali Hai law it couldn't bar them. So it charged stiff landing and docking fees by way of discouraging outsiders.

"This is all the negotiable wealth we've got, and when it's gone we're flat," Floyt reminded Alacrity, holding up the garter Callisto had given him as a parting gift and grubstake.

We're not exactly fair maidens, but that doesn't mean we don't know how to treat the gallant rescuer!

Alacrity made a meaningless bear-sound, whether because he hated being reminded of their money problems of because no one had lavished any such generosity on him, Floyt couldn't make out. He suspected it was both.

"All right, Ho. Maybe we can check, save ourselves throwing money away." Alacrity raised Lebensraum starport control on voice-only commo to avoid giving authorities a look at himself, Floyt, or the interior of the *Lightning Whelk.*

"Can anybody down there tell me if the Hecate Thrill-show is still in town?"

There was a moment's silence from the ground; it wasn't speed-of-light lag and Alacrity knew it wasn't because they were busy, because Lebensraum's traffic was light. In fact, the arrival of a nonfreight starship should be a big occasion. Floyt swapped troubled looks with him.

"All right, whoever you are," the response came. "Read me, we don't need troublemakers down here. If you have no business to conduct with the Lebensraum Company, I would suggest you keep moving."

Alacrity was thinking about what to say to that when

another voice came up, a woman's. It was throaty and vibrant. "Out-system ship, switch to common-use freq three!"

Starport control was still yelling about improper commo procedure as Alacrity searched through the data banks to find out which one was common-user freq three. Evidently a starship *was* an event, and people monitored when one showed up. Alacrity switched over.

"You bet your bum I'm still around," that same female voice proclaimed. "This is Hecate speaking, Queen Hellion of the Third Breath, Keeper of the Precursor Mysteries and Dirty-Fighting Champion of Wherever I Happen to Be! Now bring up your visual; let me get a look at you."

"Not just now," Alacrity fended. "But we want to meet with you."

"Is that right? What are you, talent scouts? Promotors? Maybe Hecate hasn't got anytime to waste on you, mystery voice. Maybe you're just another company pest?"

Alacrity thought for a few seconds. Then he set his proteus into an adaptor in the control console and manipulated it. Eerie tonalities played out over the commo, troubling but lofty. They reminded Floyt somewhat of the sounds of the causality harp back in the Precursor site underneath Epiphany. They seemed to go right through him, and did strange things to his cerebrocortex. But it became melodic, and he lost track of time.

Alacrity retrieved his proteus, slipping it back on his wrist. "What d'you say to that, Hecate?" Floyt blinked, coming awake again.

She was slow in answering. "*Huh*! All right, come to my bigtop tonight; anybody can tell you the way to the Wicked Wickiup. You can see Hecate in action, and my show's *worth* a star-hop. Afterward we can have a chat."

The contact broke.

"Alacrity, what were those sounds?"

Alacrity was rubbing fingertips on his proteus. "Precursor music, I think you could call it. I got it from my folks. If Hecate knows what it is, she'd be the real item, except that I'm not so sure she knew. Only a few people have ever heard that recording."

"I couldn't tell whether she recognized you or you just flummoxed her."

"Me either. At least we get to talk to her. We'll know soon enough if she's Hecate."

"And if she is?"

"I'm on my way to being Master of the White Ship."

"Let's just say she's not?"

"Then it'll happen some other way." Alacrity thought for a bit. "I wonder what the local firearm laws are like?"

As it turned out, they were even more stringent than on Windfall. Like most authoritarian governments, the Lebensraum Company got hysterical at the mere thought of an armed populace. The Captain's Sidearm and the Webley stayed locked in the ship.

Lebensraum's star, Invictus, was large and amber and its only starport was a drab, outdated industrial terminal. Floyt studied both out the ship's cockpit viewpane, stretching his fingers and feeling his lips and fingertips, as Alacrity locked down the console. Their peripheral neuropathy was completely gone.

Lebensraum had been explored around the end of the Second Breath, nearly two hundred years before, by expeditions from Shalimar, a more idyllic planet in the Invictus system. A brief flurry of interest occurred when indications of Precursor artifacts were observed, but no significant finds were made.

With no economic enticements to be found, Lebensraum was soon ignored by all but a minor research project, then out of touch completely for nearly one hundred years after an apocalyptic battle on Shalimar at the end of the Second Breath.

An expedition some one hundred years before Alacrity and Floyt rolled out of Hawking revealed that there was still a tiny human population, hovering on the verge of extinction, and that there was very considerable wealth to be taken from Lebensraum with new mining techniques.

Through political leverage and judicious bribery, the expedition's backers managed to wangle a mining company charter for Lebensraum from the Bali Hai Republic, neatly outflanking the Shalimar government. Lebensraum Mining and Development slapped a cloak of secrecy on its operations. The human survivors were relocated to a small reservation, though most succumbed to diseases brought in by company workers, or dissipation, or simple cultural absorption.

There was also a very successful species of native wildlife, huge herbivores called gawklegs, that had the bad luck to enjoy grazing on lands coveted by the company. The management techniques used in dealing with them weren't mentioned, but the endless, teeming herds of gawklegs were, in a shockingly brief time, reduced to a handful of scattered bands.

Somehow, Hecate had showed up there twenty years before, becoming the darling of the workers, charming top company officials into letting her look into Precursor rumors and lending her all support. She became the planet's unofficial royalty and star attraction until at last she dropped from sight.

"I guess the old brolly'll be about all the protection we can carry," Alacrity said. He hefted his Viceroy Imperial, a product of Outback.

"Most kinds of small blades are legal groundside, Ho," Alacrity added. "Maybe it wouldn't be a bad idea if you carried that survival tool whatsit you got at the Grapple—oh!"

Floyt had turned and raised his fatigue jacket and sweater a little to show that he had already set it in a belt pouch at his waist. The do-all survival tool incorporated various blades, a compass, assorted tools, brass knuckles, and a radiation detector; also, you could scale fish with it.

"Great. Do me one more favor, Ho? Wear your Inheritor's belt?"

"If you want. Do you think it will prove how much this supposed Hecate really knows?"

"It could happen that way."

So Floyt fetched the heavy belt of plaques; if Hecate actually knew Precursor secrets, perhaps she could translate or explain the strange symbols on it. He fastened it high around his waist, covering it with the military-style sweater he'd taken from Plantos's locker.

"You know, Alacrity, I've lost a good deal of weight since we left Earth—the first time, I mean—but this thing fits me just as precisely as it did then."

"It's probably just trying to impress you. You ready?"

"Let us proceed."

They locked up the *Lightning Whelk*, using a built-in touchpad rather than the code-key, and stepped out into a golden dusk out of a Flemish masterpiece as Invictus disappeared below the horizon. They'd acclimatized gradually during the trip; Lebensraum's lower air pressure didn't bother them. To Floyt it smelled weird as hell, just as had every other XT world. He felt light on his feet in ninety-odd-percent gravity.

The starport was situated at one end of town, in a deep depression, the locals not trusting starcraft not to blow up or release radiation and yet not wanting the port too far from their center of governmental control.

Horselaugh, Lebensraum's only city, was actually just a modest company town, built in functional, uninspired Aerospace Doric. It was mostly admin and operations structures and company housing, interspersed with blankly identical service/retail centers.

Here and there noncompany businesses or dwellings were mostly crammed in the crannies, hovels, and arc-shelters, marked by eye-catching lightsigns. Horselaugh was a workers' town; what the Lebensraum Company couldn't stifle in human nature it had to learn to live with.

Alacrity gritted his teeth as they entered the customs

shed. Floyt got the picture when he saw that the currency-exchange and assayer's booths were side by side with the inspection station. The two visitors were given med and immunity tests, then scanned and searched and questioned in a local language that was not too far from Terranglish, by surly officials dressed in the ominous black of the company police.

In due course Floyt exchanged the resplendent garter at a surprisingly fair rate, was immediately hit with a ruinous tax on the transaction, and signed over much of the rest of his money for docking fees and security. The only break they got, as far as Alacrity could see, was that the actual starport operations were overseen by Bali Hai officials. With any luck, that would mean company goons wouldn't have access to the *Whelk*. Over strenuous objections, Floyt accepted his change in company scrip.

There were frowns all around when the two listed their business as "Talent Promotion," and three different officials told them what terrible things would be done to them if they strayed beyond Horselaugh without permission. All told, what with approach, landing and interminable bureauwanking, it was over four hours after hearing from Hecate that they were given visas and permission to explore Horselaugh.

They ventured out into the evening along an elevated walkway. Company police were patrolling, swinging clubs and chukas, watching. Traffic cruised by below and the sky was open above except for the occasional cop aircruiser or company limoflier.

Alacrity wore a shipsuit, his pathfinder boots, and a big blue bandanna. Floyt had on bush fatigues—high-waisted pants and thigh-length jacket over the sweater—and lug-soled lace-up hiking boots that reached above his ankles. The boots were a bit narrow but long enough, so he'd chosen them; Floyt had long since learned the kind of things you can step in, in a starportside town.

If the two didn't exactly blend in with the locals, at least they didn't stand out too terribly.

These were contract miners, but not the pick-and-shovel variety. Most worked hard for their money, but their standard of living was adequate and their off-duty clothing showed it. They looked prosperous, but similar. The fashion in women's hair ran to a white cotton-candy look, floating like spindrift. Clothing tended to be comfortable and durable. Perhaps as a reaction to their industrial surroundings, many of the Horselaughers wore or carried fresh flowers.

In the midst of all this, Alacrity and Floyt got a few strange looks, but nobody bothered them.

The company employees would retire comfortably—offworld—if they did their jobs and behaved; that benefit had enormous appeal in the uncertain times of the Third Breath.

Alacrity had in his proteus a legal transaction program he'd prepared with Floyt's help and frequent references to the various legal data stores inboard the *Welk*. If he could just get Hecate to validate it with the proper Interested Party codes, it would give him voting power over her long-dormant shares. In one stroke, he'd go from nonentity spacebum to major power broker.

There was no visible boxtown at the Horselaugh spaceport, a fact that surprised Floyt and aroused caution in Alacrity. The fact that no technological slum had arisen there where there should have been one meant Lebensraum was tightly controled indeed, even if it gave the Bali Hai Republic lip service.

They passed on the cramped-looking cabs and crowded public transport to stretch their legs after the long confinement of their Hawking jump. Alacrity asked some locals for directions to the Wicked Wickiup. The couple looked at the two offworlders curiously, but obliged, saying Hecate's bigtop was within easy strolling distance.

Alacrity found his way as much by instinct as by the city map he'd cadged in the customs house. Every turn took the two friends onto seedier streets. Soon company cops were patrolling in threes and fours.

Steerers and gatehawks beckoned passers-by into shows, things like customers'-choice sexshows, toxin races, and badger-in-the-barrel. Still, Floyt noticed none of the wax-skinned addicts or hollow-eyed starveling children he'd seen elsewhere in the Third Breath. On Terra, under the Earthservice, there were none either (or at least, none to be *seen*) and yet he'd rejected it and had no regrets.

Floyt and Alacrity turned a corner in a district that seemed to consist mainly of awful-smelling breweries and came into sight of an extruded-glassfroth hemisphere covering two or three hectares of ground a few hundred meters beyond the edge of town. The blossoming light-effect fireworks, goodtime music, and crowd-tumult didn't leave much room for doubt, but a revolving holo-flash sign, like some Old Testament show-stopper, announced THE WICKED WICKIUP.

There was some crowd-press as they got close to the entrance, but it wasn't bad; the place had opened at dusk and the main performance had been going on for almost two hours.

Inside, it smelled in ways Floyt could never hope to describe, especially the odors drifting in from that part of the dome set apart as a menagerie.

The Lebensraum wildlife on display there was interesting but sad to see, and the few offworld specimens downright depressing. Floyt traded bleak looks with a couple of them and didn't mind when Alacrity said that they should be seeing to business.

They passed an assortment of Karmic readers, growth hosts and other freaks, radiation eaters, and similar side-show fodder. Vendors and concessionaires offered food, drinks, drugs, and souvenirs, particularly Hecate memorabilia.

The main arena of the Wicked Wickiup was crowded, even though the next day was a workday for most of the people there. In the center was a traditional ring bounded by low blocks, carpeted with shredded cellu-line. Above were the retracted riggings for aerial and highwire acts, bounce-jousting, and such. Floyt and Alacrity had arrived too late for Hecate's animal taming and knife-throwing performances, but in time for her finale.

An act was just finishing up, a mock battle of some kind, attended by very effective and convincing special effects, imitation blood gushing as blades glittered and swung. The acting wasn't very good, but the crowd loved it, rooting for one side and then the other, whistling piercingly and stomping their feet so that the Wicked Wickiup shook. Having seen the real thing, Floyt watched with a certain queasiness. Alacrity looked on indifferently.

The seating areas were sold out, occupied mostly by well-heeled company execs. Floyt looked up and around and noticed a box with only one occupant, a motionless, silent figure in a hooded robe, face concealed by the cowl's deep shadow.

Like most of the others Floyt and Alacrity jostled their way up onto the low, sloping terraces of gluefused dirt. Each terrace was only a half meter above the one before, and only three meters wide, with a few rows of railings to lean on.

People were eating tiny, glazed birdlike delicacies that were swallowed whole, bones and all, and skewers of dog and cat meat. Shots of aquavit were popular, and strong dark porter in vitrilex mugs cast in the shapes of squatting totem figures. Popular local drugs were brainspark, jangle, and perceptimax.

The throng was predominantly male and rowdy. It was obvious from the smell of the gluefused terraces that a lot of them weren't troubling to search out a urinal when the urge hit. There was a lot of scuffling, and several fights were in progress. The ones Floyt could see well weren't too interesting.

The phoney bloodletting ended, and the fake casualties were taken away. The lights lowered. Expectant silence—or at least a lowering of the general commotion—prevailed. Free-floating lighting cones swooped in to focus spots on a semicircular gate. A fanfare blew as the gate opened and a mounted figure plunged into the arena in a convergence of spots.

Everybody who was sitting came to their feet; those standing threw hands, hats, glasses into the air. Floyt and Alacrity winced from the volume as the whole house shouted, "HECATE!"

She cantered her mount around the ring, a splendid figure in her high-gloss black bodysuit with its glittery silver stitching, padded shoulders built in upflared tiers, cleavage cut below her navel to show off the taut, sinewy body. Hecate wore tall cavalier boots, and a low-slung gunbelt supported a pair of pistols riding in deep scabbards, butts forward.

A silver fillet held to the center of her forehead a frosty blue-white moonpure at least three centimeters wide; her jet-black hair streamed and tossed behind her.

She rode the standard Lebensraum saddle animal, a Clydesdale-size thing that put Floyt in mind of a tapir with an extra set of legs and delusions of grace. Its horns were flecked with motes of sparkle and its saddle and tack inlaid with gold.

The audience was still going wild, shouting her name. She waved to them, throwing kisses with both hands.

"Alacrity?" Floyt yelled, to make himself heard. "Does that woman look to be in her mid-sixties to you? She doesn't to me."

He was staring down at the smooth, cameo-lovely face and full breasts that seemed to linger in the air for a split-instant longer than the rest of her at the top of each bounce, rooting for them to bob free of the wonderful bodysuit.

"Tough to tell, Ho. She might've troweled on that stage makeup. Or maybe she's just in fantastic shape. Or she could've gotten treatments. But yeah, I was just thinking the same thing."

He was thinking, too, that she might know Precursor secrets that would make time and age irrelevant.

Hecate set herself in the saddle of her tapir-beast, which was known as a hoofalong, its ancestors having been imported from Shalimar, and began doing fancy riding tricks as the creature pounded patiently around the ring. She turned completely around in the saddle, then hung off to either side and did touch-and-go remounts. She hung off behind, pulled along by the hoof-along's tail, and vaulted back into the saddle, then clambored completely around the thing, sliding under its belly and hauling herself up again on the opposite side.

She did a handstand on the yoke-saddlehorn, then knelt on her steed's back, arms out to receive her ovation. Next, Hecate stood on her mount's bobbing croup, body rolling with its gait, hips moving in wave-curls.

"Look at this; they love 'er," Alacrity said. They did; the people in the Wicked Wickiup, especially on the terraces, were cheering themselves hoarse, women as much as the men or more.

"Quit salivating," Floyt advised Alacrity. "The White Ship, remember?"

Floyt meant it as a kind of weary joke; the effect wasn't so funny. The salacious look left Alacrity's face, and he inclined his head to himself a few times, taciturn and distant. "Mm-hmm; the Ship," he mouthed silently.

This sense of destiny stuff is starting to take precedence over his libido; it's completely out of hand! Floyt decided. But he held his peace. The terraces of the Wicked Wickiup were no place for a shouting match over the causality harp and Alacrity's dangerous secrets.

But as soon as we're back inboard the Lightning Whelk, Floyt made his mind up for the dozenth time . . .

Target holos orbited down into place, projected minitures in shapes of celestial bodies, strange life forms, and darting starcraft.

The woman dropped back into the saddle and drew both long-barreled pistols, and began potting the targets out of the air. Each shot was a filament of yellow-green energy; each one popped a holotarget out of existence in a *girandole* of spark swarms and novabursts. New ones moved down from the darkness to take their places.

"I thought firearms were forbidden here," Floyt said at high volume, so that Alacrity could hear him.

Alacrity made an unsure face. "Bird guns, or maybe just flashlights, harmless. Or maybe she's just the exception to all the rules."

All at once Hecate swung around to ride backward, firing with the same speed and accuracy.

The targets started coming faster. She lay on her back plinking them from the air. On the next lap she was standing on her mount's croup again, both guns blazing, skeeting targets that destructed like skyrockets. Flowers and coins and gifts were showering around her.

A sunflare hoop was lowered, and a bed of up-ended bayonets. She took the jump expertly and trotted to the center of the ring to take her bows standing on the hoof-along's back. Only the antipersonnel repel field around the ring kept the smitten, aroused, and buzzed crowd from swarming down to show their feelings more emphatically or kidnap her or perhaps make her mayor of the planet.

Hecate was still bowing to mass adoration when Alacrity and Floyt worked their way down off the terraces. No one else seemed inclined to leave. The stomping, handclapping, cheering, and whistling echoed through the dome's back corridor as the two finally found the door leading backstage.

Leaving, Floyt happened to notice the lone, hooded occupant of the box. Whoever it was was still seated, motionless in the bedlam.

When at last they made their way to the dressing-room section, Floyt commented, "On ancient Earth they used to call this type here 'stage-door Johnnies.'"

The way was guarded by a trio of big, burly men with bouncer written all over them. Held at bay were assorted admirers, swells, playboys, and suitors, and some quite stunning stage-door Janes, all trying to get in to see Hecate.

Gifts ran to extravagantly wrapped boxes and bottles, and exotic flowers. Diverse bribes, ruses, and pleas were being plied on the door guards, who looked immune. Floyt and Alacrity forged their way toward the front of the crowd.

A Johnny in an erminelike robe scowled at them and barked, "Repair from here! Hecate has sworn to have dinner with me!"

Alacrity got ready to do a little detail work on the man with his brolly, but the remark provoked the toff in the silken lounging suit, standing nearby, who was under the impression that *he* had a firm date with the Queen of Lebensraum. They were soon pushing and shoving one another; Alacrity and Floyt bore on.

People began to notice their offworld clothes. That gave them a certain leeway to attract the attention of the Three Heads of Cerberus, at the portal.

"Now, how d'we get in?" muttered Alacrity.

As answer, Floyt pulled out his Wonderment, the gift he'd been given by the Sockwallet Outfit on his first visit to Luna. It was a commemorative coin with Yuri Gagarin's face on it, encircled by the inscription, *April 12, 1961–April 12, 2461*, and TERRA: 500 YEARS IN SPACE.

Alacrity watched admiringly as Floyt showed it to a guard, saying "I believe we're expected," then flipped it to him. The coin spun, throwing off light, as many people watched it, willingly or not. The Head of Cerberus snatched it from the air and inspected it.

"Right this way," he said. The two hustled to follow him through the door before the crowd could recover and get ugly. The corridor led partway around the curve of the dome's base. Eventually the guard stopped at another door and knocked, then opened it and leaned in to say something Floyt and Alacrity couldn't catch. He pulled back out and motioned them in.

Floyt, in the lead, paused with his empty palm in front of the guard's face, snapping his fingers. The husky glared but returned his Wonderment. The sidekicks entered, and the Head of Cerberus closed the door behind them with a bang.

Hecate was sitting at a makeup console, multiple

pickups and imagers showing her face, neckline, and hair from all angles. The dressing room was filled with bouquets and wreaths. There were also stacks of gifts, most still wrapped.

She was glamorously lanky, her breasts too generous for the long-legged body. She still wore the guns and bodysuit, its exaggerated shoulders suggesting athletic padding, or armor. Seeing it at close range, Floyt couldn't decide if the material was leather, fishskin, dynamaflex, or what.

Her eye makeup made her look like a female pharaoh; her thick, musky perfume mingled with the cosmetics' smell, her perspiration, and the fragrances of the flowers. She looked to be a biological age of twenty or so, Alacrity saw, and had bright-red duraglaze glamornails on every finger.

She was pouring herself a shotglass of some violet liquor and inspecting them curiously, dark eyes shining and penetrating. "How'd you like the show?" She flipped the drink back and started pouring another.

"I thought you were superb," Floyt declared.

She raised her shoulders casually, accepting her due. She looked to Alacrity for another compliment but he blankfaced. "Do I know you two?" She rested the heel of one hand on a pistol butt.

Alacrity'd been ready to swear they weren't real weapons she was hauling, but suddenly he wasn't so sure. "Yes and no," he replied. "We've got something for you."

"And what might that be?"

"Some news," Floyt put in. "And an offer."

"We know about Loebelia Curry," Alacrity went on. "We know about her stock in the Ship. If *we* can find you, believe me, other people can, too. We've come to strike a deal. If you won't vote your stock, I want you to empower me to." He began slipping off his proteus.

She'd become uneasy. "I think you'd better go. We have nothing to discuss."

"Before we do, we should warn you," Floyt interrupted calmly. "Whoever you are, you're in over your head pretending to be Hecate. Your life's in danger, or will be soon if anybody's picked up our trail."

She was on her feet, taller than he. "What d'you mean, 'pretending'?"

"You enjoy the spotlight, wealth, and presents, and you still remain on Lebensraum. If you truly *were* Hecate you could have more of those than just about anybody alive, simply by going and claiming them."

Her eyes were slits painted for drama as her teeth clenched. "The company *did* send you to make trouble for me, didn't they? All I have to do is yell for help—not that I need it—and you two'll be ripped into such little pieces they won't be able to find you without *litmus paper*!"

"We didn't expect to meet you!" Alacrity protested. "We came looking for the real Hecate! You gonna have us killed for a thing like that?"

"I may have to." But her hands hung at her sides. Alacrity and Floyt relaxed minutely. There was a knock at the door.

"Well?" she yelled.

Another of Cerberus's heads poked into the room. "Crowd's gone and we're closing down the house, Hecate. The landau's ready, but some o' those lover folks are still hanging around the back exit."

She thought for a moment. "I have business to talk over with these two. Wait about ten minutes, then drive around to the front. I'll let us out the main entrance and meet you there."

When he showed hesitation, she stamped her heel. "I said get going!" He got.

The woman who claimed to be Hecate was hooking a travel pouch on her gunbelt and swirling an expensive spectralux evening shawl around her shoulders. She fastened a proteus, a pricey bracelet thick with lava pearls and ardors, around her wrist over her long bodysuit sleeve.

"All right, what's this about? When you said Ship you were talking about the White Ship, right?"

Floyt looked to Alacrity for a cue. Alacrity thought it over. "We were gonna lock down a deal with the real Hecate; mutual profit, and all of that."

She was looking at him thoughtfully. "Well now, maybe we can still do a little business here. After all, I *am* Hecate, hmm?"

But he was shaking his head. "This kind of con will get over on a bilge-class world like Lebensraum, but fooling the people *I* have in mind would be just about impossible. They'd run a full I.D. scan on you, and you'd need access codes and computer passwords. The only thing *you'd* get us is shot straight into the Null Set. Sorry."

"Don't be so hasty!" She pounced at him. "Give me a second to think about it, here, mystery man!"

"Perhaps you could tell us what happened to the real Hecate?" Floyt suggested delicately, to head off what would most probably have been a snide rejoinder from Alacrity.

She shrugged again, the layered flaps over her shoulders rising. "Take your pick of the rumors. Most have her dying, or heading offworld never to come back. Some say she never returned from her last expedition into the wilds. She was supposed to be pretty dough-brained by that time anyway. My guess is that the marrowbugs and drillworms recycled the last of her a long time ago."

"Any heirs?" Alacrity asked.

"None that I ever heard of. Except that I cashed in on her name."

"And you appear to have done quite well," Floyt commented.

She put on a half-pleased, half-ironic smile. "It's not easy. But I grew up on a saroo ranch, and I put in a stint with the First Mounted Rifles on Mephisto. Oh, I've been here and there. I taught dancing and survival skills and I picked up quite a bit of cash modeling. It all seemed to come together in the Wickiup."

They followed her out and waited as she locked her dressing room, then fell in three abreast—with Alacrity taking the center, naturally.

"What happened was," she resumed, "I was a little too smart for my own good, or a little too choosy. I thought I had myself a free ride with a high-roller who had his own starship. But when we got here, out at a company executives' retreat, he told me my end of the bargain. Gentlemen, I'm all for a good time, but there are some games *this* dame doesn't play. So he stranded me. No money, no way home, no documents.

"But I *did* meet the house surgeon. He was a sharp old duffer, a Hecate buff from when he was a kid, and he had a plan. I was a pretty close match as it was, and he tailored the rest to fit."

"So you just pretended to wander in from the wilderness?" Floyt asked. "And they bought it?"

She paused as they came to the entrance to the arena. "Doc pulled a few strings and got some company records altered so I scanned out as Hecate. And what the hell, people loved the show, even when we started out small. You can see how things've been going."

She gestured around proudly at the Wicked Wickiup, then saddened. "Only the good life was a bit too much for old Doc. The pile he made by being my silent partner was enough for him to whoop it up all the way to the mortuary." She thought for a moment. "I'll say this for him, though: he went out laughing."

"Well, good," Alacrity said, "but all that doesn't help us very much."

"Wait, now," she said. "Don't rush me; I'm thinking. It's time I got off Lebensraum anyway."

That brought Alacrity up short. "Yeah? Why? And why'd you think we were someone the company sent around to give you problems?"

She gave him a guileless look. "Because men tell me things."

"Oh?" Floyt asked, uncomprehending. She put her hands on her sleek hips, arching her back, holding her head just so, the shawl falling open. The effect was devastating.

"Oh . . ." Floyt said.

"Knowledge is power," she went on, "and there're a few things I know about the company that'll stand this place on its ear. And I can help you, if you get me off this rock. After all, I'm *already* Hecate as far as the company's records are concerned."

"There is possibly some angle there that we can exploit, Alacrity," Floyt ventured. Alacrity inclined his head slowly.

She clapped her hands. "We can leave tonight! I know a way I can get to your ship without the cops causing any problems. What d'you say, gents?"

They walked together across the shredded celluline of the empty ring. She was wide-eyed with excitement, practically panting. "I just have to get a few things from my townhouse."

"Nothing that's going to make your bone-breakers or anybody else suspicious," Alacrity cautioned.

"I *know* how it's done, big boy."

Floyt broke in to head off another exchange. "Ah, what shall we call you?"

She spun on him angrily. "Hecate! Get that through your head; that's who I am: Hecate."

A sudden sound rose, a banshee wail that grew and grew as they realized they weren't alone. Floyt glanced up to the source. In the box was the hooded figure he'd seen before, slowly rising to its feet, pointing down at them like Death itself as the wail got louder still.

"Whatinthehell," Alacrity muttered. And inside the Wicked Wickiup, *a wind began to rise.*

The hood fell back and for a second or two the trio below couldn't tell if the apparition was male or female. Yellow-white tangles of meters-long hair snapped and fluttered in the gale. Eyes like glowing coals beamed light down upon them. The robe blew back to show layers of crudely tanned skins and furs over tattered synthetics. A moldering gunbelt held a pair of rotting pistol scabbards to its sides.

Then it spoke—an old, cracked voice, incredibly loud and very high. A woman's. It was extremely angry.

"Hecate? You think it's that easy to steal *my* name? Slut! *Puta!*"

The young woman Floyt and Alacrity had come to know as Hecate moaned and made to back away. The vengeance demon wasn't having any of that, though, and gestured. Lightning bolts crashed overhead and a cyclonic wind blasted the celluline up around them. The gorgeous evening shawl was torn loose, to disappear into the swirling jetstream like a crippled highsheen bat. The arena's equipment and rigging swung and clanged like bells. Floyt dimly heard roars from the menagerie.

"What do you know of Hecate? What do you know of the First Ones?" the old woman ranted. "Nothing! Nothing!"

The ground suddenly threw them from their feet. Impossible as it seemed, Alacrity knew, it wasn't seismic activity or a local nuke that was doing it.

"We've got to get outside!" Floyt hollered, but they couldn't even get to their feet. The air was hotter and thinner than it had been, difficult to breathe, charged with ozone.

Of all the rotten breaks we've had, it occurred to Alacrity in a split second, *this takes first prize! Getting here just in time to be killed for something we even didn't do!*

A tornado funnel of black wind and spitting starflare foamed around the real Hecate. "Do you have any idea how badly you've *pissed me off?* I heard you; I heard you all! And I heard you on the commo, playing the First Ones' tones!"

Floyt tried to get some words out, wondering how and why the madwoman monitored the *Lightning Whelk*'s ship-to-ground communications. But she wasn't giving them a chance to answer.

"I'll show you how far short you fall of Hecate, you miserable mortals! I'll show you all!"

She gestured. The dome overhead suddenly lofted away through the air as if were a paper hat lobbed up and out of sight. The cyclonic wind howled louder as arcs and serpents of crackling electrofire snaked and spat. Alacrity grabbed Floyt's shoulder and started a desperate low-crawl escape, but they were yanked up from the floor and sucked into the funnel. Space and gravity didn't feel like they were doing business as usual, and it seemed time might be engaged in a job action, too.

Alacrity heard the fake Hecate's cry and a yell from Floyt that was cut short. And above it all sounded hysterical shrieks and laughter from the woman who'd assumed the name of an ancient night goddess and ruler of the Underworld.

CHAPTER 8

WISH WE WERE THERE

"WAKE UP! HEY, WHATEVER YOUR NAME IS, SNAP OUT OF it!"

Alacrity didn't want to. He had the vague feeling it would be a bad move. But somebody was slapping his face. "Wake up, both of you! That crazy woman will be back any second; we've got to do something!"

The fake Hecate shook Alacrity again and he felt the first stirrings of a monster headache. As he was trying to open his eyes, he heard Floyt moan nearby, stirring.

"'As the world comes back into focus...'"

"Before I go to the trouble, Ho: is it worth it?"

"*Mff*! Why...yes, I think you'll find this amusing."

Alacrity rolled over onto his stomach to lever himself up. He was lying on a cold flat surface that felt like it was spinning under him and he tried to clutch at it.

The place was enormous. The ceiling was lost in a void, but the smell made him suspect he was underground. It was an indefinable scent he'd first encountered in the subsurface Precursor site on Epiphany.

Floyt was rubbernecking from a sort of front-end pushup pose. They lay on a niellolike surface in an open space two hundred meters across or more. In all directions, rearing up in levels like a jungle, was what Floyt recognized after an addled moment as an intricate, artificial construct of some kind, nothing organic, though that was what its form suggested. The components weren't pipes, wiring, or anything else so obvious, and there was a certain flow to everything, like a water sculpture. Some of it suggested shapes Floyt had seen in the causality harp.

"Alacrity, it feels like—back on Epiphany. Are we in another Precursor site?"

"What else?" Aside from the place itself, there was the matter of the real Hecate's astounding powers. What she'd done, especially with no visible equipment, was impossible to any human technology Alacrity knew of. The impact of that brought him around fully. What it meant to his campaign to win—win *back*, as he thought of it—the White Ship was almost as strong a stimulus as his survival mechanism, which had sweat standing out all over him.

He rolled over to the impostor, who knelt next to him, making a grab for her as she yelped, "*Chikusho!*" Before she could counter, he snagged one of her handguns. It *was* merely a lousy flashlight, a low-intensity beamer good only for producing pretty light effects and triggering holotarget detonations. No wonder the Lebensraum cops let her use them.

"Where'd she go?" Alacrity snapped. "How long's Hecate been gone? Did you spot a way out of here?" The Epiphany site had had a wide adit allowing easy access. There didn't seem to be one close to hand at the moment though.

Floyt was sitting up, rubbing his temples and eyes. For the first time he noticed that Alacrity's brolly and the impostor's evening shawl were lying nearby, though there was none of the debris and wreckage the real Hecate had kicked up back in the arena. That suggested an astonishing degree of fine control.

The impostor shook her head, brushing black hair back off her forehead so that the moonpure flashed blue-white. "I only came around a minute ago myself. I heard her off laughing, somewhere in the dark. Over that way, I think. She was moving away from us, by the sound."

Floyt glanced around, saying "Maybe it's best we exit in the opposite direction, eh?"

"Napoleon couldn't have said it any better, Ho. C'mon, angel; we'd better—"

That was all he'd got out of his mouth when Hecate came screeching down at them out of the darkness like a harpy, wild hair fluttering, lit as if by St. Elmo's fire, shedding green flame and comet bursts.

They ducked and Alacrity almost fired at her with the useless target pistol, but thought better of it. As she swooped on them the place grew bright, light coming from the terraced systemry jungle. Hecate pulled up short, barely missing the impostor's head, then soared away again. The smell of her was ozone, unwashed body, and rancid, rotting clothes.

She banked and came rocketing down again, to decelerate and alight without a jar, strobing with power and throwing off multicolored streamers of energy, her aura seething and rotating. The younger woman backed away from her with a desperate look on her face and hands raised for defense. Against his better judgment, Alacrity found himself moving to intervene. He wanted very much to avoid violence. He wanted even more to wrest from Hecate, by whatever means it took, the Precursor secrets the deranged hag had discovered.

"You! Lying cow! What's your real name?" Hecate's voice made the place resound. She set her claws on the butts of her corroded pistols.

The impostor swallowed loudly before she could get out an answer. "Paloma. Paloma Sudan. I haven't done anything to you! Let us go!"

"Not done anything? Only stolen my name! Only traded on my reputation! Only shamed me, you ugly little *pendeja*!"

Hecate advanced on Paloma Sudan, her long, cracked claws raised. Alacrity automatically took a step to restrain her, but Hecate's aura touched his fingertips and it felt like every joint in his body was being tractored apart, the flesh sliced from him by flensing beams.

Hecate seized his shipsuit and tossed him aside. Alacrity flew like a sack of clothes, losing the pistol, to bounce across the black floor, nearly out again, seeing motes of light whirl before his eyes. *Oo-oo! Lookit all the pretty neuron firings!*

Floyt began easing toward the umbrella; bare hands plainly weren't much good.

Paloma tried to dodge but Hecate's responses were down in the single-digit millisecond range. She instantly grabbed a handful of Paloma's hair and let the aura die away. She was oblivious to Paloma Sudan's hysterical kicks and punches.

Winding the handful of hair tightly, Hecate forced Paloma to her knees. Then she threw her free hand up in a grand gesture. The cascading systemry flowed with brilliance and gave off rich, strange tones stopping Floyt in his tracks as he planned his attack. Parts of the instrumentality appeared to be moving.

Alacrity paused in trying to regain his feet, transfixed. No one anywhere had ever done anything to compare with what he was witnessing. Mad Hecate had made a major, probably pivotal breakthrough in penetrating the secrets of the Precursors—the First Ones, as she called them.

"This is Hecate's power!" she trumpeted, coal-eyes blazing. "Take a good look at it, dearie, because in a moment I'm going to cram you into a tiny pocket of limbo and leave you there forever!"

She pointed a finger. A green globe appeared, pulsing like a Cepheid, going from one meter in diameter down to the size of a handball and back up again every few seconds.

And Ho and me are here as witnesses, or will it be cellmates? Alacrity wondered. The hair stood up all along the deep V-mane that grew down his spine, and the blood drained from his face at the thought of being wadded up in some miniverse until the end of time.

Floyt's thoughts were running along the same lines, and he was also concerned for Paloma's life. So he discovered his mouth was shouting a very unwise thing:

"Why should we believe you? This doesn't prove you're the real Hecate!"

The laser eyes swung to him, and he discovered that his knees were knocking. He realized that he had the brolly raised, and brought it down to lean on it.

"So, you don't believe I'm Hecate, you little *germ*? Well, I've got a simple remedy for that! In you all go *together*. The more the squirmier! You'll have eternity to figure out how badly you just *fucked up*!"

The green globe began to expand, large enough to take three bodies inboard at its maximum, shrinking back to a toy with the same regularity. Winds came up in the far corners of the chamber. The sphere drifted closer to Floyt. Alacrity got set to give Hecate his last, best shot.

But Floyt got a grip on himself and spoke first. "Th-there's a much simpler way, if you *are* Hecate." The storm died a little; Hecate's eyes narrowed suspiciously, sending out flat, fiery swaths of light.

"The true Hecate owns shares in the White Ship, from long ago when she still went under the name Loebelia Curry. Loebelia Curry, yes, that was her name. Hecate would recall that."

Alacrity held his breath and Paloma froze. The old woman's lips were shaping the name *Loebelia Curry* over and over, eyes unfocused, releasing orange radiance into the distance, thoughts flung back far through space and time.

Apparently befuddled, she abruptly looked back to Floyt. He followed up on his sally desperately. "You owned voting shares in the Board of Interested Parties, do you recollect that? But you haven't exercised your franchise in a very long time. Er, perhaps you remember the ownership code numbers? And the access passwords?" He activated the pickup for his proteus's sound-recording mode. Alacrity silently did the same, sucking in breath through clenched teeth.

But instead of blurting the codes, Hecate roughly pushed Paloma aside, set her fists on her hips, threw her head back, and shook with high-pitched laughter. It was a partial transformation; there was less demented cackle to it.

Hecate laughed until she was out of breath, until she clutched her middle, slapping her thigh. The captives held their poses. The old woman waved at Floyt, as if telling him to stop. At last she ran down, trying to straighten.

"Hoo! I'd forgotten how it feels, this body, when it laughs." Then she was off in another paroxysm as the others swapped uncertain glances. "That ship, that... White Ship!" Hecate managed after a while. "Are those fools still working on her? I'd forgotten all about her. Oh, that's the funniest thing I've heard in a star's age!" The beams from her eyes danced.

"Those pinheads! They wouldn't listen to me, no! Oh, that's ripe!"

"Could you let us in on the joke?" Alacrity hazarded. "We could use a chuckle." Paloma was on her feet, watching Hecate guardedly.

"I told them years and years ago," the old woman managed. "I told them, 'This White Ship project will *never* be finished!' I saw that they'd never *wring* the secrets of the First Ones out of the universe. 'You don't grab Creation by the scrote and *twist* revelations out of it!' I told them."

"And they were too stupid to listen,' Floyt steered deftly. "Too stubborn and arrogant to do it your way."

She suddenly looked crafty. "My way, yes. You want to know what my way is, hey? Do you, germie? All right, but it's nothing you'll ever use. It's nothing anyone will ever use but Hecate!"

She gave them a twisted grin. "You don't force secrets out of the artifacts of the First Ones. You entice them out. You *seduce* them out. Now, how do you seduce someone?"

The three looked at one another helplessly.

"Oh, you numbskulls! You *join* with them. You *mate*

with them. You marry yourself to the secrets of the Precursors body and soul and spirit and mind!"

And go insane in the doing, Floyt thought. Perhaps human beings could only uncover Precursor secrets through madness. He glanced to his friend, wondering if Alacrity would be willing to.

Alacrity was carefully stifling his urge to leap at Hecate and beat the secrets out of her. "You mean, you've got all their knowledge? *Trois fois merde!* You're up there with *them*, the Precursors!"

She laughed again, but bitterly. "What year is this? Ah, never mind; I have eternity to play with now. No, I'm barely a zygote on the scale of the First Ones, but you . . . you're not even alive! And you never will be!"

The power of the instrumentality strobed brighter. Alacrity tried to gulp but couldn't.

"But you're still one of us," Floyt said, trying to lay on conviction he didn't feel. "No matter how different they are, humans are still human. I know; I'm a genealogist. Human beings all share—"

She didn't vaporize Floyt on the spot, which was what Alacrity expected to see. The fires swept up from her, coiling and expanding.

"Genealogy? What an absurd pastime! I became bored with it long since. Would you like to know how you little homo-ape-ians connect to me, perhaps? I doubt that mudpie you call a brain could encompass it."

She raised her hands high. A megadetonation of luminosity and sound staggered the three captives. Floyt leaned back to look up, nearly teetering back on his rear end, and saw a family tree, or at least part of one. It took him a few seconds to figure out what he was looking at.

The thing was infinitely complex. Details seemed to spring out at him and leap into clarity as he focused on them, then retreat as he scanned on—the names or identity quanta of more human beings than there were stars in the galaxy. The ones he focused on he saw vividly, feeling he knew them and had a grasp of their lives.

More, there were connections, the whole webwork of

human history in four dimensions, lucid and immediate, so that the connections between any two or more, living or dead, were emphatic and plain enough to understand. A part of him speculated on whether he was seeing into Hecate's mind, her instrumentality, or some wisdom of the First Ones. *Something like the causality harp?* he wondered. *Or has every sentient being somehow left its mark on Infinity?*

He tried to scan his Overvision back to the beginning of things, but a numbing disorientation came over him and he felt his grip on himself slipping away, breath short and blood kettledrumming in his forehead. Hecate was right; his brain wasn't capable of what he was attempting.

He renounced his Overvision, terrified. The great family tree was gone; Floyt was back on the floor, groaning. "That's a little of what I can do." Hecate sniggered. "Do you still think I'm one of you? What should I care about your White Ship for?"

Paloma looked around at the forest of instrumentality. "No reason, when you've got Precursor machines serving you."

Hecate scowled at her, some of the anger coming back, then cackled and slapped her thigh again. "Precursor? That? Why, you daffy little tramp! *I* built that! What'd you think I've been doing all this time?"

"You?" Floyt and Alacrity both yelped at the same time.

The expression Hecate gave them was almost coquettish, in a loopy way. "Who else? It's not much. It's like exploring the Central Library at Spica and barely learning the alphabet. But it *is* so wonderful, my god-lover! Who do you think heard the songs of the First Ones you were playing in space and brought them to my attention? And that's when I found out there was a faker using my name."

She gazed about at her god-lover/instrumentality. "It is so wise. In fact, there are some regions of it I don't quite understand myself."

She shook herself, looking back to them slyly, and signaled the green globe to approach. "But enough about me."

"Hecate, we're convinced," Alacrity said. "And we'll tell them everything you said, there at the White Ship. Then they'll know you're right and they're wrong, and everybody will be talking about you again."

"That'll put that whole Ship crowd in its place!" Floyt seconded. "Think of it! You'd be rubbing their noses in it!"

"That is, if we can get into the board meeting and speak as Interested Parties," Alacrity segued. "We'd need codes and passwords, of course."

Hecate cocked her head at them like a chicken sizing up three bugs. "Beta-Thud-Actual-Tau-Hecate-Epsilon-Kl'marth-Manila," she said after a moment's sidelong stare. "Shares 1,780,000 through 2,120,000."

That causality harp was right! Alacrity exulted. When the board met in session, he could gain entry with his one share and vote Hecate's stocks, assuming all the perks of a major shareholder.

"Only what makes you think I'm going to let you leave here?" Hecate went on, relishing the looks on their faces. She winked one glowing eye at them, an eerie and dismaying thing to see. "Do you think I'm going to share my holy-lover with anyone, or let anyone else have one?"

"We're no threat to you!" Floyt yelled as Alacrity hollered, "No! No! We won't tell anybody anything!"

"Forgive me! Let us go!" Paloma Sudan begged.

Hecate brought her hands up over her head. The metatechnic jungle erupted with light and reverb; the green globe grounded, waiting. "I'll let you go into this little world without end, here, that's what."

Floyt, the only one armed—with the brolly—steeled himself and charged Hecate, to do his duty or go out trying.

He was the only one who hadn't grappled with her yet. Even though he'd seen her uncanny speed, it came as a shock when she had the umbrella out of his hand, picked him up by his web belt, and slammed him down in one move, tittering foolishly.

The impact sent him sliding a meter or so, sprawling. The breath was driven from him and only by a reflex—hunching his shoulders; tucking his chin as hard as he could—did he avoid having his skull broken against the floor. Hecate stalked after, to finish him.

And as suddenly as that, she was staring down at Floyt in utter horror, the fiery eyes big and round. She screamed in a way they hadn't heard from her before. It took him a few shellshocked seconds to realize what had her so unhinged.

His sweater had been pushed up in the tussle, exposing his Inheritor's belt.

Hecate stood rooted, pointing to it, shrilling something over and over in a language like no other Alacrity had ever heard. Her god-lover/instrumentality began to go dim around her as Hecate foamed at the mouth, yammering the phrase.

Then it was no longer yawning blackness overhead but a shifting starswarm. Rays stabbed down to play over the Inheritor's belt, trailing over it, inquisitive. Floyt felt the belt vibrating at his middle, humming like a tuning fork.

He clumsily unclasped it and pushed it from him, afraid it would explode, undergo lethal shrinkage, or perhaps turn into a cobra. None of those things happened, but the alien symbols on the plaques, symbols no data bank had been able to translate for him, were incandescent. A few of the searchlights played over him, forcing him to blink, creating a rainbow nimbus around him.

All the while, Hecate was ranting. At length she turned to her green Cepheid globe. "Take them! Take them all! *Do what I tell you!*"

Instead, the overhead beams fixed on her for a moment. She squealed.

With no more warning than when they'd come into existence, the motes overhead vanished. There was a cliff's-edge moment of silence, except for Hecate's frothing. Then the Cepheid was on the move, homing in.

Hecate tried to fly from the globe but only managed a pitifully weak little jump, tried to run from it but could only totter slowly. The sphere expanded to envelop her, then zoomed off, dodging in among the terraced flow forms of the instrumentality. Floyt, Alacrity, and Paloma Sudan watched it go, none of them saying a word.

They almost fainted when the whole system came blazing to life again—above, around, and even under-foot, as luminous sections of the nielloed floor shone.

"What's it mean?" Paloma shouted at Floyt. "What's this place doing?"

They found out. Hecate's instrumentality began to *ungrow*, vanishing in on itself. At the same time the open area shrank and the very feel of the place began to change radically.

"It's folding in on itself!" Alacrity roared. The open area was getting smaller fast. "It's rabbit-holing, to go someplace else!"

Floyt looked stricken. "Alacrity, *it* may be able to do that, but it's just one of those tricks I never learned!"

CHAPTER 9

THE GLITTER RUBS RIGHT OFF

"THERE! LOOK OVER THERE!"

Paloma was yanking Alacrity's arm, pointing. An arc of darkness had appeared, a tunnel mouth, off where there'd been celestial pinball god-lover systemry moments before.

"It might be a way out!" she said.

"It's a better shot than we've got here; let's go!" Alacrity grabbed for her hand, but, an impressive runner, she dodged him and headed out, slowing only to scoop up her evening shawl. Floyt retrieved his Inheritor's belt and tossed Alacrity the umbrella. Alacrity grabbed the fallen target pistol and the two dashed off after Paloma as space diminished toward them.

They sprinted for what felt like an awfully long time, disoriented and unsteady. The semicircular opening came up at them, then they were pounding along in darkness, footsteps echoing in the confined space. There was light ahead—far ahead. Floyt swore breathlessly at the inactivity of two consecutive Hawking jumps for leaving him in such poor condition.

At last they raced into the sunlight, winded, to throw themselves down a slope of reddish soil dotted with tough tripwire plants. Invictus was bright and hot overhead; it came to Floyt that unless they'd been unconscious for a long time, they were far from Horselaugh.

121

They panted, looking down on a deep bowl of valley with a lot of lush flora, including tree-size plants and a good deal of open grassland—or what looked like grass. Alacrity could see animals moving around in the distance, apparently grazing. Very big animals. In the far distance was a range of lavender and gold mountains, with a sextet of snowcapped giants rearing into the clouds.

Floyt was on hands and knees, gazing back the way they'd come. "Look at this! Something's happening!"

The peak behind them, out of which they'd raced, was high and sheer. It wasn't exactly collapsing or going into subsidence; it was being drawn inward and down. There was a little shaking-loose of rubble and some flying things were frightened into the air, but aside from that it seemed a calm, almost placid process as reality adjusted to the departure of the Precursor site. When it was over, the peak was a great deal smaller and the passageway was gone.

Like the Pied Piper's place, it occurred to Floyt. He got up and slowly clasped his Inheritor's belt around him, then became aware that Alacrity and Paloma were staring at him. "Did you happen to understand what Hecate was saying about this, Alacrity?"

Alacrity shook his head. "Pure gibberish to me, m'friend." He held up his proteus. "But I've got it down here." He deactivated it, as Floyt did his own.

"I guess Hecate really *didn't* know everything there was to know about her consort machine," Alacrity added thoughtfully, regarding the peak. "Must've been some things it just wouldn't let her get away with. Like limboizing somebody carrying Pecursor I.D., for instance."

He turned to survey the countryside. "Whew! First thing to figure out is—hey! Paloma!"

She turned back, having started off down the hill, her wrap over one shoulder. "You two lugs can stand around here breezing if you want, but I've got things to do."

Alacrity waved at limitless wilderness that stretched as far as they could see. "Such as?"

She gave an arch smile. "First things first. I'm going to get some directions."

"Directions?" Floyt puzzled.

She angled a thumb over her shoulder, downslope at the grazing giants. "From them."

They hurried to catch up, kicking loose stones and loose soil, as she hiked down the hill, making some adjustment to her proteus. She picked her route carefully, keeping away from overhanging branches and dense undergrowth. Floyt took out his survival implement and opened its biggest blade—twelve centimeters. In the silence around them he could hear yapping, twitterings, stridulations, and other noises in the distance. There was also an odd throbbing in the air, like faint vibrations from a distant quake.

The two friends sized up the great grazers, which Floyt recognized as what the locals called gawklegs. "Suppose they decide you're lunch?" Alacrity inquired.

She tossed back her luxuriant hair. "Oh, I don't think so. By the way, I'll take my pistol back now."

It wasn't much use anyway. He handed it over and shifted his brolly to his right hand, removing and pocketing the ferrule cap. "Are you going to let us in on where we are? We've got to work together."

She gave him a maddening smirk. "Are you asking or telling?"

"Look, me and Ho are in this fix because you've been running around pretending to be somebody you're not! And if it wasn't for us you'd've been inside that green squeezeball till hell gets recess! So just stuff the cuteness in a convenient lacuna, hmm?"

Floyt stood back, just in case. She crossed her arms and glared at Alacrity. "And what does that mean? That I invited you to come trying to make deals with me?"

"A-ha! You were already throwing in with us when Hecate showed up, remember? Anyway, what I'm saying is, we work together or else get used to the idea of being dead."

Floyt broke in. They'd both more or less forgotten he was there. "Paloma, can you really use those animals to get your bearings? Do they orient on a fixed point or have a migratory pattern or something? They're gawklegs, isn't that correct?"

She studied Floyt for a moment, then relaxed a bit. "I'm going to talk to them. If I'm lucky, they'll listen and help. If not, I imagine they'll stomp me like a paper cup, if they can catch me. Gawklegs have plenty of reasons to hate humans."

Alacrity's brow creased. "Those things are intelligent?"

"Your grasp of the obvious is remarkable." She turned to continue her way. The other two fell into single file behind. "I told you I knew some things about the company. I'd be dead already if they knew how much. Yes; once upon a time the gawks were a very successful species. Quite intelligent, but dumb enough to be friendly to human beings."

"But what makes you think they won't decide to do the two-step on us?"

"Six-step," Floyt corrected.

She shrugged. "I'm just hoping they won't. I hope they'll hear me out, because I have a general idea where we are, and I doubt we can get out of here alive without their help."

"Hear you out?" Floyt pursued. "Are you saying that you can speak their language?"

"Something like that."

"If you know where we are," Alacrity postulated, "where are we?"

"If those mountains over there are the ones I think they are, the nearest human outpost's a couple or four hundred kilometers west of here. Horselaugh's almost halfway around Lebensraum."

"God in the Void," Alacrity snarled. The meeting of the board was only weeks away. It cheapened the value of the universe, his being stuck with the voting codes for 340,000 shares out somewhere a death march away from the *Lightning Whelk*. He considered for a moment how many shares he'd be willing to trade for a junker sky-crate with no warranty.

A lot.

It was a long descent, hot work and rough on the toes since it was unbroken downhill. Alacrity stopped to adjust his pathfinder boots accordingly, and Floyt relaced his own so his feet wouldn't move around inside them. There was no adapting Paloma's glossy cavalry footgear; she didn't comment or complain. She did, however, point out a fractal-looking plant whose branches were easy and safe to saw off with Floyt's survival tool, and made good walking staffs.

Floyt tried to remember points he'd picked up in his reading and from Alacrity, trying to be aware of his toes, soles of his feet, and knees. He leaned slightly forward to help keep balance in case of a slip, using his staff, taking short steps and cushioning himself with bent knees. Advice like that was a lot easier to read or listen to than it was to apply.

All around were tall-bladed plants that looked like some sort of wild grain in vermilion, and substantial-looking growths that put Floyt in mind of brain coral. Lower down, what had looked like high grass resembled, at close range, enormous lichen. It stained their boots and Floyt's trouser legs with green-brown and smelled pleasantly fragrant when crushed underfoot. They could feel the subsonic throbbing intermittently; it seemed to be getting more intense.

Being almost completely ignorant of the planet, Alacrity and Floyt took their cues from Paloma. She went carefully, pausing every four steps to scan all around and listen, sniffing the air. Floyt and Alacrity were watchful, too, without really knowing what they were watching for, or what was dangerous and what wasn't.

We really do need her to get out of this alive, Floyt realized. *Or even live through the afternoon.*

The slope gradually leveled off to meet the valley floor. The gawklegs ignored the humans except for an occasional long-necked swing of the head to gauge their approach. The creatures grazed and chewed, their pendulous upper lips rather prehensile, at just about any kind of flora that struck their fancy.

What the things most resembled in Floyt's opinion was something that might result if a seal-skinned, giraffey beast had a fling with a mottled six-legged triceratops. *Season lightly with moose and jackal. Add curled horns and strange articulation to high, strong legs and you wouldn't be too far off,* he reckoned. Their markings ran to Lebensraum tones of soil and vegetation—vermilion and rust red, grays and green browns. Facial color patterns were vivid and varied. Little hummingbirdlike things darted around them, to land and feed on tiny vermin that fed off the gawks.

The low-frequency throbbings had increased.

"They've probably been aware of us since we left the site," Paloma said. "Their senses are very acute, which is odd in a species with no serious natural enemies to speak of except humans, who arrived so recently."

"Nothing's surprising in a place with Precursor artifacts," Alacrity replied. That gave Floyt pause for thought. There'd never been a single Precursor artifact found on Earth or Luna or in surrounding space, not one.

"Those infrasonics are coming from the gawks?" Alacrity asked.

Paloma nodded. "Ten to twenty-five Hertz range. They do it with a membrane that covers the nasal passage in their skull. Most of their communication's audible to us, though.

"Anyway, I'm sure they've seen us and caught our scent, probably heard us, too," Paloma said softly, watching the things.

"As long as they don't want to touch us. Or taste us," Floyt murmured. "See here, why don't we at least *attempt* a rescue call? After all, Alacrity's proteus and mine may or may not get through to the Lebensraum SATNET, but couldn't yours, Paloma?"

"Doubt it," she said. "No satellite receiver's aimed in

this direction, that's pretty certain, and nothing ground-side for a long, long way.

"But that's beside the point. You have to understand, the Lebensraum Company means what it says about serious penalties for trespassing into the wilds. We'd spend weeks or months in detention even if we got them to believe what happened, which I doubt because I can hardly believe it myself. So we'd likely pull down ten years' hard labor, minimum."

"Sorry, Hobart and me have other things to do," Alacrity announced, not cautious about giving his partner's name away now that Floyt had betrayed his. "Let's see what the heffalumps, over there, have to say."

As the humans approached the herd, the larger ones strolled forward unhurriedly to protect the calves and smaller adults, whom Alacrity assumed to be females. The curled horns swung and dipped.

Alacrity tapped Paloma's back as they drew even with the last substantial tree-plant. It was like a gigantic asparagus tip. There might be some nasty life forms crawling among the imbricate fronds, but he'd prefer finding out about that firsthand to being stomped to a low spot in the road. "If you have a directional sound projector on that proteus, I think we're close enough to use it, Paloma. In fact, we're probably too close. The gawks look like they can move fast when they're in the mood."

Paloma nodded, adjusted her proteus, and spoke into a pickup. "Greetings to you, herd family."

The proteus gave a running, amplified translation much as Albrecht did back on Windfall. It was surprisingly loud and undistorted, great ambient sound, which was only right, considering how pricey it looked. It, too, produced infrasonic vibrations.

"We wish you no harm. We know and observe your decorum. We are lost and wish you to tell us the way to our homeland."

Moist rumblings and snortings went through the herd, along with horn tosses, tail flicks, postures, and other unspoken language the proteus couldn't register or translate. But to Floyt's surprise, the proteus rendered the sounds as a belligerent laughter.

One behemoth, large but not the largest, minced a step or two forward to make snorting, foaming, lip-smacking, raspberrying sounds, its triple nostrils flaring, ear cones swinging this way and that, and throwing in something between a pig's squeal and a yak's belch. And the humans could feel infrasonics seeming to go right through them.

The proteus translated it as "We're not afraid you'll harm *us*, vermin! Go away, or *we'll* harm *you*!"

Paloma pointed to what Floyt's survival-tool compass insisted was the west, to the six snowcapped peaks. "Can you tell me which mountains those are? Are they the Churchill Range?"

Her proteus made the translation. Alacrity wondered where Paloma'd come by such a linguistic program.

The gawk shook its monstrous head. "That's one of their names. To us they're the Hooves of the Sky. Now if you wish to make the Long Trek back to your own kind, do it before we moisten our forage with your blood!"

He dug a giant, curved hoof into the ground, flinging up five kilos or so of turf and soil, and charged at them a step or two, horns lowered, bellowing so that the valley echoed with it. The little hummingbird things took to their wings.

The humans almost fell over one another while lunging for the asparagus tree. The herd made sounds again; the inaudible throbbings chorused. Paloma's instrument served it up as mocking, bovine laughter.

Alacrity shook his brolly at them furiously. "*Va te faire foutre!* If I had an RPG pistol, you'd be *slipcovers*!" He ranted on without benefit of translation, subsiding only when Floyt and Paloma each grabbed an arm and towed him off.

"Maybe we can come up with a way to *buy* their assistance," Floyt mulled as they went back the way they'd come. "If we catch them on a good day?" The herd was grazing again, lookouts staring to make sure the humans didn't return.

Alacrity sighed. "What if this *is* a good day? Paloma, d'you believe them? About where we are?"

"It adds up," she decided, then dangled her shimmering proteus before him. "If I could hook this up to a display screen, I could check some maps, but I don't see any around."

Alacrity tapped his own prote. "Got just the thing right here. Let's find someplace a little less *al fresco* and see what we've got."

Floyt indicated the thick foliage ahead. "I'm not so happy with all that yowling and coughing going on up there." He meant the forested valley sides, where a late-afternoon chorus was tuning up. Animals in their natural habitats always sounded famished to him.

Just then there was a loud, throaty rasp from the open land on the valley floor, in the high lichen-grass. It was answered by several more. "On the other hand a nice, tall tree might be just the thing," Floyt mused.

"Seconded and carried," Paloma ratified.

They made a cautious search, as Floyt learned a new definition of patience. Alacrity was practiced at survival scouting, but it became plain that Paloma Sudan knew more about naturecraft, especially where Lebensraum was concerned.

They made their way to a perch she'd spotted some hundred meters along the valley side from where the Precrusor site exit had been. It was a perch up in the middle of some tilted slabs of rock, five meters above the ground, and took some scrabbling to reach. The soles and toe surfaces of the pathfinders were helpful there. Alacrity got to the top and gave the other two a hand up.

It was a rock-trough redoubt of about nine square meters' usable surface. They could find no evidence that any other creature had a claim on it. Invictus was going for the ridgeline; the three agreed to stand pat there for the night. A gawkleg might be able to give them trouble if it came up with a good reason; so would any sizable predator that was sure of foot. Still, the spot was safer than open ground and less of an unknown than the trees.

"We'll need fuel and a fire soon," Floyt said, surveying the land.

Paloma, pencil-thin blue cigarillo between her duranailed fingers, looked dismayed. "I forgot my igniter back in my dressing room! Well, men, unless one of you is carrying a—oh!"

Floyt was holding up his survival gadget, flicking its friction-wheel firestarter. "Also, you can scale fish with it." Paloma lit her cigarillo and gave him such a glorious smile, raising his blood pressure, that he found himself blurting, "I'll gather some wood, and you two can plot us a route home."

While Alacrity dug around in a pocket to see if he had the right adaptor to hook up the proteuses, looking for the little kit he usually carried, Floyt cautiously scrambled back down, regretting his offer already. He glanced around for deadwood.

"Stay in sight, Ho," Alacrity warned. Floyt waggled a hand over his shoulder. His staff was ready in his other hand.

Luckily, there was plenty of fuel laying around for the taking; the idea of cutting a large supply with the survival-tool blades was too unpleasant for words. The staff near to hand, he began gathering branches fallen from a plant resembling a poison hemlock. They were lightweight and spongy; he gathered as many as he could, assuming they'd burn quickly. He soon had the hang of scrambling up the redoubt to just short of the last, most difficult portion of the climb, and heaving his burden up onto the bivouac surface. Alacrity and Paloma were bent over their proteuses together.

Floyt worked until the dusk had him too nervous, then hauled himself up to the redoubt again. Alacrity had mated the proteuses and Paloma had accessed a map and located the Churchill Range, switching to larger and larger scale to bring up details and land features that would help them locate themselves. The map was pro-

jected up into the gathering darkness by the little holodisplay of Alacrity's high-end-tech proteus.

"Here's more or less where we are," Paloma was saying, "if your pal's compass is accurate. And there's the
high desert."

"It's accurate," Alacrity said absently, engrossed in
the map. *How many weeks left? Seven, maybe. Or six;
I'll have to do a conversion a little later.* "Too bad your
compass isn't a lensatic, Ho. I have a feeling that could
come in handy real soon."

"Don't worry; the gawklegs know the way," Paloma
assured him.

"To them we're just mobile salads. Forget 'em."

Floyt began arranging a fire, something he'd done
only a few times before. Mostly, he was trying to stay
out of the debate. Alacrity was his friend, but he had a
feeling Paloma was right.

"Are you considering trying to slog it out of here on
foot?"

"Why, you see any bus stops? Did I miss something?"

"Would you like the bad news all at once, or gradually? This isn't a good spot, but there're even worse ones
all around us. The shortest route out of here, by a thousand kilometers, takes us *that* way, through some of the
more hostile territory on this world, and Lebensraum's
got no shortage of hostile, either." Operatic belching
erupted from a gawkleg somewhere in the distance.

She looked to Floyt, who was arranging the wood,
shaving off long, fine curls of it for tinder. "The thing is,
we won't last very long here, even if we scavenge
enough to eat, because there aren't any diet-supplement
dispensers or imported food sources. We're looking at a
slow death from deficiency diseases—something to do
with Lebensraum amides or proteins or whatever. Now,
there's only one way to get to the nearest outpost so we
can steal ourselves some transportation: do it quickly
and do it without getting killed and eaten by the more
truculent life forms between here and there. And the

only way we'll accomplish *that*, fellas, is with help from *them*."

She said it with an inclination of her head to the gawklegs, who were bellowing and chorusing. Alacrity glared at her.

"Didn't you hear what that big bull said? They'll squash us flat and jump up and down on the stains! You know what 'human being' probably means to them? 'Dangerous when armed, delicious with onions!' "

Paloma was undeterred. "If we can talk to them, we can talk them into it."

"Yeah, while we're on the subject, how'd you do that? Talk to them?"

"The original survey contingent from Shalimar, the ones in the research project who were stranded here, they and their descendents worked out a translation program. It's still kept in a top-secret company archive."

Alacrity shook his head. "And next you're gonna remind me how men like to tell you things, right? But how come you care about the gawklegs?"

"I just started hearing rumors about what had been done to them. The company covered everything up, of course, because intelligent autochthons would've been inconvenient."

Alacrity had his chin on his fist. "Head 'em up, move 'em out, huh?"

"*Rub* 'em out, for the most part. Y'know, there used to be millions and millions and now there're only a couple-three scattered little herds. You think these ones stay out here by choice, when their prime grazing areas are in company operation sectors? They talk tough, but they know what would happen to them if they strayed someplace that antagonized humans."

She thought for a moment. "I was planning, when I finally got off Lebensraum, to see what I could do about it. All it would take is a few words in the right place on Shalimar. They've been dying to get hold of Lebensraum for a long time and this is the perfect excuse. Shalimar goes to the Bali Hai Republic, beats its chest over what's been done to the poor gawks, and gets to be the new landlord."

"Not that Shalimar's any wholesale outlet of virtue, from what I heard," Alacrity said.

"It's not," she conceded. "The gawks'll never get their planet back all to themselves, but at least they'll have a better shake. Anyway, that was what I had in mind, and I could use a little help. Humans have done so much *to* the gawks that it's only fair humans do a little something *for* the—"

"You don't have to preach to the choir," Floyt, who'd gotten the tinder going, was saying in between blowing softly on the little flames. They caught fast, the stuff burning like fatwood. "We'll help you."

Alacrity hadn't been consulted on the decision, but after a moment's thought he grinned to his friend and nodded. Floyt went back to tending the fire, smiling.

"But if the gawklegs are afraid of humans, that's an even bigger reason why they're not gonna take us anywhere," Alacrity pointed out. "Especially toward human settlements. Unless you think they're stupid enough to let you lead them into a duckshoot, which I assume you don't want to do anyhow."

"You know damned well I wouldn't," she snapped, giving him a dangerous look. "But they wouldn't have to take us all the way to the nearest outpost; just through the most dangerous country."

"But you heard for yourself, they don't want anything to do with us except maybe as shoeshine rags—Ho, would you stop playing around there and back me up?"

"Hmm?" Floyt looked startled. He'd been pursuing certain engrossing thoughts of his own, nearly forgetting their dilemma.

Alacrity gazed at him disappointedly. "Aren't you even a little bit curious about whether or not we're going to survive this one?"

Floyt half smiled. "Oh, I'll find out one way or the other, won't I?" He was feeding small pieces to the growing fire. The spongy fatwoodlike fuel burned brightly but quickly. There were still some odds and ends lying around the foot of the redoubt; he got ready to make a last foray but stopped with one foot over the side to listen to Paloma.

"Men," she announced, "I have reason to believe I can talk the gawklegs into it. But first I want to study up on some of the company wildlife files and maps." She flicked her fingers at her proteus. "Then I'll let you in on the whole thing. First, though, we can figure out our route."

She made sense; Alacrity yielded to the inevitable. "All right, let's just see if we can get some contour lines on this map, then try to adjust it for—"

He stopped, and all three of them went statue, at a gargling rattle that wasn't a snarl or roar but had the same impact. Floyt was frozen a pace or two from the base of the redoubt.

Less then fifty meters away a creature had emerged from a patch of undergrowth that looked like a kelp forest. Six-legged, about the size of a lion. It carried a kill clamped in its four-segment, rock-crusher jaws. The prey was a four-legged animal, like a delicate cross between a fawn and a cricket.

Behind the killer's narrow head, flat along its neck, was a webbed collar of bright green-and-silver wattling. As it spotted Floyt, the hunter lifted the collar all around its head like an evil flower in warning display, vanes holding the webbing taut. It whipped into view a tail with a sting that slid in and out like a kinetiblade.

The killer looked up to where Floyt's fire was beginning to burn high, its globular eyes reflecting the light in red. It made a low sound of irritation, debating attack. Floyt eased his back up against the rock slab behind him, holding the puny knifeblade ready. Alacrity edged his hand to his brolly, gathering himself to jump down if the thing charged. Paloma reached for her staff.

Then there was another not-roar; a second, larger predator sprang into the clearing to confront the first, neck wattle spread wide, stinger high, jaws mashing. It slunk at its rival, head low and extended to grab the prize from the other's maw.

The newcomer was leaner, almost emaciated. With the two predators occupied with one another, Floyt turned and went up the slab of rock in the nimble tradition of his primate forebears. Alacrity and Paloma each gave him a hand and they landed in a tangled heap as he overbalanced them. There they lay, watching the drama below and wondering if they'd be on the menu. Floyt rolled over to throw more wood on the fire, not sure it would help.

The first creature scuttled backward a few paces, glancing around it undecidedly. Seeing no avenue of quick retreat or shelter, it dropped its kill and sprang at its rival.

The two things locked in gouging, snapping combat, rolling over and over, spending most of their time in the air. The sheer ferocity of it was spellbinding. The brilliant neck ruffs, at full deployment, battered and flopped. The animals tore at one another's hide and dark blood streamed; the stingers plunged and stabbed. They had to be immune to their own species' toxin, or they'd both have been disabled in no time.

The bigger one got a telling hold. Its jaws clamped down with power-vise pressure as it braced itself against the other with all its legs, ripping. There was a *crack* of bone and some tearing of tissue. The smaller hunter lost its right foreleg from the center joint down. The stump gushed blood for a few moments, then the bleeding all but stopped. Alacrity expected to see the thing keel over or at best beat a slow, maimed retreat. Instead, it streaked for cover, a blur disappearing back in the upright, dry-land kelp bed.

The attacker dropped the mutilated foreleg and chased its opponent for a dozen lengths, then skidded to a halt, gurgling in a way that Floyt could only characterize as self-satisfied. It quickly returned to the abandoned kill and began sniffing at it.

"Scare-flare," Paloma Sudan identified it tightly, with out taking her eyes from it. The creature noticed the humans for the first time, gurgling, opening its warning ruff at them wide, snout antennules waving for their scent. After a few moments it lay down by the dead prey and began feeding with noisy enthusiasm.

"If it leaves scraps that draw scavengers, that could be bad for us," Alacrity said.

Paloma had her target pistols out but she was shaking her head. "I might be able to drive it away with a little lightshow, but on the other hand I might just get it mad. And anyway, as I recall, there're no scavengers in this area that would be very dangerous to us. The scare-flares are our main worry; they're really called Morgan's scorpions."

Floyt gave a sudden yell, slapping his neck, startling the other two. He was pulling an insect-size thing off his neck as blood ran from the spot where it had opened an exploratory well. The pest was about half the length of his thumb, a hydra with wings like mayapple leaves. "What is it?"

"Drillbug," Paloma supplied. "I didn't know they infested this area."

"Poisonous?" Floyt was pale. Alacrity scanned the air for more.

Paloma was shaking her head. "No, but they can be nasty. They inject an anticoagulent, so that bite's going to bleed for a while, I'm afraid."

She, too, looked around for more. "Lads, this isn't good—even worse than scare-flares. The atmospheric pressure on Lebensraum's lower than Standard, so our bodies put out a lot of odors, and that's liable to get them swarming. I don't think they can get through our clothes, but unless we can cover up our hands and faces with mud or something, or find better shelter, I guess the fire's our best bet.

The feeding scare-flare disinclined them to search around in the gathering gloom for a cave or other refuge.

"That is," she went on, "unless one of you has repellent or a keepaway field generator."

They didn't, but Alacrity opened his big Viceroy Imperial umbrella. As Paloma watched, he began freeing up its drop-netting.

"Well, aren't you the well-equipped travelers, though?" As she helped Alacrity clear a spot where they could all take cover, Floyt prepared a pile of firewood and kept an eye on the scare-flare.

Unbothered by the drillbugs, the creature finished its meal with incredible speed and glared up at the humans again. Their inaccessibility, the fire and its recent meal combined to discourage it. The scare-flare ambled over to a sausage-boled tree, its bark a delicate, lacey white. The creature sniffed at it, looking it over carefully. On the bole there was a series of deep, parallel gouges in the wood.

The thing reared up, raking at the bole to leave new clawmarks, deeper and higher off the ground than its former rival's. Then it dropped back to all six and wandered off.

Alacrity and Paloma had selected a spot in the middle of the redoubt, about the only place where they'd all be able to fit comfortably under the brolly. They paused long enough for Alacrity to swat a drillbug that had landed on his hand. Floyt batted at another that was circling him as Paloma lowered herself to the rock surface.

"Quick, they're swarming!" she called. They sat with their backs together, feet extended in different directions, the umbrella propped up between them; it wasn't the first time Alacrity had taken a night's refuge under an umbrella, and he'd bought the Viceroy with that, among other things, in mind. Freed up, the tough netting was diaphanous and plentiful; they tucked it under their legs and tried to make sure there were no openings. Paloma had her evening shawl around her for added protection, and had closed a flap of her costume's sheer insert to cover her risky cleavage.

Drillbugs began orbiting in squadrons, bouncing

against the netting, attracted by body heat, blood, sweat, and other aromas. The trio squirmed to get as comfortable as possible. "Will we have to spend the whole night like this?" Floyt asked with dread. His behind was already getting numb; his back felt like it was planning to kink up in the near future.

"It looks that way," Paloma said tiredly. "Do either of you two buckos know any good, *lo-oong* jokes?"

CHAPTER 10

SHALL WE COMPARE THEE TO A SUMMER'S COLD?

IT TURNED OUT THAT THEY ALL KNEW A FAIR NUMBER, from the quite funny to groaners, though after months together Alacrity and Floyt were familiar with one another's repertoires. Paloma had good delivery, but Alacrity noticed that she stayed away from anything overtly sexual.

Still, for the most part the conversation revolved around how they were going to get back to Horselaugh —or if they stood any chance of it—as drillbugs bounced off the netting. The things preferred flying to scuttling, so it wasn't much problem keeping them out. Down below, the gawklegs had begun a peculiar droning, like two-ton Buddhist monks inside an echo chamber, and the infrasonics had gotten intense, an impossibly deep pipe-organ concert.

The three shifted and resettled a lot at first, trying for more comfortable resting positions, backs sliding and rear ends squirming, but each time one moved, it disarranged the other two. Accusations were exchanged. In time, with a certain amount of bickering, they achieved a compromise that all three could endure, at least for a while.

Every so often Floyt would snake his hand out into the open long enough to toss another piece of wood at the fire, then snatch it back before the slow-witted drill-

139

bugs could pounce on it. He wasn't as particular about his aim as he was about avoiding more bites, so the fire became rather haphazard. It popped and hissed as confused drillbugs blundered into it.

Floyt and Paloma were sitting with legs off to either side of the blaze. Alacrity, facing away from it, was comfortable enough in his shipsuit for the time being but knew it would get colder fast, and wished he'd had time to pull on his suit insert. He was also worried about the prowling noises he heard from time to time in the darkness. He held a short cudgel of the spongy firewood in his lap. His best weapon, the brolly, was their only drillbug defense.

Floyt kept the survival tool ready, blade open, and was trying to whittle a stabbing stick for Alacrity without poking a hole in the netting or jarring open any gaps in their flimsy palisade. Paloma had her flashlight pistols and a few throwing-size rocks. The wood supply wasn't adequate for the night; they didn't talk about what might happen when the fire burned itself out.

Resigning himself to being uncomfortable, Alacrity began examining Paloma's planetological info file again, fast-forwarding through it as the little holoprojection lit his face and Paloma and Floyt twisted their heads in an effort to see. "Jeez, Paloma, you got everything in here."

"I wanted to know all there was to know. Planetography, flora and fauna, climate and the rest—how else was I going to sound like someone who'd spent a long time in the wilds?" She removed her fillet with its big gemstone.

"Well, you knew what you were saying; hell's entropy, this'll be a rough trip even *with* those big derricks helping. Without 'em..."

"I doubt we could make it very far before we became too weak to go on," she gauged coolly, "aside from predators, mountains, rivers and the rest."

"Perhaps we ought to rethink signaling?" Floyt ventured. "With a big fire if not with proteuses. If someone lands, we jump them and take their craft."

"First of all," Paloma told him crisply, "this whole area's very lightly inhabited. I doubt anyone flies within visual range of here once in several years. But if we did attract attention, it'd most probably be from a boatload of company police. Still, what you're talking about is the kind of thing we might have to think about, further down the line."

"I wonder what the Precursors were doing here," Floyt mulled.

Alacrity had been thinking the same thing and couldn't come up with much. He hadn't had much time to ponder it through, but at least one thing was definite: of all the Precursor manifestations he knew of, the two that had yielded the most amazing connections to Precursor knowledge were the only two located on or under a planetary surface. He also tried to envision where Hecate and the site had rabbit-holed to.

"You've got high desert, where we can travel and survive *if* the gawks help," Paloma said, "because they're good at finding water and can carry it for us, besides which they cover ground a lot faster." She was trying to see the map Alacrity was studying. "That's our first big barrier, if we can't win their help."

"What's this here?" Alacrity held the projection up so she could see it, pointing out a map feature. A half meter or so away, drillbugs bounced against the netting like pixie vampires. "Beyond the mountains, I mean. Savannah?"

He caught her nod, and moved the map around so Floyt could get a look at it.

"You read it right," she confirmed. "A gruesome place for humans afoot, but no great shakes for a herd of gawks. And beyond that is Lake Fret, which is a problem I haven't quite worked out yet. The gawks are supposed to be able to swim a little, but I don't think they can make it across a stretch of water that big. And besides, there's a good deal of surface shipping there, and some meat eaters in the water."

"Yeah, that's what—thirty, thirty-five kilometers

across at the narrowest point, there?" Alacrity said. "Of course, it's a couple hundred extra to go around in either direction, but if we have to—"

"Uh-uh." Paloma was shaking her head. "At that end, beyond the company operations sites, there're mires and bogs pretty much the whole way to the sea, impassable to gawks. At the opposite end, it's open country, barren, with lots of company activity. We might be able to go around, but we'd end up in some very cold country. I don't know if the gawks could take it—or if we could."

Floyt, already chilly despite the fire, shivered at the thought of a snow trek, even on gawkback. *Especially* on gawkback. "What about rafts, for the lake?" he proposed hesitantly, picturing a fifty-klick row with something the size of a gawk trying to keep its balance. "Or could we leave them behind at that point?"

"Not a chance," Paloma said, "because the selling point of the trip, as far as the gawks are concerned, will be that they can go on from the opposite shore of Lake Fret to link up with another gawk herd down in those plains there a few hundred kilometers south. I'll explain the whole thing to you, but for now that lake's our big problem.

"And we can't let the gawks be seen anywhere close to company operations, or everything the company could get flying in the air or moving on the ground would be out blasting away at them."

"But then what does that leave?" Floyt wondered.

"I'm working on that, Hobie," she told him. Floyt started. *Hobie?*

"Well, keep us updated," Alacrity said. Then he added, *"Whoa!"* as something the length of his forearm whipped down into the firelight in a quick swoop and was gone again. "What-all in perdition's plenum was *that*?"

"Ringwing," Paloma said. "I didn't know there were any in this area. But then again, I didn't know the drill-bugs lived on this side of the mountains, either."

Another ringwing dove through the light and into the dark again, and another, eel shapes with multiple wing-sets that seemed to meet and form circles at the top and bottom of each stroke, oaring the air. Then more shot through the firelight as drillbugs began disappearing.

"Makes sense, though," Paloma said. "The drillbugs probably came along when the gawks did; they lay eggs in the dung. And the ringwings eventually blundered into a huge drillbug population and prospered."

Floyt could see that the fast-moving ringwings were proficient feeders, getting a drillbug or two on every dive, like bats grabbing insects. He gulped. "And do ringwings have a taste for human blood, too?"

She considered it dispassionately. "Mmm, I wouldn't think so. They're pretty specialized predators, and we're too big for them."

"Fast, too," Floyt commented. The air was cleared of drillbugs—not because the prey was very good at avoiding predators; the drillbugs seemed to be singleminded blood seekers, like leeches—in just a few minutes of ringwing feeding.

It was like being in the middle of some bizarre dog-fight. Except for the flutter of wings, the hiss of air as the ringwings passed, and the occasional bump of a drillbug, it was played out in silence. The fire sounded quite loud in the middle of it all. The ringwings' guidance sense was uncanny; as close as they swept to the brolly, not one so much as brushed it. The humans watched spellbound for a total of seven minutes or so.

Then the air was clear of bugs and 'wings alike. Ala-crity cautiously poked his head from under the netting. "Well, I'll be."

"Great, isn't it?" Paloma said cheerfully. "Let's all hear it for ringwings."

Floyt emerged from the netting, grabbing for more wood. With a sudden dread of the dark and a determina-tion that the flames would not die out, he fed the fire. The gawks' droning still rose and fell in the distance. Other nightfliers were venturing out, bioluminescent mites and fluttering, transparent things like ghostly, airborne hairpieces. Decaying matter and plant parasites gave off eerie phosphorescence, making the woods look menacing and haunted.

"Look, Paloma," Alacrity said, carefully laying aside the brolly but leaving it open just in case. "This stuff about wiping out the gawks and driving them out here—how long does the company think it can get away with a thing like that?"

She raised her shoulders and let them fall, making dismissing gestures with her hands. "People have better things to do than go nosing around the Lebensraum Outback. And most of the very few who know the real truth have a vested interest in keeping the secret. Besides, nobody's counting on it lasting forever.

"What I'm getting at is, you have this company exec, and how much do you think he cares if the truth comes out thirty or fifty or a hundred years down the line? By then he's long since retired somewhere with his money, or dead. But they all make sure nothing gets out while *they're* on the scene, and that's the way it's been all along."

"Some secrets have been maintained for a long, long while in more or less that fashion," Floyt said, the fire set up to his liking again. Alacrity could just about read his thoughts: the Camarilla had lasted two hundred years.

Floyt took the mated proteuses and began flashing forward and back through gawkleg data, looking over some very old company zoological studies. Alacrity tossed more wood on the fire so that it was disarranged; Floyt took a moment to square it away to his own satisfaction once more, with a proprietary air. The brolly and the data and wilderness savvy might be someone else's, but the campfire was Floyt's.

"I think it'll be all right," Paloma said, meaning the fire. "If we run low on wood we can take torches and get more; there's enough nearby. I don't think even a scareflare would bother three of us with burning brands."

"Now, while we've got a minute," Alacrity brought up some old business, "just why is it again that you think the gawks'll go along with your invitation to convoy us cross-country?"

"In a way, the gawks need us just as much as we need them," she said.

Floyt, the professional Earthservice accessor, had found what he was looking for. He looked to Paloma. "Only to convince them of that might require a little nature study of our own, am I correct?"

She gave him a congratulatory nod and a smile Alacrity found himself coveting. "You're a fast man with a file, Hobie."

"All right, all right; I'm lost," Alacrity confessed. "Now will somebody please tell me?"

She gave him a surprised look. "Why, we're going to take a headcount on the gawklegs, of course."

"Day shift coming on." Floyt yawned, looking down at some little rodent-thing scampering from cover and back again. "I hope the scare-flares are late sleepers." He rolled in his mouth the pebbles he was using to try to keep his mind off thirst. He rubbed his side to get the blood circulating after a torturous night of trying to sleep on cold solid rock. As a mercy, though, the drillbugs hadn't returned. As he watched, an enormous flock of avian-things took to the wing, blotting out Invictus and darkening the sky.

Alacrity looked up from where he was hardening his spearpoint in the coals and wondering if he was doing it right; he'd only heard about that sort of thing. At the very least, Floyt's multitool was a promethean blessing, a hip-pocket machine shop of sorts.

Alacrity squinted at the dawn. Gawklegs were on the move in the distance, their infrasonics apparently silent. "Time to go house hunting, what d'you say?"

Paloma stood and stretched, hands against the small of her back, groaning as she arched. Alacrity watched admiringly. "First, how 'bout some food hunting?" she proposed.

"That sounds wonderful," Floyt enthused. "My stomach's rumbling so loud, the scare-flares must be cowering in their dens. Or nests, or whatever."

"Usually in a burrow down on the flatlands," Paloma clarified. "And today's the day we start convincing them they better stay the hell down there and away from *us*."

"What've you got, landmines hidden in your girdle?" Alacrity blinked. He was scattering the fire, grinding embers and covering them with ash; the area was dry and he had no desire to find out what a local wildfire was like.

"Trust me; I'm the legendery Siren of the Wilderness, remember?" Paloma followed Floyt down from the redoubt, both of them alert against attack, holding their sharpened walking staffs as spears.

Alacrity moaned tiredly, gathering up his own spear and meticulously brushing off and refolding the brolly. He thought a moment, then left the cap off its sharpened tip.

"A drink of water's first on the list as far as I'm concerned," Floyt announced. "And, er, another brief stop."

"No argument here," Paloma assured him. "Only first let's see what's left of the scare-flare."

They went with Paloma leading because she knew more than either of the men. Floyt held the center and backed her up while Alacrity brought up the rear. They moved in close order; it wasn't a combat patrol wherein one round might get them all. It was instead a survival march in unfamiliar wilds without firearms; grouped defense, grasslands-baboon style, was their best bet.

Unless, of course, some gawklegs elected to come up from the plains and romp and stomp on them, in which case even a tree probably wouldn't be much protection and they'd all three very likely become so much toe-jam.

Floyt's thoughts strayed to their conversations in the night. Alacrity had questioned Paloma and combed her proteus for all the local data he could find. Floyt mentioned general survival rules and Alacrity explained, "General survival rules that don't stand a chance of making you die young, you can count on one hand.

"I heard this story once, when I shipped in the Salty Dog. Guy was one of a survivor party, so this big whatsit comes charging outta the brush and he shinnies up a tree. Well, who wouldn't? Besides, he was from Adam's Apple, and that was what he was used to.

"Only, it turns out, the thingie he was running from was this harmless spore-strainer, but the tree he picked out was a carrion eater with toxic bark. So his account got stamped *closed* brother."

Floyt sighed. "At least I wish we had our guns. Especially the Captain's Sidearm, with those pouches. We could certainly use more equipment, survival equipment."

Alacrity had half turned to him in the firelight. "*What* survival equipment? Those pouches are just for cleaning equipment and ammo and a lanyard and like that, Ho. The Captain's Sidearm's not meant for survival groundside; it's meant to keep you from *losing* your ship!"

And then Alacrity looked out into the darkness, adding softly, "God*dammit* anyway..."

"Oh! Sorry, Alacrity."

"Forget it, Ho. Wait'll you see what we do when I've got that Ship back."

Bigger scavengers were done with the leavings of the cricket-fawn's carcass; the smaller and smallest were almost finished. Bones were cracked, marrowlike contents gone. Most tissue and skin had vanished, too.

"Thank goodness," Paloma breathed. "That foreleg's still here." She grabbed the defeated scare-flare's dismembered leg and began knocking tiny feeding things loose from it with her spearpoint and by banging it against a tree.

"What would you want that for?" Floyt asked, thinking of fishhooks and arrowheads.

Alacrity was watching with an air of knowledgeability.

"Like she sez: we're gonna see to it the scare-flares stay clear of us."

Paloma glanced to him suspiciously. "Now, how would you know about this? I thought you'd never been to Lebensraum before—and this trick *isn't* in the proteus."

Alacrity tested the wicked needle claw with his thumb. Its tip was as sharp as his brolly's. "S'right. But the trick's a classic and it translates well, Paloma."

Floyt almost shouted out a demand to know what in the world they were talking about, then decided not to give them the satisfaction. Instead, he scanned the countryside, spotting the gawklegs a kilometer and a half down the valley.

"First things first. You two stay together, here, for a second," Alacrity bade, checking out a nearby asparagus-tip tree to see if anything dangerous was hanging around it looking for a meal. Then he sauntered off around it. Paloma muttered something about "pushy"; the awareness that he'd have to wait his turn made Floyt's bladder that much more insistent.

Paloma went next without asking, the two men standing guard. "Although pity the poor thingie that jumps her," Alacrity muttered.

To take his mind off his own urgent need, Floyt said, "Alacrity, have you noticed anything about Paloma's, um, 'look'? I mean, the high-allure outfit and the two horse-pistols—it puts me in mind of crazy Constance." Floyt was referring to the woman who'd served Dincrist and tried to end their lives several times.

"Yeah, but you got it backward," Alacrity answered. "Both of 'em are copying the figure Hecate cut in her heyday. People patterned themselves after her then and they still do. I wonder what they'll think when the truth comes out."

Floyt reached the limits of his endurance and went off before Paloma got back, heedless of Alacrity's objections. When Floyt returned, vastly relieved, Paloma and Alacrity were talking almost civilly.

"How shall we do this?" Floyt inquired. "All go house hunting together? Split up, with someone beginning the headcount?" He didn't admit that the idea of dividing forces upset his stomach. He'd gotten over much of his Terran prejudice against intelligent XTs in the course of his wanderings with Alacrity, but any animal too big to fit in a carport still made him queasy. "After all, we're working against time."

"No, we'll stay together for now, until we know the land and what the dangers are around here," Alacrity decided.

Paloma stared at him for a moment before she said, "Yes, that's correct," as if she were grading him on a test.

They're both so used to giving orders, Floyt thought resignedly. *Tao, give me strength!*

Paloma led the way without any argument or advice from Alacrity. They went off along the valley's slope in the opposite direction from the onetime Precursor site. At last she stopped where an outcrop of rock thrust out of the hillside like an enormous, layered chisel blade. Foliage and undergrowth were darker and more lush there. Following the others' lead, Floyt helped pull back masses of netvine, cutting bushes out of the way with his survival tool, probing carefully with his spear before he touched anything, trusting Paloma to know what plants were unsafe. They uncovered not one but two tiny water seepages.

One was useless for the time being; it ran down a rock face from higher up and they had no way to collect it short of licking the rock. The second dripped and dribbled in a deep, vertical cleft only a few centimeters wide. There was one small catch pocket ten centimeters or so back, where a teacupful of water accumulated. Floyt gazed at it hopelessly, licking dry lips.

Paloma looked around, then borrowed the survival widget and cut a length of reed, trimming it as a drinking straw. Alacrity and Floyt wouldn't hear of her not going first. The survival tool had a built-in water purifier of questionable efficacy, but there wasn't any way to use it in configuration with the drinking tube. Floyt was so thirsty that he didn't give a damn, trusting to his immunities and eagerly awaiting his turn at the reed.

Fortunately, the catch pocket refilled quickly, ready for a second emptying almost as soon as Paloma made way for Floyt. Alacrity drank next, then they all had a second go-around and a third, longer turn.

Eventually they started off again, working their way along low cliffs, moving cautiously, spears up. They noted a few outcroppings and eroded crevices, but nothing that offered decent protection against weather, predators, or drillbugs. Once or twice, though, they saw trees marked by scare-flares.

In time, they came across an overhang of blue-gray rock under which a low, narrow opening stretched back into darkness. It looked to Floyt unpleasantly like prime housing for something large, aggressive, and carnivorous, like a scare-flare.

"I think this was the loser's lair," Paloma said, gesturing with the amputated foreclaw. She glanced around; several trees in the neighborhood were claw-marked. "Yes; it must be."

She shied a stone into the cave, then, when that brought no response, fired some light effects into it with her target pistols. Alacrity and Floyt fronted for her nervously, spears ready.

"Nobody home," she concluded, "or it'd be out here facing off with us by now. The wounded one either died or moved on." She looked around at the nearby trees. "Time to advertise. Can you hold me up on your shoulders, Alacrity?"

"Relax; I'll do the honors," he said.

She handed him the claw and he put his brolly and spear aside. Floyt finally began to understand. Alacrity knelt and did something to the expensive pathfinders he wore; climbing spikes clicked into place at both insteps. Paloma gave a whistle of admiration. "Best damn boots in the universe," he said simply.

He didn't bother improvising a climbing belt; he wasn't going far. He went up quickly but very carefully while Paloma and Floyt kept watch to all sides and stole periodic glances up at him. Alacrity came to a stop with a grip on the lowest branch, climbing spikes seated firmly.

He started scraping at the bark with the claw a meter above the previous scare-flare marks. "So," Floyt said, back to back with Paloma. "Now the biggest, meanest scare-flare there is, is warning all the others to stay away, hmm?"

"You hit it. We've got a lot of marking to do, though."

"This bark's thicker than a landlord's wallet," Alacrity reported. "Ho, toss up that hip-pocket hardware store, will you? I'm gonna cheat." The tool had a V-gouge wood chisel blade on it.

It was nevertheless more than ten minutes by Floyt's proteus before Alacrity came down again, after dropping the claw to Paloma and the tool to Floyt.

"Well, it seems like some monster scare-flare about the size of a hovercab with claws like augers just took up residence in these parts." He looked up, admiring his work.

"I just hope the scent pads hold their smell long enough for us to mark a perimeter," Paloma said. "That shouldn't take us more than two days at this rate, I should think."

"What about the smell in the cave?" Floyt thought to ask. "Won't rivals know that it's no longer a scare-flare headquarters?"

"There're ways to cover that," Paloma dismissed the matter. Alacrity had opened the crotch of his shipsuit, facing the tree he'd just marked. When he turned back, its base was damp.

He smirked. "Picture some newcomer sizing up the territory. 'Holy Buddha in a bunnysuit! This local scare-flare's a thyroid case! And what's he been eating? And drinking, *ugh*!'"

As a last precaution, Floyt tossed a couple of lichen

torches into the cave from a distance. When nothing happened, they braved to look in. Flashes from Paloma's pistols showed that the place was empty, a low crawl-space reaching back four meters, with less debris in it than Floyt had feared.

"I saw some knucklenut trees as we came along," Paloma said. "I propose that Alacrity and I go gather breakfast while Hobie builds another of those great fires."

It was agreed, and Floyt set to work, careful to keep vigilance all around. No fire except natural ones had ever burned on that part of Lebensraum; the place was a deadwood supermarket. He began with a small blaze, feeding bigger and bigger pieces of fuel, then saw things were getting out of hand. He built a ring of stones under the overhang and transferred operations there.

Floyt found a powerful, difficult-to-understand fasci-nation in the work, something strong and vastly comfort-ing. The phrase *keeper of the flame* kept recurring to him. The fire seemed so ephemeral, the dangers of the wilds so close to hand.

It took him some time to realize how much time had passed. He checked his proteus, then tried to picture the distance they could've traveled and estimate the time it would've taken to collect the nuts, whatever that en-tailed. The whole effort was hopeless and dispiriting.

He tried to raise Alacrity by proteus but got no re-sponse. Nothing ominous about that necessarily; land features might be interfering, or Alacrity could be busy, or in a situation where he didn't want to make noise. Floyt kept working, glancing around every few seconds in hopes of seeing them return. His stack of firewood grew high.

At last he gripped wooden spear and survival knife determinedly and set off to find them. His first few paces back under the tree canopy brought him to a halt as it occurred to him that he didn't know where he was going or how to get back.

Wasn't there something—oh, yes! He checked his

compass to see in which direction he was headed, proud of himself. Then, even prouder, he recalled how Scagway Scanlon had dealt with this sort of thing in the deathless penny dreadful, *Scagway Scanlon, Wilderness Wildcat*.

Floyt made a very unpracticed blaze in the soft, flaky bark of a slender tree. Drawing a deep breath, he sighted on the tree where he would make his next blaze. Just as he was about to sally forth, Alacrity and Paloma came into view not ten meters away, slightly uphill from him.

"Oh! I was—"

He stopped before he could tell them how relieved he felt. He saw from their faces that something had happened, that they shared some knowledge from which he was excluded. He exchanged looks with them, thinking *All right; now everybody understands what everybody understands*. It was beyond the realm of possibility that he was wrong.

He abruptly felt left out and resentful, betrayed really, not from envy or desire for Paloma—though those were there, too—but because it wasn't a trio anymore but rather a couple with a satellite. And because some accord had plainly been struck around and above him, which pointed up a certain disregard he found it hard to endure.

Oh, swell! And here we are, the three slap-happy throwbacks—two lovebirds and an irate spare wheel, just waiting around for trouble in paradise.

Well, not a chance! I like them both too much.

So he twirled his spear and said lightly, "There was a commo call while you were out. The neanderthals in the next cave invited us over for toddies and an evening of grunting."

Alacrity's face broke into a skewed grin. "What, on a school night?" He came Floyt's way with a certain swagger.

But Paloma rammed him aside. "Oh-hh, no!" She walked toward Floyt with wide paces, leaving Alacrity to catch up. "Now, hear me, Hobie: this is strictly an alliance for survival purposes. I'm nobody's cuddle or camp follower. That's what I told libido brain over here and that's what I'm telling you, so we're clear on it all around.

"We're three partners. Equals. If either of you tries to act hypermasculine or change the bargain I'll strike out on my own, I swear it, and leave the pair of you to poison yourselves on the wrong kind of berries or disappear under the mire because you can't read bogsign!"

Floyt saw he'd gotten things wrong. "That's fine with me, Paloma. Just so long as you stop hollering."

She guffawed and got herself under control at the same time, looking at Floyt in a way she hadn't looked at him before. Alacrity was red-faced and sheepish, but he was laughing, too, and for a strange but wonderful moment they were all on an equal footing, alive and hoping, companions, with something quintessentially human and rueful floating in their laughter.

Back at the den, Alacrity and Paloma emptied their pockets. Demonstrably, they'd been busy doing other things beside establishing social boundaries. There were dozens of the little shining-bronze knucklenuts—the size and shape of a periwinkle—and some roots they'd found, shaped something like ginseng but looking like they were made of black iron.

The nuts were a disappointment, hard to crack and dig the meat from, and tasting like gravel. Paloma's sculpted glamornails of superhard duraglaze turned out to be a lot more than fashion embellishments; they were like a fingertip tool kit, very useful for nut-picking, among other things.

The roots, formidable as they looked, turned out to be juicy and crisp, with a flavor somewhere between radish and celery. Floyt bit into one; the juice squirted across his mouth and down his chest. He hummed with delight at the flavor. Paloma showed them the proper technique so as to waste none.

But when it was all gone they'd barely cut their hunger pangs and thirst was on them again. The good news was that Alacrity and Paloma had found a tiny runnel not far off, making water less a problem.

"This is gonna be a very tough day," Alacrity said. "So, *if nobody objects*, we can try to gather more food and do the tree markings at the same time. If it doesn't work out, we just go back to concentrating on one thing at a time; mark fewer trees and eat less."

All three of them had eaten well on the day Hecate showed up to Oz them away to her Precursor lair. Real hunger hadn't begun to hit them yet. The plan was carried unanimously.

Floyt regretfully banked his fire and they moved out with Paloma at point once more. Floyt was again amazed at how long a day could be—in this case the Lebensraum day, some twenty-seven Standard hours. As a comfortable Earthservice accessor—if not a free or happy one, or permitted much dignity—Floyt had lived a not-much-varying routine that, mercifully, made time not seem to hang heavily upon him. At least, not unless he thought about it.

He worked a straight day schedule and that was a tremendous plus, going from his apt to his work carrel and back. There was his accessing, a succession of minor absorptions, broken up by periods of light office exercise and a midday meal. In the evening he returned home to watch media with his family, indulge his hobby of genealogical research, or occasionally have a night out at some recbureau function. Freedays, he liked to bicycle, his worst eccentricity.

But for the most part days had drifted together in a comfortable routine sameness, blurred so that they passed with an easy timelessness. Only now and then would Hobart Floyt get the twinge, in his carrel in the morning or his apt living room at night, *Didn't I just leave here?*

That first morning, like Floyt's experience on a couple of other worlds, was utterly different from functionary life. To the distant booming, belching, and flatulence of the gawklegs, he and his companions stole through the brush, alert to peril, watching for trees to mark, searching for scare-flare signs, careful of their footing, wary of noxious plants and insects. The first half hour had them perspiring in spite of the morning chill and was so uncomfortable, demanding, and fatiguing that it seemed to Floyt longer than a workweek, even a dull and toilsome one, back on Terra.

They found another knucklenut tree but passed it by when Paloma Sudan judged that the nuts were unripe enough to make them sick, possibly be lethal. A midge-like thing tried to crawl into Alacrity's ear to explore, others being drawn to mouths and nostrils by warmth and smells. Less than two hours after dawn, the temperature was already 20° C by Paloma's proteus. They paused for a long drink at a runnel. Just after that, Floyt stepped in some unidentified fewmets.

They came to a tree that seemed suitable—the scare-flares only used certain types—and Alacrity borrowed Floyt's web belt to join with his own and use as a climbing belt. After extending the climbing spikes, Alacrity took position while the other two stood guard.

Most wildlife was unfrightened of them, but none they saw was inclined to attack. Three adult humans were too much for any rock-eel, ringwing, flapcat, or kobold to tangle with.

They passed the day marking out territory around the lair, gathering food when they could, eating most of it on the spot. They also discussed the gawkleg census.

"From a distance is how we're gonna do it," Alacrity said. "Preferably by intelsat."

"That *would* be nice," Paloma answered, "if it were possible. But we've got to do it accurately, and that may mean getting uncomfortably close, because if we haven't got our facts right the first time, those beauties will probably never listen to us again."

Floyt gave Alacrity a hand down from the last tree. "We don't have a lot of time," Alacrity said yet again.

By late afternoon they'd finished a fair perimeter of

marked trees, pretty well using up the scent in the fore-leg paw pads as far as Alacrity could tell. All three were dirty, tired, hungry, and thirsty despite water stops and intermittent foraging of berries and other things okayed by Paloma's data. They were also sweaty and increasingly rank. Floyt had been fantasizing about a sylvan bathing scene, jungle-romance style, finding a pool or a safe, deep part of the little river that wound through the middle of the valley, until Paloma mentioned sliverworms, stingfish, and similar noxious life forms liable to be prowling any stretch of deep water not claimed by the gawks. A sponge bath began to sound grand.

Invictus was getting lower. They could hear the cavorting and eructations of gawks happily traipsing around in an environment where little could harm them unless they were badly injured or sick.

Well, maybe not completely happily, Alacrity thought. *They're smart enough to know something's wrong. All we've gotta do is get them to admit it and then believe we have the answer. Good luck...*

"We'll have more time for food gathering tomorrow, now that the Walls of Jericho are finished," Paloma said. "I wouldn't mind a little more to eat, but I really don't feel like stumbling around in the dark, especially with drillbugs."

Just then a scare-flare gargled somewhere and another replied, from across the valley. They tended to become active around dusk. "It certainly seems an advisable time to draw the wagons into a circle," Floyt declared.

The gawklegs were starting up their droning again; they sometimes did it by day, but always in the evening, Paloma's info said. The kicker was, the droning wasn't simple animal herd sounds; it was a blend of recitation and something a lot like prayer.

The three moved back to camp quickly. They checked carefully, but the former den was still empty. Alacrity supposed that the fire ring with its ash might have something to do with that. The new occupants used short branches as rakes, pulling out debris and loose dirt. Then they refloored it with leaves and heaped more to the side to use as covers. The den didn't smell so much rank as oily. To Alacrity, scare-flare scent was redolent of old machine parts.

Then they built up the fire, readied plenty of wood, and each made a last commo with nature while the others did sentinel duty. Alacrity gently detached the drop-netting from his brolly and hung it across the mouth of the cave, weighting the bottom and filling in gaps with dirt.

As the fire burned down, they waited for the next drillbug onslaught. The night came on. "Maybe the fire's keeping them back from the overhang, or they're someplace else?" Alacrity speculated.

But just then a miniature hydra shape, then another, bumped the netting. As if that was a signal to relax, the three settled down in the crawlspace cave to watch. Paloma dug into her pouch and came up with a sweetspeck dispenser.

"I was saving it for a morale booster," she explained, and carefully flicked a tiny flavored dot onto each man's palm. The sweetspecks tasted wonderful; they dissolved in moments, but the taste lingered. Stomachs growled like gawks' droning.

There was no swarming of drillbugs, just assaults from roving individuals and small groups. Alacrity guessed that the smoke and heat of the fire were masking the humans' scent and body warmth. It was full dark before a ringwing zipped through the firelight, taking a drillbug on the fly.

After another half hour Floyt volunteered to go out and test the air. His fire was burning low and he couldn't bear the idea of watching it go out. "Just another caveman," he muttered.

The drillbugs had again disappeared. According to Paloma's data, they fed on fruits and plant sap when there was no blood source available, and didn't much like spending time in the air. Alacrity and Paloma joined

Floyt by the fire and they went back to talk of the gawk-legs' recruitment drive.

"I've been thinking about it," Alacrity said, tossing a length of wood on the fire carelessly. Floyt frowned and rearranged everything more to his high standards in fire esthetics. "And I have an idea," Alacrity went on.

Floyt sighed. "Just when things were getting restful."

CHAPTER 11

MIDDLE-OF-THE-FOOD-CHAIN BLUES

"I MAKE IT FIFTY OF THEM IN THIS GROUP," FLOYT INsisted.

He was quite comfortable stretched out on his stomach, where he'd been for two hours; he'd learned a hunter's stoic patience from Alacrity and Paloma. He no longer reacted to or worried about midges, for example, and as a result they seemed less interested in him.

"And I'm telling you it's more like seventy-five," Alacrity repeated. "Just count the number you see in the area we measured off by those trees and multiply by—"

"See here, Alacrity, I understand the procedure and I'm not blind."

"Oh, forget it!" They were on a boulder low on the valley's side, less than two hundred meters from where some gawklegs were grazing. As they watched, one cow reared and shied away abruptly from something in the grass, trailed by her calf. The men saw a flash of green and gunmetal and knew she'd almost stumbled on a scare-flare. The two species usually gave one another wide berth; a gawkleg could, of course, trample one of the predators to pulp, but if the scare-flare got its sting into a vulnerable area, a gawk could become quite ill, though death was unlikely.

The scare-flare sprang away through the high lichengrass. Alacrity shifted his weight. "We already know all

160

we have to. I say it's time to talk to those ladder-legs again. Today. Now."

Floyt shook his head. "We should try for one more count, closer in." He rose a centimeter or two and eased back off the boulder, moving cautiously, circling to get closer to the valley floor. He moved with an ease acquired over long days of stalking, knowing the local dangers.

Floyt had learned other things, as well, like banging out his boots before putting them on, no matter how short a time he'd had them off, and how to blow his nose with his fingers and other facts of outdoor hygiene that Scagway Scanlon and his ilk had somehow never gotten around to mentioning.

Alacrity resignedly trailed after. They kept track of the wind to make sure the gawklegs didn't pick up their scent. The two came down onto the open stretch and stalked toward a good vantage point, one from which they'd have a good view of the gawks and still be fairly safe. Then a sudden, minute sound came to them both, a tiny shifting of weight among branches only meters away, as twigs and leaves rustled against tough hide.

They both froze, turning their heads slowly, slowly, quick motion being a sure way to draw attention and be spotted, or attacked.

A gawkleg was watching them from ten meters away. It couldn't possibly have crept up on them through the foliage, given its size and horns and weight. This one was a male, one of the smallest of the adults, whom Paloma had named Nosey.

Floyt's first thought, after total shock and just as he began casting about for the nearest tree, was *But they don't stalk or lie in wait! Gawks just don't* do *this kind of thing!*

But then, Nosey wasn't like the rest of his kind. He was quick, but too small to compete in the bull battles and so, as a nonbreeding male, had little status in the herd. He was curious, even eccentric, always rooting around and prying into this and that.

Alacrity grabbed Floyt's arm just as Floyt was about to bolt. "Don't you get it, Ho? *He's* observing *us!*"

Nosey watched them steadily, rocking from side to side as gawks did when passing time, a sort of contemplative sway, except that Nosey hadn't done it while he was waiting to get a better look at them.

Alacrity must be right, Floyt realized, not daring to speak, *because Nosey isn't taking off or using us as doormats. And that is something new under this particular sun.* He nodded, to show he understood.

Men and gawkleg stood there in tableau, dappled by the shade, until Nosey let out an *oink*ing belch. It was muted for a gawk, not doing much more than stirring the men's hair and carrying a strong gust of herbivore-breath to them. Then the gawk turned ponderously, bending a small fractal sapling, and trotted away.

"There's no record here of a gawk ever doing anything like that," Paloma concluded, scanning her data as Floyt operated the linked proteuses. She scratched a leaf-mite bite on her arm; all three had them from their bedding, but the bites were preferable to shivering through the long nights.

They were sitting on the ledge in front of the den, eating wheyberries that had just gone green and ripe. The gawks were droning and bellowing in the afternoon light. "That doesn't change the fact that it happened," Alacrity reminded her.

"Here's something from back when the first human research group became isolated and started allying with the gawks," Floyt said, pointing out a bit of info he'd projected with the holofeature.

"Hey, how'd you find that?" Paloma answered her own question. "Oh, that's right; accessing was your specialty, hmm? What's it say?"

"Rather what we might have supposed. Gawklegs assumed that swaying, peaceful mode in talking to humans, just as they do when they're doing their droning. Not that any of them have talked to a human in a while, except us."

"What it boils down to," Alacrity said slowly, "is Nosey was treating us like kin. Or, at least, neutrals—not enemies."

"So?" Paloma prompted. "He's only one young male and not a very important one at that. In fact, some of the dominant bulls seem to have it in for him."

"So maybe he's just the errand boy," Alacrity reasoned. "Maybe they're all curious, and we can finesse 'em."

Floyt, unconvinced, shook his head, feeling that some sort of contact had taken place when Nosey stared at them.

"All right now, Alacrity." Floyt got back to more fundamental matters. "Don't you think it's time for you to let us in on your idea? How do we treat with them without being flattened by some three-ton isolationist?"

"The only smart way, of course. Like I said: from a distance."

"Sure," Paloma cut in, "only the volume of my proteus doesn't go loud enough for the gawks to hear a translation at anything like a safe remove, and neither does yours or Hobie's."

"Ahem." Alacrity looked a little tentative. "Well, yeah, that's true . . . as long as somebody's *wearing* the proteus."

That took a second to sink in. Then Paloma clapped a protective hand over her jeweled instrument/bracelet. "I will *not* risk having this thing tromped on or eaten up! It cost me too dearly, and besides, it contains things I just won't sacrifice. Toss your *own* bloody proteus out into the middle of those honking bloody tanks!"

Alacrity was elaborately disingenuous. "Gee, I thought your heart went out to them."

"That's all right, Paloma." Floyt stopped her as she was about to sail into Alacrity, at least verbally. "Your proteus isn't compatible with mine or Alacrity's for commo, remember? And this will require a conversation, not a recorded message."

He looked to his friend. "And I know you're not about to hazard your own. But what about the things I've stored in *my* data files, Alacrity? They're as important to me as yours are to you."

Alacrity was nodding vigorously. "I never said they weren't. But we can transfer it all over into mine for safekeeping. Mine's got megastorage galore; that one the Earthservice issued you—it's just not as much of a loss."

Floyt was slipping off his proteus, exhaling deeply. "You're right; you win."

Alacrity took it and began matching with his own for the transfer. "When we get out of this we'll get you a new one, I swear. Something really top end, good as mine or better."

He hesitated. "Or at least, good as we can afford."

Floyt barked a laugh. "You're hedging! Now I *know* you're confident we'll make it!"

"*Curnutie!* Wouldn't you think they'd move a *little* faster? Even grazing?" Paloma fumed under her breath at the distant gawklegs. She popped another ripe green wheyberry into her mouth.

"They move fast enough when they want to do the Antarian Handkerchief Dance on somebody's spinal column," Alacrity agreed softly.

Sure enough, the main herd of gawk was wandering in the general direction of the tree in which Floyt's proteus had been secured, but the approach had taken most of the day, with a lot of reversing field and digression. As the three humans watched, a scare-flare showed its webbed mantle, scuttling out of the way as a dominant bull backed from it in swift reverse. That started a general repositioning away from the wired fractal tree.

When Alacrity selected the tree at the edge of the grazing area that morning, he'd figured the herd would be in the vicinity fairly soon; they ate huge amounts of vegetation and moved almost constantly. Now he swore in a whisper at the perversity of all species that hadn't evolved to the level of civilization where there were saloons and taxi stands.

"Maybe what we need's a little come-hither," Floyt reasoned, shifting his whittled toothpick and trying to readjust his Inheritor's belt so that it didn't dig into him as he lay on the great-girthed limb where they'd been perched all day. "What about that sound they make when they get romantic?"

"Give it a try, Alacrity," Paloma said, groaning and stirring uncomfortably on blistered, convoluted bark, vigilant against any more of the biting and stinging things that inhabited it. "Anything's better than this."

She was good to look at, even after days in the wilds, though her hair was more matted than windblown and with smudges on her face instead of makeup. That made it that much more frustrating to Alacrity that she'd kept him at arm's length, showing him no more cordiality than she did Floyt. She'd continued to pull her weight, though, and treat them both as teammates, even sharing her few remaining sweetspeck candies.

Alacrity checked to make sure the gain on his proteus was set to max. Floyt's cheap instrument's reproduction might be far from ambient—distorted, in fact—but they were hoping for the best. The hookup seemed adequate when they'd tested it at the cave.

Alacrity fiddled with his heavy black-green wrist-torc of a proteus and began transmitting the lowing, curious sounds that preceded many gawkleg exchanges and nonverbal interactions. It was B-flat, a sound the cows, in particular, made when they wanted a little attention. It was a synthesized, amplified lure.

Floyt gripped his shoulder and pointed; Nosey had his head up, at his usual place on the outskirts of the herd, looking straight at the tree where the proteus was fastened.

The undersize gawk male trotted for the tree as Alacrity sent another call echoing from Floyt's proteus. A few of the herdmembers watched indifferently.

Nosey moved up close to the tree. The humans knew enough about gawkleg body language to see that he was neither belligerent nor aroused, but simply inquisitive. The gawks, being an intelligent species, demonstrated a fair degree of curiosity, but Nosey much more so than the rest. The runty nonbreeding male spoke to the sound-source in his language, and the hookup sent a translation back through Alacrity's proteus, using the linguistic program copied from Paloma's data files, giving a running translation.

"I find this puzzling. How can a tree be in need of sexual easement? You smell all wrong," Nosey told the tree.

"Yes. That is, you're right," Alacrity responded.

Nosey snorted, the loud blast taking a little longer to reach them through the open air than it did through the proteus hookup. He dug in a hoof to fling a bucketsize hunk of soil arcing back into the air. "So, this is some (untranslatable white noise) of the two-leggers, then?"

"A what? Try again."

"A trick, a boogum of the—humans. Those three who have come *are* humans, aren't they? I notice this voice comes from a strange, shiny fruit up there in the branches. I have never seen one like that before, but it looks tasty."

"It's not, it's not!" Alacrity hastened. Nosey huffed a strange sound that the proteus rendered as laughter.

"Well, what do you know?" Paloma chuckled. "He's clowning on us."

"The Verities tell us that the humans could speak to us once," the thing said. "Is that who's speaking through this horny tree? Humans?"

"You're smart," Alacrity conceded. "What's your name?"

The thing huffed and snorted, but there wasn't much of the body-english the gawks often used among themselves. The hookup translated, "I have a name, Meadowbreeze, but my use-name has gotten to be Poke-snout."

"Oh. What're the Verities?"

"Lore/History/Law/Legend." (The proteus did a surprisingly good job of overlapping it, to make the castaways understand that the Verities were all that.) "Haven't you heard us recite and discuss the Verities?"

Nosey/Pokesnout made the dirgelike droning the humans had listened to every night since their arrival. The century-old linguistic program turned it into "The First Ones called to the Herd, and the First Ones were the Light, and the First Ones gave to the Herd a smaller Light of their own, in each and every one . . ."

Precursors! Alacrity wanted to hear more about that but Pokesnout was already on to other things. "Question! What do you want? It better be no danger to the herd! This skulking about and talking through trees makes no sense to me."

"I guess that's no surprise," Alacrity responded, wondering just how the program would translate it. "But you heard what we tried to say to the herd leaders?"

"We all did. This Long Trek that you have in mind for yourselves is more arduous than you know. But it will be interesting. You will see many strange things. That is intriguing."

"Good, because we want you and the others of the herd to carry us."

Pokesnout snuffled and honked laughter. "Say more; I hope to hear all I can before the others make you part of the ground."

Alacrity covered the sound pickup with his hand. "We got a droll one here." To the pickup, he added, "You wouldn't like to go?"

"Not enough to be burned by sky-flame. And then, too, it goes against the Verities. Not the Old Verities, but the New Verities, which were chanted after humans cut the herds from many to few, with fire."

Alacrity looked to Floyt and Paloma, who watched

him wordlessly. "The thing is," he said, "we have a reason the herd should come along, for its own sake."

"Even to listen to this runs counter to the Verities," Pokesnout announced.

"But you're already doing that!" Floyt put in.

"I don't always agree with the Verities, but then I will probably be outcast soon. But there is no reason that will make the herd listen to you."

Paloma leaned over the voice pickup to say "We can tell you why the herd is growing smaller and smaller, and how to save it from dying out."

"Wait, while I gather the others," Pokesnout said, trotting off at urgent speed.

It took an unholy amount of honking, squealing, and bellowing on Pokesnout's part to get even a few others of the herd to approach the proteus tree. The infrasonic impulses stormed.

The humans watched from their spying place, eating wheyberries and sipping from a canteen improvised from a hard vegetable suggesting a tubular gourd, and scratching their various bites, rashes, and sores.

More than one male seemed inclined to batter horns with Pokesnout rather than listen to what they considered an amorous plant. But it turned out that the survival-of-the-herd argument was, as Paloma's info indicated it would be, powerfully persuasive, even in the face of the Verities. At last one of the big, dominant bulls approached the tree while hundreds looked on.

"I have to speak with you," Alacrity said. The male immediately lowered his head and charged the unoffending talking tree. The tree trembled to the blow, several fractal-veined leaves shaken loose. They'd chosen the sturdiest tree feasible, yet the bull had nearly tilted it.

Pokesnout reacted at once, charging the bigger male. The male turned to give battle. The humans expected to see one of the gawks' highly ritualized combats, with the usual posturings and protocols.

But Pokesnout altered the rules at the last moment,

sheering off and avoiding a horns-to-horns collision. It was the first time the castaways had seen a gawk use such a trick. But then, as they were starting to understand, Pokesnout wasn't like other gawklegs.

The bull stood his ground, straddle-legged, confused by the unauthorized change in procedure. But at least Pokesnout had made him forget his determination to bring down the strange talking tree. The runt male stood off a way and harangued, bending his head back so that he could give full throat to it.

"We should at least listen to the amorous tree!" the proteus interpreted. "For the sake of the herd!"

"What can a rutting tree tell us?" the bull lowed.

"I can tell you this,"Alacrity intervened. The gawklegs turned to hear out the tree. "I can tell you you haven't got many generations left before there's no more herd, and you already know that yourselves. This herd used to number thousands, and there're barely three hundred of you left!"

Several bulls dropped their heads combatively, pawing and braying. A few of the cows, though, were moving closer and paying attention to the proteus, calves keeping close to their mothers' flanks.

Even the translator program's pseudo-AI couldn't sort out what was going on; there were overlapping snatches of outrage and animosity. "What does a horny tree know?"..."teat-biting liar!"..."fix this up with a good knock of the head"..."driven Pokesnout out of the herd a long time ago!" The uproar kept the hummingbird vermin eaters from alighting.

"You're having fewer and fewer calves, and fewer of those live!" Paloma yelled into the pickup. "A disease that affects one of you affects all! *You're too inbred!* You blithering numbskulls, you're dying out!"

Hearing that, the bull who'd attacked the tree did so again, joined by several others. Pokesnout shifted undecidedly; trying to stop them would probably get him trounced and driven from the herd, outcast or perhaps even killed. But just then the herd's alpha-male, the top bull, trotted for the tree, lowering his head. Pokesnout held his place.

The other bulls hit the tree one after the other, from different angles. On the third hit the tree heeled over, dragging up roots clotted with red-gray soil, pulling and snapping taproots. Two more charges and it went down.

The bulls moved in among the branches. They reared and stomped and butted; limbs and branches gave way. The commo link went dead as hooves flashed.

The gawks didn't stop there; they went on bashing and trampling, peeling big areas of bark with horns and hooves, jolting the heavy trunk around like a piece of athletic equipment. Floyt watched sadly, even though all data from his proteus had been transferred to Alacrity's. The cheap Earthservice proteus had been with him since his misadventures first started. Paloma chafed his hand between hers sympathetically. "You'll have a new one, I promise, Hobie."

Floyt's hand felt like it had a corona around it. He'd been aware of her day and night, her lissome stealth in the woods and her soft breathing as she lay wrapped in her stained evening shawl, asleep under mounded leaves. He'd watched Alacrity and Paloma circle one another, seen the standoff tested and reaffirmed a half-dozen times; he conceived hopes of his own every day and each night, only to quash them in the name of friendship, of teamwork, coexistence, and other things that he tried not to question too closely.

The top bull wasn't joining in the tree-stomp. His head was high in the air, the three great nostrils flared, sniffing in the humans' direction. He started moving, a creature five times the size of a Cape buffalo, stronger and meaner in proportion.

"Uh-oh," murmured Paloma.

"Don't anybody move," Alacrity whispered. "But if he starts coming this way, run for the rocks. And don't stop, *no matter what*!"

The alpha-male moved almost daintily, picking up one or two feet at a time, poising, sniffing. The humans hesitated, hoping he wouldn't get wind of them; their tree was far downslope, almost out on the flatland, and a gawk at full speed could cover ground at an appalling rate, making escape a long-odds bet.

As they wavered, the top bull was prancing closer. Paloma had her mouth open to say something just as the big male began gathering himself by centimeters, like a cat getting ready to pounce, for a charge.

All at once Pokesnout was cantering in the humans' direction. Instead of lowering his head for a butting duel, though, he was belching and braying to the gathered cows and their calves. He was too far off for the proteus to give a translation, but the females milled uncertainly and the other males stirred around, undecided.

Always watchful for a challenge, the top bull turned, forgetting the human scent. Pokesnout continued his foghorn tirade, galloping in a wide detour around the alpha-male as, one by one, the cows set off in a wide circuit to follow.

The top bull, legs spread wide, watched, angry but bewildered. Pokesnout skirted him, slowing to a brisk trot, cutting a course straight for the tree where the humans crouched, wavering.

"He's bringing them down on us! But no, that can't be," Floyt contradicted himself.

"Not with the females and calves following him," Paloma said. "I wonder how he got them to come along."

"If we don't talk these hefties into helping us we're probably dead anyhow," Alacrity said. "What the hell; not much chance we'd make the rocks. Let's see what happens." He kept his spear across his lap.

The alpha-male and other bulls began following after Pokesnout, the cows, and calves, gathering speed as herd instincts warned them the herd's future was going into possible danger.

Pokesnout led the females and young right up to the tree where three apprehensive humans sat clutching the bole and fingering the bark nervously. Pokesnout spared them only a brief look with huge, liquid eyes green as wheyberries and a hawking sneeze of acknowledgment. Then he got the cows and calves bunched around the tree. Nonbreeding males and females were watching from nearby.

Alacrity and Paloma had their proteus' pickups at max by the time the bulls arrived and the argument began. The bulls were pawing and butting for a crack at the tree, but the females wouldn't get out of the way and the calves followed their mothers automatically. The bulls would shove one interloping cow away—neither savagely nor gently; herd instincts kept them from harming females and young—only to have another take her place and the displaced one circle around to rejoin the jostling.

Floyt, Paloma, and Alacrity watched open-mouthed, pulses racing, as the horns dipped and tossed, and hooves dug. Even the relatively lesser jockeying of the females to protect the tree-perch had the tree swaying and jarring.

All the while, the proteuses were having intermittent luck translating snatches of the argument in assorted synthetic male and female voices, not bothering to interpret the calves' bawling, puling, and farting.

"Out of the way!" ... "hear what they have to say!" ... "my hoof on your horns!" ... "Stand clear!" ... right about our calves! Think how few we" ...

Then Pokesnout was yelling over all, somehow making a lot of noise even for a gawk, so that the humans, shrinking back from the din of it, almost missed the translation.

"They're in a tree; where can they go? Hear them, hear them! If they raise our tempers, we still have them. If they won't tell us what we want, we can let them feel our horns and hooves then. This agrees with the Verities!"

The bulls were uncertain as it was. Soon the herd had turned to the alpha-male, who was standing to one side, head lowered. After a while they were all quiet except for the unceasing snuffling, pawing, and lowing.

Alacrity spoke carefully. He was no expert in nonhuman psychology, but it didn't take a headboarded synergenius to figure out that the key to the problem lay with herd behavior. It would either motivate the gawklegs to help Floyt, Paloma, and himself or drive them to bash the tree down and play hopscotch on them.

"The reason the herd is dying isn't your fault!" he yelled by means of the proteus. "It's not the fault of the cows and not the fault of the bulls!"

There was more agitation in the milling and trumpeting when the gawklegs heard that, although they went on listening. *I wonder who's been blaming what on whom?* Floyt thought.

"The reason's something you can't see," Alacrity pushed on. "As invisible as—as the wind, or your herd instincts."

The top bull's head came up. "Do you talk about the All?" He sounded ominous. "Are you saying the All is punishing we who are part of it?"

Oh, my aching ass! They've got a religion! "No, no!" Alacrity yelled to cut in over the babbling, holding his proteus far from him as its directional sound projector turned his words into gawkleg sounds at highest volume. That was barely high enough.

"Not the All. The words in my language for what you've lost are 'gene diversity.' You have to—to renew your blood with another herd!"

That was good for a small hurricane of sound, like a thousand alligators in a sing-out against a million bullfrogs. Pokesnout somehow managed to trumpet over it, "But what are we to do? We have to save the herd! How can we save the herd?"

The feisty runt-male was looking better and better to Floyt, who was once again overcoming his Earth-bred aversions. In moments the doubts and hesitations had all vanished into an all-embracing concern for the survival of the group, a gawkleg instinct that took priority over almost all others.

"The herd!"... "How shall we save"... "The herd!"

"I'm telling you," Alacrity hollered. "You've got to mingle your bloodlines with another herd! We can guide you to them. We'll go with you."

"The Verities forbid the Long Trek!" "They also forbid letting the herd die out!" "The humans' death-from-above will kill the herd more quickly than the dwindling of our calves!" "Sky-fire is only a chance, but I have dropped three stillborn. I say we go!"

"But Pokesnout said—" some female's voice came, and another cut in. "That nub-horned calf! A bad one, from bad stock, him and his Shadow Verities! We should have driven him out long ago!"

A strange thing happened as the debate-cum-jostling match went on. The herd jockeyed its way back to more open ground by habit and instinct, the humans ignored for the time being, until the proteuses couldn't pick up the exchanges anymore. Some arguments were punctuated with a butting of heads, nip, or kick, but the disputes didn't unravel into the riot the humans expected to see. The gawklegs honked, switched their tails, droned and jounced one another as Invictus sank toward the horizon.

The onlookers gradually realized that Pokesnout was studying them from below. "Go back to your bedding place," he said when Paloma pointed her proteus his way. "There won't be any decision tonight, perhaps not tomorrow."

"What are the Shadow Verities?" she asked.

"There are the Verities," he replied, "straight and simple and uncomplicated, the way we like things. But there is also a special body of lore for things and times the Verities don't cover. They are grim and complicated, and they upset many herdmembers, so the knowledge is passed down in confidence, as my mother passed it to me. It contradicts many of the Verities. This knowledge is the Shadow Verities."

"We need to ask you more questions," Floyt said.

"And I would like to hear more from you," Pokesnout answered. "But I must join in chewing over this great decision, or it will surely go against you. And I must prepare." He swung around and trotted off.

Alacrity was already shinnying down the fractal tree. Now he stopped partway and, clinging with one hand and his climbing spikes, held out his proteus to ask "'Prepare?'"

"Heads decide things in the herd," Pokesnout threw back over his shoulder. "Sometimes with thought. More often with horns." He continued on for the restive herd and wouldn't look back when Alacrity called out after him.

"Heretic," Floyt said affectionately.

"Alacrity, what've you done to your hands?"

"Nothing, Ho," Alacrity assured him, joining Floyt and Paloma on the flat rock from which they'd been watching the herd-milling through most of the day. "Squeezing up a little wheyberry juice. I'm betting we can ferment it."

"Well, we could've used your umbrella," Paloma said snappishly. "It's hot out here."

"Sorry; it's back up there." He gestured vaguely toward the lair. "Still no decision from the Steering Committee, huh?"

"No, but we think something's happening," Paloma said, pointing to the herd with her chin. "They've been breaking off into two groups, coming together and breaking off again, for hours now."

"Somebody's about to call the question," Floyt predicted.

"Let's just hope Pokesnout's not in the middle of it," Alacrity said. "One of those big bulls could do him in with two hooves in a trench."

There were very strict rules for gawk ritual combat, most of which would work to the disadvantage of diminutive Pokesnout.

Down on the valley floor, one group, by far the more numerous, was made up of the cows and calves and the majority of the nonbreeding males and females. The other was mostly the alpha-male, his lieutenants—or betas—and the rest of the bulls.

As the trio watched, Pokesnout, standing between the two factions, belly-*oink*ed and thrummed infrasonics at the holdouts, the dominant males. One of the betas took an uncertain few steps to join the bigger group. The top bull whirled and bellowed at him, rocking his huge horned head in warning. The would-be defector got back in place.

The alpha-male, a bull named Treeneck, whirled in a space no longer than his massive body and went thundering at Pokesnout.

"Oh, damn, I *knew* this was coming!" Paloma raged. *Watch your tail, Poke!*"

Pokesnout couldn't hear the translated warning, but didn't need it. As the little male threw himself at the alpha, Alacrity wondered how much a night and a day of jostling and wrangling had weakened the contenders, and who had the edge. Treeneck was traveling like a gravrail freighter, but Pokesnout somehow managed to duck under his charge and hit his shoulder.

"That's not in the rules," Floyt yelped. "He's *cheating!*"

It was more than a mere transgression of form; the herd would react as one against an individual who violated its Verities, especially Verities pertaining to something as central as ritual combat. As far as Floyt understood, Pokesnout was making himself outcast, even if Treeneck didn't kill him. For now, though, the herd simply watched the fight. And, against all Verities, Pokesnout started to win. The humans almost fell off the boulder, rooting for him.

Pokesnout broke the rules over and over, snaking under the top bull's head, avoiding impact where he should've met it straight on, and hitting his opponent blindside when the other wasn't in position to defend.

Treeneck tried to spin and take Pokesnout from the side, but the little gawk was fast, eluding the strike and smashing into the alpha-male's chin in one quick butt that struck Alacrity as *practiced*. And Pokesnout had said he was going off to prepare.

How long's he been preparing? Alacrity asked himself.

Pokesnout nipped the side of the top bull's face, drawing dark, purple-red blood, then sprang away, coming around end for end on the fly as his enemy lurched at him. Pokesnout kicked with his hind legs, connecting with the alpha's jaw.

The hind legset hooves crashed into the top bull's chin and his forelegs gave out. He dropped to his front knees, dazed. Noting Pokesnout's blasphemy, the herd made a hostile, concerted noise; the beta-males pawed and trumpeted furiously, indicating that they might intervene.

Alacrity slipped back off the rock; Floyt and Paloma, screaming and cheering for Pokesnout, were too preoccupied to notice.

Pokesnout rushed his foe just as Treeneck was beginning to rise, butting the bull's neck and the back of his head as hard as he could while the dominant male was still struggling.

The fight was taking place very near to where the castaways were watching. Alacrity made his way out toward the battle, hoping he could get away with simply yelling a warning to Pokesnout against sneak attack if one shaped up; the betas were looking ornery. But Alacrity had a cold-stomach feeling that a diversion would be called for. He thought of tons of horn, muscle, and antisocial behavior charging at him and sweated, clutching his brolly the harder.

I can't let Pokesnout lose. I've got a White Ship to win!

One of the more assertive beta bulls had broken from the group and was trotting closer to the fight, not wanting to warn his victim with a ground-shaking charge just yet. Alacrity shouted and shouted to Pokesnout, but the undersize challenger was busy finishing off Treeneck with unauthorized butts and kicks; there was no hope of getting his attention.

Alacrity crouched lower in the vermilion lichen-grass, hoping the beta's gawkish singlemindedness would work to his advantage. The ambusher came cantering in Alacrity's direction; Alacrity scurried into a better position, keeping well down. He made a frantic calculation between speed and surprise and gathered himself, moving into the beta's path, praying the thing wouldn't start going any faster.

And when the beta was almost on him, Alacrity sprang at it, thrusting his brolly up out of the grass into its face, opening the umbrella with a sudden *pop*.

The gawkleg got a brief glimpse at the brolly and nearly piled up on top of himself in a chop-hoof, hysterical attempt to reverse field, kicking up grass and soil. He came to a sliding stop partway on his rump, chin almost in Alacrity's lap, thrashing for a frantic retreat.

Alacrity partway closed the brolly and popped it again as the beta, his sneak attack forgotten, galloped off the way he'd come. The conventions of herd behavior gave every indication of having gone into the converter, and Floyt wondered if it wasn't due in part to Pokesnout's Shadow Verities as well as the situation and doctrinal conflicts. Alacrity's strategem had given Pokesnout's supporters a chance to position themselves to stop any more intervention by the dominant bulls. Some very rough jostling was going on, vicious ram-jousts really, Pokesnout's adherents barely holding their own against the betas. Alacrity heard yells behind him and turned to see Paloma and Floyt racing downslope at him, pellmell, astounded that he hadn't been trampled into pasture carpeting.

Alacrity looked to where the dominance fight still raged. Pokesnout was using his iconoclastic style still; he had Treeneck reeling.

Cheating sometimes pays, Alacrity decided. As he watched, Pokesnout charged, reversed field just short of the alpha's lower horns, and kicked him in the head again with hind hooves, side on. Alacrity suspected that the runt male could've shattered the alpha's jaw and muzzle but chose not to; certainly, accuracy didn't strike Alacrity as one of Pokesnout's problems.

Treeneck's knees wobbled and he keeled over in a cloud of dust shaken loose from the long lichen-grass. "It looks like we're going to town!" Alacrity grinned, as Floyt and Paloma Sudan bore down on him with every sort of imprecation and accusation, too short of breath to do it right.

"Moron! You almost—"

"Of all the dipshit stunts! What were you—"

Alacrity held up a hand stained wheyberry green for silence, then casually opened his brolly for them. He'd decorated it in a passable imitation of a scare-flare's wattle in warning display. The color was a pretty good match; not surprising since the predators often hid among the vines. It stood out dramatically against the vermilion lichen-grass.

The other two stared at it in mute shock, still panting. "What if...it didn't work?" Paloma huffed out at last. "What if...that big bull didn't fall for it, or couldn't stop? You'd be dead, and you're even more worthless to me and Hobie dead than you are alive!"

"I'm too busy to die," Alacrity told Paloma. "At least for the immediate future. Long enough to reach Spica, at a minimum." He raised his shoulders and dropped them carelessly, smiling his most maddening smile, closing the brolly slowly because the berry stain was drying and starting to flake away; nothing stuck to the shiny metallic fabric of the Viceroy Imperial for long.

Pokesnout, satisfied he was the victor, sniffed at his fallen opponent, threw his head back, then bugle-grunted to the herd. The gawks looked confused and immobilized now that their Verities were all in disarray. Paloma swung her proteus's pickup, aligning it on the runt, nonbreeding male victor.

"The Verities won't keep the herd alive," Pokesnout was saying. "The Shadow Verities might. This is not an unclear decision."

"I'd say they're buying it," Paloma said in a hushed

voice. "Or else they would have hopped him flat by now."

"And, after all, he does have the monopoly on Shadow Verities," Floyt reminded her.

"Well, anyway; there's too much to do for me to die," Alacrity said cheerily. "It's fate and that's all there is to it." He started off to talk to Pokesnout.

Floyt and Paloma Sudan looked at one another. "Tempting to prove him wrong, isn't it?" she snarled, whacking her wooden spear against her palm.

"Constantly," Floyt said, flat-toned.

CHAPTER 12

AT THE RISK OF SOUNDING FOOLISH

"LISTEN, FITZHUGH, I'LL ONLY TELL YOU THIS ONE more time: it's not worth the effort," Paloma said yet again. "The exertion of building deadfall traps will use up more calories than we'll get out of them. The bigger life forms are especially wary."

"Not if we build barriers along the game runways, twiff brain! We could nail one of those leaf-eaters that looks like a boilerplate badger, or even catch ourselves a scare-flare. Unless you're becoming fond of larvae pudding."

Paloma Sudan made an exasperated noise. "We're eating well enough. But I thought your first order of business was making every possible preparation for the Long Trek?"

"It is, it is," he grumbled. "But I *am* getting a little sick of roots, grub stew, roasted nuts, and the occasional side order of ringwing or snakefish!" He rubbed his shrunken middle, which, given his height, nearly touched his backbone. Paloma didn't look much better. All three humans had lost weight and acquired real and dangerous medical problems out beyond civilization in the Lebensraum wilds.

"Well, graylock, if you're not happy with what we're getting from the hanging snares and figure-fours, you're free to dig yourself a pitfall big enough to catch a gawk

for all I care. Only don't whine to me when the Long
Trek's postponed!"

"Lay off, lay off," he chanted. "So now you know
how to win any argument. I surrender. But where's
Pokesnout? I thought he was gonna be here with the rest
of his advance party."

The first major obstacle to the Long Trek was a narrow stretch of high desert that lay a day's gawk-march
along their route. The Verities and the Shadow Verities
referred to something there that translated as "scuttle-
death." Alacrity had convinced all parties that a recon-
naissance was in order, and Pokesnout was doing his
best to bring one together.

To his credit and the credit of the gawklegs' intelligence, the little nonbreeding male was maintaining his
leadership—more by his special knowledge of Verities
and Shadow Verities and innovative thinking than by his
combat victory. At another time he'd have been killed or
made outcast at the very least for it. But in time of
danger to the herd, necessity took priority over custom.

"Hobie went to find him," Paloma said. "It's surprising how your sidekick's warmed up to the gawks; it takes
him a while to get around that Earth upbringing, doesn't
it?"

"Yup. He didn't exactly hit if off with me at first either, but—" He reached out and took her hand in his.
She didn't fight it. "I have this winning personality..."

For a second he thought she was finally going to let
him kiss her, but then she drew back, turning her head
aside, dropping her eyes. Alacrity threw down her hand
in mock disgust.

"Hey, Hot 'n Cold! Lemme know when you make up
your mind!"

Paloma laughed and struck another of her model
poses. Even in the wilds she could be a beguiling, high-
style performer. Her hair was drawn back into a tight,
high horsetail, gathered with a clip from her pouch, and

she smelled great again, now that the humans could use
the river to bathe under gawk protection.

"All this attention is very flattering, Amber Eyes, but
why do I wonder about your sincerity?" She dropped the
act a little. "If you want try again once we're out of this
jam, we'll see. But not here; I just refuse to feel...
convenient. Maybe you'll look at things a little differently when we're free to go our separate ways, hmm?
And I'll see the back of you?"

Alacrity thought about what the future held for him,
thought especially that somewhere there was Heart,
whom he loved so much that there was very little room
for any other woman, really. But of desire there was
plenty, at least in Heart's absence.

So he counterattacked. "What about you? If you don't
want me at all, just say so and we won't ever talk about
it again, you have my word."

She gave him a long look. "For now I think I'll file
that one under 'creative evasions.'"

He thought she was opening the way for him to press
her about it, but the chance slipped by as Pokesnout
trumpeted and they saw him trotting their way. On the
gawk's back, struggling to keep his seat, rode Floyt.
Vermin eaters circled, *birr*ing angrily at his invasion of
their domain.

"Well, here's me with my mouth open!" Alacrity
cried, jumping to his feet.

Paloma let him give her a hand up. "It looks like he's
pretty adaptable," she said, meaning Floyt.

"Comes from a big gene pool, I guess."

They gave Floyt a little cheer as Pokesnout drew to a
halt. "See me after the Long Trek if you want to go into
show business," Paloma added.

Floyt bowed, speaking into Pokesnout's ear via Paloma's proteus, which he wore on his left wrist. The runt
male clumsily bent his front legs, nearly unseating Floyt,
but eventually achieving a dismount position. Floyt

swung down with exaggerated care, his fatigue jacket pockets bulging with some cargo.

"I'm gratified that you enjoyed the act," he said. "Pokesnout caught on to horsey-ride right away." He reached into his pocket carefully. "He also helped me get these." Floyt drew out an egg nearly the size of an ostrich's, with a shell like green delft.

"Scare-flare," he explained. "The gawks know how to find them; they just don't care, because they don't eat them and scare-flares don't bother them much."

He pulled out his survival gadget and, holding the narrow end of the egg uppermost, hacked it open. It took some doing. Floyt had a cautious sip, then passed it to Paloma. "The first cache I found was pretty far gone toward hatching," he explained while she sampled it, "so I recovered it and went on to the next."

He angled a thumb at Pokesnout's big hooves. "It helps to have an excavating team with you. They're as good at kick-digging egg caches as they are at roots and tubers." He pulled another egg from a bellows pocket.

Paloma had taken a good swig at the scare-flare egg. "Maybe it's just hunger talking, but this doesn't taste bad!" She passed it along to Alacrity, wiping her lips on the back of her hand. "Are there many more?"

Floyt had an egg in each hand and another weighting a breast pocket. "All we can eat. Evidently the flares have a year-round laying season. Rock-eels and so forth get most of the hatchlings, so the females deposit a lot of eggs."

Alacrity got the green yolk, high-concentration protein, along with the ochre "white." It was faintly chalky, but still wonderful and rich.

Paloma took two more eggs from Floyt. "I'm going to boil these," she decided. She and Alacrity had already improvised a cooking vessel from a large joint of plia-bamboo. "It'll probably take forever, but then we can throw on some of this and that for seasoning."

"Here, try this." Floyt held out a large-denomination

Lebensraum Company scrip that he'd twisted to form a crude pouch. Inside was a palmful of coarse, dirty, large-grain salt. "Pokesnout showed me a big lick by a hot spring."

Paloma kissed Floyt's cheek soundly. "Hobie, you're such a treasure!"

"Oh, well," he said, face rosy. "There really wasn't much I could contribute while you two were debating Apache foot-snares and twitch-up traps and poisoning fish and all."

"So you went and got the straight goods from Pokesnout, which is what we should've been doing from the start!" Paloma bussed him again while Alacrity did his best to mask the sound of grating teeth.

Then Paloma accepted her proteus back and set off, the eggs clutched to her chest, her spear held ready. Pokesnout said something; by now it was second nature for Alacrity to hold up his proteus and listen for the translation.

"So you Other Male and Female like the eggs as much as Digger?"

"Digger, Ho?" Alacrity puzzled.

"Well, 'Hobart' didn't translate, and 'Digger' is close enough to 'Delver.'" That was Delver as in Delver Root-nose, Floyt's alias among the Foragers of Luna.

"So I'm just 'Other Male'?" Alacrity asked Floyt.

"'Alacrity' doesn't translate so well either. I would suggest 'Speed.'"

"Mmm. All right."

Pokesnout had been absorbing the running transla-tion, looking from one to the other, his semiprehensile upper lip curling, flapping, and everting. "Speed, eh? A good name. I will tell everyone, and that will be your name for always. Does Female have a name, too?"

Alacrity gazed after Paloma. She was moving lithely up the hill, very much aware of her svelte, glamorous appeal, secure in it and proud of it.

"Her name's 'Babyfat,'" Alacrity said spitefully.

"Make sure everybody knows. That will be her name for always."

"So, Digger, that is why Babyfat was trying to hit Speed in the head with her wooden branch and kill him? Because of her name?" Pokesnout snorted a vast breath and rolled around in the mud some more. He was a lot more confident and relaxed now that he was a breeding male.

Floyt lay stretched out on his back on the warm boulder, head pillowed on his arms, basking in the sunlight after a chilly bath in the river, gazing up at the peaceful Lebensraum sky. All around him, his rock-pounded clothing was drying. Alacrity's proteus was loose around his lower forearm.

"I don't think she was *really* going to kill him, Pokesnout. But yes, she was quite angry about the name he gave her."

Pokesnout tossed his tail, flinging mud droplets into the air. "That is what I thought, although it is very hard for us to understand. I could try to get the herd to call her something else, but 'Babyfat' is woven into the New Verities now, and it would probably only confuse things; it would muddle everyone's mnemonics terribly and disorder their thinking and, in the end, not work."

Actually, Floyt didn't much care to think about troublesome sociodynamics just at the moment. With gawklegs having accepted them and begun helping them, the humans had a much easier life, and he felt like enjoying it. Using the swift-moving part of the river to bathe, for example, where there was no danger from sliverworms, bloodflukes, and similar perils, and not having to worry about manglejaws because he had a gawk for a bathing companion, was a luxury to be savored singlemindedly.

Preparations for a recon were going well. The Verities weren't much use in guessing what the scuttle-death was, and both Pokesnout and the humans wanted to know before the main herd moved up into the high desert. Floyt had worked hard helping gather food and fash-

ion equipment, and intended to enjoy his restful interlude.

Except that the problem of the Lake Fret, the last
major barrier along their way, still bothered him. Neither
Alacrity nor Paloma had come up with a workable way
to negotiate it. Floyt had been accessing the subject, a
large body of water in the middle of a region of Karst
topography—limestonelike substrata. There was a tiny
drone substation racking-and-launching point not too far
from their route of march, stocked with seismic charge
robos, but it was of no use to the strandees; shaped ex-
plosive charges weren't much good as weapons, and the
drones were much too small to use as transportation.

But he didn't want to think about that anymore either.
He answered Pokesnout lazily, "Oh, I'm sure she'd be
grateful if you'd see what you can do about it, but not if
it's going to make communications all mixed up."

"Hobie, you wouldn't be so casual if *you* were the one
being slandered!"

Floyt rolled over onto one elbow and Pokesnout shot
to his feet in the mud. Seeing it was only Paloma, the
gawk sank back down, grunting and sending out waves.
"Greetings, Babyfat!"

"Hi, Poke," she said dispiritedly, her proteus putting
it into gawk for her. "And relax, Hobie; don't throw a
vertebrae being body-shy on *my* account. I grew up on a
ranch."

Floyt realized he looked silly trying to cover himself
with contortions and damp clothes. He stopped, and settled for rolling onto his stomach on his boulder, a few
meters out in the river. Paloma seated herself under a
cirrous tree on the bank. Her hair was combed out and
she looked more bewitching than ever.

"Anyway, thanks for trying to straighten things out,"
she said, digging her heel at the turf. "But this Babyfat
business has a life of its own." She smiled cheerlessly.
"That vindictive *filho-puta!* It's just like Alacrity to be at
his most inventive at a thing like this!"

"Actually, that's true. Um, I was right, wasn't I? You didn't kill him, did you?"

"I might have, except those damn climbing spikes gave him an edge. It'll serve him right if he sits up in that tree until the drillbugs drain him dry. Damn him and his White Ship and his damn Precursors!"

Floyt was toying with an Inheritor's belt warmed by the rays of Invictus, studying the strange symbols that had saved his life from Hecate. "I never asked you this, Paloma, but what do you think the Precursors were? Or who?"

She'd been frowning at the water; even that expression looked tantalizing on her. But she brightened, looking back to Floyt.

"Us."

"I beg your pardon?"

"The Precursors. They're us, Hobie. And sweet old Poke there, and the grass and trees. And even that treacherous *cazzo* sitting back up there in his tree. See what I'm getting at?"

"I suppose." Neither of them paid any attention to Pokesnout, who lay there in the mud waggling his ears and listening to the running translations the humans had come to ignore as background noise.

"Now I get to ask you one, Hobie. What's Heart like? The Nonpareil? In the news she always looks friggin' killer-gorgeous."

"She's—sometimes I find myself looking at her and I think, 'I'll memorize her, so that I won't stare so much.' And then I look away, but when I look back, I find that the memory's pale by comparison, and she bowls me over again. I end up staring—"

"I'm sorry I asked."

"No, no; I was going to say—it's the same with you." His face reddening, he averted his eyes. "And she's bright and courageous and compassionate like you, too."

Paloma was silent for a long time, staring at him. Then she said, "Well, who does *Heart* think the Precursors were?"

"I never asked her, Paloma. Is it too trite a question?"

She considered that. "Not from an Earther. From you, it comes honestly, not labored. You make me rethink the answer. You're from somewhere beyond the cliches and commonplaces. Or maybe it's got nothing to do with Earth. Maybe it's just you, Hobie."

Her dark eyes made a lasting contact that had him fibrillating. "It's Alacrity I'm drawn to but—you, I like better."

She got up suddenly, dusting herself off. "Drillbug time's coming up. Don't stay here too long."

"I won't, Paloma."

"How soon will we be in danger of being attacked?" Alacrity asked, leaning toward Pokesnout, holding his proteus out for translation. Alacrity was seated high on the withers of Treeneck, erstwhile alpha-male of the herd.

"Oh, back where we came up onto the high desert, the Verities say," Pokesnout answered without breaking stride. He was moving at a slow lumber, the gawkleg version of a wolf-trot, across the easy-roll planetscape of hard-packed pink sand glittery with infinitesimal specks of mica, marked by jutting prows of mauve basaltic rock. There were infrequent clumps of red or red-brown plant life—fiendishly spiny, spikey stuff more daunting than anything Floyt had yet seen in his travels.

Pokesnout led the recon party, with Floyt astride him and clinging to a rough surcingle improvised from tight-rolled netvine. Floyt's hands were raw from gripping the surcingle, and he'd taken to wrapping a cloth around whichever hand was doing the holding. The cloth had become available because Floyt found that his stylish but tight underdrawers tended to chafe in the rigorous outdoor life he was leading, and a crotch rash was something devoutly to be avoided.

At least the gawks' withers were comfortable for riding, almost made for it. All three humans had taken to their new mounts, and carried long, sharpened saplings as lances.

. Treeneck was slightly behind Pokesnout and to his right. Alacrity was surprised at first how quickly and without qualm the herd accepted the little maverick as leader. Apparently something in the droning Verities covered the situation—or, at least, Pokesnout's clever arguments convinced the herd it did—and the gawks' reaction became just about a reflex: crisis made them close ranks behind their leader literally and figuratively. Treeneck became a loyal lieutenant, if a bit slow on the uptake.

Strung out behind them were three more gawk bulls, one carrying Paloma, who had devised the surcingles. Jets of air from the gawks' nostrils and mouths steamed in the cold air, as did the humans' breath. The gawks had become saddle animals without much problem; chief virtues of having a sophant for a mount were companionship and matchless cooperation.

An expedition like the recon, away from the herd, went against instinct, but Pokesnout and his Shadow Verities and New Verities had overruled that. Alacrity had begun wondering if the new herd leader was a mutant, some sudden jump in evolution. Certainly, aside from him, there was a striking uniformity to the herd. It was Pokesnout who'd given an explanation for something that bothered Alacrity.

As Alacrity put it, "Why, of all the wide-open spaces on this planet, should one of the last remaining gawk herds be here, now? I mean, it's a lifesaver for us, but it's too big to be called a coincidence."

"We like the Tingling Mountain," Pokesnout told him. "The one you three came out of. It was a special place for the herd and gave us good feelings, until it got smaller."

So the Precursor site coopted by Hecate somehow attracted them until it rabbit-holed. That set Alacrity wondering about Precursor influence on the gawks. It wasn't unknown for herbivores to develop intelligence, but it was unusual enough to insure that the creatures would be studied carefully if and when the truth and the Lebensraum Company's misdeeds came to light.

Paloma's mount and the two riderless bachelor males were gawks who'd become disciples to Pokesnout, enthralled by his Shadow Verities and odd ways of seeing and doing things. The two riderless ones carried net-vine paniers of leaf-wrapped food and water gourds. The gawks were well adapted for going without food and water for long periods and for scrounging even in a Lebensraum desert.

"Whoa. If we're in a danger zone, let's call a halt and look the place over," Alacrity said.

Pokesnout slowed up. Treeneck veered off to come up even with him. Rockhorn, Paloma's mount, almost rear-ended Pokesnout until he realized the group was stopping. A snort from Treeneck had Rockhorn and the two behind him hurrying to sort themselves out. Things got straightened away in another couple of seconds, with Paloma drawing up next to Floyt on the other side and the two riderless gawks looking around grazing fashion, finding nothing to eat nearby except pink sand.

"What's our next move?" Floyt asked. He was feeling better than he had on the morning's long final ascent through chilly shadow to the high desert. Alacrity had the thermal insert in his shipsuit against the cold, and the hood unrolled from its compartment in his collar. Paloma's sheer bodysuit insert, its décolletage flap closed, appeared to be keeping her comfortable, besides which she had the shawl. But Floyt's outfit just wasn't as heavy as it should have been for the weather, and the cold was giving him problems though he didn't mention it. Invictus had started warming him, though, and Pokesnout's body heat helped.

"Whatever this scuttle-death is, it killed a lot of the gawks when they fled here," Alacrity said. "Let's not get too far away from safe ground until we know what we're dealing with."

"I agree," Paloma said. "Anything that can give gawks a hard time is something to be wary of."

They peered into the distance. The high desert crossing wasn't too wide, twenty kilometers or so according to the maps, but it loomed in the Verities as a killing ground.

Treeneck exhaled like a storm. "I'm not afraid." His horns churned the air.

"Why didn't scuttle-death follow the herd down to its new home range?" Paloma asked.

"It couldn't. That is all that we know," Pokesnout said.

"But it's up here blocking the way back," Alacrity mused. *Maybe what we've got here is a bogeyman? Invented to keep the gawks from going back to be slaughtered by the company?*

"I like this place," Pokesnout proclaimed, looking around and sniffing. "And yet I do not trust it. Shall we go a little farther? The edge of the desert isn't far behind, and you know how fast we can move."

"Yeah; like a flea on a hot griddle." Alacrity swept the place with his eyes, shifting uneasily. The high desert looked unthreatening, but then again he didn't know what he was trying to spot. *Maybe it's some kind of seasonal critter that's not around right now. We could bring the whole herd over the high desert in one day, if we moved hard—*

"*Yiii!*" the proteus translated as Pokesnout bucked straight-kneed into the air with a bawl to split the sky, one great hoof cocked up close to his barrel belly. Several little things were clinging to the gawk's hock, Alacrity saw in the moment before it slammed down again with a jolt that almost knocked Floyt from its back, even though the Terran's knees were under the surcingle. The gawk's frantic low-frequency signals pounded.

Suddenly Treeneck reared and caracoled, a couple of the things hanging from his hock, too. Paloma was shouting advice or orders, fighting to stay mounted on

Rockhorn, as the glittering pink sand seemed to come to life.

Alacrity, lurching against his surcingle-hold, abrading his hand, didn't see how so many of the things could live so close together in the lean environment of the high desert, didn't see how it could support them. Gawks were rearing and bucking, amazingly limber and deft. The midair maneuvers weren't planned as a way to unseat riders, but felt like a good bet to do it. Hordes of the little things closed in, the color of the sand, and the air was filled with a sharp, corrosive, mephitic smell.

The scuttle-death, insofar as Floyt could make out, were rabid little sand dwellers about mouse-size and build, with some tarantula influence. But the front third of their bodylength was fishhook teeth in snapping jaws.

And they weren't made for climbing; that much was plain because the ones on Pokesnout's leg couldn't improve their purchase at all or do much of anything else except hold on. The things' attack concentrated on the lowermost parts of the gawks' legs; the teeth were penetrating, though Alacrity wouldn't have believed gawk leg-hide would be vulnerable to a sheetmetal screw.

Still, the scuttle-death fangs did it somehow. Gawk efforts to stomp the little terrors into the sand did no good; the scuttles' carapaces protected them. They were sand hunters, after all.

"Back to the rocks!" Paloma shouted over and over into her proteus, pointing it at Rockhorn's ear and Pokesnout's and the others'. Alacrity, hauling at Treeneck's mane, did the same.

Somehow, in the throes of excruciating pain, Pokesnout ignored his own suffering and acted as leader.

He turned and got the other gawks moving with butts of his head and vicious nipping and kicking. Treeneck somehow reasserted himself enough to help. The party curvetted and bucked into retreat, the few scuttle-death that were on the scene trying for a grip but failing, the legions of reinforcements not close enough yet. The riders barely kept their seats; if Floyt and Alacrity hadn't had instruction from Paloma and practice under her coaching, they'd both have died. The gawks ran, the two riderless males picking up more of the tiny furies. Then, somehow, the whole group was back on the stone trail that led to the gawks' grazing lands.

On the trail, things were different. Some of the scuttle-death had dropped off along the way; those that were left clung savagely but were eventually wrenched off or batted loose by the humans, or simply jarred loose by the gawks then dashed and mashed. No attackers were clinging above the hock level; the scuttle-death were diggers, not good at jumping and lacking any effective means to advance their grip. They were also very poor at making their way over rock.

"Rocks aren't their place. We're all right," Floyt said, crushing a last squirming scutter under his heel and then bending to examine Pokesnout's wounds. The frightened gawks were starting to settle down. "But if they caught a gawk out there on that desert, they'd bring it down in time, and strip it at their leisure."

Alacrity's proteus picked up the words and translated them; the behemoths trembled.

"Sand devils!" Paloma spat. "I should've thought of it!"

"You knew about those things?" Alacrity snapped at her over his shoulder, trying to reassure Treeneck and the others.

As she gave him a hand she explained. "They're not supposed to be cold-climate animals. And you hardly ever heard about them; people wiped out most of them over the years—blew up every hive they saw. Besides, who'd have thought a sand devil could bother something the size of a gawk?"

"Well, they can," Floyt said grimly. "Look at the blood on Poke's legs. And that's just from a minute of it. He's been tapped like a rubber tree."

Alacrity heard the emotion in his friend's voice and realized just how fond Floyt had become of the runt bull.

"Something is not right," Pokesnout informed them,

through the translators. He was beginning to shake and shiver. "I feel unwell." A quick look around showed the other males were ill, too, even the doughty Treeneck.

"Toxin!" Alacrity hissed. "Quick, get over there in the rocks! Prop yourselves up!" Gawklegs never lay down for long, naturally. Even in Lebensraum's lesser gravity the pressure of their own bodies on their lungs could suffocate them.

The big creatures lumbered unsteadily over among the rocks of the washes feeding into the trail, with the humans chivying and encouraging and picking spots, directing and even shouldering them along. The gawklegs tried to rest their weight in notches that would help keep them upright. The three younger males were successful, but Treeneck couldn't find a small enough place. Pokesnout managed to worm in next to him and braced himself, the two keeping one another upright. They throbbed and lowed mournfully to each other.

"This won't do for long," Paloma said worriedly, glancing back at the desert. "And what if those little horrors come after us to eat á la hoof?"

"They don't appear to be doing so," Floyt observed, pulling his lower lip between thumb and forefinger, "and they looked rather specialized to me. That notwithstanding, you're quite right: we cannot remain here. Perhaps we can get a rescue party up here from the herd, to support these ones on the trip back down?"

He used Alacrity's proteus to ask Pokesnout about it. The gawk was still grunting and blowing in pain, but when Floyt got his question across the answer was reassuring.

"No, we are feeling better—a little," Pokesnout said. "And now I know why the herd's losses were so terrible on the Long Trek and why the Verities tell us to shun this place."

"And the company just blew up the sand devils' hives? That finishes them?" Floyt asked Paloma.

"Well, you can just dust them with pesticide, and most of your problems are over," she said. "Or you can throw out poison bait so that the hive queen ends up eating some, but basically you have to wait around for the hive to die out afterward, and that can take quite a while. Yeah, beam weapons, nervefields—they're plenty of ways of getting rid of them, but none we can use."

"Is the hive close by, then?"

"Probably not. As I recall it, those little warrior-workers are hatched and move out across the desert, find a spot and burrow in, waiting. They lie dormant for years, sometimes. When they sense food they come awake, get it and bring it back to the hive. Sand devils hunt and communicate pretty much exclusively by olfaction. I don't know, Hobie; if the hive's been here all this time, that stretch of desert could be pretty much carpeted with them by now."

Floyt gnawed a thumbnail. Paloma sighed then covered her proteus with her right hand while shielding Alacrity's proteus, which Floyt held, with her left.

"We'll have to find some other route. We can't ask the gawks to march into a slaughter."

Floyt shook his head resignedly. "The maps don't look very promising, but I agree. What do you think, Alacrity?"

Floyt looked around and saw that, as he tended to do, Alacrity had gone off without saying a word. Floyt found it an irritating habit.

They glanced around and saw him strolling back down the trail toward them. He'd obviously trotted back up to the very edge of the desert for another look at the sand devils. It was obvious because several of the tiny animals still clung to his pathfinders.

Those boots are even tougher than I thought, Floyt thought. His own boots were already showing signs of advanced deterioration.

Alacrity came down the trail, stamping loose one of the sand devils, which squirmed around for a moment before flopping over the edge of the trail and disappearing. He held a pliabamboo food-storage jar, examining the marks of sand devil teeth that had failed to penetrate it.

"Okay; no problem," Alacrity said, hooking a thumb to indicate the high desert.

"What'd you do, bribe them to look the other way?" Paloma asked tartly.

Alacrity kicked another sand devil loose and crushed it to jellied shapelessness under his heel. "No, although that's not a bad idea, in a way. Anyhow, the desert's our garden path, if we're careful about it."

He grinned at them. "Technology's about to come to the gawks—from the ground up."

"Hold still," Alacrity chided Pokesnout, wrestling with the hollow segment of pliabamboo. "If this thing doesn't fit right you'll probably take a spill and it'll be all over for ya, tiny." He rapped the creature's poised, trembling leg.

"This I cannot understand," Pokesnout said. "How can I walk the Long Trek this way?"

The pliabamboo, unlike its Terran namesake, was actually more a tree than a grass. It was flexible, nearly elastic, but Alacrity was beginning to doubt that it was flexible enough.

"Not the whole Trek," Alacrity corrected, cheek contorted in concentration as he tried to shove the prototype gawk boot into place. "Just the desert crossing."

He got it lined up and rammed it partway into place. "Okay; you can put your foot down easy."

Pokesnout did, very tentatively, balancing gingerly on his other five legs. With the gradual increase in pressure, the improvised footwear seated surprisingly well. It looked like the stem-joint partition at the segment's base would hold the weight, but for how long? Alacrity was resigned that the project would be all experiment and guesswork. Pokesnout tried to walk on the booted foot but instinctively favored it.

It had taken Alacrity a full morning to select, cut, measure, and adjust the pliabamboo joint to fit Pokesnout, even with the gawk's full cooperation. *Let's see: six legs per gawk, times the number of gawks, divided by a couple of boots per day each from me and Ho and Paloma, presuming there're no complications . . .* The answer was very depressing.

Nevertheless, the boot looked like it would work. Pokesnout gained a little confidence and put his full weight on it. Paloma and Floyt were watching from the sidelines.

"What if he loses footing up there?" Floyt asked worriedly, inclining his head toward the high desert.

"Can't you guess?" Alacrity grunted, not caring that his proteus was translating to Pokesnout's attentive ears. "He'll probably die. Just like the herd will die if it doesn't cross that desert and mix with new stock."

Pokesnout was experimenting, putting more and more weight on the boot. He looked to the humans. "And we would only need to have these on us long enough to make the crossing?"

They nodded, then Floyt realized the gesture meant nothing to a gawk. "Yes," he clarified.

"This is a very difficult idea," Pokesnout declared. "It drives the thought from my head! An answer so strange and so simple."

"Welcome to the Archimedean Universe," Floyt told him.

"It may work, it must work," Paloma said, "but we've still got Lake Fret waiting for us, our worst problem."

"We'll figure something," Alacrity said. "We've got to. It's an old tradition here in the Archimedean Universe."

Floyt came walking along with Paloma; both were burdened with netvine bags of scare-flare eggs wrapped in leaves. The scattered family groups of the herd had been summoned together. Gathering food was the least of their troubles, what with gawks uncovering eggs and butting fruits and nuts down from the trees and trampling paths through thorny undergrowth to the best of the berry plants.

In a similar way, the big locals had quickly become adept at knocking over pliabamboo and snapping off individual boot segments by means of their enormous strength and weight, with a little human help. Bonewearying work by Floyt, Alacrity, and Paloma, from sunup to drillbug time, had gotten the preparations for the Long Trek more or less complete in just nine days. Scattered family groups of the herd had been summoned together; tomorrow they would begin.

Paloma and Floyt came upon Alacrity, who was sitting on a rock and working away. He'd cut and patiently woven a rough square of netvine and weftweed, and sawn forearm-length pieces of young pliabamboo. He was patiently lashing it all together in some obscure fashion.

"Camp stool," he explained.

"And don't forget the mobile robobar," Paloma scoffed.

Alacrity made a vaguely dismissive *phui*! sound and went back to what he was doing. "You're laughing now, but think about how sore your ass gets sitting on logs and rocks and whatnot *here*.

"What about out *there*?" He gestured to their route of march with his chin. "Not even a stump or a dry patch of ground, maybe. I know what it's like to squat on haunches for dinner or get my landing gear wet and cold in the mud. Laugh away; just don't ask to borrow this collector's item of modern design once we're on the road."

Floyt looked at Paloma and Paloma looked at Floyt. Without another word, they put down their burdens. Floyt went off to cut some more framing wood while Paloma bent and picked up some weftweed, studying Alacrity's technique. "You do have your strong points, *shiasse*."

He smirked at her. "It's the little things that make life worth living."

* * *

Alacrity, mounted on Treeneck, took a final glance around, ready to give the order to move. He felt a spasm of disbelief; so many times in recent days it had seemed that this moment couldn't possibly come to life.

High overhead, flocks of avian things swarmed and soared. He wished for their wings, wished the trip would be the few hours or days it would take them, and not the weeks that lay ahead for the herd.

Oh, well. The sooner we start . . .

Floyt piped up, "Do you mind, Alacrity? After all, Pokesnout here is leader."

"Huh? Why, go right ahead, citizen." Alacrity gestured for him to lead off. Floyt looked back grandly as Pokesnout took position, gazing over the shifting gawks, a number of the high backs bearing panniers of netvine. Invictus glinted up at the horizon, catching the avians, lighting them like metal mobiles. Paloma's face was solemn and haunting in the dawnglow; Alacrity's silver-in-gray hair touseled in the faint, faint breeze.

Floyt was surprised to feel his fears slip away, replaced by an abrupt, vivid connectedness to the world around him, a mystic veneration for the moment. He drew a sharp breath, for the extraordinary clarity of it.

Floyt made a long, trumpeting sound Pokesnout had taught him. The proteus translators didn't read it, but when the little alpha echoed it, Alacrity and Paloma heard, "Now let us go!"

But the herd was already in motion; they'd understood Floyt. By stops and starts, the gawklegs began their Long Trek. *My lordy! He's learning gawk!* Alacrity thought, staring at his friend.

Alacrity had feared that keeping trail discipline would be difficult, that the herd would tend to scatter and hold things up while strays and laggards were gathered in. But the gawks had evolved for this kind of migration. Luckily, the calves were old enough for the trip; they kept close to their mothers, and Pokesnout's deputies kept the herd in tight formation. Doctrine in Pokesnout's New

Verities kept the gawks from spreading out or pausing to graze. The vermin eaters had gotten bold, and now fed from the gawks even when humans were astride.

The gawks' gait ate up ground even though it was leisurely and energy saving, though a bit rough on riders. The creatures moved three hooves at a time, leaving them a tripod for stability. When moving fast, gawks abandoned the static stability of the tripod for the dynamic stability of rapid motion, and the broad hooves were a blur. Alacrity dearly hoped there wouldn't be much need for that.

He thrust anxiety aside. For the time being there was the sheer joy and relief of being underway. Around mighty, blue Spica, the White Ship awaited him.

CHAPTER 13

ENDANGERED SPECIES

"STEADY, STEADY," ALACRITY SAID. BUT THE WEIGHTY old cow was too nervous and frightened at the unfamiliar feel of the boot. Even Pokesnout's imprecations and those of the other herd leaders couldn't quiet her. She set the huge foot down then pulled it back before Alacrity could seat the pliabamboo segment properly, then brought it down again with more weight. The boot, askew, was bent and a split appeared along its side.

"God...*dammit*!" Alacrity yelled. *"Dinosaurs on stilts! Christ, I must be crazy!"*

He strained to regain his temper. He'd figured on two days for getting the herd shod there in the rocky marshaling spot a half kilometer below the high desert. But three days had passed and the gawks were getting hungry and restless.

Some of the herdmembers shod earlier, wandering around looking unsuccessfully for forage, had, despite their best efforts to be careful, split their shoes, requiring reshoeing. The supply of spare shoes was getting smaller fast. But the main problem, as with the cow, was that nervousness and clumsiness simply made things maddeningly difficult. For the humans, it had been three days of anger, fatigue, exasperation, hair-pulling frustration, and near tears.

Or maybe clumsiness isn't a fair word, Alacrity was

forced to admit; the gawks were actually pretty graceful for beings of their size. It was just that the shoes were absolutely alien to them.

"Listen," he said through his proteus, gathering the shreds of his patience. "We'll try it again, okay?" He showed the cow another joint of pliabamboo. "Please, *please* try to take it easy, all right? It won't hurt you; that's a Verity."

Miraculously, the cow complied and the boot went on. Paloma and Floyt, assisting the operation, panted weary cheers.

"That's the last, unless somebody else has split a boot," Paloma reported. "What do you think: should we get moving before one of them does?"

Floyt was watching Invictus. "We have to take the trail slowly, and the desert, too," he reminded them. "We might still be out there when it gets dark."

Alacrity gauged the light, too. "Can't be helped. If we wait another day there'll be more split shoes for sure, and we'll be yanged but good."

"But what about the drillbugs?" Floyt objected.

"There won't be any up here," Paloma put in. "Or on the other side of the mountains either."

Pokesnout had been listening silently. He turned to his herd and gave a blast of basso sound. They oriented in his direction and began to assemble for the final ascent. Alacrity wondered if it was his imagination that the runt hadn't waited for the translation.

Is he learning to understand Terranglish? What're him and Ho doing?

The going was, in Floyt's opinion, better than they had any right to expect. Gawklegs weren't mountain goats, but they were surprisingly surefooted and the trail fairly negotiable. There were only three more shoe-splits, and they were replaced with gratifying dispatch.

A visible wariness and hesitation came over the herd as it reached the pink sands, an unwillingness to set hoof out on the ominous wasteland. The herd slowed, the creatures buffeting one another. Even males assigned to help lead the way faltered and balked.

Pokesnout whistled angrily and throbbed from one side, where he was monitoring things. Several bulls at the lead began nudging a trio of calves out onto the sands, the younger gawks' feet skidding and digging in their pliabamboo sheaths as the calves resisted futilely, bawling, bewildered and frantic. Their mothers answered but couldn't get to them past the wall of bulls.

Floyt held on as Pokesnout trotted forward and butted one of the bulls, bellowing. The calves took advantage of the confusion to bolt and rejoin their dams.

When Alacrity and Paloma got there with their translators matters were already sorted out, the herd in a semblance of order again, Pokesnout having faced down several large males, Treeneck backing him up.

"It's an instinct with some of us," Pokesnout explained. "When a trap or danger lies in wait, the very young, or old, or sick are sometimes driven forth to test the way. But we won't do things that way anymore," Pokesnout said. "I will lead. Sacrificing the weak is bad."

"Because you were one of the ones they'd drive into danger?" Floyt blurted. Pokesnout craned his head around at an extreme angle to study him while the translator sounded.

"You think well." Pokesnout stepped out onto the high desert, making sure the other males followed.

The herd had been told what to expect and had the danger of panic hammered into them. Nevertheless, a kilometer into the crossing, when the pink sand started moving and yielding up sand devils and the corrosive smell filled the air, frightened bawls went up and the gawklegs began rearing and kicking.

Alacrity was just thankful the scuttle-death didn't simply climb one another, mounding high enough to bite above the gawks' boots. But as he'd seen on his scouting foray, that wasn't a part of their behavior; any sand devil that stepped on another was instantly driven off or engaged in combat. Almost at once a hundred incredibly vicious duels were going on among the teeming midget monsters.

The gawklegs—the cows in particular—were unnerved by it all, but they were intelligent beings, not bovine-brained ruminants. They quickly understood that as long as they didn't fall they were safe.

And none wanted to be left behind; that was an imperative of the herd and the Verities were too strong to be denied. Pokesnout led off and Treeneck, Rockhorn, and some of the others got the rest moving. Sand devils thronged and slavered, hurling themselves at the pliabamboo sheaths. Again and again they slid off, teeth unable to penetrate the stuff. The things were sometimes trampled into the sand by gawks, only to rise and try again.

"We're barely making two kilometers an hour!" Paloma called to Alacrity. "What do you say? Is it decoy time yet?"

"We'll have to give it a try," he yelled back over the din of the herd. "We've got to make some headway."

He guided Treeneck out away from the main body of the herd, trying to block mental images of what would happen to a tender *Homo sapien* down there among the fishhook teeth.

But the big bull was steady and ploddingly calm though he had quite an escort of ravenous devils, and more were skittering in the herd's direction all the time.

When Alacrity reached a spot a half kilometer to the left of the route of march, he unlashed a stiffened fawncricket carcass from behind him and dragged it free.

Bracing himself with one hand on the surcingle and both knees thrust under it, he raised the kill and heaved it as far as he could, bouncing his heels against Treeneck's sides as a signal to get clear. The body had sand devils swarming to it the instant it hit.

And if those warrior-workers really take their prizes back to the hive, our luck's gone sour, he saw; the hive looked to lay along the herd's route of march.

Waves of scuttle-death came hurrying in response to the new olfactory message; the decoy drew quite a few devils away from the herd, but that still left an awful lot of little uglies. Still, the herd's speed more than doubled as the gawks got used to wearing their new boots in sand.

In the next four hours there were no two minutes in a row when disaster didn't loom. Calves stumbled; a frightened male took a misstep that threatened to send him foundering; a cow put her foot into a hole and nearly fell. Panic and stampede were never more than an instant away. The infrasonics made the air feel like an invisible vibrobath. The vermin eaters abandoned the herd, flitting homeward.

According to Paloma's data, sand devils normally preyed on small game and certain plants, and a single hive might claim hundreds of square kilometers as its territory, warrior-workers lying somnolent under the sand until awakened by the smell of prey or an olfactory cue from hivemate or queen. In especially hard times, excess hivemembers simply let themselves be consumed as emergency rations. Alacrity could think of a lot of ways he'd prefer to go, or see any of the others go, rather than nourish a hive of rotten little hyper-communists.

He scanned and searched, but it was Paloma who finally spied the pyramid-vent hive entrances, three two-meter-high mounds. "What do you think, Speed?"

He looked at the sea of sand devils squirming to snap at the gawks' legs. "Might as well give it a shot, Babyfat; we've got nothing to lose. Ho?"

Floyt nodded, readying his torches and friction-wheel firestarter. With luck, a little diversion might activate the scuttle-death's hive-survival reflexes or something and take some of the pressure off the herd. Floyt pointed out the pyramids to Pokesnout, who understood even without benefit of translation.

The mounds were sand hills hardened with some secretion; the shafts were meter-wide sand-devil superhighways. Floyt lit torches of twisted grass and noxious plants, and lofted one down each shaft. Then Pokesnout stumped away as fast as he could. Smoke rose from the shafts as from so many chimneys; the scuttle-death scent message changed at once, sharply.

The hive was aboil; the assault on the herd slackened. But about then the sand became loose and treacherous underhoof, and soon after a wind came up, making the humans squint and shield their eyes and their mounts close two layers of nictitating membranes over their own. Alacrity pulled his blue bandanna up over his nose and mouth; Paloma protected herself as best she could with her wrap, and Floyt fastened his fatigue jacket up all the way, closing the collar flap, burrowing his chin down.

Alacrity threw out another carrion decoy at a spot where the sand was especially bad. The third and last decoy, carried by Paloma on Rockhorn, they held against extreme need. Their hopes picked up. The wind died.

Then the duneline hove into sight.

At first Alacrity hoped that the pink ramparts of sand were a trick of the late-afternoon light, but a few more minutes made it certain: a wall of dunes had been thrown up by winds sweeping up from the rocky stretch beyond and below the high desert.

"There has to be a way around the dunes or through them," Paloma said. Darkness would be on them soon and the herd was tiring. Some of the weak and ill gawks were already lurching.

"I will do this thing you've taught, going-ahead-without-the-herd," Pokesnout resolved. "Keep them moving, keep them together," he told his deputy males and senior females, and Alacrity and Paloma as well.

Then he was charging off, Floyt clinging as best he could, praying the surcingle would hold. Pokesnout was amazingly fast and sure despite the pliabamboo sheaths.

Soon the duneline loomed up; Floyt's heart sank. It wasn't very formidable by normal standards—ten meters high, a thirty-five-degree incline. No problem for

a gawk who, churning along and sinking to its knees or
losing balance, could simply right itself and keep on
going. But a lethal obstacle when a single falter could
leave a helpless herdmember covered with clinging, ven-
omous sand devils.

Pokesnout slowed to a trot, he and his rider searching
for some solution. Floyt pounded Pokesnout's neck and
pointed, crying "Look there!"

For the first time it came to him that he didn't have a
proteus, and he wondered how in the world he was going
to get the message across. But Pokesnout craned around
to glance at his arm, then followed the pointing finger. At
the very least, he'd learned what the gesture meant. At
most . . .

He is! He's picking up Terranglish!

Sand devils were far fewer at the dunes, perhaps because of the shifting sand. But more than a dozen were
attacking the alpha's various shoes as he trotted for the
little saddle between dunes. The bull shifted to a strong
six-by-six low gear as he climbed. He was more coor-
dinated and efficient than an articulated adjustable-
suspension vehicle that Floyt had seen do the same sort
of thing once on Blackguard. Pokesnout's limbs were far
more agile and adaptable than the ASV's pantograph legs.

Floyt held his breath, hypnotized by the struggle,
clutching for all he was worth. He watched the solid legs
work, and the crest of the saddle came closer. Sand
devils circled and darted in a frenzy, showing their teeth
to each other when they bumped. Pokesnout's sheathed
feet sank in halfway to the rims of the pliabamboo segments.

The top bull took a near spill that had Floyt's heart in
need of a jumpstart. Then Pokesnout crested the rise.
His sides heaved and his head hung tiredly as he inhaled
in rapid whooshes and exhaled in unbelievably loud
whistles, foam dripping from his muzzle.

Beyond the dune ridge's base, a gentle slope led to a
rocky barrens lying between cliffs and talus heaps. There
were a few isolated patches of sand, like pink snow dis-

appearing in springtime. Though the air was rank with the furious sand devils' frenzy-smell, there were none below.

Floyt patted Pokesnout's head. "You made it, you . . . made it. You got us through . . ."

The bull huffed, brought his head back up with a shake, and whirled to start back for the herd, making his way downslope cautiously. Floyt wasn't sure the weaker calves, oldsters, and other marginals could make the upgrade, but those who couldn't had no way out but death.

Floyt took a last look back at the lowlands that lay along the route of march. In the distance, there was still the barrier of Lake Fret. As suddenly as that, inspiration came to him. He exulted and urged Pokesnout back to the herd.

"We lost two while you were gone," Paloma told him when he rejoined the others. "One calf fell, and there was a beta-male whose boot split wide open."

When Floyt explained what he'd found, she summed it up. "If that's all there is, we'll have to take it. It looks like smoking out the hive wasn't such a master stroke; there's a lot of activity back that way and the gawks have picked up some new smell. We think the hive queen may have come out for the hunt."

Floyt absorbed the bad news. According to Paloma's proteus, a queen's decision to take part in the hunt made the borderline sand devils completely crazy, as she programmed their behavior with her royal scents.

"And she's gaining on us," Alacrity said, studying the duneline ahead. Floyt thought he could make out movement back the way the herd had come.

"We have to move faster," Alacrity told Pokesnout, "even if it means casualties."

"We can't let anything stop us now!" Floyt told Alacrity. "I've figured out a way to get across Lake Fret!"

"You *which*?"

"I'll explain later."

Pokesnout gave orders. Treeneck, Rockhorn, and the other lead gawks got the herd moving at a pace that would've been suicidal earlier in the day, but the gawks had had time to get used to the leg coverings.

Weaker members began straggling in spite of everything Pokesnout could do, their tongues lolling, breath coming harshly. Alacrity thought about trying to slow things down again but saw it would never work. The herd knew it was near the end of the high desert. Fear and the need for flight had taken over; they wouldn't be slowed this side of safety or hell.

The herd strung out farther and farther. Paloma had ridden far back to drop the last decoy carrion; it did little good. The scuttle-death was coming in the tens of thousands to form a carpet, their stench thick as smoke from a prairie fire.

A stringy old bull, whose legs had been trembling and quaking since the march began, finally reached the end of his strength, missing his footing. He skidded on front knees, then struggled up to race another three lengths. He tumbled tail over horns, nearly bringing down a second male who'd blundered into him from behind. In an instant the sand devils were clinging and biting around him, still unable to climb far.

The bull got to his feet a second time, bellowing weakly, as the last herdmembers swerved around him, devils bobbing on him with their teeth fixed in his hide. He keeled over and more warrior-workers flooded in at him. The vanguard of the herd was already at the dune saddle, bunching up as gawks jostled to get ahead of one another.

Alacrity caught a whiff of something new from the sand devils, who were more agitated than ever. He looked back and saw a thicker mob of them coming, darker than the ones he'd seen so far. One particular knot of them moved as a unit, like the eye of a hurricane.

Hive queen! And she was leading a sea of her subjects; they were slaves to the royal hunt-odor now, following it no matter where or what, laying out an emulating smell so that the plague of devils coming after, blindly obedient, would sense the command, would comply, and would put out the emulating smell in turn. Alacrity held his proteus by Treeneck's ear, yelling his idea.

Paloma noticed as Treeneck swung to retrace his way. "Where are you going?"

Alacrity pointed with his lance. "You keep 'em moving, Babyfat! I'll be right back!" Treeneck cantered off at a reckless pace.

"Cazzo!" she spat, and turned to ride for the turmoil of the duneline just in time to see a calf inadvertently trampled by its elders, bleating as it died.

Many times the size of her warrior-workers, big as a terrier, the hive queen wasn't hard to pick out. Her personal scent overcame the normal sand-devil loathing of territorial incursion; in her vicinity and along her odor trail they piled atop one another, all squirming to be close to her and bask in her aromas. They were in such transport that they failed to notice Treeneck's approach, or warnings from peripheral members of the swarm, until the gawk was in their midst.

Treeneck seemed to take naturally to the flat-footed gait that was his only hope of survival. Even in the writhing mass of the scuttle-death, they couldn't reach vulnerable flesh, but it was a nearer thing; making weak, clumsy hops from mounded hivemates, devils were coming within centimeters of the gawk's boot tops. Treeneck waded on bravely anyway.

A new scent permeated the air in the last seconds before Alacrity struck, the hive queen and her escort raising an alarm. Alacrity drove his long wooden lance down into her and through her, overhand, with all his might, the fire-hardened point striking in just between her first set of shoulders, the scare-flare claw barbs sinking deep.

With an effort that nearly ungawked him, Alacrity hauled the queen up from her worshipping subjects, a few of them dropping from her. Treeneck was already turning to trample his way back into the clear. Moving faster than most herdmembers could, the big bull left most of the wriggling mass behind, but they were already in furious pursuit, sending out summons and alarm odors tinged with the queen's scents. Sand devils converged on Alacrity and Treeneck from several sides.

The queen struggled and flailed angrily at the end of the lance. Alacrity paused long enough to make sure it was firmly fixed in her, then set off, dragging the queen over the sand, leaving a scent trail. Her hordes came flooding after.

The next few minutes were sheer adrenaline unreality, as Alacrity left the trail while praying he wouldn't fall or lose the queen, and Treeneck clomped along recklessly in the clumsy boots. Man and gawk did their best to keep track of direction; to become lost would mean an ugly death. They cut a long arc away from the rest of the herd. More and more sand devils streamed along the queen's odor trail, their frenzied aromas mingling with hers, reinforcing the urgency for those behind.

Treeneck wove around rock obstacles and occasional desert plants; the nearsighted sand devils never attempted to take shortcuts or head him off, staying right on the scent-path because its stimuli would let them do nothing else.

Alacrity began to panic, fearing Treeneck hadn't understood the plan, or had become disoriented. Then the bull rounded a boulder and Alacrity saw what he'd been praying for: the spot where he'd originally begun laying down the trail. Sand devils were still converging on it from all over.

The queen was still wriggling, but only feebly; the scent she was exuding was almost visible. Still dragging her body, Alacrity urged Treeneck on. In another minute they were at the beginning of the queen's trail again, having drawn a full circle. Treeneck went into the scuttle-death stream gingerly but quickly; the pursuit had nearly caught up with him.

Alacrity dragged the queen right to the spot where her trail began, closing the ring, then lifted her high, where she could deposit no trail, bearing her away as fast as Treeneck could manage. The leaders among the pursuing scuttle-death followed her spoor right back to where they'd started, encountering the imperative, emulating scents of other pursuers who were just starting on the circle, along with the queen's own original smells.

Their genetic programming gave them no room for doubt or hesitation. The devils leading the way started around again, laying out even more scent. More and more of the little fiends thronged to the scuttle-death superconducting ring. Alacrity, still holding the wounded queen aloft, turned for the herd.

Wouldn't surprise me if they all turned into butter . . .

Paloma was at the crest of the dune saddle on Rockhorn, exhorting the gawks on. The path had been churned to a gentler incline by the herd's passage, making it easier going; there'd been a dozen-plus casualties, which Pokesnout had miraculously managed to get moved out of the way with his aides' help, mostly through careful use of hind legs.

Gawklegs who'd already made the transit were grouping on the rocky stretches beyond, where the scuttle-death wouldn't go. The herdmembers were shaken but beginning to sort themselves out once more.

Alacrity showed up, his lance bare again. He'd dragged his weapon free of the wounded queen a kilometer back, not out of clemency but to give nearby devils something else to do. It may have helped, but the trampled incline was still alive with devils.

It was pandemonium. Gawks' cries of panic and dismay were deafening and the air was almost unbreathable with dust. Alacrity pulled up his blue—now pink—bandanna again. As he drew near, the last of the herd got ready to assay the dune saddle.

Floyt and Pokesnout were about to go up, to make sure everything was all right at the crest and beyond. Treeneck fell in beside the runt alpha. Alacrity and Floyt held on tight as their mounts went up with the last few of the herd.

Then a young noncalving female in the group slipped

and, bleating and hooting, slid backward, somehow still keeping upright, her legs widespread. Pokesnout watched, gathering himself; Floyt knew the gawk was going to try to help her. Treeneck faltered, exhausted by his labors and undecided.

Pokesnout blared something at Treeneck; the big bull swung to continue grinding his way up the hill. Alacrity held the surcingle and objected loudly. He had an impulse to go after Floyt afoot, trusting to the protection of the pathfinders. But he saw it would likely be suicide; the sand was too uncertain. And Pokesnout had brought Floyt through so far. Alacrity was borne to the top of the hill in a spume of sand and flying, flailing scuttle-death.

Pokesnout slid to a stop near the female. Floyt's heart sank when he saw what was wrong: she'd split both shoes on her two forelegs and lost one of them. The other foreleg was exposed all the way to the hoof pad. She'd had the presence of mind to rear up on her two hindsets, free of sand devils so far, but Floyt didn't see how that could last long with an animal so used to traveling on all six and built for little else. She was right there yet beyond help.

But Pokesnout was trumpeting to her, buffeting her in reverse gear to get her attention, backing his rump at her then swinging around to trumpet at her again, and backing at her once more. Frustrated, the bull swung around and belched something at Floyt, waggling the vast behind again, bouncing and wriggling it.

Like the flash of insight he'd had at the crest of the dunes, Floyt understood clearly in an unexpected instant. Some strong bond had come into being between the man and the gawk; Floyt didn't hesitate.

He took the last two spare pliabamboo sheaths. They were calf-size, too small for the female, so Floyt jammed his own feet into them. While his boots didn't fill them, their length wedged into the round segments fairly well. He eased himself down from Pokesnout's back, using his lance for balance, as Alacrity screamed at him from the top of the hill.

The feel of sand devils lunging against the pliabamboo, gnawing at it, trying to climb to the tops of the sheaths only to fall back and try again nearly made him scramble back up onto Pokesnout or stumble madly for the top of the slope.

But Pokesnout snuffled softly at his ear and gave him a restrained nudge forward. Floyt swallowed his terror and started for the female, catching himself with his lance once or twice but perservering. Pokesnout was droning, Verities style, in the background.

She still had her exposed forelegs up, the whites showing all around her rolling eyes, but she was having more and more difficulty keeping her balance. Floyt went in close, just ahead of Pokesnout's backing rump.

She was nearly the little male's size. Floyt pushed up on her forelegs and chest with the lance, not because his strength would do much good but to show her what she had to do. She came to herself a little, and cooperated.

Then Pokesnout was in under her, jacking her chest up with his croup, still droning Verities. She listened, then struggled to maintain balance.

Holy Spirit of Tellurian Places! it came to Floyt. *He's inventing a Verity on the spot, to tell her what to do!*

Pokesnout dug in, legs spread for stability, trying to help her without losing his own balance.

Floyt assisted as much as he could, and batted one devil trying for the female's lashing tail. Then the two gawks were moving, but with poor coordination and maddeningly slow. Floyt shuffled and crutched along, keeping a hand on the female's flank as a comfort if nothing else, while sand devils assailed all three. The top of the dune saddle loomed in the dusk, a corona of sunset igniting the sky beyond. Floyt's soul seesawed from hysteria to exaltation and back between one instant and the next. But he looked at Pokesnout's stubborn lion-heartedness and felt a wash of fierce loyalty.

Then the female's starboard hind leg missed its footing for a moment, her weight threatening to shift and bring them all down. Floyt grabbed her port foreleg to pull, on the long chance that the extra bit of leverage might make some difference. A part of him could right well not comprehend why the life of one more gawk maiden he'd never noticed before had become so vital to him all of a sudden.

She regained her balance and centered on Poke-snout's back by dint of furious pedaling and some fancy maneuvering on the bull's part. At just about that same time, Floyt—he never figured out just how—lost his equilibrium and fell.

Pokesnout couldn't possibly have seen, but somehow he knew. The gawk managed in some way to keep things stable with his other five legs and cocked his near-mid-ships leg up and out, an altogether unprecedented maneuver from his kind, trying to arrest the Earther's fall.

Floyt lurched, scrabbling, against the leg and just barely missed saving himself. He slid and rolled off, landing on his back, beginning a pliabamboo segments-first slide down the slope as warm sand coursed around and under him.

The scuttle-death were on him at once, first a few, then a dozen. Oddly, he felt little pain—the bites were less than the single bee sting he'd received on a field trip on Earth as a boy. He didn't know if that was because of his emotional blaze or a numbing secretion of the scuttle-death.

But numbness spread fast, even as Floyt was thrash-ing and tossing, trying to get to his feet. It occurred to him that a toxin that could knock over a gawk in a short time would quite probably kill a human without very much waiting around. Still, he swiped and ripped away at the sand devils that clung to him, beating at others with his lance, furious that he was being slingshot into the afterlife with so much left undone.

He was back on his feet again, free of them for a wonder, but too late. "Isn't this *just like* the fucking uni-verse?" he asked Lebensraum's sky unsteadily; laughing was so much effort as to be out of the question. His head wobbled. Things became cloudy for a second, then unnaturally clear as he concentrated, feeling like he'd slept. He brought all his willpower to bear, knowing no one else could save him.

Concentration did no good, not even for his posture; he tilted backward, unable to get a foot into position to stop it, beginning a fall into a bed of sand devils who'd set up an eager feeding scent he'd hate forever. He waited for his back to hit the squirming, biting mass because he couldn't do much else.

A surprise, then, when he landed on something rather less yielding and felt distinct pain in his upper back and across his buttocks. Very large teeth bruised and lacerated him, teeth bigger than a whole sand devil. It also felt hot and was rather smelly. Too, there was something large and slimy-slidey under him. The Floyt was immobilized by another enormous weight/surface from the top. Woozily, he understood that he was in Pokesnout's mouth like a duck in a retriever's.

Raised high above the sand, head bobbing on a limp neck, Floyt blearily watched the sand devils running around to no effect a million kilometers below. Dusk was deeper or his vision was going. He coughed and spat out sand, chuckling to himself, immensely amused. Pokesnout was carrying the female as well as Floyt, sand fountaining back from his sheathed hooves.

Floyt decided to nap.

Much later, he came around for a few moments to find himself laid out on leaves and branches layered over hard stone, close to a fire. Gawks were gathered around him curiously; Alacrity and Paloma Sudan were moving sprightly to keep them from singeing their muzzles while investigating the blaze. Verities—and New Verities, he supposed—were droning in the background. He was so woozy, he could hardly feel how saddlesore he was.

"Hobie! You're *back*!" Paloma cried, dropping to her knees near him and kissing his brow, cradling his head with her hands.

"Good. We were just gonna dock you pay." Alacrity

winked. He flung an arm out in a grand gesture. "Long way to go. And some water waiting along the way. Listen, d'you happen to remember what you were telling me about Lake Fret? Your solution?"

It was the first Paloma had heard of it. "Hobie, you never cease to amaze me."

Floyt looked around sleepily, moistening his dry mouth. "We'll *walk* across."

His face lolled against Paloma's bosom and he was out again.

CHAPTER 14

WHO'RE WE TO ARGUE?

"BIG LAKE."

"A too-*damn*-big lake, Paloma," Alacrity commented. "The map says Lake Fret's—lemme see—something like twenty-five kilometers wide at this point, and this is as narrow as it gets."

Lake Fret was too choppy to reflect the sky, too shallow and silty in most places to have a true color of its own; it was an unhealthy gray-black. Alacrity lay back watching it with his head pillowed against Pokesnout's ribs, patting them absently, scratching his own various bites. The gawks had attracted a new air fleet of vermin eaters, who seemed to accept the humans as part of the gawks, but the assorted tiny pests were a constant bother nevertheless.

Floyt's beard was still fairly well maintained, thanks to the survival tool's scissors. Alacrity had no need to shave, having put a hold on facial hair growth years ago, for the same reasons of convenience that had moved Paloma to stop her menstrual periods soon after she'd begun getting them.

And both men had let fingernails grow, finding them utilitarian, as other primitives did.

Alacrity studied the sky but saw no patrolling aircraft. The herd had taken careful concealment under heavily leaved candelabrum trees along the lakeshore, where they'd lain doggo for two days while the human trio sallied out in an effort to deal with the obstacle of Lake Fret.

Alacrity, Floyt, and Paloma had lit no fire since their second night down off the high desert, and chosen the route to the lake to maximize cover and minimize the dust the herd raised, taking every precaution to avoid detection and the air strikes it would draw.

There was a fair amount of traffic on Lake Fret, mostly ore barges. But none of it was likely to stop where the human and gawk expedition hid under lakeside foliage. Paloma, closer to Pokesnout's head, gave his chin a brief, thorough scratching with her red duraglaze glamornails. Pokesnout closed his eyes blissfully.

Humans and gawklegs were worse for wear, but Floyt was, after fifteen days' additional Long Trek, having fewer and fewer nightmares in which sand devils devoured their way into his eye sockets.

More than twenty additional gawks had died since the herd left the high desert. Alacrity confidently predicted that the human fatality rate over that same ground, given the prowling jackjaws, the flash floods, the bogs, zapfrosts, cruising dragon-kites, rockslides, and brushfiends, would've been right around 100 percent. Throw in a personal convoy/bodyguard of two- to three-ton gawklegs evolved to thrive on Lebensraum, though, and all the equations changed. The humans had suffered no casualties but the gawks had, and Paloma, Floyt, and Alacrity were painfully aware of the connection.

Things between the humans had changed, too, but in ways that were hard to define.

At the end of the first day's journey down from the high desert, Floyt accepted Alacrity's and Paloma's word that there must be no more campfires after that night; the humans had thrown in their lot with the gawks irrevocably, and detection would likely mean death for all.

So Floyt stared into the last fire, exhausted and still a bit bleary from the scuttle-death toxin, feeding the tiny blaze while Alacrity was off trying to get a location fix from surrounding land features and Paloma was gathering some menu extenders.

Then Floyt realized Paloma was standing at his shoulder. She put down a meager double-handful of hardscrabble up-country nuts and roots on a flat rock, took her much-repaired camp stool, and joined him by the fire.

"Just tell me this," she said suddenly. "Tell me what makes *him* so cocksure, huh? What're those little signals between you two? Why's Alacrity so smug about this White Ship business?"

Floyt stared into the flames, debating where the next piece of wood ought to go, despondent about the nights that were to come, when there would be no light or warmth, but especially no light, and knowing he would miss, as well, his station as Keeper of the Flame.

At last he sighed and gestured to the fire with the stick he held. "You think this is much of a light? Or that a bonfire is? God, Paloma, you should've seen the causality harp!

"It was a Precursor artifact—at least I *think* 'was' is the right word; I'm fairly sure it was blown to oblivion. It was a—I don't know; a nebula, a living fire fifty meters high that sang and revealed Verities of its own, and what is to be."

Paloma's face had clouded. "So what are are you telling me? You found some kind of Precursor crystal ball?"

Floyt looked around at her suddenly, paused to consider, then nodded slowly. "That's exactly what I'm telling you; that's exactly what happened. Except that the crystal ball is more like some sort of wind chime that registered... well, I'm not sure *what* in creation it registered. *Causality*...

"And Alacrity went out to it—almost into it—and asked it a question, asked it whether he'd be Master of the White Ship."

"It told him yes, of course." Paloma frowned, on one knee by the fire. "And so now he figures he's got Destiny by the ass, hmm?"

Floyt wanted to tell her everything but wasn't sure where to start, or how much it was fair to tell her about Alacrity's delusions in view of the fact that Floyt hadn't worked up the nerve to tell Alacrity himself.

"S'right," Alacrity drawled, coming out of the dusk to balance on his teetering camp stool.

Paloma looked him over. "And why should you control the Ship? Are you so much better than the Ghh 'arkt? All *they* want to do is find the Precursors so they can pray to them. The rulers on Egalitaria claim they're going to administer all findings to benefit all life forms if they crack the Precursor mysteries. The Interested Parties want to show a profit, but at least they're a committee, or whatever, with some checks and balances. What makes you so special?"

Alacrity made a sour smile. "Because I've been getting ready for it my whole life, and I don't owe anybody anything—no government, no god, nobody. Because the Ship's gonna be the greatest source of power of all time, and she's not to be controlled by the people who *rule* and the people who *own!*"

He smiled again, self-deprecatingly, Paloma thought, drawn to his answer against her will.

"And I haven't done much of either," Alacrity added.

"But more to the point, you're the Anointed of the Causality Harp," she shot back, with a wicked set to her jaw, eyes slitted.

That wiped the smile off Alacrity's face. "Besides," he said grimly, "that Ship means more to me than she does to *any* of them! I just—"

He looked up at the stars. "It's got to be done fairly and justly. Precursor secrets're gonna dictate what happens to this universe; they have to be used *right!*"

Paloma had moved from irritation to anger. "And that's what makes you so sure you know what's right? Some Precursor fireworks display?"

Alacrity looked as if he was going to say something pompous and provoking; Floyt braced himself.

But abruptly Alacrity's lopsided smirk appeared. "To level with you, yeah. And nobody's more surprised about it than I am."

He shook his head, chortling, and rose to stroll back into the dusk, hands in his pockets and head tilted back to inspect the sky.

Pokesnout and the humans were looking out at a string of acre-size turbo barges being guided and bapped as needed by waterjet workboats. For the Lebensraum Company, with its aged and limited industrial and technical base, surface shipping offered substantial savings over airfreighting; Lake Fret saw a lot of use.

Clouds had closed in late in the day, giving the sky the textured grays and sepias of an old Earth platinum print. "The data says those schools of snapping whoosies and the rest of the lunch trade in the water there would tackle a human *or* a gawk," Paloma brooded. "If Hobie's idea doesn't work we're going to be turning in a very bad afteraction report on this one."

"I don't see why it shouldn't," Floyt maintained. "You read the info and the calculations yourself. They may be guesswork, but they're good, informed guesswork."

Lake Fret was a basin area formed through the solution of the underlying deposits of limestonelike sediments. Over the ages it had changed back and forth a number of times between a lake and a marshy prairie with areas of open water. But company documents said a vast, eroded cavern system typical of Karst topography remained beneath it. When occasional leaks developed in the limestone cap, company engineers were quick to reseal them with force-injected aquacrete composite on reinforced duralloy matrices; Lake Fret was important to the balance sheets for operation in that region.

"'We'll walk across,'" Paloma quoted Floyt, patting

his hand. "You really yinged me with that one! I saw us pulling off some New Testament extravaganza."

"Or maybe Old Testament," Alacrity suggested, "parting the waters."

"But you'll recall I never said anything about water," Floyt reminded them. "Now, when are the drones due?" He was checking his compass.

Paloma read her proteus. "Let's see; they have fifty klicks to cover. If we programmed them right, they'll be here any time now."

The company survey station, an automated facility, hadn't figured in their plans since it offered nothing of use. Mostly it was simply a seismic monitoring post and remote-controlled launch point for seismic sounding-charge drones. Then Floyt's brainstorm made it the linchpin of their survival. And so the three had left the herd long enough to break into the station and reprogram the six drones stored there. Company work records and maps showed them their exact targets.

"Hey; here we go." Alacrity was pointing to the east. All six drones racked for launch at the station were programmed, but only three of the small shapes hove into view out of the cloud cover.

"The rest must be on target already," Alacrity concluded. The other three objectives were closer to the station; the main one, out near Lake Fret's narrowest section, was vital and so the saboteurs were giving it double redundancy. As they watched, the chubby metal insects swung out to zero in on their objective.

The trio settled down again to wait, sharing the little remaining food. They checked insect bites, blisters, injuries, and running sores acquired along the way. They spoke little, and only Pokesnout seemed relaxed.

There was less tension among the humans, though. An elegant system had evolved among them, vectors of attraction and friendship running in different directions and balancing each other, and caution running in opposite directions, canceling each other in at least one case.

And so they were in a close partnership of adversity, with conflict very much in the background. Moreover, as Floyt had discovered, the hardships of a cross-country odyssey left a lot less time and inclination and energy for romance than the books, films, and holos might give one to think.

But he suspected that if and when the three got to safety, the extreme circumstances of the Long Trek traded for comfort, privacy, and leisure, Paloma Sudan would let her desires come to the fore. He suspected, despondently, that her chosen lover would not be him.

"Fancula! I'd give anything if we could tap into the company commo nets!" Alacrity fumed. A breeze stirred the trees, and gawklegs shifted around restively, eager to feed on the foliage but unable to because the New Verities included a lot of doctrine about staying hidden from possible observers, especially aerial ones. An adult gawk could put away more than one hundred kilos of forage a day, but the herd had been on thin rations for most of the Trek.

Floyt was finishing the last of the food he'd saved, some freshwater shell creatures they'd dug from the lake's shallows with their lances. They wouldn't have appealed to him a few weeks before; now he prized at one with his survival tool, mouth watering and jaws aching in anticipation. As he did, the ground gave a distinct tremor and he nicked himself.

"Alacrity! Was that—"

"Had to be." Alacrity was on his feet, looking out over Lake Fret. Of course, there was nothing to see. "The other shock waves'll be a while longer getting here."

He turned to Pokesnout. "We'd better move back from shore a little, just to be safe. And tell 'em they can come out from cover a little after dark to feed, as long as they don't strip the trees we're using for camouflauge."

He looked out over Lake Fret. "And tell 'em we're coming into the home stretch."

They kept lookout by turns that night, up on higher ground. The shore was in disarray, undergrowth and small trees draped with lake plants and battered by the miniature tidal waves kicked up by the blasts. It already stank of decay and death; the humans could hear small land animals moving around in the aftermath, feeding off beached lake dwellers and plants. Insects were swarming; luckily, there were no drillbugs in the area, but Alacrity opened his brolly and the three shared it as they had that first night.

Paloma woke the other two around first light. Out over the lake, some sort of aircraft moved, showing an arcade of lights, playing spots, detector-lasers, and monitoring beams over the waters. A frightened groan went up from the hiding gawks until Pokesnout belched at them for silence.

As the group looked on, the aircraft dropped some kind of tech buoy or probe robo far out over the water. Then it left.

A short time later the light showed them, bit by bit, that the face of Lake Fret had changed; a mudflat over two-hundred meters wide led out to murky waters. The mud was draining, exposing pieces of embedded wood, silt-covered rocks, struggling, stranded lake creatures, and decomposing plants.

A choking stench lay over everything. Flocks of flying things were gorging on the unscheduled feast, and scores of small, furtive shore animals who were predators or scavengers, as opportunity dictated, were sating themselves on the mass stranding. Insectlike life forms were out in clouds.

"And there'll be bigger things along soon, to feed on those in turn," Paloma said, alluding to the breakfast contingent. "We'd better stay close to the gawks."

"The limestone plug that gave way in that place on Terra—how long did it take to drain?" Alacrity asked Floyt as they took in the scene.

"Paynes Prairie Lake? It took a week. It stranded

steamboats and so forth, much as this will do. Of course, that lake was a good deal smaller than Lake Fret, but on the other hand the holes we've punched into the underground drainage are much, much bigger than the one that did the job on Paynes Prairie Lake, which was fairly modest.

"I'd conjecture that it's just a question of how fast the drainage can handle water, and it's rather damned enormous, according to survey maps."

"Fast enough, it looks like," Paloma agreed. "I'd say shaped deep-shaker seismic charges are a lot more efficient than a little chunk of stone giving way."

"Just guessing," Alacrity said, "but it looks to me like we're due for a real low tide tonight." He consulted the holo lake charts and pointed. "Right across there. I do believe we're gonna make it."

Floyt glanced at him. "I thought you were certain all along?"

Alacrity hunched his shoulders, dropped them. "Oh, I believe it real hard, for about thirty seconds out of every hour or so. It comes and goes."

"I never thought I'd say this, but don't start doubting now," Paloma told him. "We're a long way from home free."

The mud was adhesive and deep, a sucking mire reeking with rotting microorganisms and higher life forms, still impassable to humans. But by nightfall a narrow isthmus had emerged from the receding waters. The three compared charts and depth readings and decided their chance had come.

"Another day or three and that would be baked marl, an easy walk," Paloma estimated. "But that doesn't do us much good." The cover of darkness was essential, and there was no telling what problems another day's wait would bring.

That mud was no great annoyance to the herd; gawk-legs were used to mud, built for wading when necessary, and for enjoyment, and they had excellent night vision.

The herd pushed off just after full dark. The humans couldn't do much but cling to their rides and hope; it all lay with Pokesnout and his people. One of Paloma's wilderness survival files had tipped them to a local plant, and now the three rode with all exposed skin rubbed down with leaves of cabbagelike stenchweed. It kept most of the swarmers from landing on them but not from circling maddeningly, whining and buzzing and ratcheting in the gloom.

Seldom troubled by mud above the calves' knees, often in stuff that was less than hock-deep, the herd smelled and spied out the highest ground. Then too, since most of the weak and the sick had died along the way, the herd made good time.

A few individuals got stuck, but the gawks constantly showed how adept they were at helping one another when they weren't hampered by sand devils. Every so often, as the exodus went on, Alacrity and the others heard strandees flopping and thrashing weakly in the mud. Those seemed fewer out along the isthmus, though; Alacrity reckoned that most of the lake's denizens had had time to make it to deeper waters. He was also assuming the Lebensraum Company had no intention of letting Lake Fret revert to prairie, thereby costing the company a fortune for a new air or dryland freighting system.

At least, there was a lot of sky traffic, though less than there'd been during the day. Given the relative scarcity of flying craft on Lebensraum, Lake Fret was evidently an emergency-priority crisis. Most of the effort looked like it was going into moving crews and machinery to work sites after a day of evacuations and survey overflights.

The herd forded on, dragging hooves from the clinging ooze to put them down again. Every so often an aircraft would rush by, sometimes at low altitude. The entire caravan froze then, though if the company was using detectors and looking for unusual movement there wasn't a prayer the herd wouldn't be spotted.

"I don't know; that last one seemed to slow down for a second, there," Floyt said of one flyover. "How far do we have to go?"

"Not far, I think," Alacrity said. "Pokesnout, how about it?"

"We smell land very close, Speed. Do you not?"

"I mostly smell me," Alacrity began, and heard Paloma gasp.

"They've found us!"

From the southeast came a flight of aircraft, several smaller ones and two giants, running lights blazing, megacandlepower spotlights playing back and forth across the water. They were bound straight for the herd.

"Not much else they could be looking for out here," Alacrity agreed. "And anyway, they're bound to see us. Okay, Pokesnout: remember what we told you. Let's go!"

Pokesnout threw his head back and brayed loudly. The other gawks had seen the oncoming airships and knew the signal. They wuffed and honked among themselves, preparing to run. Pokesnout gave a brief, stertorous sound; the herd broke into a sloppy, desperate race.

Mud was everywhere, hurled up by the broad hooves. Alacrity could only cling to Treeneck's surcingle, burrowing his head against the bull's neck. The mudflats shook to the cannonading. Almost from the first there were mishaps; gawks lost footing or collided with one another and went down, only to flail up again. They were the winnowed-out herd, consummate survivors, quick to rebound and incapable of giving up.

The flight of aircraft was breaking formation, the individual ships spreading out slowly and deliberately, taking up what Floyt assumed to be attack positions. Some hung back as others moved right and left, and a lead vessel bore down right on the herd. It was then that Alacrity and Floyt heard Paloma calling out their names.

"Rein back! Stay with me! Maybe we can stall them somehow so the others can make it!"

It was sure that those gawks burdened with humans would never outrun aircraft. *We'll be captured or killed whether we run or stand*, Alacrity concluded. *At least this way some gawks might live. It's the least we can do for leading 'em into this.*

Floyt made the same decision; in another moment the three were sitting side by side with Pokesnout, Treeneck, and Rockhorn rubbing shoulders under them as the lead ship closed. The gawks shook their horns, made bellicose sounds, and flung up muck with their hooves. Paloma, in the center, reached out to squeeze each man's shoulder.

Alacrity was reviewing the alibis and lies he'd thought up over the weeks since Hecate whirled the trio away from the Wicked Wickiup. He hoped he'd get a chance to try one or two of them instead of being scorched on the spot. Just as he was making up his mind which one to go with first, the lead ship stopped, hovering, its spots raising their aim from the water and fixing on the two large ships, which had taken up station close to the lake's surface.

"I—what— Look, it's hooked to them by a cable!"

Floyt wasn't the only one who'd spotted it, a long gleaming metal line the ship had paid out. In the flash of the running lights and spotlights, lines could be seen running from the other small ships to the large ones, or rather to something slung under the two brute cargo haulers, something like a shaped, skeletal crosshatch dome with long, hooked anchor prongs, four meters thick.

"A duralloy matrix," Alacrity said wonderingly. "They're here to plug a leak!"

"But we didn't position any charges here," Floyt reminded him.

Alacrity made a helpless gesture. "We must've weakened something, I guess."

They both looked to Paloma, who was smiling into the backwash of light from the construction operation as the matrix was lowered away, touching the lake's surface.

"Let's go get cleaned up," she said serenely, showing white teeth through her mud mask.

"That way," Floyt said, showing the direction. "About four days' easy march for you, you'll begin seeing members of another herd. Make sure you keep to cover, the way we taught you, until you find them, Pokesnout."

"Yes. Yes." Pokesnout looked that way. "Their scent will lead us to them."

"And the company won't notice that the gawks' numbers have increased?" Floyt frowned to Alacrity. Decline in population was, after all, a major reason for the company's leaving the gawklegs alone.

"Naw, not unless they start tagging and doing a detailed headcount," Alacrity said. "And even then, the numbers're gonna be lower than they were generations ago. At least until the two herds make friends—plus gestation, of course." He patted Treeneck's lowered muzzle.

"What will happen when you meet the other herd?" Floyt wanted to know. "Will you fight, Pokesnout?"

"Verities are Verities," Pokesnout pronounced with great composure. "It will be all right. Digger; Speed; dear Babyfat! We wish you well. All this is part of the Verities now, and so are you, for always."

Paloma hugged Pokesnout's neck as Floyt dried his eyes on his hand. "We'll do our best for you, on Shalimar; we'll get things changed as soon as we can," she promised.

There was more of the same, farewelling with Treeneck and Rockhorn. But Invictus would be up in half an hour, and the herd had to find shelter for the day.

"Take care, Pokesnout." Floyt squeezed the neck so thick that he couldn't get his arms around it. Pokesnout put the huge mouth that had saved Floyt's life over Floyt's shoulder, exerting infinitesimal pressure, an embrace.

The three bulls moved off after the rest of the herd, tails switching. In a few moments they were gone.

The various plans of action they'd worked out were all unnecessary, given the state of the company outpost when the worn trio made it there late the next day.

It had swollen to twenty times its former size, a make-shift workcamp crowded with exhausted construction and survey crews, overworked study teams, and exasperated, badly organized managerial types who gave contradictory orders based on conflicting information and cross purposes. It seemed the diverted lake drainage had also damaged a large dam and jeopardized a major company mining operation. The workcamp reminded Alacrity of a scuttle-death hive.

The three came into the place nonchalantly, their lances discarded and the top of Paloma's costume hidden under Floyt's jacket, her gunbelt slung over her shoulder beneath the jacket and her evening shawl wound around her middle. She and Alacrity each had one of the target pistols concealed on them, ready to try a bluff if they had to.

The first order of business was stealing worksuits, then finding out which of the shuttling airfreighters was leaving for Horselaugh next. Bumming a ride wasn't very hard; personnel, supplies, and equipment were being hauled *to* the improvised camp with all possible speed, but there was plenty of room on the return leg. Manifests, routing slips, passenger clearances, and all the usual security details had been brushed aside in the emergency. Paloma kept in the background, work helmet tilted low, as she, Alacrity, and Floyt climbed onto the cargo bed of the lugger and it lifted off.

From high up, Lake Fret was a collection of shrinking pools in a huge, baking mudflat.

Even Horselaugh was in a hoo-ha over the Lake Fret crisis, crews and equipment being tallied, vehicles jock-ied around for transshipment while apoplectic foremen and expediters got into shouting matches and purple-faced cargo masters tried to get a straight answer out of somebody. The only notice anyone took of the three arrivals was when a loading dock super screamed at them to get the hell out of her way so the robos could get the lugger's next cargo aboard.

They scrambled out and found themselves near a large freight gate, where the guards and scanners were so busy checking what was coming in that scant attention was paid to who was going out. A minute later the trio stood by a city intersection, blinking and looking around with not much less amazement than Pokesnout might have.

Alacrity spotted a day-date-time panel and was relieved to see that it matched his proteus in both local time and Standard. There was still time to make the White Ship meeting.

Somehow, through it all, Alacrity had hung onto most of the scrip he and Floyt got when they traded off Callisto's jeweled garter. He took the folded, wadded money, faded from assorted dunkings and salt-frosted from his sweat, from an inner pocket and bought a bottle of fortified fruit juice from a corner vending machine. All three drank deeply.

Paloma wanted to see what had happened at the Wicked Wickiup, but Alacrity vetoed the idea. "The company might still be keeping an eye on it, hoping you'll show up to explain things. Same with your town-house."

Floyt agreed with that; Paloma dropped the idea. "But I kept a sealed apt unit in a complex across town, under another name, a kind of safe house. And the rent's paid a year in advance. *That*, at least, damn well ought to be all right."

She pushed a summoner signal at the curb and the next groundcab that came along popped its gullwing doors for them. They piled in, still passing the fruit juice around. Eight minutes later they were at the apt. It wouldn't open to her palm ID. Paloma drew back a fist to hammer at the plate, but Alacrity caught it.

"Your paw's too grimy." He sloshed fruit juice on it, drying her palm against his chest, as she endured it stiffly. The lock opened on the second try.

The place was nothing extravagant, comfortably but sparsely furnished in Industrial-Mosque *Cosmique* in soft pastels, with a commanding view of the dreary company town. Paloma dashed to the bath chamber first, while Alacrity used the lavatory and Floyt rummaged through the kitchen storage, digging for vitamins and medicines as well as food and drink.

When Paloma emerged she was wearing a travel suit that might've been nondescript if it hadn't been on her. Alacrity and Floyt had shot glasses of ice-cold peppermint schnapps and were tossing back megavitamins and cramming cookies into their mouths. They'd found coveralls in her closets and jammed into them with only hasty washing-up, leaving their own clothes in a heap by a dispose-all.

They were now attentive to her media terminal, poring over a search program Floyt had set up to screen newsfiles, public announcements, police blotter reports, and similar sources.

Paloma accepted a drink, motioning to the bath. "Next? And what do you men say we throw about six or eight meals in the heater?"

"Uh-uh," Alacrity said. "We can eat in the *Whelk*, or grab something on the way." He motioned to the media terminal. "Nobody's looking for us, and you're just listed as missing. So grab whatever you're bringing and let's breeze. Next stop, Spica."

Paloma stopped in midmotion. "Spica?" Her brows met. "You mean Shalimar, *then* Spica, don't you? Or have you forgotten the gawks already?"

"I haven't forgotten. But they're safe for now. All that's just gonna have to keep for a while. Paloma, *I can't miss that board meeting!*"

"You won't!" she snapped. "But how long can it take

to put a bug in somebody's ear on Shalimar? They just need an excuse under Bali Hai Republic law to take Lebensraum away from the company, and we'll give it to them."

His mouth thinned to a ruled line. "And suppose Shalimar decides it needs us as witnesses or something, and locks us up? I'm not taking that chance."

"No, but you'll take a chance that somebody will notice the herd's moved and wipe it out, is that it? We might not get back for months! Anything could happen!"

Floyt was torn, knowing Alacrity's desperation and very real fear, but sharing Paloma's apprehensions for Pokesnout's people. "Alacrity—"

But Paloma drowned him out with her proteus's playback mode. The other two recognized it after a second, the gales and Precursor thunder of Hecate's lair. Even a recording sent needles of fear into Floyt's nerves but called up a Vision he regarded very differently, too.

"Beta-Thud-Actual-Tau-Hecate-Epsilon-Kl'marth-Manila," said the crazy woman's voice.

Paloma shut it off. "And I've got the share numbers, too. Now, we can go after the White Ship as allies or as enemies, Alacrity, and if you don't help me do right by the herd, you'll be making the choice. But crooks should stick together."

He fought the urge to hit her, was nearly driven to it. She saw it in his eyes but stood her ground. He was in an attack posture, face scarlet.

"Crook?" he shrilled. "Call me crook? The White Ship's mine and my family's!"

"That's what everybody on that board claims: *'It's mine!'* " she howled right back at him. "You think you're unique? The only one claiming divine right?"

"Yes." He'd gotten hold of himself so suddenly at what she'd said that it left her, flushed and quick-breathing, alone and off-balance on the field of battle. "Yes, that's dead-center correct, Paloma. All right, then: Shalimar."

She looked doubtfully to Floyt. He nodded; he'd

never known Alacrity to break his word to a friend. She lowered her proteus. Alacrity and Paloma inspected one another, then dropped their gazes.

"I don't have much to bring," she told Floyt. "I'd like to pick up some things from my townhouse, but—"

Something occurred to her and she touched out a commo call, leaving the visual pickup off at her end. A face appeared, one of the Heads of Cerberus, her bodyguards from the Wickiup. He spoke at once.

"Condition shog, here. Fallback bromide." The image was still for a moment, then repeated the code exactly. Floyt saw then that it was a loop.

Paloma broke the connection. "Well, the police aren't hunting me, but I'll have to stay away from the townhouse. Legal trouble, I expect. That's life; the gang will handle things until I get back."

She pulled on a flight jacket, quickly stuffing this and that into her pockets while Alacrity and Floyt gobbled up the rest of the pack of cookies and opened a box of chocolates. Paloma ate some, too.

Alacrity saw that she had a number of cash drafts and credit plaques, and assumed she had the moonpure fillet with her as well. In a few minutes they were cabbing to the starport.

At the terminal entrance, Paloma dumped a handful of candy into a pocket and went walking off without a backward glance. Floyt and Alacrity raised their eyebrows to each other, then entered, Alacrity's brolly *tok*king the hard floor with its ferrule cap back on.

Outprocessing was a lot less rigorous than inprocessing. Floyt exchanged their scrip for Bali Hai currency at a much less favorable rate than conversion the other way. As Alacrity waited, he studied the displays listing ships in port: status, destination, port of origin, and so forth.

Fortunately the partners' visas hadn't expired and still showed gold in the computer system. The only hitch was when an officer reviewed Floyt's initial declaration to make sure the Inheritor's belt wasn't some kind of smuggled artifact. Take-off and field access clearances from the Bali Hai officials were *pro forma*.

They walked out across the wet hardtop of the grounding area under floodlights, slick rainbows of spilled lube splashed here and there under their boots. A few freighters and ore-lifters were around, and lit with worklights and preparing to make weigh, a beat-up ten-passenger intrasystem shuttle was being serviced. The *Lightning Whelk* rested where they'd left her, a contoured, tired old seashell in the glare.

As the pair walked along, a shadow separated itself from others and joined them. "Made it, huh?" Alacrity grunted.

Paloma chuckled, twirling a lock of hair around her glamornailed finger. "Oh, that Tepilit—he always had an eye for my second-best sunstreamer choker. Shall we go?"

She took Floyt's arm to head for the *Whelk*, but Alacrity stood in their way. He gestured with his head to the interplanetary shuttle.

"She's lifting for Shalimar in three hours," he said. "I checked while we were processing. You'll be there in eight hours, Paloma. If you don't have the fare, we'll give it to you. She's a Shalimar vessel, so once you're inboard your troubles are over and the company can't fool with you."

She spoke slowly, stunned. "Your word never meant anything to you. You don't care shit about Pokesnout or the herd or anything, do you?"

Floyt groped, "Alacrity—"

But Alacrity cleaved the air with his hand. "Think what you like! I promised Shalimar, and that's where you're going. But I have to get to Spica *now*, not later."

Her lips were drawn back, teeth locked. "And you end up with one less competitor, how perfect, eh? What if I say, 'Fine, let's up-ship for Spica?' And we make it back and find the company's wiped out all the gawks? Could you live with it?"

Alacrity met her stare. "I can't help any of that."

Floyt, a deep breath held, let it out and set himself in front of Alacrity before Paloma could launch herself at him. "This is beneath you. And it's pointless; the White Ship isn't going to be yours, Alacrity. Ever."

Alacrity drew his chin back and aside a bit, as if Floyt had taken a swing at him. "Listen, I know how you feel about Pokesnout, but—"

"The White Ship won't be yours! So stop deluding yourself and at least help someone who's helped you!"

"God *damn* you, Ho, I don't have time to get into this with you right now—"

"Oh, yes you do! You were wrong about the causality harp! Shall I tell you why? Because you saw what you wanted to see! Alacrity, I changed the input before you went out on the gantry and touched the harp. Is this getting through to you? *The harp was answering a different question!*"

Alacrity was breathing as heavily as if he'd just run to Horselaugh from the Precursor site, or fought an army of enemies. He was long moments answering. He sounded almost calm.

"It's Paloma, isn't it? Go; go with her. I don't blame either of you, I mean that! I'll come back for you if I can. Or send somebody if you prefer..."

Floyt went to throw himself at his friend. "You're not some kind of avatar! Your family failed and you'll fail! *I'm not letting you get away with betraying people and wronging them just so you can live some fantasy!*"

But Floyt's grasping hands missed because Paloma pulled him back, restraining him. She was taller than Floyt, strong, and, moreover, had gotten him in some sort of very effective hold. He couldn't shake her loose.

"It's no use, Hobie! He heard Fate play his tune on that harp!"

"*I don't care if he heard Krishna blow it through a tuba for him!*"

Alacrity caught one of Floyt's clawing hands and slapped the rest of their cash into it. "You two're gonna need this more than me. I'm lifting as soon as the

Whelk's warmed up." He hesitated. "You're gonna be great together." He pivoted and went off.

Floyt subsided, watching him go; Paloma eased off her grip. "God, I hate it when he acts noble," Floyt seethed. "Worse than when he acts like a shitheel, even! Did you hear him? *Exit speeches!*"

Paloma hummed a short laugh. "You'd better get moving, Hobie."

He spun on her. "But—the herd—"

"Oh, I guess I can handle that. No, let's be honest: I know I can. But I'm not so sure you two can deal with whatever he's about to get you into, so watch yourself."

Floyt clasped handfuls of his thinning hair. "He wasn't always like this, you have to trust me." He felt like weeping. "He didn't leave me to fend for myself when he could have and had every right to. And maybe should have, given what's happened since."

"If you say so, citizen. You'd best get going, before he raises without you. But I *mean* this—"

And Paloma Sudan put her arms around Floyt's neck and put her lips close to his, so that he inhaled her sweet breath. "I almost made the wrong pick, there, once or twice, Hobart. I hope we find each other again. I want that a lot."

He had her in his arms and kissed her, embracing forcefully, just as content to make it a grinding, snail-tongued kiss as she was. It conveyed more feeling, meaning, and intent than any other language Floyt knew. The world pinwheeled.

And they were apart. She caressed his cheek; he kissed the palm of her hand. Then she was just beyond his reach, pulling up the collar of her flight jacket. Paloma made for the shuttle, heels clacking on the hardtop. He watched her until she'd disappeared up the boarding ramp, but she never looked back.

Alacrity had left the *Whelk*'s hatch open; Floyt secured it behind him. An odor caught his notice as he moved cockpitward, and he traced it to the minuscule ship's head. The smell of undertow hung above the basin and drain. The empty bottle was in the refuse bin.

Floyt seated himself on the pulldown jumpseat, saying nothing, watching Alacrity ready the *Whelk* for lift-off.

"We forgot to lay in supplies," Alacrity said after a while, still tending his boards. "We'll be on emergency spansules most of the way."

"Alacrity—"

Alacrity swung the pilot's chair around to face Floyt, control banks and instrument panels automatically moving out of his way. He'd seen the farewell kiss from the bridge, realizing that nothing had happened between Floyt and Paloma on the entire Long Trek, and didn't know what to think or say.

"Look, please, Ho...you're the best friend I've ever had, that's all I have to tell you. But—let's not talk for a while, okay?"

Floyt settled back in his seat to wait, as the starship's engines came up.

CHAPTER 15

DAMNED IF WE DON'T

AND SO AT LAST, SPICA. FIRST MAGNITUDE JEWEL OF the Virgin; blue, short-lived supergiant; homeplace of the mightiest Precursor work yet confirmed: the Carousel. Twenty-three E-type paradise worlds in a single impossible orbit, blazing gems in an imperial diadem, with no clues as to how the trick was done, confounding and enrapturing *Homo sapiens* (and incidentally giving lots of people the conviction that their species was the Chosen of the Precursors).

Spica, in the wrong place on the Hertzprung-Russell diagrams for its impossible brood, centerpiece of the human race in the wake of the Final Smear—the disastrous climax of the Human—Srillan War—at least until hapless, harried Hobart Floyt and misadventuring Alacrity Fitzhugh brought the Camarilla conspiracy down around the ears of some of the most powerful individuals in known space.

Floyt and Alacrity weren't precisely back on their old footing, but their friendship had held and the tension was mostly gone. Floyt had tried to broach the matter of the causality harp only once during the trip; Alacrity refused to discuss it. Floyt gave the matter long and deep contemplation and then resigned himself that what would happen would happen.

The *Lightning Whelk* left Hawking with Alacrity prepared to point out a few of Spica's spectacular sights once he got his bearings and took care of the checking-in yangtwang the rules required. But the half-ducat sightseeing tour wasn't to be.

"Holy Shiva's snatch!"

"Alacrity, what *is* this? We've stumbled into a war, is that it?"

"Dunno yet. Sit tight." He was displaying more information on the media-mosaic, assigning the commo system to monitor and cull, to give him some idea what was going on. In the meantime, Floyt gazed by means of scopes and the late Plantos's vision enhancers at several flotillas of warships floating in the vicinity of Nirvana, the system's capital and most populous world, power base of the Spican sphere of influence.

Floyt couldn't resist gaping a bit. Strung along in that same orbit were Xanadu, Heaven, Utopia, Eden, and the rest, worlds that had no business being there except that the Precursors had seen fit to arrange things so. As for the warships, they appeared to represent a number of different governments or factions, but there were also an awful lot of Spican Navy battlecraft on the prowl and at full alert.

Alacrity had no time to spiel about Spica's tremendous energy runes, or the Five Great Anomalies, or the Shepherd Forces; he was venting spleen at the commo rig. "*Psjakrew cholera!* The White Ship Corporation's under a news and commo blackout as of yesterday! What *is* all this with our awful timing, anyway?"

The Spican Military was at max alert in part because of the upcoming board meeting and the visiting flotillas that were permitted then by law; it seemed several major shakeups were in the offing among the Interested Parties. (*Wait'll they hear* my *scoop!* Alacrity sneered to himself.) But a lot of the furor had to do with another vessel that had shown up.

News pickups showed the starship in a holding position down near Spica itself, in a more or less stationary spot relative to Nirvana and the White Ship, Alacrity noticed queasily. It was bigger than the White Ship, bigger than anything humans had ever made, and bigger than many of the worlds they inhabited.

"You just don't see many of those," Alacrity told Floyt a little numbly.

"What is it? It looks like—I don't know; some great big radiolarian made out of glow-filament, maybe?"

"For all anybody knows, you're right. That's a Heavyset starship. The Heavysets've never been much interested in what humans are doing, and if you ask me it was safer for us that way. But here they are."

"And, 'By the pricking of my thumbs...'" Floyt quoted quietly, face lit by the displays.

"Huh? Oh, never mind! What in God's own data bank are Heavysets doing around Spica? Almost *in* Spica?"

Floyt bunched his shoulders and dropped them to show he couldn't supply the answer. "You're asking the wrong person. Maybe they heard we were coming?"

"Not funny. Look, there's no time for tourism; Nirvana Control's calling. Let's get down there and see what we can find out."

"If the Precursors could do this," Floyt said meditatively, scanning the magnificent Carousel as Alacrity made his approach, "and if they could make the causality harp and the Biomass of Rigel and all the things reports claim—if they could do that, then tell me why they never did any of the things mankind is still trying to do. Dyson spheres, and all the rest of that."

Alacrity made an impatient, nonanalytical sound, most of his concentration on his instruments. He wanted to holler at Floyt for not worrying about what *he* was worrying about. But they were more circumspect toward each other in the wake of the Lebensraum business.

So he said, "Why build high-density housing on Mount Fuji if a hermit's hut is what you really want? And all you need?"

When Nirvana Control came up, typically stern and condescending, for final approach, the little, outdated, ragtag *Whelk* was treated to some of the famous local surliness. Until, that is, Alacrity gave Control a business-affairs visa request accompanied by an ID code based on his White Ship stockholder's registration.

There was, as far as he'd been able to find out, no other Interested Party—no shareholder in the White Ship Corporation—who held fewer than ten thousand shares; few, indeed, all told. And for a generation, every other attendee at board meetings had been a mover and shaker on a scale transcending mere interstellar governments and alliances.

So there were perquisites and prerogatives in place for *any* Interested Party. Nirvana Control came back with a lot more verve then, jumping the *Whelk* to the front of the line for her landing, respectfully giving her a prime grounding spot and best wishes for a safe setdown.

Groundside, Alacrity and Floyt made no bones about having been through tough times. They stepped from the scarred, contoured snailshell of a ship in working clothes that had seen better days, Alacrity with his warbag and umbrella, and drew deep, satisfying breaths. Spica shone gargantuan and blue, its harmful radiation filtered out by the same human-friendly atmosphere that enveloped all the Carousel worlds.

There was no point trying to use aliases; in the Spican system they were famous and notorious, prominent in the scandal and fallout surrounding the Camarilla unpleasantness, which had already resulted in the imprisonment and in some cases the execution of dozens of important men and women. The Spican customs people didn't have much reason to delay them, except for a very courteous inspection to make sure Floyt's Inheritor's belt was on his declaration statement. Everyone was polite and in fact quite jolly; matters were concluded with dash.

The two friends asked no questions about the White Ship Corporation and deflected the few oblique ones that were asked them. Interested Party status won Alacrity —and Floyt, in the bargain—a permit to carry weapons, much harder to come by on Nirvana than on Luna. One thing it didn't overcome was woefully low exchange rate for their Bali Hai currency. Alacrity brushed the issue aside like it was pin money instead of the last cash he and Floyt had. Floyt concluded that it was the way in which an Interested Party was expected to behave.

A liaison officer was eager to get them conveyance to the White Ship Corporation's Nirvana headquarters but Alacrity declined; the two didn't dare go among enemies —especially *certain* former enemies—until they'd seen to a very critical item on their agenda. Alacrity grabbed his bag and he and Floyt boarded the golden VIP swan-boat that had been assigned to take them wherever they wished in the terminal complex.

Alacrity's first stop was a bonded warehouse, where he used a code in his proteus to claim a storage strongbox. "You left luggage here?" Floyt asked.

Alacrity shook his head. "My old man did, long time ago. So I could show the colors, I guess you could say."

Alacrity took the box and they proceeded to a rental spa. There they cleaned up thoroughly, lolling in it after the very limited comforts and conveniences of the *Whelk*. Floyt emerged from the max-regimen's abuses and indulgences, icewater-hosed and automassaged, pore-purged and at peace with Creation, to behold an Alacrity he hadn't seen before.

"Good lord! You're an admiral? What time is the parade?"

"Awright, awright," Alacrity growled, but most of his attention was on the figure he cut in the vanity imager, adjusting his waist-length jacket.

He wore a captain's uniform of midnight blue spectra-flex, heavy with gold trim—embroidery and brocade, floral stitching, fourragères at the shoulder, gleaming piping along the seams of his tight trousers. There were stripes of rank at his cuff, and on his stiff, high collar were insignia: the arc-and-cross symbol of the White Ship, same as the ones on the yellowed ivory grips of the Captain's Sidearm.

Floyt began donning the tuxedo the roboflunky system had prepared so exactingly to his specifications. "Well, at least we look the part—until someone hands us the bill."

"Moth balls!" Alacrity said, misusing a Terranism he'd come across. He checked minutely in the imager to make sure his cleaned and burnished pathfinders looked right with the uniform.

"I'm an Interested Party, Ho, remember? It says so on my visa. That's good for a lot of credit, if you know how to work it." Alacrity buckled the shoulder strap of his Sam Browne belt, settling his father's pistol.

Once more Floyt was into his tailcoat, his stiff shirt and wing collar and white tie resplendent. His dancing pumps gleaming like polished onyx; he made sure the Webley was comfortable under his left armpit. His Inheritor's belt didn't clash with the outfit; the barbaric splendor of it somehow set off the impact of his Terran wondersuit.

"You mean we don't have to live in the *Whelk*, or a packing crate?" Floyt sounded amazed, adjusting his tie. The exact starting time of the meeting hadn't been announced yet, since those in charge were waiting to see who would attend. That left an uncertain amount of time to fill.

"Never again," Alacrity pronounced, fluffing the fringes on his shoulderboards. "Life's too good to waste on mere survival."

An hour later, two stretch skylimos set down at the 250th floor landing stage of the Sceptered Isle, the best hotel on Nirvana and, in fact, a chartered duchy under local laws. The stage was crowded with the wealthy and privileged, the preeminent and astoundingly attractive. Dress ranged from depilated nudity to what looked like radiation suits; nonhumans abounded in outfits impossible to classify. Live porters sprang to offload the mounds of baggage stowed in the second stretch; the first carried passengers only, of course—two of them—since respectable people simply didn't ride with luggage. The steamer trunks, cased systemry, portmanteaus, pressurized containers, valises, data troves, and reinforced lockboxes passed from hand to hand to gravcart.

Floyt and Alacrity stepped forth into Spica's blue glory, the Inheritor's belt glinting against the high white and deep black of the tux suit, the White Ship captain's uniform speaking for itself with its insignia. They drew every eye there.

Conversations stopped midsyllable and people froze like statues. Everyone knew who they were from popular penny-dreadfuls and from the newsspews. An erotiholo star who'd been getting healthy press coverage of his departure found himself abandoned by the reporters; mediaghouls flocked to the tall, lean-faced young man with the pistol on his hip and the Earthman with his air of authority and *class*.

Alacrity and Floyt got a perceptible nod of the head from the doorman, a looming, bioengineered Cossack of a man from Moloch who seldom deigned to give the run-of-the-mill tyrants or power brokers the raise of an eyebrow. Alacrity returned a Prussian dip of the head and Floyt a generous half smile.

The Wicked Wickiup would've fit in the lobby of the Sceptered Isle with room to spare for a trade fair. It was a tech-deco cavern, oozing a swank exclusivity that scorned the merely filthy rich. The lobby was busy in spite of—or perhaps because of—the hotel's severe admittance policies.

Their faces caused a minor upheaval among the otherwise unflappable clerks at the registration desk even before Alacrity showed his Interested Party visa. The two sidekicks were duly and almost instantly signed in, their luggage ushered away to a prime-class suite in the Imperial Domain tower. Floyt nearly had a fainting spell when he got a quick glimpse of the rates; Alacrity didn't even glance at them.

To cover his nervousness, Floyt plucked a gorgeous, outrageously costly blossom from an art-display floral arrangement, sniffing it ecstatically and inserting it in his lapel as a boutonniere. His pretended confidence was such that nobody thought to comment for fear of looking gauche.

It took stubborn insistence and an additional tip to convince the concierge that they preferred to find their own way to their own suite. Alacrity took Floyt's elbow and indicated the banks of guest liftshafts and shoot-chutes and carriers on the other side of a lobby the size of an amusement park. The scale of things was important; being noted and admired promenading around it was, for most guests, one of the main draws of the Isle.

Alacrity waved away whisk-platforms and flying lounge modules, preferring to walk. For one thing, it was a good time to start attracting a certain notoriety. For another, he liked floor level for the cover and fields of fire it offered, even though the hotel's security was legendary, and he doubted an ambush (or at least, a very good one) could be set up in so short a time.

He thought he had everything under control, but an unexpected hand settled onto one of his brocaded shoulderboards. Alacrity whirled, pulse hammering; he'd been just about sure nobody would try anything in the lobby.

She was, in Floyt's experience, short for a non-Terran, a few centimeters under his own height, slim and fragile looking, with a high-crested shako hairstyle in rust red and an all-over coat of zebra pattern dermafrosting that made her look like something good to eat. Her eyes were covered by a high-fashion wraparound commo visor. She wore minimal soleskins and no jewelry; Alacrity couldn't see any weapons, but that didn't mean she wasn't well furnished.

"Waitwaitwait," she hastened. Alacrity, taking in her charms, let himself be importuned for a moment, there close by a pillar that resembled Waterford crystal. Floyt stood by with watchful curiousity, not missing the fact that his friend opened the thumbbreak over his pistol, and all the while Alacrity smiled right back at the girl like a Cheshire cat.

"You're going to the Imperial Domain?" she asked anxiously, almost vibrating. "You'll be living up there next to Circe Minx's place?"

"Flash that one past me again?" Alacrity wasn't quite sure he should shoot her, Floyt saw with relief.

"Circe Minx! *Circe Minx!*" she hissed with quiet annoyance. "Where've *you* been living, sport? In a cachesleep wrapper? Circe canceled her reservation at the Babylon and checked in here to shake the press. She wanted the whole Domain, but somebody else has the western suite and that's you, right? You'll be up where Circe Minx is?"

"Oh, she's the—" Floyt chose the word diplomatically. "Celebrity" would've done, but a lot of people would've substituted, variously, "sex icon," "siren," and in some cases, "hoyden."

"—actress?" Floyt finished.

"Aw, yeah, yeah," Alacrity placed the name. "So?"

"So, Circe Minx just got through diz-bonding her marriage to those three clone brothers she found on Tara," the zebra-hide said. "My name is Salome Price! If my network gets an exclusive on who her new dunk is, it'll mean a ten-point audience jump!"

Alacrity was by then fending her off. "Sorry, kid; I've got no idea what—"

Salome Price was fast, Floyt saw, as fast as she was hungry. She pressed an info-wafer into Alacrity's palm. "Attend: you tip me to anything you see or find out up there and I'll make it worth your while! I'll split the bounty!"

A reference to money got Alacrity's undivided attention. "Start again; what is it that you want to—"

He forgot what he was going to say next as a hand the size of a buzzball mitt closed on her shoulder. All around the three were big, alert, well-dressed men and women. They had the air of hotel security, but they were much tougher and more agile looking than most of the breed that Alacrity had seen before.

"You know the rules," a square-jawed, handsome

killer-type said to the scandal-hound. "You stay off the premises or we punish you." He and a woman had the girl secure with pinpoint nerveholds. She knew enough not to move.

"Nah, nah, it's all right," Alacrity intervened. "My mistake. Suppose she just leaves and we forget it, huh?"

The security people looked to their leader, the one who'd grabbed the newsghoul first, for a sign. He looked eye to eye with Alacrity for a second, then nodded. His crew closed in to escort the girl away. She was gazing at Alacrity, truly seeing him for the first time.

"Hey, hold on!" Salome Price breathed. "I know you! You're . . . Fitzhugh! And that's Floyt! Oh, Allah, Captain Fitzhugh, I want to talk to you!" She struggled. "Leggo!" The security crew paid no heed and in seconds she was gone.

The crew boss turned to Alacrity and Floyt, giving them an understanding smile; they mirrored it right back at him. The man apologized on behalf of himself and the Sceptered Isle. They assured him he should think no more about it.

He cleared his throat, hand going to the structured marsupial pocket of his expensive suit, which movement didn't *quite* make Alacrity reach for his gun again. "If you wouldn't mind, Captain Fitzhugh; Mr. Floyt? For myself and my severalmates and even more for the kids, you understand."

He held a slim, costly qwikgraf and a copy of *Hobart Floyt and Alacrity Fitzhugh Versus the PSI-Mongers of the Yodeling Wormhole*.

The western half of the Imperial Domain and its lift were theirs, the eastern belonging to Circe Minx and her entourage.

"I always like a sunset view," Alacrity explained.

The lift wasn't an elevator or chute; nothing so common belonged in a Domain of the Sceptered Isle. Alacrity and Floyt stood on a polished disc of semiprecious stone called tidalquartz, from Adam's Apple. It was fifty meters across and it began rising and kept doing so, past shaft walls lined with art objects and stained glass—so many things that Floyt couldn't begin to take them all in though he trotted this way and that trying, head swiveling.

"You're not supposed to." It came to him after a while. "Become familiar with all of this, I mean."

"First of all, who could afford to stay here that long, Ho? Besides, I guess the management would get some new stuff in here if it came to that. Novelty, y'know; big selling point. What good's money if you're bored?"

After a time the column stopped at a higher level with a giant round door like an old-fashioned camera shutter before it, a genuine antique. They were in a vaulted rotunda with friezes, niched statuary, paintings, mosaics, and lightshapes, its ceiling open to the sky, and a marquetted floor that was a study in exotic woods. Here and there around the walls discreet illuminated symbols marked accessways to quick-transport systems for guests in a hurry.

Alacrity was opening his uniform collar and unbuckling the Sam Browne. The senior bellhop and his four assistants, in uniforms as elaborate as Alacrity's, stood by at attention. Them Alacrity tipped lavishly too, with just about all that he and Floyt had left. The bellhops were all smiles as they disappeared into a service chute.

Floyt stared glumly at the sad little sum they had left. "We may have to *walk* from here on in."

Alacrity brushed that aside as the shutter door unspiraled for them. "From here on in we don't *pay* for anything, Ho. We *sign* for it."

"What happens when the bill comes due?"

Alacrity halted, looking around. He wasn't sure the place was wired; the Isle also had a reputation for scrupulous discretion, and most wealthy guests' staff-members would routinely sweep and debug their accommodations. Still, it was wise to be careful. He tapped his proteus. "They know an Interested Party's always good for it, and I am."

Floyt understood then that Alacrity already considered Hecate's inactive shares to be his own. Alacrity went on, "Besides, they know we've got the *Whelk*, and a starship's sound security *anywhere*. And you can bet that crate's not moving a millimeter until we settle our tab."

They entered the foyer of their suite, the western half of the Imperial Domain tower's top seven floors, as Alacrity slung his gunbelt over his shoulder. "And what's more, our luggage is here."

The windows were ten meters high, a whole wall of them showing glorious Spica and Nirvana's capital city, Avalon. The drawing room was just a short hike from there, considerably bigger and brighter, with an exactingly flawless formal garden overlooking the city. The whole place was done in sinister, unrelentingly expensive Fantasia-*Robotíque-Noir*. A lot of the furniture was built to heroic scale: chairs big enough for two; beds of triple length and quadruple width.

They explored, and found the place easy to get lost in, especially up by the sybaritorium and down in the servants' quarters. The main kitchen, pantries, various bars, and room larders were stocked to capacity. There were no guides or directories, since there was supposed to be a full-time staff of five. Alacrity had insisted that they be absented from the suite, more of his natural wariness. The concierge made it clear that the rate was the same regardless, but that full-time personal assistance was available by hotline, round the clock, to do, explain, obtain, or assist in anything.

Their clothes and other luggage had been unpacked and stowed. Floyt found that funny. The closetsful of offworld garments, many of them only generally Floyt and Alacrity's size; the safelike security modules and lockboxes loaded with paperweights and gravel; esoteric alien artifacts—all those had been bought only that afternoon in pawnshops, thrift exchanges, and recycling operations along Rocket Row, outside the starport.

"The sight of a mountain of luggage gives your hotel

people a nice, secure feeling," Alacrity had explained during the shopping spree.

"What's next?" Floyt asked, loosening his snowy bowtie and undoing his top shirtstud, the wing collar flapping open. "Do we take care of—*you* know..."

"First item. I've got a few calls to make. Maybe you could find out why the White Ship board's so jumpy."

Floyt began accessing and orchestrating in the main information studio while Alacrity disappeared to find another commo terminal. By the time Alacrity got back twenty minutes later, his jacket open, Floyt had not only reviewed and winnowed down a large body of information about items of interest but had also located the studio's autobar and had it mix him a meltdown. Alacrity requisitioned a double and joined him.

"There's absolutely no word on what that Heavyset's doing here," Floyt updated him. "But people are worried because nothing like this has ever happened before. Heart and Dincrist haven't arrived yet, though there are still references to a falling-out between them.

"And there's something else. It appears a person by the name of Reno Magusson has died, a major shareholder—"

"*The* major shareholder," Alacrity said flatly. "He didn't like Dincrist, but I think his heirs do. *Bagaya-ro!*" He took a long pull on his drink.

But Floyt was shaking his head angrily. "Will you *listen*, for once? Magusson was sick for a long time, some neurological thing they couldn't pin down."

"Ah, the old sod lived twice as long as he should've anyway," Alacrity said, then made a hasty placating gesture to Floyt. "Sorry! What else?"

"He didn't leave his White Ship stock to his family or any of those, that's what. There was a therapist-holician with an experimental treatment, and she'd kept him alive for almost a year through constant work. All the shares went to her."

A face appeared on a screen, a brown-skinned woman who appeared to be past middle age but still struck Alacrity as strong and canny, even a little fierce, with peppermint-striped hair cut short. It looked like a shot out of a professional journal or 'cast; she wore a pearly clinician's tunic with doctor's insignia and red-starburst medical patches.

"You're looking at Dr. Sibyl Higgins, specialist in pansystemic therapy, behavioral allopathy, and neurological wholism healing."

"Doesn't sound very specialized to me, Ho."

"I confess not to understand what it means either," Floyt replied. "But Magusson's revised will was held valid and impervious, so it appears that Dr. Higgins is the new power to reckon with. I'm pulling all relevant data now—"

He was interrupted by an autosignal, the suite's private landing stage being requested for clearance. Alacrity gave it. "C'mon; we can go through that stuff later. I've got somebody you're gonna like knowing."

The main landing stage was just outside the drawing room. It was chilly and the wind snapped and tangled their hair. Floyt would've described the man who emerged from the robocab as unhealthily vibrant. His movements were quick but jittery, skin pale and papery although his cheeks were ruddy. His eyes were animated but glassy.

The cargo compartment of the cab was loaded with equipment cannisters and automachinery, and the new arrival carried a shoulder bag. "Still burning that candle bright, huh, Doc?" Alacrity asked him, offering his hand.

The man didn't take offense; the hand that grasped Alacrity's was thin and white, glittery with rings and bracelets. "They're executing you at dawn? I can't think of another reason you'd be getting this treatment, Alacrity."

"I won an election bet. Oh, and this is Hobart Floyt. Good man."

The doctor eyed Floyt. "That's not what the erstwhile Prosecutor-General said when they flash-fried him for being a Camarilla member. Nice to meet you, Citizen Floyt."

His hand was moist and very warm, its tremble broadcasting misgivings directly into Floyt's brain. Alacrity grinned. "Ho, say hello to Nils Van Straaten, the only MD I know who gives refunds. Providing you're well enough to sign a receipt. Nils, can we give you a hand with your ballast there?"

Van Straaten took a deep breath of something from an inhaler. The twitching lessened at once. "To be sure; I also brought that, ah, special gear we discussed. Where shall we work?"

"Um, what about the drawing room, there?"

"No objections. Shall we spread a dropcloth or do you think bloodstains will come out of the carpet?"

The three men muscled the cargo inside. Under Van Straaten's direction, they set up medical apparatus all around the drawing room, but no dropcloths. The cab was ordered to wait, a command it was programmed to accept on a Sceptered Isle landing stage. The good doctor had also fetched along a variety of debugging modules and seekers. The seekers cruised off through the air like so many levitating spider crabs while Alacrity and Floyt and Van Straaten plugged scan modules into all the suite systemry.

The place read clean; the trio got down to cases. Van Straaten scanned the two friends with a selection of detectors and analyzers. "Nasty." He clucked.

"We already know," Alacrity replied tightly. "Can you find 'em and can you get 'em out?"

The doctor looked surprised. "But of course. And I don't even have to dissect you to do it. All I meant was, whoever implanted those actijots in you two was devilish." He was pulling long, baggy white skinfilm gloves up past his elbows, like opera gloves.

Van Straaten looked from one to the other. "Who's first in the barrel?"

"Her name was Constance, and she was sicker than

most people I ever saw running around loose," Alacrity said. "And I'm first. Jacket and shirt off?"

Van Straaten had activated the gloves' microfields. They tightened up, lumpy over his sleeves but like a coat of spraypaint on his hands, his jewelry sharply outlined. "Take it all off if you care to, but it's the pants that have to go. This Constance really had it in for you, eh?"

"Nothin' *I* ever did," Alacrity grumbled, dropping his trousers. Van Straaten, running a sterilizer over his gloves, laughed.

On their way to Blackguard, a kind of perverse sporting preserve owned by certain Third Breath notables, Floyt and Alacrity had, while unconscious, been furnished with the tiny internal actijots that let them be traced, punished, and controlled with all-embracing pain, and that would have executed them if things had gone a little differently.

The companions-in-mishap had no idea where their jots were located. Every muscle spasm, nerve twitch, and itch was a possibility, inviting the crudest kind of surgery. There were horror stories about people lopping off a foot or tongue or whatever, hoping to escape, only to find out they'd guessed wrong.

Dincrist, Heart's father and sworn enemy of Alacrity and Floyt, was one of Blackguard's rulers. Possibly other White Ship shareholders were as well. It would only take the brush of a jot control unit's beam to kill them both or, probably worse, make them slaves again. The jots had to go before they could come to grips with the White Ship meeting.

The doctor picked up a thing like an ultratech puppeteer's handset, instrumented and fitted with complex controls. Radiant, infinitely fine wires issued from it, curling and corkscrewing and straightening again as though alive. Alacrity held still while Van Straaten beamed a desensitizer on the subject area.

Floyt decided he didn't want to watch and sat over at the bar, prescribing himself another meltdown. Van Straaten donned an involved goggle-headgear affair and jacked its leads into the handset, concentrating on his work.

"What d'you know about this Sibyl Higgins, Nils?" Alacrity asked, to pass the time.

"Stop talking or I'll knock you out and lock you in clamps," Van Straaten said distractedly. A moment later he added, "A tough old bird, Higgins. Director of the Nirvana Med Institute and became incensed over some new policies, so she quit and went back into private practice. And made that Magusson connection, of course."

Van Straaten straightened, pushed the visor up, and switched off his handset. "She spent ten years as night-shift supervisor in the penal system behavioral allopathy clinic, *that's* how tough Higgins is, kiddo! All right, Hobart; we're ready for you now."

As Alacrity hoisted his dashing trousers back up again, Floyt put down his drink and steeled himself, putting a hand to his second shirt stud, his open collar wings bobbing. His forehead glistened. "Where—ahem; what shall I, ah, remove?"

"Mmm? Oh, nothing, nothing. Keep your clothes on and just come sit down over here in front of me and don't jump around, that's all."

In another moment Van Straaten had fitted an intricate servomounted mask device over Floyt's head, making it fast. Floyt sat, seeing nothing, hearing perfectly, experiencing no pain but knowing tiny fibers were probing and worming within his eyes.

"So what's the penal alleotropic whatchamacallit?" Alacrity demanded.

Van Straaten's voice had that distracted sound again. "The behavioral allopathy clinic? Let's just say the cases nobody else can handle end up there. And if an aide or restraining mechanism is even a millimeter too far away, they're sufficiently far away to get you killed. So all clinicians take continuing martial arts training from the Strike Recondo masters and get combat enhancements. The works. I was consulting there one time and I saw this tiny ward nurse who probably bought her clothes in the kids' department fold up a brain-scrolled berserker like she was just pushing buttons. Dispassionate precision and, oh my, was she ever fast! And your Dr. Higgins, well, she was—"

"—shift supervisor, nights, ten years," Alacrity anticipated. "But I mean, what about her? Herself?"

The mask pulled away and Floyt was silently elated that his eyes worked again. Van Straaten scanned him, then patted his knee. "You're clean, sir."

He turned to Alacrity, accepting a frosted martini glass. "I don't have a clue, really, about Higgin's setup. Bit of a martinet, I seem to recall." He pulled out a different inhaler and took a wheeze off it. His eyes grew brighter.

"Um, Doctor, might I have that jot as a souvenir?" Floyt asked.

Van Straaten's grin was very wide as his thumb caressed the inhaler. "I could sift it out from the disposal unit for you, I suppose, but—where would you keep it? You could lose it in a *pore*, dammit, Mr. Floyt."

"Ah. Anyway, thank you; you know how much you've done for us."

Alacrity was at the nearest transactions terminal as Floyt and Van Straaten shook hands. "Business for a second, here. What d'we owe you, Nils?"

Van Straaten, putting his equipment away, stopped to look at him. He said very slowly, almost unwillingly, "I would say that I am still in *your* debt, Alacrity."

Alacrity's mouth curved down, bracketing. "Or my father's, huh? Look, it's all on the tab, Nils, but the hotel will pay you up front and give itself a healthy service fee. Besides, I'm an Interested Party in the White Ship."

Van Straaten rubbed his hands together, going for the terminal. "Well, in *that* case . . ."

A few minutes later they'd shaken hands all around, Van Straaten admitting, "I don't even know what to caution you about, Alacrity; Hobart. But do be cautious. And I'll tell you one other thing I heard about La Higgins: Precursor sects, White Ship Company, crime *aparatchiks*—she's got her reasons to hate them all, and she *does*. That Reno Magusson, he must've had *some* sense of humor!"

Just like Weir, when he named me in his will, it occurred to Floyt.

"And there's that Heavyset starship and the whole Dincrist/Heart square-off," Van Straaten was saying. "Don't forget what I'm telling you, boys: the fangs are showing, and you're not a very big bite, I think."

Then the cab was lifting away over Avalon, which was coming alive with light as dusk came on. "More news updates?" Floyt proposed.

"Let's take a break and let the programs rummage around some more. What d'you say we abolish pain out in that big formal garden?"

They each got another meltdown and wandered out across the obsessively faultless garden, which ran down a gentle slope to a picturesque pond. A bare, pristine-white flagpole stood there, flying Earth's globe-and-olivebranch in Floyt's honor, though he had no idea how the hotel had found one and gotten it up there on such short notice.

The sward was blue-green, softer than fleece; Floyt couldn't name any of the flowers, shrubbery, or trees. Spica's glow still brightened half the horizon, and Avalon looked like a photon refinery, some huge petrochemical plant pumping out splendor.

They paced along beside an intricately detailed wall topped by big, jagged sawteeth. "When there are enough shares represented, the meeting will be convened, Alacrity?"

"Yes." Alacrity looked up to where several of Nirvana's sister planets had already appeared. "And then we get ferried up to the Ship, and if we live through that, things *really* start to boil. This Sibyl Higgins—I just don't know how she's gonna change the equation, here."

"It would seem to me, Alacrity, that anything that changes the *status quo* could very plausibly work in your favor." *My god! If he proves the causality harp wrong there'll be no living with him! But no; I'd welcome that kind of exasperation.*

"True enough, Ho. Now, I figure that if we stay alive long enough to get there and start intriguing without any more surprises—"

A sound—a full, contralto bellow, actually—had been rising in the background. *"Tim-ber-rrr!"* Something heavy and metallic *bong*ed down on the wall right by the spot where they stood, with a death-toll sound like the universe's time was up, breaking off the top of one of the sawteeth, knocking fragments and dust every which way.

CHAPTER 16

PUT 'ER IN THE LONGBOAT TILL
SHE'S SOBER

ALACRITY WAS HUGGING THE TURF, THE XANTHOUS EYES
wide. Floyt, aside from shielding his face, had stood his
ground.

"Goddammit, Ho, geddown!"

"Why? Are assault troops generally in the custom of
crying '*Timber!*' when attacking, in your experience? Or,
for that matter, 'Yoo-hoo!'?"

Alacrity grudgingly shook his head no, but "Yoo-
hoo!" was undeniably what that same rich, sultry, high-
decibel contralto was calling out.

"You win; you're right." Alacrity stopped trying to
recall where the Captain's Sidearm was and scrambled to
his feet. The thing that had crashed down on the wall
sawteeth was a thin, snow-white cylinder that looked
troublingly familiar until Floyt placed it: a flagpole just
like the one in their own garden, only its red, white, and
blue flag displayed a coiled-rattlesnake emblem. The
voice sounded louder, lilting and huskily coy.

"Yoo-hoo! Neighbuhs! Ay!" There was a piercing
fingers-in-lips whistle.

Floyt looked at Alacrity and Alacrity looked at Floyt;
they both stepped over to a wall planter filled with lush
blossoms, climbed up into it, and waded across to peer
over the wall. The flagpole ran from their rampart to that

261

of the Imperial Domain's east wing, a matter of a mere ten meters at that point in the figure-eight floorplan.

"Hello, ge'mun," she purred, a *loud* purr. "Ah thought somebody ovah theah might be up foah a game o' Grafenberg hockey. Why, ge'mun! Whut's wrong?"

They did look a little foolish; slack-jawed and frog-eyed. She was standing across the way, in a white gown that shone blue in the dusk and threw out tiny speckles of starlight. It was tight as sausage skin on a truly awesome shape.

She was that same startling female persona they'd seen in dozens of holoflix and tapes, with the honeyed, stand-clear voice. Her windblown coif was no one color; it was all colors, a spectrum or rainbow that shifted around her face and neck and shoulders.

And, where they just about had to chin themselves on the wall, she was leaning *down* on it, a tumbler looking small as a fruit-juice glass in one long hand. Floyt and Alacrity looked down at the planter on which they were standing, and at each other again, and back to their neighbor.

"Look heah, hons: the least y'all could do is say good evenin' and invite me ovah theah! Oh, well . . ."

She put the glass down behind one sawtooth and vaulted up very neatly for someone in a designer sheath gown, to stand with one foot on either side of the make-shift assault bridge. The fabulous floor-length dress had a walking slit that reached all the way to her treated, jewel-threaded pubic locks.

The two friends squeaked like a pair of gerbils and bumped into each other, hands outflung to ward her off, not sure what to do but anticipating catastrophe.

"No! Circe, you can't—"

"Don't! Miss Minx, *please*! I beg you, stay back!"

She put fists on her hips and thrust out her lower lip at them. *If the scale is the same at her end*, Floyt proc-essed, *she's about three and a half meters tall.*

"Now, ge'mun, *ah* come fum Damfino, which is a

planet wheah folks inner*duce* themselves to one an-othah! So, heah ah come!"

She put one big, pink, bare foot out onto the flagpole; Floyt sprang to brace it but Alacrity dragged him back, afraid he'd only jostle Circe Minx.

Circe Minx—after Hecate achieved her tremendous fame, the whole pantheon had been pillaged by people in search of catchy stage names, pseudonyms, and aliases —walked the balance-beam of the flagpole with a definite air of authority, the long, wide feet grasping, toes reaching and feeling for purchase, gripping. Air traffic passed by in the distance, beyond the Sceptered Isle's restricted zone, and low-level fliers and ground vehicles streamed below in rivers of light. She was out beyond the climate controls, where the winds carried Avalon sounds from far away and the fall would be long, long . . .

"Alacrity, shouldn't we call somebody?" Floyt whispered harshly.

"No! No, don't leave me in the middle of this! And anyway, who would you call? Just get ready to grab the pole if it bows too far, but don't let it drag you over the side if we can't save 'er."

Circe Minx's weight—no fan publication or publicity outlet ever revealed it—caused a pronounced dip in the composite flagpole, but then again she was halfway to her destination. She held one cross-tie, stiletto-heeled dancing sandal in either hand, arms out for balance like a circus pro. Except she was giggling.

Alacrity and Floyt waffled between shielding their eyes and watching fascinatedly. Alacrity couldn't help thinking what a splat *the* reigning sex symbol of the Third Breath would make if she misstepped.

One moment she was doing fine, hair tossed by the breezes; the next, she was in trouble, arms windmilling slowly, brows knotted as if she couldn't recall something. "Uh-oh . . ."

Alacrity breathed *"Vaina!"* to himself and got ready to grab for the pole or go after her or something. But Floyt jumped up to brace his elbows on the parapet, to yell through cupped hands.

"There's a commo call for you here, Miss Minx! Something about you not having script approval on your next feature!"

She dropped both big sandals. *"What?"* The shriek hurt their ears. She finished the walk one foot in front of the other, arms outspread, so quickly that the two friends fell to either side so as not to be trampled.

Circe Minx hit the turf with a solid thud and a swirl of sense-satin. "Where the hell's that commo terminal? *No script approval?* Would you two ge'mun be gallant enough to 'scuze a gal while she goes and toe-asses a little butt?"

"Yes, well now, how shall I put this?" Moisture beaded on Floyt's forehead and in his mustache. "I'm afraid I made that up. Heh-heh!"

"To get you in off that flagpole. I mean, really," Alacrity hastened. "You had us kinda scared." They both gulped, staring up at her. Alacrity estimated that she came in at three hundred kilos and a good deal more, but distributed on that amazing frame it all looked healthy and dynamic, fetchingly proportioned if voluptuous, but under the circumstances, frightening.

Uh, where is that gun?

Floyt was more contemplative, recalling things he'd read. Height was a matter of some introspection to him, what with most non-Terrans running to extratall according to his standards, by way of nutrition, eugenics, bioengineering, and what-all. Circe and people her size were about as far as human physiology could be stretched and not run into prohibitive troubles like osteological breakdown, critical loss of coordination, and square-cube revenge. As it was, cardiovascular glitches almost always cropped up, necessitating transplants, implants, and synergics.

Despite that, Circe Minx struck him as a big, healthy woman in her early thirties who'd adapted about as well as anybody could be expected to. She'd started out in

erotic entertainments that were still prized and praised
as high paradigms. Her lackluster dramatic vehicles only
pointed up the fact that she was bright, funny, well read,
and woefully underserved by the material given her.
Much better things came with time.

As a performer and actress, her main problem was
that there were few enough costars of *any* height with
talent to match hers, much less leads who could play a
scene opposite Circe without recourse to a forklift. Of
people her size with her comedic timing, singing, and
dancing ability, there were just about none. That notwithstanding, she'd almost singlehandedly made the
"larger-than-life" school of holo and multimedia enormously popular and profitable, and become the fantasy
figure of billions of people.

Still, all that mass was more than a little intimidating
up close, especially to someone who'd just conned her,
Floyt decided. *Where* is *that Webley?*

Circe scowled down at them for a beat, then broke
into a smile warm as a fireplace. "You did it foah feah of
mah safety?" The big hands bloomed, somehow graceful
as Japanese fans. She affected to be a little breathless.
"Such *noble* ge'mun. Are y'all sure yoah not fum Damfino?" The magnificent bosom rose and fell.

Oh, Freud in the Void! If she faints, she'll crush us!
Alacrity thought, a little unkindly, wanting to yell *timber!*
himself but refraining, because he figured she'd probably
become sick of height jokes long since.

"Just admirers of yours," Floyt said honestly.

She threw her head back and laughed. When she
spoke again, a lot of the Damfino accent was gone. "Well
then, you're forgiven for userpin' my favorite half of the
Imperial Domain. You mean you didn't know? Who'd
you *think* that economy-size furniture was for, gents?
Trained polar bears?"

"Won't you come and sit down in some of it?" Alacrity invited, the only thing he could think of to say.

"Hold up, now." She was looking at them closely.

Circe Minx pointed at them with an elegant forefinger the length of a tentpeg.

"You two fine darlin's are Alacrity and Hobart, now aren't you? You look just like your pictures, but not a thing like those book covers! My, my! Aren't you just the most *dappah* things ever?" She clapped the big hands, a small explosion.

They squared away uniform and tux as best they could, trying to live up to the billing, Floyt mumbling, "You're too kind, I'm sure."

"Things weren't any fun over at your place?" Alacrity asked.

"Aw, everybody says they want to comfort me about the diz-bonding, but mostly they wanted to freeload and try and take a canoe trip up the Delta!"

"We were sorry to hear about your divorce—your diz-bonding," Floyt lied a bit.

She nodded tiredly. "Blix 'n Frix 'n Strix are good ol' boys, but I ask you: do *I* look like a gal who's gonna settle down and help run just one l'il ole planet?"

They shook their heads energetically.

"Aren't you sweet! Anyways, so here I am, high and dry again, with all the debts those stinkin' triplets ran up, and lawyers pouncin' down at me outta the trees, an' a yacht Ah cain't be spacin' in 'cause it holds so many sad mem'ries."

Alacrity and Floyt sighed for the tragedy of it. Circe thumbed at her suite. "So I sent 'em all packin'! Then I decided to see whut was goin' on over here at your place, because if I'd sat there alone I'd've ended up blubbering for the first time in almost twenty years now."

She seemed about to cry anyway. "That's a funny thing," Floyt told her, "for, you see, *we* were just about to yank out *our* flagpole and drop it over *your* wall."

"Well, darlin'! Th' evening's young! Now, which of you is gonna offer me some refreshments?"

An expedition was organized to ransack for food and drink, the food being optional. Floyt, trailing along on rearguard, gave the western suite flagpole a little tug, then a considerable heave.

Nothing.

They ordered up two pitchers of dogfights—one for Alacrity and Floyt, one for Circe Minx—and returned to the garden, the men taking chairs and the woman settling into a wrought-composite couch with such limber nonchalance that it looked small rather than she, large.

They talked some more, during which time Floyt denied, "Just because we've got a lot of problems, don't mistake us for heroes," and Alacrity and Circe laughed. A little later, what with Floyt being an Earther, Circe made them harmonize with her on "Irene, Goodnight."

"Well, that's what I get for bonding with somebody again," Circe said at a certain point. "Should've learned better by now. Hwa-*thoo!*" she added, spitting over the wall practicedly, as a sort of editorial.

"My feelings exactly," Alacrity said a little blearily, wondering what in the world he was saying and how it might bear on his bursting love for the Nonpareil.

"Love," Floyt explained to Circe Minx.

"Oh, yes! You and that Heart, right, Alacrity? That Nonpareil? I saw about that on one of those gossip shows. Woof, she's such a *looker!* Wish I wuz a chill beauty like that!"

"Stop looking suicidal, Alacrity," Floyt said, and they all touched glasses.

"Listen: why don't one of you sell me some White Ship stock?" Circe proposed.

When she saw how guarded that made them, she added, "Now quit bristlin'! Forget ah said it! It's just that ah've played most of the other games there are, and one of these days the looks'll go and the bod'll give out— probably right at the same time, given my luck.

"Bein' an Interested Party'd be just the pastime for me when ah git to be this blousey old coot with a few compromised helmet gaskets." Circe Minx twirled her finger next to her temple. "Ah'd like to poke my nose into that mess.

"Ah got interested in it a while back, but it's been a year and a half now and ah still haven't found a single share for sale. Except for one old foop who wanted, well, you might say, more than it was worth. Ge'mun, ah came close to *hurtin'* him!"

"More than it's worth is what they all cost," Alacrity intoned, crunching an ice cube.

"That's life for you, all right, sugar." Circe nodded. "Listen: I have something I want you boys to see..."

She rose unsteadily and headed for the improvised drawbridge. Alacrity and Floyt swapped frantic, resigned looks and dove for her ankles, rattling around like castanets but eventually bringing her down, mostly because she didn't resist. To their vast relief, she was laughing.

"All right, nevah mind!" They led her back across the lawn and somehow got her onto the couch while she was still helpless with laughter. She put a giant hand on each man's shoulder.

"Look, we'll just leave it at this: I'm tired of performing. If there's some stock around, you jes' let me know."

Alacrity had his chin on his chest, abruptly more pensive and reluctant to banter than Floyt was used to seeing him. "I'll try my best."

Circe kissed him hard enough to tilt the two front legs of his chair off the turf, even though she did it with an artful restraint. She smelled wonderful and was a sufficiently marvelous kisser that Alacrity started fantasizing with no thought to possible sprains and torn cartilage. Or whatever it might take.

Circe beamed. "Now I'll do somethin' for you luvs. A party! That's it! Gawd! We'll invite all the—"

But Alacrity had stopped her. "No good; outsiders." Circe slouched but nodded.

"I'll tell you, though," Alacrity went on. "Ho's proteus got trampled by...that is, it just got stomped to smithereens a while back. And had a tree pushed over on it, quit looking at me like that, Circe! So we're putting a new one on the tab and quit yelling, because you can't buy it, but I thought you could suggest something, maybe help us pick one out."

He showed her Floyt's watch chain, a venerable herringbone pattern, which looked so striking against Floyt's white vest but had only a fob on it—the heavy keepsake coin celebrating Terra's first five hundred years in space, with Yuri Gargarin's features on it—and no watch or proteus.

"So I thought, some big pocket model," Alacrity said. "If you could tell us the best place to—"

But Circe Minx was making her way to a commo terminal. She drawled a few quick orders with winsome *noblesse oblige*. Within minutes, attractive, beautifully dressed, amazingly eager-to-please people were pouring into the place with gorgeous wooden, leather, and precious-metal display cases of pocket-watch-configuration proteuses, at prices that made even Circe lift her long brows.

Floyt felt like shielding his eyes against the blaze of gems, gold, silver, and the rest. Circe was in her element, friendly and familiar with the clerks but demanding, too. Alacrity suspected that was because, for a change, she was helping pick out something for somebody else and her money had nothing to do with it. She was being protective of Floyt.

All the argument, testing, and comparison went on for three quarters of an hour. At one point, Circe and Floyt were happily yelling at one another about the relative merits of beauty and function, which discussion they both took personally, while Alacrity refereed.

A decision came to pass; Floyt held up the winner as the other two gathered round to admire. The case was an exact duplicate of a gold seventeenth-century John Willats watch, but machined from a solid block of super-alloy and strong enough to carry out-suit on Jupiter. The case showed gamboling figures in deep repoussé, so that some of the limbs were actually free-standing. The instrument had a face, chapters, working hands, multiple dials, and crown just like the original, but under the back cover were displays and instrumentation and controls that would let Floyt do pretty near anything he cared to, short of raising the dead. When he tried it on his chain, tucking it into the watch pocket of his white waistcoat, Alacrity said, "You look like Old Money."

The price of the proteus more than quintupled their hotel bill; Floyt followed Alacrity's example, registering the purchase with a world-weariness. When the supervisor asked if Floyt would like an inscription on the outside of the case-back cover, Floyt thought for a moment then turned to Circe Minx.

"I hope this won't sound too forward, but, since you picked it out—would you mind?"

She blushed, and wrote out the inscription in a beautiful, fluid, and draftsmanlike longhand, gnawing at the end of the tintstik as she decided what to set down; the engraver beam-etched it into the metal in reduced scale: "TO HOBART, MORE THAN JUST ANOTHER HERO. WITH ESTEEM, CIRCE."

In light of the very tidy profit she'd just turned, the supervising clerk threw in, free of charge, a likeness of Circe Minx carved into a wafer of glittering ice-lense, a popular item whenever she was in residence, mounting it in the inside of the case front cover.

The clerks withdrew, high-spirited as if they'd just won a buzzball championship. Floyt, Alacrity, and Circe Minx adjourned to the garden to celebrate. Alacrity dug out an adapter and let his own proteus do a complete sweep of Floyt's new one, to make sure it was free of logic bombs, saboteur AI's, sleepers, and other booby traps.

"Oh, *ge'mun*, that was fun!" Circe's eyes were moist and she ran the back of her hand under her nose, but she was more sober than when she'd shown up. "Ah don't get to *do* things for people, y'know? Ah mean, ah don' even get to *meet* many people."

"Good flagpoles make for good neighbors," Floyt observed grandly. Circe sprayed out part of her glass of dogfight and Alacrity broke up.

"But really," Circe forged on. "I'm not singing one of these 'poor little me' type numbers to you; after all, I'm lucky I'm not freakshowing somewhere or busting heads in an arena, or going catatonic in some flesh emporium. That's the kind of stuff people like me are slated for, in case you didn't know.

"What I run into's usually some *avant-gardeoisie* who sneers at what I do for a living until I hint around that I might hire him to write for me. Then all I have to do is yell 'frog!' *Hwa-thoo!*"

Circe massaged her neck. "You know when the last time was that somebody asked me an intelligent question? *I* sure don't."

"Well then, where'd the Precursors go?" Floyt popped out owlishly.

She considered. "Well, it's funny most sentient races we've found are more or less on the same footing, now isn't it? Almost impossible, if you look at the odds. Maybe the Precursors cleared the decks, *retired*, if you catch what I'm saying. Maybe, in order to love Creation —I mean, to love it in spite of itself, in spite of the unpleasant parts, they had to withdraw from it and contemplate it from afar. From Outside. Hey, this is great! Ask me another!"

Floyt hiccupped. "That was one of the most inneresting hypothesis I've ever heard. And it makes more sense than most."

Circe let go a long breath. "Nobody ever wants my opinion on stuff like that. I can visit twenty starsystems and never see a blessed thing, ta-*taaa!*"

She struck a pose. "But oh, *you* two guys! You really live!"

"Nothing to it," Alacrity said. "First thing you do is, you throw away all your money."

"And if you happen to get more, make sure someone steals it from you," Floyt chimed in. "Preferably while they shoot at you."

She looked at them sidelong. "Are you two sayin' you were happier before all this happened to you?"

They didn't answer right away. Then, at almost the same time, Floyt said, "Nope," while Alacrity muttered to his pathfinder boots, "You got us there, Circe."

Alacrity went on, "Yeah, but: it's still no fun being Life's Makiwara-board. And speaking of adversity, you're in a position to do us a favor, if you feel like. I'm figuring we're gonna run into trouble trying to get to the White Ship meeting; people will be watching our crate, the *Whelk*, maybe even impound her or something by the time the meeting's called. But you've got a lot of pull around Spica; we might need a ride."

She patted his knee, her hand covering it. "Don't give it another thought; I'll get you there. Who're we up against?"

"Everybody," Floyt said sourly. "Like always."

"Worry no more." She took another sip. "Did I tell you I shot a musical number in that White Ship for my last Special?"

They talked and drank a lot more, swearing eternal fealty with some kind of complicated triple handshake Floyt had never seen before. Circe left by a connecting door between the two suites that opened only to a two-part combination, one part supplied by her and one by Alacrity.

Floyt and Alacrity found their way to their rooms. Floyt, head spinning, expected to go to sleep at once, but found himself thinking, instead, of Paloma Sudan, and wondering where she was.

Then all at once, Alacrity was shaking him and Spica's first light was pouring through the window.

"Hey, wake up! The board meeting! Ho, they've called it!"

CHAPTER 17

OR WHAT'S A HEAVEN FOR?

HAIR METICULOUS AND FLUFFED FROM THE AUTO-grooming suite, Floyt was fastening himself into his freshly laundered and starched tux when Alacrity came trotting past his door.

"Make sure you've got everything you want to take, Ho. There's gonna be a limo here for us any second, and chances are we won't be back this way."

"But Alacrity! I thought we were going to take up Circe on her offer of a ride. I thought you said the *Whelk* isn't going to be permitted to raise."

Alacrity, who'd disappeared, backed up into the open doorway. He had his warbag in his hands. "Could be; I gave Circe a call and she'll be here in a few minutes, so hurry!"

Floyt did, but there wasn't much more to do and not much he wanted among the junk luggage they'd bought on Rocket Row. He took loving pleasure in settling his fob, chain, and new proteus into his blindingly white vest.

The limo was rakish and new, much bigger than the one they'd arrived in. Alacrity had ordered it so, with Circe in mind, but it was just as well for the chauffeur, too, a real ogre, bigger than the Sceptered Isle's Moloch doorman. His uniform, cap, and low-caste mask were all resplendent. He opened all passenger doors briskly and came one precise step into the drawing room.

"Number of passengers, sir?" the muffled voice said.

Alacrity was busy at a terminal. Floyt was looking through the provisions in the drawing-room larder, looking for something they could take along for a make-do breakfast-in-transit; he was ravenous and vitamin-starved from the drinking bout. Hangover remedies from the bath chamber pharmacy had taken hold and food was very much on his mind as he sipped at a tumbler of fruit juice.

"Three passengers, and just get the one bag, hmm?" Floyt gestured to the warbag; the chauffeur went to fetch it.

As the man passed by, Floyt caught a whiff of some strongly evocative scent, something the man's hygiene sprays and aromatics didn't quite overpower. It reminded Floyt vividly of some other specific time and place. He couldn't resurrect it, though, and was about to go back to his rummaging when he got a last faint whiff. And then it hit him.

Old Four Smokes Wallop! He'd smelled it for days, there in the *Whelk* before the traces had been absorbed by the ship's atmosphere regenerator, and had that one sickening swallow of the stuff the Golem drank, and would forever connect it with the Golem's huge make-shift bunk.

Floyt suppressed his first impulse, which was to drop the fruit juice and yell. Months of tight-sphincter situations in the company of Alacrity Fitzhugh had given the onetime Earthservice functionary object lessons in timing and the importance of that moment of deliberate setup.

Still bent at the waist in front of the big open larder, he set down the juice tumbler quietly and drew the bulky Webley from its shoulder holster, pinky hooked down to keep the lanyard ring on the butt from clinking, shielding the motion with his body. Floyt turned calmly, bringing the revolver up with both hands, cocking it with both thumbs.

"Alacrity!"

Floyt had to yell; jacket drawn up, the enormous chauffeur was pulling something from his waistband. Alacrity began to pivot and the chauffeur's head swung toward Floyt, the weapon coming clear with great speed.

But Floyt had already fired. The dum-dum round *crack*ed, batting the air hard against their ears, impairing hearing, even in the vast drawing room, putting smoke and fire into the air. Whatever the intruder was pointing had almost but not quite come to bear; the hours Floyt had spent practicing on the target range at Old Raffles paid off in that he scored a first-round hit at some ten paces, a very respectable piece of marksmanship in the insanity of a pistol fight. Alacrity was frozen, his discarded Sam Browne and sidearm in Floyt's line of fire, near the chauffeur.

Gentry Standing Bear felt himself a human flame, as he always did on the hunt and especially at the pounce. It didn't bother him very much that his plan had gone wrong; plans were only a general guide anyway. Except he couldn't quite figure out how Floyt had pierced his disguise, which gave Standing Bear a vicious disquiet.

If his mission had been a mere execution, it would've been over the moment Standing Bear stepped in off the landing stage. But the orders had been changed; Langstretch wanted answers to some questions about the White Ship, and that required live prisoners. Standing Bear didn't usually tolerate that kind of restriction, but he felt a personal vindictiveness toward Fitzhugh and Floyt for the way they'd killed Plantos on Luna and for inconveniencing him, Standing Bear. And so he'd agreed.

He'd been inclined to hit them with the stungun from the doorway, but the angles of the halls were a little funny and suspicious, and there was no way to be sure, from there, that there was no one else waiting to take a shot from ambush.

And so he'd gone in, to see for himself that he wouldn't take a beam, or one of those deranged split-slugs like the Earther fired, in the back while loading the unconscious Floyt and Fitzhugh into the limo. Standing Bear now had Fitzhugh's weapon spotted and knew Alacrity couldn't get to it without the risk of getting shot by his sidekick. The Earther had only a bullet gun, as intel reported, so as far as Gentry Standing Bear was concerned, things were still pretty much on schedule.

But that was just about the time Floyt's first dum-dum round missed Standing Bear's midsection and made a hit —almost square on the muzzle of the stungun. The stungun jumped in the giant's hand, fragments and pieces of bullet tearing at his clothes, his hand jolted and chewed up, blood weltering.

It numbed Standing Bear's right hand a bit and rendered some of the fingers useless, and the blood loss would have to be seen to. But beyond that the shot was no great bother; Standing Bear had long since concluded that he didn't feel pain as others did; he was in fact contemptuous of it.

But Floyt knew what he was doing; the Earther fired again, right away, single-action for accuracy, not waiting to see what the first shot had done. It was like the Langstretch reports said: Floyt wasn't some shakey little Earthservice functionary anymore. Standing Bear almost admired his calm.

Another dum-dum round hit, this one squarely, as Standing Bear heaved the stungun at Floyt, missing. The dum-dum broke against Standing Bear's body armor, ripping up the chauffeur's jacket. Standing Bear lurched for Alacrity's Sam Browne belt with a fierce exultation. Floyt fired again, this time missing, chewing up some textured wallpaper.

Alacrity saw the huge interloper going for the Captain's Sidearm and dove to beat him to it, yelling so that Floyt would notice him and not accidentally shoot holes in a pal.

But the big man was very fast. Alacrity bounced off

him, not something Alacrity was used to, being swung aside and jounced into the air by the swing of an arm thicker than his waist.

Knowing his hand would never fit inside the pistol's basket handshield, nor his finger inside its trigger guard, Standing Bear grabbed the gunbelt and tossed the whole affair high into one of the lighting sconces.

Floyt held fire until he saw Alacrity smashed aside, then he let fly again. This time Floyt was sure it was a hit; the round broke up against the man's upflung forearm and pieces of it ripped at the mask.

None penetrated; Floyt realized the chauffeur's disguise was bulletproof and regretted that the Webley didn't throw something with a little more heft—like exploding tunnelpoints, or depleted transuranics.

Then Standing Bear was charging at Floyt. Floyt planted his feet, held the pistol in both trembling hands, thumbed back the hammer coolly, and fired for the right eye. And missed.

Standing Bear felt safe attending to the Earther before taking care of the breakabout; Fitzhugh seemed stunned when he was flung against the sculpture pedestal. To Floyt it looked like he was being charged by a rhino in a chauffeur's suit, but he did his best to steady his aim, squeezing the trigger again.

The hammer fell with a pinging click. Floyt had kept an empty chamber under the hammer, and five rounds were gone.

Standing Bear didn't hit Floyt full tilt. That would've snapped the Earther's spine across the bar and almost certainly killed him with various fractures and concussions and massive internal injuries. Standing Bear's giant hand, dripping his own blood, closed on Floyt's throat in a blood-choke hold, and the Langstretch stringer pulled out his injector kit.

But as Floyt began to go under, pinned and straining, helpless as a hatchling, Standing Bear took a quick look at Fitzhugh to make sure he hadn't come around yet. As he began to turn, he took a bar stool full in the face.

Alacrity had fallen back on doctrine, pretending to be hurt worse than he really was. The stool jolted Standing Bear's head around, wrenching the low-caste mask loose and opening a gash on his forehead that seeped blood, but not bothering him much otherwise. But he dropped the limp Floyt to see to this more immediate problem.

Alacrity made the mistake of looking at Standing Bear's face. It was distorted and horrific from old wounds, much of the nose gone and teethmarks still showing on what was left, which was also flattened and crooked from uncounted fractures. Eyes ridged with thick, scarred tissue stared at him madly, quite madly. The cheek was distorted from some terrible, ripping wound.

The sight made Alacrity a half-tick slow, and though he got a good hunk of Standing Bear's forehead with the second swing, it wasn't enough. Standing Bear rolled with it, coming up at Alacrity like an avalanche in reverse.

Standing Bear blocked a third lick with his invulnerable arm, which he then brought down across Alacrity's collarbone, dashing Alacrity back and bashing the remains of the bar stool from his hands. Standing Bear pulled his follow-up elbow-strike quite a bit, so as not to stove in Alacrity's chest, and stretched him out straight, first in the air and eventually on his back.

Standing Bear turned to get his injector kit, flipping it open one-handed on rows of prepared dosages. Floyt and Fitzhugh would be nice and quiet for the limo ride, and more than ready to talk when they got where they were going, entranced and ready to babble.

Alacrity had bumped his head and lost consciousness for a second; now he came back into focus as a titanic weight settled on his chest and arms. He winced up at the ogre, remembering what was going on after an instant, but at a loss as to even one move. Standing Bear knelt on him, bringing an autostyrette into line with his neck. Somewhere in the background, Floyt was wheezing and gasping pitifully.

And the next thing Alacrity knew, Standing Bear was arching back and up, the swing of the styrette missing Alacrity's neck by a few centimeters, the Langstretch man yanked partway off him. Standing Bear stabbed the styrette at the forearm, broad as his own, that had locked around his throat, but the pneumostyrette triggered against thick leather, the sleeve of a battle jacket, and puffed its charge harmlessly.

Standing Bear was limber as a snake in battle. He turned and secured some kind of hold; he and his opponent both lost balance and sprawled. Luckily for Alacrity, they fell away from him, and so he wasn't crushed.

Circe Minx tumbled and rolled clear, trying a kick to Standing Bear's head as she did. He barely ducked it, chopping hard at her ankle, but his slab-hand only slid along her calf. The floor drumrolled under their huge weight. Standing Bear tried to capitalize on his offensive but brought himself up short, Circe's snapping, backhand blow barely missing smashing in his face.

They were up in an instant, in fighting crouches—amazingly low and limber stances, considering their sizes. Circe had the reach and weight, but there was no telling about brute strength or skill, except that both of them had plenty. The wounded hand didn't hamper Standing Bear much.

Circe kicked an antique table out of her way with the flick of a foot. Gentry Standing Bear smiled hideously; *her*, at least, he didn't have to take alive. Too bad there wasn't time for more fun with her . . .

He went in low but was rocked by her first two-handed blow; thereafter he kept his head pulled in, blocked with forearms and legs. Circe was amazed when Standing Bear took the best she could throw at him and kept coming. She didn't take time out to chide herself for not bringing a gun when she'd heard the commotion in the western suite; she got on with the program at hand, which was, in short, to plant the monster for good.

Standing Bear got in under a kick—because she was out of practice, Circe was positive; she'd never missed in the old arena days—and started to footsweep her. But she hopped over the footsweep and rammed an elbow around into the side of his head, and he growled like some animal.

Circe was unbelieving that she hadn't knocked him unconscious; she'd concussed much bigger opponents with that same shot. Standing Bear grappled close with her, the two losing balance and hitting the thick carpet. She bridged, almost reversed his hold, but he resisted her with more strength than she'd ever come across in someone so much less than her own size. Standing Bear tried to knee her in the crotch but she twisted away, also avoiding the headlock he attempted.

They were rising to their feet. Circe Minx got in a hip throw, slamming her enemy down hard enough to knock a painting off a nearby wall and shatter the bones of a lesser opponent. Standing Bear grunted out a little breath but was squirming to come at her again almost immediately, unhurt. Panting, she left herself open a little; as he went for her eyes and got a one-knuckle punch into her short ribs, she grappled. A gorgeous antique settee fell to splinters under them as they went down again. Circe got him in the mouth with her fist as they fell, drawing blood but knowing it wasn't enough to stop a demon like this.

Then Alacrity was swaying over them with another bar stool. Alacrity couldn't reach his own gun and had no idea where Floyt's ammo was, and there was no time to go looking.

Circe was working a chokehold on Standing Bear from beneath. The stool came down, the blow jarring Alacrity's shoulders, without doing much more good than the first. The monster swept out an arm and grabbed Alacrity as Standing Bear wove and gathered Circe in, too, because she was hampered by not wanting to hit Alacrity.

Standing Bear began exerting pressure, hugging, gathering them tighter. Circe couldn't maintain her braced chokehold on Standing Bear without risking breaking Alacrity's neck in the press.

Circe Minx reflected on how the folks on Damfino would be disappointed if a local gal got herself beat by some overmuscled runt three quarters her size. She tried fingers to Standing Bear's eyes, but he buried his head against her and his chest, and tightened his grip, making Alacrity groan in agony.

The sound of that explained why Standing Bear didn't detect Floyt, who was staggering his way. Floyt half knelt, half fell across Standing Bear's back, swung two hands wide, and brought them in to strike at both sides of the huge man's neck. Standing Bear batted him away with a brief snarl. Floyt was knocked back, dropping the two autostyrettes he'd snatched at random from the injector kit.

Bit by bit, Circe felt the machinelike pressure slacken. She was careful to push the thick arms loose without exerting more pressure on Alacrity, who was out. Floyt was trying to get to his feet, to help, without much success.

Gentry Standing Bear was unconscious, but his eyes were open, staring at the ceiling. And, whoever the man was, he *liked* violence; Circe could see that clearly from a certain very pronounced physiological response he'd had to the fight, one that was visible through the chauffeur's uniform.

"Langstretch, all right," Circe pronounced a short time later. She was examining the injector kit. Floyt and Alacrity had come around and didn't appear to have any serious injuries. But they were a bit dopey and a lot shaken.

"Yeah; I think I've been using his bunk inboard the *Whelk*," Alacrity said, kneading his scalp. "What'd Ho shoot him up with?"

Circe squinted at the markings on the two empty styrettes. "Some sort of hypnoblank, looks to me. The fella 'pears to have a clean slate, here."

True enough. Standing Bear hadn't moved or done a thing since Floyt got the twin dosages into him. He simply sat on the floor, gazing off into space, mouth hanging open, a little saliva falling off his chin in a thread every so often.

"Hey, buddy! Close your mouth!" Circe said. Standing Bear did.

"I think I know what this stuff is," Alacrity concluded. "This ex-Langstretch agent, Victoria, told me about it back on Blackguard. This guy is a wipe, all right. Complete personality dump."

"Well, whatever it was, it wasn't what he was going to use on *us*," Floyt said, tending a bump on his head with an iced towel. He was holding the styrette Standing Bear had been about to use on him when Circe showed up. "This thing has the same markings as that other concoction Victoria showed us, Alacrity—that conversational elixir? At least Langstretch isn't trying to execute us outright these days."

Alacrity drew a sharp breath in pain, rubbing his sides. "Circe, we got you into something a lot more dangerous than we—"

"Ferget it," she said flatly. "Ah need a little voltage every now and then, or ah git bored and borin'. Let's git goin'."

Floyt gestured to Standing Bear, whose eyes were wide and childlike. "What about the Golem?"

Circe, fists on hips, looked Standing Bear over. "*Fearsome* little runt, h'ain't he? Y'know, think ah'll jes' bring him along."

"That'll confuse somebody," Alacrity said. "Okay, go get your stuff and we'll take the limo."

"Haven't got much; didn't bring much important junk along with me. Ah'll be right back."

But when Circe returned with a tote bag over her shoulder, she found Alacrity in front of the commo terminal and Floyt looking worried. "The limo's locked down with some code that this fellow is in no condition to tell us," Floyt said, meaning Standing Bear. "And the hotel sounds like it's in on it; they won't permit any more vehicles to land here."

A severe-looking woman in police-brass uniform was gazing out at Alacrity from the commo display. "And since your vessel, the *Lightning Whelk*, has turned up on the Wants and Warrants Network, I'm afraid we'll need to speak to you in some detail before we can allow you to move her."

"But I'm an Interested Party, and the board meeting's been called! And you know that! You have no right to hold me!" The set-jaw tone was clear in Alacrity's voice.

Her smile wasn't very merry. "But we're not holding you. We are merely impounding your vessel, although" —her mouth gave a tug—"you may have a little trouble getting up to the White Ship. And, of course, your problems with your hotel bill are your own affair. Besides, I'm not at all convinced the holder of a single share is any great shakes as an Interested Party, are you? But be that as it may, I'm sure we can have all this straightened out in a few days."

"*Days!*" Alacrity hammered his fist to cut the link and whirled on Floyt and Circe. "By that time the meeting'll be over and the cops'll be able to arrest me!"

"Us," Floyt corrected mildly. He closed the reloaded Webley—six full chambers this time—with a loud *snap* of the barrel catch. "And if we try to go through the lobby we run into the opposition?"

Alacrity nodded. "Bet on it." He'd recovered the Captain's Sidearm and was buckling it on.

"And how'd the law come to know how many shares you own?" Circe asked him. "That's supposed to be confidential company info, no?"

"It is unless somebody's got it in for you," Alacrity said despondently.

"Well, I'll jes' call another limo on *my* terminal and we'll get you up to that White Ship in my yacht, the *Tramp-Royal*," she said.

But hotel service wouldn't cooperate with her any more than it had with Alacrity. The excuse this time wasn't credit problems but rather difficulties with the hotel's defensive systems; the management was terribly sorry, but anything that flew close to the Imperial Domain tower—and, by implication, from it—was liable to be shot down.

Circe cut the link with a curse. "They want to make sure you don't get out of here no way 'cept down. That lobby *must* be covered."

Not the cops. Alacrity thought, chin on fist. *They'll most likely stand back and let Langstretch do the dirty work.*

"What about the service transport systems, or the utility shafts?" Floyt proposed.

"Uh-uh," Circe vetoed. "How many times d'you think somebody's tried 'em over the years? I expect they're covered, besides which they'd be a little cramped for me, and you're gonna need me to get *Tramp-Royal* into the air. *Shoot!* Damfino gals're s'posed to be able to look after their men by theirselves, but . . . What about if I hire us some private security to come get us?"

"I'm not sure who we could trust," Alacrity decided. "Langstretch has an awful lot of pull. They might co-opt or scare away hired muscle from some other—hey! Lemme at that commo terminal! We'll give 'em a crowd scene they won't forget!"

"Could be tapped," Circe cautioned about the terminal. "But I've got a scramble relay link. Use that." Circe opened the link and handed over the ornate proteus she carried in armlet configuration.

Alacrity took it. "If this works, get ready for some jostling."

The three stepped out of the lift from Circe's suite right on the dot, Alacrity resettling his warbag and brolly. In an effort to spread the enemy thin and by dint of a lot of last-second dashing around, they'd managed to dispatch or summon various service carriers, chute skids, and cargo whisks from both suites at just about the time they started down.

There seemed to be a fair amount of bustle in the lobby—deliveries and early-morning check-ins, and the coming and going. But there were also more bellhops and service staff than usual; Alacrity and Floyt spotted at least two members of the security crew from the day before.

The threesome stepped out of the rotunda carefully. Heads turned to them, but that was only natural; Floyt and Alacrity stood in their distinctive outfits alongside Circe Minx, who was decked out in a high-fashion traveling ensemble and a battle jacket. Behind them, vacant looking but frightening, obedient as a robot, came Standing Bear. They'd cleaned him up as best they could, dressing his wounded hand and the forehead gash. Several bystanders, seeing him, exchanged troubled glances.

It was Alacrity's theory that the Langstretch people and hotel security would be disinclined to shoot in the lobby. He was also hoping that they would presume, at least for a while, that Gentry Standing Bear, as the giant's I.D. gave his name, had the situation under control. Besides, the opposition was under the impression that Alacrity and company had been isolated.

The lobby was a long, long way across, and the ambushers would have insured that escape routes were all dead ends. The enemy could afford to wait a bit before making its move, do things as nonviolently as possible. At least, that was the way Alacrity had things figured, and Circe agreed. If the stunguns, dazzle beads, blitzgas, and whatnot came into play, there'd be nothing to do but fight, and most likely lose.

As they moved across the lobby, the three, followed by Gentry Standing Bear, registered the various crews— opposition disguised as guests, servants, and the rest. Floyt found himself sweating, and his mouth was dry.

C'mon, c'mon, Alacrity urged silently, praying the timing was right. Then he saw it.

A shrouded neo-Coptic Elder, his wives and harem

guards and family and votaries, all on their way to register, suddenly threw open their robes. Their rich luggage was opened to reveal some kind of gleaming hardware.

It was sophisticated recording and transmitting gear, portable lighting and such. One of the "wives" was the little scandalhawk from the day before, Salome Price.

Chattering a running commentary, Salome rushed up aiming an aud-vid pickup as lights converged on them. "This is your Uncensored Network correspondent, Salome Price, coming to you live from the lobby of the hotel Sceptered Isle, with an exclusive scoop on the newest twist in the troubled and tormented love life of the undisputed sex goddess of the Third Breath, Circe Minx!

"Circe! Mistress Minx! Do you have any comment to the hundreds of millions of fans *who are watching you at this moment*? Can you tell us your feelings about your sudden elopement with these two firing studs, Citizen Hobart Floyt of Terra and Master Alacrity Fitzhugh? Does this mean you recant your denunciation of lifelong relationships?"

"That's how it looks, doesn't it, sugah?" Circe responded, batting lashes eight centimeters long and tossing her rainbow-shimmering hair.

"Citizen Floyt, can you tell our viewers how long you've been intimate with Circe? Where did you meet? And would you tell us, please, when you knew that it was going to be love forever?"

"Er, that is, um, it was all rather abrupt, but I've been an ardent admirer of Miss Minx's—uh, Circe's—for some time now, I would say—"

The three, flanked by Standing Bear, were in the middle of a growing crowd of gossipghouls, tech crews, and support personnel, augmented by gaping bystanders who were only beginning to realize something extraordinary was going on. Security crews and Langstretch field ops were gazing at one another in confusion, not sure what action to take in the middle of a live broadcast being watched by hundreds of millions of fans.

Salome pounced again. "Master Fitzhugh, what will you say to Heart Dincrist, the so-called Nonpareil, with whom you were reputed to be engaged in a torrid love affair?"

"Something real brief and truncated, I bet."

More media teams had come out from under wraps and disguises: a portly woman who turned out to be an aud-vid director and whose children were actually commo-link specialists. A hotel security woman and her partner made a tentative move to stop the interview, but two large Utopian business moguls suddenly reverted to a pair of strongarm men from the network's own security department. A strangely silent scuffle broke out, neither team wanting to attract attention.

Chauffeurs and guests and valets revealed themselves to be Uncensored Network people, numbering dozens. A protective ring was formed around Salome, Circe, Floyt, Alacrity, and Standing Bear as they were convoyed across the lobby, Salome keeping up a constant barrage of questions. All around them, muted, furious engagements were being fought, with everyone trying to avoid involving innocent guests.

Salome was trotting to keep up. "Circe, do you plan to repeat the kind of formal, planet-mobilizing celebration you had for your bonding to Blix and Frix and Strix Bledsoe?"

"Darlin', ah'm jes' a country girl at heart, so ah think we'll keep it simple!"

Salome's face clouded. "But as I've been telling our viewers, the Uncensored Network has rights to exclusive coverage of this romantic surprise story of the year, isn't that right?"

The lobby doors were getting closer. Circe's smile was frozen and staplegunned into place. "Why, hon, y'all kin come to the *consummation* if you h'ain't doin' nothin' more *interestin'* that evenin'!"

"And there you have it, ladies and gentlemen! Proof once again that the Uncensored Network brings you the biggest stories first, best, and at their most intimate! Citizen Floyt! Do you plan to have children right away?"

"If we don't get out of this lobby soon, it's more likely to be *kittens*," Floyt confided.

The ambushers no doubt thought they had the main landing stage covered, in that no cab or hire-flier was there to help the group escape. But the erstwhile Coptic Elder's skycraft caravan was suddenly in place, doors open, guarded by burly men who'd discarded their robes. Langstretch backup people, taken by surprise, had no time to get blocking vehicles into position and suffered much attrition in some very spirited knuckle jousts.

Alacrity, Floyt, and Circe reached the truck-size saloon flier in one sustained rush from the doors, Circe still mother-henning the dazed Standing Bear. One overexcited Langstretch backup-crew leader dove headlong, bulling his way through the Uncensored ranks, hand going under his jacket. Floyt was tugging at the Webley and Alacrity fighting to get the Captain's Sidearm free, both of them hampered by the press.

Standing Bear's mouth was open again, his eyes apparently unfocused. Yet he reached out and closed his left fist unerringly around the op's handgun and hand as it swung in Circe Minx's direction. Standing Bear had the weapon away from the op in a move that left the man nursing a separated wrist and several fractured fingers. Gentry offered the pistol to Circe with doglike devotion; the Langstretch muscle began to break contact.

Back at the doors, the Uncensored strongarm teams were making sure the opposition kept at bay. Floyt saw one of the men who'd grabbed Salome the day before, the square-jawed killer type, his right arm hanging limp and looking broken.

"Don't worry," Salome had said when Alacrity warned her, during his call, that there would likely be trouble. "Those hotel goons've messed up quite a few of our people over the years, and gals and guys on our scuffling crews'd like nothing better than a chance to get even. Besides, the press has to break a few heads every so often, so folks know we're not punching bags."

Someone was pushing Floyt into the saloon flier behind Circe and the others. The luxurious flier was big enough for Circe to sit upright. In no time Salome was practically in their laps, pickups were in place, and the interview was in progress again.

"Now, Citizen Floyt," Salome cooed, "can you give our audience a quick rundown on the sexual practices you three are looking forward to?"

CHAPTER 18

IF YOU CAN'T JOIN 'EM

CIRCE MADE LOUD AND COLORFUL PROTESTS, BUT ALA-
crity wouldn't yield the point. He and Floyt would make
their connection to the White Ship in the *Tramp-Royal*'s
gig, Circe herself standing away and making for her vast
estate on Eden.

"We don't want you getting any more involved in this,
Circe!" Alacrity shouted, the blood vessels standing out
in his neck and his face growing dark, because that was
what it took to get something across to her.

"I expect things to go my way at this meeting, but if
they don't, there'll be a lot of badges up here real soon!
And if the board decides it wants a little revenge, you'll
think you've been run over by a posthole drilling machine! And unlawful trespass is something they could
make stick, at the very least; Interested Parties are only
allowed one companion apiece at meetings, and Ho's
mine."

"Hellfar," Circe Minx pronounced. "Ah got a Chinese
Obligation to y'all now." She sighed. "And this's been
more fun than ah've had since ah don't know when. But
if that's the way y'all want it, darlin'..."

They were in the cockpit of the yacht *Tramp-Royal*, a
swift, handy, and responsive starship with disproportion-
ate headroom by most standards—sufficient for Circe
throughout. She was in the outsize pilot's chair, Alacrity

290

in the more conventional copilot's. Gentry Standing Bear was belted, uncomplaining and inert, into the weather bridge's Circe-size pilot's poz, aft. Floyt stood between Alacrity and Circe, taking in the view.

The White Ship, a scant ten kilometers away, wasn't the biggest starship he'd ever seen, but she was in the running. She resembled a sleek, spacegoing iceberg, surprisingly aerodynamic.

Floyt stared at her and wondered what lay ahead. Board meetings were critical to the operation of the White Ship Company because they were just about the only time the farflung Interested Parties all came together. They were times of power-brokering and machinating; because of travel lags and communications delays, jockeying for leverage and influence was time consuming and frustrating—almost impossible—when conducted across interstellar distances.

As Heart had explained it to Alacrity, the meeting, huddling, and maneuvering went on in marathon fashion; the strategic and tactical situations could change from moment to moment.

Floyt let out a deep breath. *And we're going in short on sleep, biffed and bruised by that brute Standing Bear, and wanted by the authorities.* The only comforting aspect was that he and Alacrity had been in worse shape and worse jams.

"Uh-oh; warn-off signal from the Ship," Circe said as a holodisplay flashed. "Take us back and hold at minimum distance, hon," she told the *Tramp-Royal.* The starship came onto a new course. It was best not to provoke the White Ship; AI's in charge of her security were provided with a lot of discretion, but they were also suspicious and not hesitant to defend. There'd been a number of attempts to board and hijack her over the years, some quite bloody, none successful.

"The gig's ready for you," Circe told them. "Hang onto her as long as you need to. I'll be on Eden for a while, I expect."

"What about that Standing Bear creature?" Floyt asked.

Circe gave a high-voltage smile. "Well now, you know, I think I'll jes' hang onto him for awhile. *Lordy*, he's ugly, but he's got me mighty impressed."

"Yeah, we saw that when you patted him down for weapons," Alacrity observed.

Circe hooted. "I think he's got possibilities, now that the meanness is gone."

Alacrity was climbing out of the copilot's poz. "Sorry we had to tell all those fibs to that gossip ghoul, Circe."

"Don't bother your head about it. A little scandal now and then's good for a gal's career, and anyway, ah'm *expected* to be licentious. Now, y'all better get movin'." They kissed her and moved out. Circe honked, blowing her nose, and turned back to her controls.

The *Tramp-Royal*'s gig was like a little bit of the Taj Mahal in a spaceboat, done in a confectionary Erotodynamic-Baroque motif—with meters of headroom, of course.

Alacrity launched and the *Tramp* peeled off, headed for Eden. The gig received a warn-off, but this time Alacrity responded with his shareholder's code, was voice-I.D.'d, and got a wave-on.

The gig was assigned a boarding lock far forward in the White Ship. A dozen other ships and boats were already there, several of them company VIP shuttles. As Alacrity and Floyt cycled through the lock, they were subjected to detector scans.

The Ship spoke in a serene, precise female voice; the voice and warning displays pointed out that the two men were carrying firearms, contrary to the Ship's rules. An armored storage bin slid open to collect them.

Alacrity tried to keep back the Webley and just surrender the energy pistol; the White Ship wasn't fooled. Guns and holster harnesses went into the bin and were withdrawn from view.

The Ship informed them that her board meeting was due to convene shortly in the Vale. They could drop off their luggage at their quarters and freshen up, but there wasn't a great deal of time.

"Yeah, listen, I want to make one stop first, at a company transactions terminal," Alacrity told the Ship. "You've got 'em up here, right?"

The Ship's voice made Floyt think of some virgin high priestess. "Of course, Shareholder Fitzhugh. Or would you prefer that I refer to you as Shareholder Jordan Bowie?"

"You had it right the first time." He ran a hand along the hatch frame. *And before too long you'll be all mine, doll!*

A passageway tram was waiting for them just outside the inner hatch. Alacrity threw his bag in the back, joined Floyt up front, and the tram glided forward. "There is a transactions terminal just aft of the Vale," the tram told him in the Ship's voice. "All shareholder business can be conducted at that station."

Floyt saw that he was plainly in a working starship, not an overdecorated palace, but there was still an expansive feel to the big passageways. He'd learned enough in his travels to see that no labor or expense had been spared.

In her thirty years of construction, the White Ship had been through work stoppages, major rebuilds, and radical design changes, been the cause of several near wars and an awful lot of corporate bloodletting. She'd been through assorted renamings, too: *Culminator, Onward, Jilleroo, Firebird.* But those never stuck and she was only and uniquely the White Ship. Floyt, who'd hated the whole concept of space travel only months before, now looked around him and understood on a glandular level why Alacrity was ready to fight and connive and even die in his campaign to win her.

The tram eased to a stop outside a wide hatch. "The transactions terminal compartment, sir," the Ship said. Floyt followed Alacrity to the hatch, only to bump into his friend's back as Alacrity stopped short. Alacrity didn't move, so Floyt peered down under his arm, which was braced on the hatch frame.

"Why, hello, Hobart." The voice was rich and musical. "And you, too, of course, Alacrity."

"Hello yourself." Alacrity didn't move.

She was sitting in a high-backed tech's chair before a workstation, in the most advanced accessing facility Floyt had ever seen. It was oddly appropriate that Heart, the Nonpareil, the most beautiful woman Floyt had ever beheld—he had a brief tussle with his loyalty to Paloma on that one—should be sitting there in a big, baggy coverall that hid her marvelous figure, with her chalk-blond hair gathered in careless doggy-ears, wearing a pair of scabrous shipside scuffs on her feet, and no makeup.

She'd been called an ice sculptor's wet dream; Floyt knew that most of her cool appearance was a facade, the self-defense a stunning, enormously wealthy young woman needed to survive. Just then, though, she was simply a very easy-on-the-eyes female of nineteen or so who looked like she could use some sleep.

What rattled Floyt was what had brought Alacrity up short and made his greeting so clipped. Heart was sitting with a man who was poised with one hip on a console, bent down to watch whatever Heart was doing at the terminal.

And *he* made quite a first impression, an Adonis with ringlets of light-brown hair and beard, ruggedly classic good looks, and the build of a Xanadu muscle dancer well served by his revealing crimson suit-of-thongs. His proteus was in the shape of an artwear pectoral, a burnished, gemset crescent.

Floyt hated him right away and could only imagine what was going through Alacrity's head. *He let her go, and now she's gone and fallen for this damned demigod!*

Heart realized why they were staring and motioned to her companion. "Wulf and I were just trying to get the final point spread on the meeting. Have you two been briefed?"

Floyt rallied first, peering under Alacrity's arm. "No,

we're all at sea as usual, one jump ahead of reality, as it were."

Wulf flashed a brilliant smile at that. Heart pointed to a couch near her. "Maybe you'd both better sit down right over here, and we'll fill you in."

Alacrity's lips barely moved. "Not if we're interrupting."

The Nonpareil's eyes suddenly went wide and her fingertips flew to her lips. "Oh-hhh!" The heroic vision named Wulf turned his head aside decorously, so as to mostly conceal the grin he couldn't suppress.

Floyt heard Alacrity's teeth grinding. "Yeah; well. See you around."

She sprang up, crossing the compartment to him in two athletic bounds. Her smile was devilish. "I should *let* you go, you know that?"

She'd grabbed Alacrity's hand, but now she threw it down again. "In fact, go—go on, leave if you want to! But Hobart at least has a right to know what he's gotten into."

She'd taken Floyt's hand, which instantly started to sweat. Floyt wasn't sure what to do but was appalled by the thought of struggling with her, so ducking under Alacrity's arm, he let himself be led into the compartment.

Alacrity looked unresolved, then slouched after, telling himself, *If you lost her it's your own fault. And if that's the price of the White Ship, so be it.*

"Wulf is Chief Operating Officer of the Haviland family," Heart explained, naming one of the most powerful of the Carousel clans. "He's voting their shares and he's on our side—or, at least, mine. Now sit; I'll have to give this to you in big bites."

They sat, and she began bringing up displays, a data mosaic ten times bigger and more complex than the one back in the *Whelk*. And Floyt could see it was only a part of what the workstation could do; he followed the accessing procedures carefully, memorizing.

"My father and his group—what we call the Old Guard—have the majority of active shares over us, but only by a little," Heart said. "You two know some of his allies: Baron Mason is here, and Praxis. They're all pretty much used to having what they want, and what they want now, and what they have a fairly good chance of getting after years and years of plotting and conniving, is to make a complete break with what the White Ship is *supposed* to be and make her completely theirs.

"Except Reno Magusson changed everything on them when he went and left Dr. Higgins his stock. Sibyl's so radical, she's not even sure there ought to *be* a White Ship, much less one in the hands of the Old Guard."

She stopped and swung her chair back toward them. "That Reno! I think he respected Doc Sibyl a lot and decided the board needed a counterbalance."

Alacrity was only half listening, the other half being a void of longing for Heart. "But the Magusson shares— Dr. Higgins's—don't give you a majority?" Floyt said.

The Nonpareil shook her head, the slightly frazzled doggy-ears swinging. "And that's in spite of the fact that a lot of other things changed, due to the Old Guard types who are out of the picture now because they were Camarilla members—*grazie*, Floyt and Fitzhugh!

"Rules prohibit proxy voting of inactive shares, so that only leaves us in the New Faction a *little* out of the winner's circle."

Wulf gestured to the workstation. "We feel that the White Ship and the company have certain obligations to the human race—to all species; to the common good, if that doesn't sound too florid. And so the New Faction is going to try to make its move."

His voice was deep and sure. Wulf had a direct, searching gaze that Floyt found himself trusting. "So we're looking through everything we've got on every Old Guard member. If we can just leverage another vote or two our way, we'll bring it off."

"But so far, nothing looks promising," Heart added. "And we're just about out of time. The Ship will be calling the meeting soon."

Alacrity was staring down at the deck. "Listen, you never know. Something could break for us."

Us! Floyt looked at the walls of systemry to hide his feelings; Alacrity had made his decision and, Wulf or no Wulf, was going to do right. Floyt's chest swelled with pride.

Heart looked puzzled, a fine crease coming into view between the long, arched brows, the flawless curves of the lips parted and about to speak. As had happened to him before, seeing her mouth that way, Alacrity found that his own lips had opened. He clamped them angrily, just as the compartment's hatch opened again.

Another man stood there, in the same striking crimson suit-of-thongs that Wulf wore, its stretched strands glittering like ice and blood. He was younger, not so filled out, but with the same cut and curl of beard and hair.

"Wulf, Dr. Higgins wants to talk to you before she calls the rest together for a final war council prior to the board meeting." He was inspecting Heart, Alacrity, and Floyt as he delivered the message, with something Floyt couldn't quite put a name to, something that had undertones of suspicion. "She also managed to obtain a little of the Heavyset data. She wonders if Citizen Floyt and Master Fitzhugh would take a look at it."

Wulf got up, squeezing the Nonpareil's hand affectionately and moving to the younger man, saying "Very well, Yester." Wulf put his olympian arm around Yester's shoulders reassuringly, kissing his forehead and cheek gently.

And to Floyt he said, "Citizen? If you'd do us the favor of talking to Sibyl?"

Floyt checked to see Alacrity's expression. It looked like somebody was standing on Alacrity's foot but he didn't quite know what to do about it. "Of course."

"We'll be right along, Hobart, Wulf," Heart told them. Floyt readusted his Inheritor's belt and went off, trailing Yester and Wulf. They climbed into the tram Yester had brought.

"You're the one who does those genealogies, right?" Yester smiled, jealousy assuaged, as the hatch closed. "You know, I've been meaning to do my family tree for a while now—"

Heart turned back to her accessing. "Oh, and by the way, Alacrity: congratulations on your engagement, and the same to Hobart and La Minx. I expected you and Ho to be wearing lifts in your shoes, at the very least, or maybe flying harnesses."

"C'mon, lay off; you know it was just a stunt! *Ho-ino-wale, wahine!* How could him and me live someplace where we had to stand on a stepladder to take a piss?"

She laughed out loud, that full-throated melody he remembered from the first minute he'd met her. Then she gave him a rueful look, a tilt of the head that would've had a mischievous curl bobbing across one eye if her hair were free.

"I'm glad the stunt worked and that you and Hobart got here safely, but I'm not letting you take over the New Faction or the White Ship, you know."

"I have an idea: let's save this tub from your old man and his gang and *then* iron out the details. And just for the record, there're *two* things I want more than everything else combined: this Ship, and to make you love me again. Because I still love you."

She was disarmed completely, blinking as though she'd taken an electrical shock. "Oh, but Alacrity! I still love you, too! We were going to mate for life, like swans, remember?"

He moved to kiss her and she met him halfway. The kiss was harsh and drawing one moment, tender the next, and then harsh again, tongues gliding like mating constrictors then suddenly tentative as hummingbirds.

After some minutes they moved, still clasped so that he was sitting on the couch, Heart maneuvering herself to straddle him, settling onto his lap. Her baggy suit was all seals and buckles and adjustment tabs, but there was a long convenience seam running from the navel region to the coccyx. She opened it down, under, around, and up while he threw the captain's jacket aside and worked the waistband on his trousers.

Afterward, she lay draped along him, their arms around each other, touching noses and foreheads and lips and chins by turns, lapsing into long kisses and parting again to peer deep into lover's eyes.

"I forgot how very, very—"

"Yeah, me, too; I only *thought* I remembered." He let out a breath. "I worried about you all the time, even when I was busy worrying about myself."

She drew her fingertips along his cheek. "Same here. After you and the rest made your break for Earth, and Victoria and I got the *Astraea Imprimatur* into Hawking, we did what we could for poor Janusz's injuries, then we patched up the ship and limped to a real fringe world called Easy Street. That's where Victoria told me you'd given her practically all those novaseed gems you had."

He grinned, pleased with himself. "Figured you'd need 'em worse than me."

She reached down, squirming a bit, to give him a very special caress. "Good guess. So, we got Janusz into a decent med facility and eventually got the *Stray* repaired, although we ended up having to sell off a lot of her beautiful fittings.

"And we had plenty of other crises, too, some very rough spots, but later for those. Eventually Janusz and Victoria dropped me off on a planet where my credit account was good and flew off to lay low together for the next century or so. I knew there'd be no reconciliation with my father, so I've been rushing around trying to get ready for this showdown and find out what happened to you and Hobart after you ducked out of the party on Earth."

It was good to hear that Janusz and his lover, the renegade Langstretch op Victoria Roper, were together and safe. But at the moment there were greater and more immediate joys to celebrate. He'd responded to her gentle stroking and moved his hips under hers, easing himself in . . .

Just then the Ship's voice came into the compartment. "Shareholders Fitzhugh and Heart Dincrist, your presence is requested in the Vale by Shareholder Higgins."

"That tight-ass voice is the first thing to go when the New Faction takes over!" Heart started to lever herself up and off, but he held her for another kiss.

"So now I get to meet Sibyl Higgins?"

"Um-hmm. She's really a great old dame under it all. I *think*. There's a small head off the compartment there; we'll have to freshen up one at a time—*me first!*"

It was close, but he lost the race and lay laughing on the deck as she roared hysterically from within, over the sound of running water.

Then his eye fell on the transactions terminal. *Shaitan! I forgot all about it!*

He leapt for it, almost falling over his half-mast trousers. Getting himself slightly reorganized, he took off his proteus and fed Hecate's codes and passwords into the Ship's network, taking control of 340,000 shares without a hitch or a glitch, and was credited with accrued dividends in an amount that was more than he could quite picture.

He set his own codes in place and was about to conclude the transaction when an interrogatory came up: QUERY TO LAST REMAINING FOUNDING SHAREHOLDER HEIR-DESIGNATE: CHANGE CODE FOR SAMPSON OPTIONS?

He entered: DISPLAY MENU SAMPSON OPTIONS.

He sat for long moments, face lit by the flaring displays. His expression flattened, went cold.

Something has moved me along, all my life, to this moment. This is all as it is supposed to be. And the causality harp proves it, and that business with Hecate proves it, and now this confirms it. Like it or not, I'm just what Ho called me: the White Ship Avatar . . .

CHAPTER 19

QUANTUM MUTATUS AB ILLO

WHEN ALACRITY AND HEART ARRIVED, MEMBERS OF the New Faction were still circulating and chatting. Floyt was still glancing about him wonderingly.

The Vale, like a lot of other amenities, had been installed in the White Ship on the assumption of a prolonged mission in inhospitable regions and the likelihood that the Ship's compliment would need a change from decks and bulkheads. In that respect she was like many vessels that had come and gone before, but Floyt doubted many of those had had an environmental compartment to match the Vale.

In Floyt's mind the place was reminiscent of an elven glen out of Earth legend, miraculously set under a crystal dome in space. As that part of the Ship faced away from Spica or any other source of strong direct light, stars shone down.

The Vale's flora all came, like the Vale itself, from Paradise, and was bioluminescent in pale blues, grays, and greens. Even fruits and blossoms, and what looked like insect chrysalises and huge gossamer nests, glowed.

The trees resembled parasols, anchored balloons, pipe organs; shrubbery might be clouds around a sunset here, a flight of softly radiant birds there. The grasses underfoot were a phosphorescent fog, the curling, twisting blades infinitely fine.

301

The sounds of the place were of tiny creatures trilling, birring, and chirping. And the lush "Forever Endeavor, Amen" played, the symphony whose theme was the Precursors great works and the long effort to penetrate their mysteries. Floyt had never heard it before he left Earth; it was becoming very familiar.

A long table had been set out down in the center of the Vale, a score of tall chairs around it. Serving automata floated about, dispensing food, drink, and other refreshments, data, or whatever else the attendees might require. The shareholders already present were putting off the moment when they would sit; they faced a lot of long hours in those chairs.

Floyt heard someone chafe that the board should adopt more modern meeting procedures: holographic conference linkups that would let people rest in comfort, for example. As an Earthservice functionary, Floyt himself had always found that the more comfortable people were at a meeting, the longer it went on and the less got done.

He'd look over the other New Faction members. Sibyl Higgins was off to one side with Wulf and Yester and a nonhuman of a species that called itself the Ghh'arkt, a furred, stork-legged thing. Busy with her young turk lobbying, Higgins barely accorded Floyt a nod of the head and a wristclasp, but various people appeared eager to introduce themselves.

They accorded him a great deal of courtesy as he stood there in his snow-white tie and black tails, the Inheritor's belt gleaming, the first Terran any of them had ever seen in the flesh. In a fairly short time he received two sexual overtures, three inquiries about Terran genealogies, several compliments on his exploits as described in books like *Hobart Floyt and Alacrity Fitzhugh Challenge the Amazon Slave Women of the Supernova*, and at least a half-dozen requests for Circe Minx's autograph.

And naturally in this gathering it took no more than a

word or two to trigger diverse theories about the Precursors from assorted Interested Parties.

An ascetic-looking young man called Chancellor Peale-Vuttruck, who claimed to have used part of his enormous inheritance to set up his own think tank devoted to Precursors matters, said he had proof that the Precursors still existed—and always had—in the realm of the neutrino and the tachyon. To them, humans and the substantial cosmos in general were a mist, intangible but perceived through certain secondary effects. The so-called Precursor artifacts were merely probes and efforts at communication.

Yester's conclusion was that the Precursors' massmind conscience had obliged them to take themselves outside of ordinary reality, to give younger races a chance to develop. A quite striking dowager held that the Precursors had presumed to attempt to reorder Creation more to their liking and been banished for that by a Higher Power.

Floyt could see from their faces that Alacrity and Heart were back on a truce footing and a lot more, the two wearing cream-in-whiskers looks.

Heart had changed from the slop-around shipsuit and now wore a stupefying black sheath of high-sheen skinfilm, not quite transparent, so sheer and taut that it seemed it must burst, molding parts of the Nonpareil that didn't really require molding. The chalk-blond hair was full and perfect again, weighty locks of it that framed her face and the wide, encased shoulders, and one curl that bobbed mischievously across her eye. Her spike-heeled evening slippers of smokey duraglaze chimed faintly with each step on the pathstones and made her Alacrity's height and more.

She wore the proteus Floyt recalled, an Impéria Optitech that looked like a chic manacle, made of precious metals set with natural wavestones, ardors, and Satan's tears.

As for Alacrity, he was as heroic and noble as could

be in his splendid captain's uniform. Their appearance alone made them a formidable couple, an impact to be reckoned with. Alacrity gazed around rapt at the Vale, which had long ago rested on a planetary surface—in Alacrity's grandfather's backyard on Paradise, to be exact.

Sibyl Higgins spied the two and didn't hesitate for a moment to block their way, making Heart less ebullient and Alacrity mistrustful. "So, Fitzhugh, you made it here alive! Against the odds! I have heard a good deal about you, and read the files. Young man, you do not strike me as the sort of chap who'll die in bed!"

"God knows, I try, ma'am."

Heart stifled a kind of *yimph!* of laughter and fought to keep a straight face. Higgins nearly smiled. "How very nice for you both, I'm sure. Shareholder Fitzhugh, your friend Mr. Floyt knows a certain amount about what's about here tonight. I suggest you join him. How you vote is your decision, of course. Your sympathies seem to lie in the right place; I hope you are with us as a matter of morale, even though you don't represent much stock."

"Thanks." *Have you got a surprise coming, Granny!*

Higgins went to make final preparations, joined by Heart and the rest of her privy circle, One-Vote-Fitzhugh pointedly excluded. Alacrity ambled over to Floyt, who was savoring a cup of coffee that tasted far better than any the Earthservice ever served up to a functionary third class.

"Hecate's in the bag," Alacrity slurred, so that Floyt had a hard time catching it, Alacrity unsure of who might be watching or listening. "What've you found out?"

Floyt sipped again, eyes closed in rapture. "Just that the White Ship is practically a sideshow, in some ways, at this point."

That made Alacrity's big, oblique eyes go nearly round. "Wha? Look, spit it out; we haven't got much time."

Floyt set the delicate cup down in its fragile saucer

precisely. "There are the many, many patents and licenses that have come out of the White Ship and Ship research, of course, and they represent a huge income. But even those are secondary. Alacrity, that Heavyset ship? The one down near Spica? *It's here because it heard the White Ship!* The Ship's AI's summoned it, or were talking to each other, or something, in Heavyset, or modified Precursor symbology, or some combination of the foregoing. Nobody's sure."

"They—who—how—"

"Don't interrupt, and I'll endeavor to make this painless."

A serving robo drifted by and Alacrity got it to cough up a pisco sour. He debated over an inhaler of perkup; the contusions and other hurts he'd received in the scuffle with Gentry Standing Bear were starting to ache again. So he shrugged and took a wheeze or two.

He wished there was a little more recuperative time available. A half-grain hit of kick might do as a substitute, but it would be a bad idea to overdo and be playing Tarzan out on a Vale tree limb someplace while Dincrist and his contingent made their move.

In the meantime Floyt brought Alacrity up to date. "I've been listening to these people here and accessing a little, and I tell you, the Ship's brain and the AI's it uses to run things—well, they're very good, but they were drawn from everywhere, put together piecemeal and updated very, ah, *haphazardly*. Stuff right out of military R&D side by side with stuff that had been extracted from older starships, do you see what I mean? What I'm saying is, the right hand doesn't necessarily know what the left is doing.

"And so what happened was, Dincrist and that lot began making inroads with the Ship, starting some years back. They were using data that were of interest to the Ship to open up operational areas of its brain to them, so they could window their way through to a position of power, at the same time as they were putting together a majority of voting shares. They've got the shares, but they don't seem to have that window, at least not yet."

Floyt stopped for a deep breath and another sip of coffee. Alacrity sipped the pisco sour and curbed himself from interrupting.

"But what the Old Guard *did* feed in—Dincrist did, mainly—were Heavyset/Precursor correlations. Symbols, impulses; I don't quite understand yet. Alacrity, I think some of it came from Weir. That in return for the Blackguard intelligence Dincrist gave Weir—and that Dincrist thought Weir was merely going to use to become a landholder on Blackguard, instead of using it to throw down the Camarilla—Dincrist got some of the Heavyset/Precursor stuff I'm talking about." His voice had dropped to a stage whisper.

Alacrity's forehead was ridged with lines of thought. "Maybe as his Inheritance?"

Floyt held up his hands helplessly. "I wish I could tell you. I won't have a clear idea until I do a lot more accessing, preferably someplace private."

The perkup had Alacrity feeling alert, dynamic, unhampered by injuries, tingling. Floyt said, "Put down that inhaler and listen, damn you! Somewhere in the labyrinth of the Ship mind, in some information pocket no one's been able to isolate, is the basis for the first real contact humans or anyone else have ever had with the Heavysets! As long as you're going to stand there with your mouth open, drink."

Alacrity did, but not much; he was too distracted.

The Heavysets were almost as much a mystery as the Precursors. There were those who thought the Heavies *were* the Precursors. Except that the Heavysets seemed more or less contemporaries of humanity and were anxious to solve the Precursor enigmas, too. Certainly, the Heavies avoided contact with *Homo sapiens*, and just as certainly their technology gave humans every reason not to push the issue.

A few observations had been made, like the fact that Heavyset ships apparently zipped in and out of singularities as they pleased, and a few conclusions, such as the one that the Heavysets had visited the Galactic Core and other galaxies as well. They preferred extreme-gravity worlds and situations; thus their name.

An exclusive pipeline to the Heavysets could amount to a throne from which the human race and most other known intelligent species could be ruled if the wrong party or parties controlled the White Ship.

Sibyl Higgins, swiping her peppermint hair out of her eyes, was clearing her throat and calling for attention. Alacrity, looking at her, wondered if she'd worn her white clinician outfit for prestige or simply because she figured there might be some medical emergencies before the meeting was over.

"As leading shareholder of our faction, I believe I'm to speak for us all. Unless someone objects? I hold four hundred fifty-five thousand six hundred shares in the White Ship."

Nobody said anything. Alacrity seemed very interested in the bioluminescent grass, so like cotton candy, underfoot.

"We are met in that very same Paradise Vale where the original Ship founders convened and threw in their lot together these many years ago," Higgins went on. "This very beautiful place that was later transported up *in toto* and made part of the Ship." She gestured around her at the faerie beauty.

"I shall put our case at the full meeting, as we've agreed, and we'll see whom we may sway on the other side. Failing an upset, it seems, we must turn our efforts to public opinion and to every avenue of acquisition of more shares."

As if Dincrist and his bunch would care about public opinion if they get a hotline to the Heavies, Alacrity thought. *I sure wouldn't.*

A tone sounded through the Vale, not out of phase with the humming of XT insects and the susurrus of a light breeze that came from no source Floyt could see.

"The meeting begins directly," Higgins said. "Please

take your places." The Nonpareil took Alacrity's hand and led him to his assigned place. On the way, Higgins intercepted again and drew Alacrity aside.

"Your family was well intended, from what I can find out. But good intentions are not enough. Don't disrupt what we are trying to do here for personal vendettas. I hope you're made of sterner stuff than your mother and father."

Heart and Floyt held their breath, and Floyt readied to jump into a brawl again. Alacrity said in a low, scorching voice, "Look, I know all about you and that Strike Recondo training, but if you ever say anything like that to me again, I'll *drink your blood*, understand?"

Once she saw she'd gotten him angry, Higgins became as serene as the Ship. "If I've given you rage, channel it toward our opposition, as shrewdness."

"Madam, you are crotch curd."

Alacrity assumed his seat, face burning. Floyt stood behind it, as the other advisors and companions were doing for their principals, and asked himself which side Sibyl Higgins was working for.

Yester, behind Wulf's seat, looked like a graven image. Sibyl Higgins sat at one end of the table, all the New Faction to her right, Heart the closest; no one stood behind Heart's chair, or Higgins's.

From among the trees walked a file of newcomers, about an even balance of males and females, along with two nonhumans, wending their way down through the magical Vale. Dincrist led.

Heart's father came to stand at the other end of the table; those who followed him went to their places at his right. The nonhuman pair was Srillan, and Floyt had a momentary feeling of pleasure; though Srillans had laid waste so much of Terra during the Final Smear, the two members of that species he'd met personally turned out to be good friends and allies. But he saw that neither the aardvarklike alien in the chair nor the one who stood behind was Maska or his nephew Corva. Floyt's Earthbred loathing overcame him again.

Alacrity scanned the newcomers, too: Dincrist, regally tall and fit and tan, silver-maned, sworn to kill Alacrity and Floyt. Clearly the leader. Next along was Praxis, head of the Church of Human Potential, Saint of the Irreducible I, textbook-class mental defective. Praxis had the white hair and distinguished looks common to his type, a holyman of self-forgiveness and self-understanding. His secret vice, known to Alacrity and Floyt and a very few others, was subjecting clones of himself to unutterable abuses.

Floyt recognized most of the others from the files he'd read—well fleshed but hard-eyed, all, including the several women among them.

Watching Alacrity with predatory hatred was Baron Mason of Styx, once a Better of Blackguard until Alacrity and Floyt had to bring all Blackguard's ugliness down to get away with their skins, and also because the universe was better off that way. Mason was the biggest person there, half a head taller than Alacrity, vigorous looking, with direct, piercing black eyes. He had a head of thick, curly black hair touched with white—not gray —at the temples. His beard projected in two menacing spikes, the middle of his chin being clean shaven.

And standing behind Mason...

Alacrity's mouth twisted. "Well, hey, Constance! Up and around, huh? I figured they'd still be busy replacing that brain of yours with something a little better, like for example a half-watt bulb."

Constance, once Dincrist's creature, now stood behind Mason's chair, from where she gave Alacrity a seething, teasing look. Constance had helped waylay Alacrity and Floyt and implant the actijots in them. She no longer worked in tandem with her pirate-partner/lover Sile because Sile wasn't very presentable after Alacrity shot him dead.

Constance's eyes were long, painted ellipses—eyes blue as Spica, Alacrity had once observed to himself. Floyt compared them to cornflowers. She was olive-skinned, lean-flanked as a boy, with lemon-yellow hair barely long enough to hold a part. She wore soleskins and a minimal V-shaped garment of white glove leather, crotch to shoulders, her skin glitterflecked.

Constance crossed her arms, tapping herself absently with fingers encased in long golden mandarin-style sheaths set with gems and painted in enamel to look like dragon's claws. Alacrity knew the fingernails within were bitten to the quick. Floyt thought of Hecate, and of Paloma Sudan.

"'Lo, cupcake," she purred. "You don't know how much I wanted to see you again. And poor old dippy Hobart Floyt, there, too, it goes without saying! But, oh, Fitz-*you*! *Tch!* The *score* we have to settle!"

Constance shook her head and rolled her eyes. Floyt felt the hair stand on the back of his neck. Constance's main thrill was pain, and he knew enough about her to be scared. Further along the table the Nonpareil was staring raw death at her.

"Enough."

That one word from Captain Softcoygne Dincrist, Heart's father, was enough to cut through the murmuring at the table and end the sideshow. Constance subsided, running one talon along Baron Mason's chair sullenly, as everyone looked to Dincrist. His place became the head of the table with his presence, since Higgins was seated. "We have business at hand." He rapped the table with a large signet ring that carried his family crest.

The Srillan who was seated, the shareholder, slapped paws together, sleepy-eyed but animated. His silver-black pelt was beginning to show the russet frosting of old age.

"Indeed! Here at last we'll have one of the shortest board meetings on record!" His Terranglish wasn't bad but, as with all his species, it was like listening to somebody talking through a rolled-up rug.

Alacrity put the arm on a passing robo for a refill. Dincrist gave a death's-head grin. "Yes, a very succinct meeting. Now: the usual agenda is set aside. The question before us is: shall a research team as specified in the proposal addendum be constituted as described to isolate from the White Ship's AI's the basis of this apparent communication with the Heavysets and render a detailed report to my committee?

"Now, speaking for my group, I cast a majority vote *aye*, in advance. Debate will be limited to five minutes, and then—*Fitzhugh! Stop that!*"

Alacrity was rapping his knuckles on the robo who'd given him his drinks. "Hey! Paracelsus! How about a readout on that? The majority, I mean?"

The automaton said in the Ship's voice, "Impossible to compute until you declare your preference, Shareholder Fitzhugh."

Dincrist's snowy brows lowered. "What's this? That young whoreson votes only one share!"

"As of sixteen thirteen Ship time, this date," the robo corrected in the virgin-priestess voice, "Alacrity Fitzhugh holds voting power over three hundred forty thousand and one shares."

There were open mouths all around except for Floyt. Floyt reached around the chair and whapped Alacrity's shoulder triumphantly. Heart rayed him with a smile that made his whole life worthwhile.

Alacrity raised the pisco sour. "Some of us are born to greatness; others don't see anything wrong with swiping it."

"What's that one share for?" Wulf leaned out over the table to ask. "Luck?"

"To grow an inch," Alacrity said, leering at Heart. He turned back to her father.

"Anyway, I vote against this motion, or resolution, or whatever you want to call it. Motion denied, Paracelsus?"

"Motion rejected by a vote of one million four hundred seventy-nine thousand four hundred twenty-five shares in favor to one million five hundred twenty thousand five hundred seventy-five opposed."

Dincrist shook a big, browned, very impressive fist. "This is a fraud! He's rigged the computers somehow!"

He pointed at Alacrity. "You're not going to cheat me again!"

Mason had risen and walked off to one side of Dincrist's chair, the Srillan shareholder waddling to the other, both of them calming him. Constance drew slow breaths, nostrils flared, pursing her lips at Alacrity. Heart's dimples appeared first, then her full smile was directed his way as Alacrity felt a distinct increase in his vitamin D level.

"This is an important vote," Baron Mason said after a quick, whispered conference with Dincrist. He glared around the table. "The bulk of the information the Ship used in contacting the Heavysets came from Captain Dincrist's sources, and he has the right to litigate to deny you access to the final product! And then no one profits.

"Now then: what I propose is that our faction withdraw from the Vale for a few minutes—say, five. We will caucus, and you here may reconsider the matter among yourselves."

What must it have taken to make these two sworn enemies allies? Floyt wondered.

Mason moved around the table as the other Old Guard members rose to follow along with their escorts. Alacrity saw with surprise that the baron was coming his way.

Floyt wasn't sure what to do, but Alacrity gave him a nod, so he made way. Any transgression would be picked up by the Ship herself and dealt with, and Alacrity knew Mason was smart enough to be well aware of that. Alacrity rose and met the baron partway though, to have some maneuvering room just in case. Others there did their best to appear not to be staring.

"You have something that belongs to me," the baron whispered harshly, glaring.

"Your proteus, you mean?" Alacrity smiled innocently. "Well, I'll tell you, now, it looked like you were going to use it to get me and the others blasted as soon as you could get free of that riot, and it looked sort of valuable, so I just took it for safekeeping."

"Don't toy with me, you little nobody! That instrument is of no value to you, and you'll soon have all the trouble you can handle and more if you don't start using common sense, believe me! Now, what have you done with that proteus?"

"Oh," Alacrity said, pretending Mason's threats hadn't rattled him, "why don't we talk about that a little later? And why don't we also talk about how you're going to vote your shares for the rest of this meeting?"

Baron Mason's eyes went wide, but Dincrist called out to him, Constance was coming nearer, and the rest of the Old Guard had already withdrawn. Nodding balefully, Mason went, flanked by Constance, to join Dincrist. They followed their allies up the path.

Alacrity walked back to his place as murmured side exchanges began to die away. After a short silence, Sibyl Higgins put the question, "I believe I'm safe in saying none of us cares to change his or her vote?" Nobody contradicted her.

"Then I see no reason to prolong—" Higgins had just begun when hatches boomed closed, reverberating, and a voice filled the Vale. It was the first time any of them had heard the Ship speak with any voice but her own; it was nothing short of terrifying that it was the voice of Dincrist.

"Now hear this! You people in there have only one thing to consider: the next vote is going to be unanimous, and so you will either reverse your position or you'll die."

Everybody at the table was talking at once. Alacrity was the first one to his feet, moving to grab the Nonpareil's hand and race off up the moon-garden path by which he'd arrived, heading for the only hatch whose location he was sure of, making sure Floyt was close behind. The balance of the New Faction bolted after.

But the hatch was secured and wouldn't open. Others gathered behind as Alacrity and Floyt struggled with it. It took only a minute or so to accept that it wasn't going to budge. There were no tool lockers or equipment stations in the Vale, no airlocks, or spacesuits to use even if there had been.

The Ship herself was supposed to be final arbiter of rules, the failsafe insurance that the laws laid down by her founders would be abided by, the final safety factor in the system. The Ship was supposed to see to it that this sort of thing couldn't happen, and she always had. But now, somehow, she was compromised, at least in part, and the New Faction was boxed.

"Was there anything about this kind of tactic in the data you obtained from your father?" Wulf asked Heart.

She shook her head, the heavy locks swinging. "Absolutely nothing."

"You know your situation," Dincrist's voice boomed at them. "But there are...those among you whom I—we—would rather spare. So then: change your vote. Tell the Ship! And we continue with our great endeavor!"

"How can they expect to get away with this?" someone yelled.

"Hell's payroll!" Wulf's deep voice answered. "If they get the Ship to let them dig out the Heavyset-contact secrets, they'll be able to write their own ticket!"

"Um, why doesn't the Ship stop them, Ho?" Alacrity muttered to Floyt. "She kept 'em from bringing in guns, or they wouldn't've had to try this lock-in stuff." He didn't dwell on what would happen if the Ship leeched away the Vale's air supply.

"I *told* you, Alacrity: the Ship's personality isn't one AI. It's an interlocking constellation. It's gotten very big and I think it may be starting to break down with this Heavyset business. And the subparts, well, they *leak*. Back and forth. And I don't have the access to get us out of here. The left hand doesn't know what the right hand's doing."

"Pay attention," Dincrist said resoundingly. "I am going to begin bleeding the air from the Vale. You have perhaps half an hour. The decision rests with you."

"He couldn't have complete control of the Ship,"

Wulf mused, fingers toying with the thick ringlets of his beard, "or he wouldn't need a majority vote."

The immediate New Faction idea was a motion, passed unanimously, that the Ship open the hatch. But somehow in his poking and tampering, Dincrist had found a way to nullify that.

The next decision came from Sibyl Higgins. "I don't know what this will come to, but Dincrist and the others *have* us. Human life is sacred, and so I say that we concede."

"What about the human lives of people who're gonna have to live under Dincrist and his gang, and die under them?" Alacrity drawled.

She dealt him a wintry look. "Our deaths will not affect that one way or the other, it appears. Why?"

"Just running a spine check, as it turns out." Alacrity smirked. He looked around, spotted the nearest Ship pickup, called to it.

"Shareholder Alacrity Fitzhugh. Identify."

"Shareholder Alacrity Fitzhugh, confirmed," the Ship's voice said.

"Sampson Option. Menu."

"Sampson Option menu, aye! Menu: Option One: event, mutiny. Option two: event, piracy. Option three: event, incontrovertible infestation. Option—"

"Stop!" Alacrity drew a breath. "Sampson Option three: event, incontrovertible infestation. Run it."

"Sampson Option three: event, incontrovertible infestation, running, aye!"

People were looking at each other with eyes the size of pingpong balls, Floyt included. There was no real sense of movement, but everybody was aware of the change in the starfield overhead and looked up to see that the Ship was changing course. The crystal dome polarized for a moment as Spica swung into view and then past, the Ship realigning herself.

"Alacrity, wouldn't you like to tell us what Sampson Option three is?" Floyt hinted quietly.

"Something the Founders put in, my grandparents

and the others who sat right at that same table in that same Vale down there, back when the Ship was just a dream! Contingency plans, and all that. I didn't know it was in there any more until I took over Hecate's shares; her access was linked to the Sampson Option. I guess all other accesses were expunged."

He pointed up to the dome. The glow of Spica, coming from forward, lit motes in the upper air. "Anyway, you can see for yourself, can't you? We're heading into Spica. Ultimate decontamination. And nothing gets into the Ship now, and nothing gets out. And she'll evade or repel rescue attempts, even presuming somebody gives that a try."

"And if Dincrist decides you're bluffing?" Higgins asked coldly.

"Then he finds out I'm not."

"Query!" Heart spoke up to the Ship. "Estimated time of destruction?"

The Ship voice came. "Presuming no contact with stellar prominence activity, entry into Spican photosphere in thirty-four minutes. Destruction of this vessel within six minutes of that time, plus or minus estimated twenty-five percent." The Ship sounded above it all.

Alacrity whistled. "We're really movin'!" To the pickup he said, "Put that out over the PA." The Ship's death sentence echoed across the Vale.

The furred-stork humanoid, Clizzixx, click-spoke. Its translator device rendered, "This does not seem sensible."

"Amen, brother," Alacrity shot back.

The Nonpareil's expression was all misgiving. "Alacrity, my father will never give in. Remember the Regatta, when he wouldn't divert course to finish us off because he wanted to win? Well, he never stops once he's committed to something!"

Alacrity, a little surprised, studied her. "And you think I do?"

"It's getting hotter in here," somebody quavered.

"Only 'cause you're sweating," Alacrity said, inspecting the hatch again. "The heat differential's so huge, passing it along to the interior of the Ship wouldn't make much difference. The Ship'll keep us cool pretty much until she's done for." *And I'll kill us all before I give up this Ship! She belongs to my family; she belongs to me!*

"Let's get something to eat in the meantime; I'm starved," he lied. He started back down the path, leaving a babble of argument behind him. Floyt dashed to catch up. Heart was neck and neck, fast in chiming spike heels.

"When do we pass the point of no return?" she asked, falling into step just as Floyt did.

Alacrity shook his head and said slowly, "I'm not sure, and I don't want the Ship putting it out over the PA. *Pheew!* Once we're down by the photosphere, my friends, one good Spican prominence would probably put us out of commission for good."

He got Paracelsus and ordered another pisco sour. Floyt loosened his white bowtie and wing collar; the Nonpareil massaged her temples and tried to think. Maybe it *was* imagination, but Alacrity felt hotter, too.

Heart looked up to the blue-lit motes floating in the dome. "My father won't give her to you," she said, hugging her arms to herself. "Maybe you believe it's better that the Ship be destroyed rather than fall under his control. Maybe you're even right! I don't know anymore! But he's just as ready to die as you are, and I thought you were better than him, that way. But you're both so *fucking* ready to die!"

"If I really was, we wouldn't be here, Heart. You should've heard some of the other Sampson Options."

Alacrity set the pisco sour aside without having tasted it. "I'm not betting on your father; I'm betting on those soulbenders he's in with. He's not some heroic one-man expedition this time; he's saddled with a bunch of greedy, self-centered slime smears."

There was a furor on the footpath. Higgins came

down the trail, leading the others. Wulf brought up the rear, dignified and deliberate, Yester trailing him.

Higgins came up close. "Master Fitzhugh, this has gone far enough! The issue is not worth innocent lives!"

Alacrity almost laughed. "You seen any of those around here?"

"Stop talking nonsense!" She took a step nearer and her small brown hands took on odd, martial shapes. Alacrity tried not to sweat, but everybody knew stories about those superhumans, the undefeated Strike Recondos who'd trained her and given her her enhancements.

"You *will* revoke your instruction to the White Ship, Master Fitzhugh, or I shall be obliged to make you do so."

Alacrity thought about nerve holds or maybe even injections, if she'd brought along styrettes. Recondos had infamous ways of getting information, but those probably weren't a patch on what somebody learned in ten-odd years running a penal ward.

Alacrity leaned back a bit, afraid; height and weight and reach didn't mean a damn in this context. Gentry Standing Bear would probably be easier to deal with. He debated plunging into the undergrowth, dodging and hiding, anything to give his plan time to work.

But he chose to stand his ground in his grandfather's ship, glowering. "No."

Floyt intervened, facing Higgins and the rest. "You gutless *children*! Get back! He's right and you know it!"

Heart came from the other side, shoulder to shoulder with Floyt, protecting Alacrity. "You're all so free with words! *What happens to the White Ship decides what happens to the human race!* Stand back, now, or strike the first blow at me."

Most of the group was undecided, but Alacrity saw Wulf slip in to stand at Higgin's shoulder, and knew a pang of disappointment. He'd liked Wulf.

Higgins went into a martial crouch. "Yes, I think we

will have to. And later there will be time to try to get what *we* want."

Alacrity, astounded, watched as Wulf brought up his big, dojo-hardened fist for a hammer blow on Higgin's neck, a risky attempt to put her out of the action with one shot, which was the only feasible way. Higgins was saying "Your last chance, Fitzhugh. Cooperate! I don't wish to do you harm!"

Alacrity must have betrayed something with his eyes; Higgins caught some hint from him and/or Heart and/or Floyt, and swung around with reflexes that reminded Floyt of Hecate. She caught Wulf's arm on its lightning descent, arresting it there, and appeared to tap him.

Wulf fell back, all the color leaving his face, blocking Yester from leaping to his assistance. Alacrity, Floyt, and Heart were about to launch themselves at Higgins when they realized somebody was yelling "Stop it! Look! Look!"

There'd been a weighty metal grinding for a few seconds as the confrontation went on, Alacrity realized, and the creak of bending alloy. And now there was a growing slice of strong artificial light across the top of the footpath, overwhelming the soft bioluminescence of the Vale.

A voice called down, "Fitzhugh! We've opened the hatch! Stop the Ship! You win!" It was some Old Guard veteran, not Dincrist. It was sweeter than anything Floyt had ever heard in his life.

Alacrity was off and running like one of Lord Marcus Perlez's rover lightshapes, dodging around the scene at the table, racing for the light. Floyt and Heart were first to follow, then the others in a rush, except for Yester, and Wulf, whom Yester had leaning on him weakly, and Higgins, who took Wulf's other side and kneaded pressure points to undo the paralysis.

The hatch had been crumpled open with force tools and power jacks liberated from a nearby tool locker. Mason, Praxis, Constance, and Dincrist were gone, but the rest of the Old Guard was there. It was what Alacrity had been betting on: not that Dincrist would lose his nerve, but that his followers would.

"Stop the Ship! Turn us back!" It was a magisterial-looking, elderly man.

Alacrity held the old man back with one hand. "Sure, all right! After you tell me Dincrist and the others give up! Where are they?"

The answer was so shrill it was hard to understand. "They're crazy! They went forward to the bridge. They say they're going to blank the Ship's memory!"

There was only one passageway tram there, a small one; by the time things got sorted out, Alacrity had jumped in along with Heart and Floyt. The other New Factioners had gathered round.

Alacrity accelerated away. "That's enough! We're too heavy already! Get more trams; follow when you can!"

The White Ship's bridge wasn't very far forward of the Vale in terms of the Ship's overall size, but the trip was four minutes of fear and forboding anyway, the tram whisking along passageways and riding interdeck chutes.

When they got to the bridge, Alacrity jumped off the tram while it was still moving and marched in without looking around for an ambush. He calculated that Dincrist and the others had had enough time to divine that they couldn't stop Sampson Option three or save themselves short of caving in to Alacrity.

He'd entered via the captain's companionway, looking out on a bridge that was twice the size of the Vale. *All those tech stations, slaved through the Ship's AIs*, he thought.

Mason and Praxis were standing by command stations, out of their depth, both of them having reason to fear what Alacrity and Floyt might do. Constance was perched indifferently on the backrest of the captain's chair, eyes unfocused, running a metal talon along her outthrust tongue.

Dincrist was checking something at a console, not too far beyond. He turned, holding up his hand to show the massive signet ring he wore, its crest now flipped up to reveal a button trigger.

"And what will your victory be worth if I loose this cyberwipe?" Heart's father asked with a bland smile. Praxis and Mason stood to one side, their misgivings plain.

Dincrist held high the ring. "It will set off logic bombs in the Heavyset material I gave the Ship." He gave a fey grin. "One can hardly blame the Ship AIs; some of them go back nearly a century and are obsessed with Heavies data."

He brought a finger close to the button trigger. "I think you're bluffing, but if you're not, just stand where you are. If you don't call off the Sampson Option right now, I'll blank the White Ship's AIs and take the choice away from you. The Ship will be a helpless hulk, and we'll all go down to glory together."

But Alacrity was shaking his head, his slate-gray hair rippling. "What happens is, you sign over your shares to me. And Mason, there, does, too, and Praxis. Or we all go into the fire, and if you disbelieve me it won't be for long."

Constance hissed at him. "Stupid child! We *know* you're faking!"

"Oh, yeah?" Alacrity pointed to Praxis. "Ask him. He already knows how far I'll go. So does the baron." Baron Mason bided his time, letting no reaction show, but Praxis looked worried.

"Right down into Spica," Alacrity said mechanically.

"Very well! All right!" Praxis burst out. "Take whatever you want! Take my shares, they're yours! Only turn the Ship around!"

"*Silence!*" Dincrist thundered, red coming in like a weather front under his perennial tan.

"No, he's right," Mason yielded tiredly, measuredly. "Fitzhugh, we only have a little time to save ourselves. Turn this vessel around and my shares are yours."

"Gimme those shares first, and it's a deal."

"There's no *time!*" Praxis shrieked.

Alacrity turned to look down at the self-proclaimed Saint of the Irreducible I. "There's enough if you hurry." Alacrity glared at him. "Don't tempt me to kill you, 'cause *I really want to!*"

They all knew the techniques of transfer, and the bridge pickups constituted a transactions terminal. Dincrist yelled in rage and Constance spat resentfully, but Praxis transferred his shares to Alacrity. As far as the Ship was concerned, the transfer was valid, whatever the courts might say later.

And by the time these beauties get to a court, I'll be long gone with this Ship. Alacrity grinned to himself. *And the secret to Heavyset contact, maybe.*

"You're next," he told Mason.

The Baron had a fey smile on his face. "How I wish I'd killed you both! You, and Floyt there!"

"Some other lifetime, maybe," Alacrity allowed.

"Very well, then..."

Mason began the transfer procedure, too, but Dincrist, unable to bear anymore, sprang at him. Alacrity had expected the first attack to come *his* way; sometimes there was no figuring people.

Mason, half a head taller than Dincrist, was borne back by Dincrist's velocity. They rebounded from the systemry.

Alacrity charged down to break it up, get the ring away from them, and incidentally do some violent laying-on of hands. Anger had hold of him and he didn't hear either Floyt's yelled warning or Heart's, or realize that he'd be passing close to Constance.

He caught Constance's movement just as one jeweled nail sheath, envenomed sting extended, swung for his neck. Floyt had a split-instant vision of Langstretch injector kits like Gentry Standing Bear's, and knew the scuffle was a ruse to draw Alacrity into range so the Old Guard could pump him full of something that would compel him to revoke the Sampson Option.

But Alacrity was brought up short, making Constance miss, and hauled back out of range, overbalanced and rolled out of harm's way by Heart, who had a grip on one of his tasseled shoulderboards and the waist of his form-fitting britches.

She lost a slipper that rang on the deck as they got out of striking range. Floyt leapt in, swinging the Inheritor's belt like a war-flail, braving the raking talons, making Constance shrink back rather than risk getting herself brained.

In another moment Alacrity, Floyt, and Heart were back by the companionway hatch. Panting and mad-eyed, Constance sank claws into the backrest of the captain's chair, slicing it.

Mason and Dincrist, their gambit failed, had released one another. Alacrity opened the collar of his uniform jacket so he could catch his breath.

"Time's about up. C'mon." He snapped his fingers, opening his palm again for the suicide switch ring. "Hand it over! This Ship isn't yours! And while you're at it, you're going to sign over your shares to me."

Dincrist and Mason looked at each other. "Do like I say or I'll kill us all!" Alacrity howled at them. "You have nothing more to say about the White Ship! *Nothing ever again!* And I'm not bluffing."

Spica filled all forward displays. Dincrist looked at Alacrity with a vast tranquility that made Floyt fearful. "I don't chose to comply, Fitzhugh. Do what you will."

"You'll choose death?" Floyt demanded angrily. "For all of us? Even for your daughter?"

"No. Fitzhugh might, though."

Alacrity indicated Floyt and Heart with a toss of his head. "They already know I'm not going back on this. *I'm not going back to being what I was, understand?* Dying with the White Ship is a bigger, better death than I ever counted on. Look: you think you're at peace with an end like this? Dincrist, *I worked my whole life for it!*"

Dincrist and Alacrity stared at one another while ten seconds went by. Heart felt Floyt take her hand.

Dincrist closed the crest cap of his ring and slouched across the bridge, defeated, meaning to slump into the captain's chair. Floyt glanced to the Nonpareil's stoic face; it was impossible to gauge how much the scene was hurting her.

Alacrity moved toward Dincrist but kept an eye on Constance. "Uh-uh, Dincrist; you can't sit there!"

The Nonpareil put a hand on his shoulder but he ignored it. "That seat was supposed to be my father's! I'm not letting—*look out!*"

The warning came too late; Constance's claw was already at target—a different sting from the one she'd been ready to use on Alacrity—sinking into the side of Dincrist's neck. She was trying to get the signet ring the rest of the way off with fingers and teeth even while he was falling, her free hand-claws spread to hold off any who might try to interfere.

The flashing finger sheaths brought Alacrity up short and kept Heart back when she would've gone to her father's side. Floyt dragged Heart back, or she would've risked Constance's poisons, after a moment's hesitation, to try to save her father. Mason and Praxis stood frozen.

Constance sprang to stand by the captain's chair with a blissed smile and the ring high-held in her left hand.

Left hand.

That tiny oddity, in a hand-to-hand situation, set off alarm bells in Alacrity, because Constance set her right on her rump rather than keep it out on guard. Constance toyed with the destruct ring and fed on the reactions of the others on the bridge.

Alacrity couldn't help wondering what her right hand was really doing. He angled a bit, and caught, in a high-gloss power panel behind her, a reflection of Constance's fingers delicately retrieving a tiny device from the minimal V-garment.

Tachypsychia kicked in, making everything seem slow motion, giving him time for calm consideration. Since there were no firearms in the Ship, he had an instant, vivid realization what the device was.

Constance whipped it out and fired. Alacrity contorted in midair, limbs outflung, the very picture of agony, landing painfully. He slumped when he hit the floor. Constance lowered the little instrument and advanced on the fetal ball that was Alacrity, palming her gadget, right-hand claws at a sort of guard, left hand holding the ring. "I wasn't quite sure that would work on you." She giggled.

"Did that feel familiar, sweetie?" she said with a voice like a sugarbath. "Oh, dear, dear babies, let's talk about revenge!" One falciform sheath tip poised over the trigger button.

"This Ship comes to me now. Only a little sooner than I'd planned." She looked to Floyt. "And now it's time for *your* little jot to make *you* dance, pet—*ahh*!"

Alacrity had worked a leg-trip on her, lashing out to seize her wrists so that she couldn't strike with those talons, forcing them to the deck and managing to snap the crest cap shut against it, Constance yowling all the while like a scalded cat, losing the actijot control unit, which was useless because Van Straaten had removed Floyt's and Alacrity's jots.

Alacrity rolled sideways, tossing Constance off, diving to make distance. Coming up with the destruct ring and not a mark on him, he heard a nearby cry—Constance's, he thought.

Sibyl Higgins beat Floyt and Heart to the battle, catching Constance's wrists in some strange grip and exerting force with odd, wheeling movements of her elbows. Constance went down, wrists hanging at strange angles as she wept and screamed.

Dincrist's eyes were fluttering and he knew he had no time left. He smiled up at Heart as she held his head in her lap. "I want—I wish—" the father said, and he passed from life to death before he could get out another word.

Alacrity stood watching helplessly as Heart closed her father's eyes. He heard a commotion and the rest of the Interested Parties and their escorts arriving. He pocketed the ring and squared his shoulders.

"Fitzhugh, it's over," Sibyl Higgins barked. "Now cancel the Sampson Option."

"It's not quite over," he contradicted. "First, you're going to hand over your shares to me. And so are all the rest of you." He gazed up at an overhead holodisplay that showed nothing but the blue annihilation of Spica. "Wulf; Heart—everybody."

He brought his gaze down to the Nonpareil. He'd assumed, in just those few moments, what Heart had heard Calendar War vets refer to as "the hundred-mission stare."

He said, "Everybody, no exceptions! I'm not going through this kind of thing twice! After today, there's no more arguing. The White Ship does what my family meant her to do."

He looked at the gathered Interested Parties, not afraid of anything anymore, squaring away his captain's jacket. Perhaps his family's errors stemmed from too much compassion; if so, that would stop.

The magisterial-looking man took a half step in Alacrity's direction. "That would make you no better than *they* were." A hand gesture indicated Dincrist and his group.

Alacrity's face seemed about to shatter with emotion. "Don't you tell me what I am! You and you and all the rest of you screwed up this Ship and bottled up the best hope of the human race for *twenty-five years*!"

The words reverberated from the bulkheads, so loud they came in again upon themselves. Alacrity's teeth were locked, fists balled. "The Interested Parties had their chance and more chances, but *it's finished*! So now I'll do it myself, or I'll take this Ship down into Spica and somebody else can make a new, clean start."

He threw a quick look at the displays. They were all alight and the whole bridge rang with impending catastrophe. "And you have no more time to think it over. We're marginal as it is. Either sign your shares over to me or find some corner and make your peace. I couldn't stop you from thwarting what my family lived and died for, but I can stop you from ever doing it again. And I'm about to."

His stare fell on Higgins. "And there isn't even time for *you* to get that cancel code out of me."

He backed up all at once, stooping over the embryonic, weeping Constance, and yanked off several of those deadly fingernail sheaths, stepping back then, ready to use their poison, bringing his back up against a railing overlooking the various workstations. A moment's monkeying got one stinger forth.

"Ho, I think I need you right about now. Cover that side, will you?"

Floyt stayed where he was.

"Ho, dammit, I *need* you!" Alacrity tossed another fingernail sheath to Floyt. Floyt's arms were crossed; it bounced off his starched white shirtfront.

"No, Alacrity. It's not fair, what you're demanding of them. *And I'm not going to argue about your parents!* You're not special! None of us are! And you just can't treat people this way!"

Alacrity looked like somebody'd hit him a good one with a neurosap. Heart put her arm through Floyt's pointedly, saying nothing, watching. Wulf came shoulder to shoulder with her, Yester by his side. Higgins took up a subordinate post at Floyt's other shoulder and in moments the Old Guard and the New Faction had joined ranks against Alacrity Fitzhugh.

Alacrity looked at his only love and his only friend, and the rest of them, and the Ship around him. All his, for another few minutes, then starfire.

He locked eyes with Floyt, and Floyt, arms still crossed, said levelly, "And I *wasn't* lying about the causality harp."

Alacrity nodded, throat working, and started to speak three times before he got out a croak. "I never thought you lied. Ever." He took in a great chestful of air and let go a lifelong dream, staring at Heart the whole time, as she stared at him.

"Attention! Shareholder Fitzhugh, identify!"

"Shareholder Alacrity Fitzhugh, confirmed," the Ship replied.

"Cancel Sampson Option three. Return to Nirvana orbit." He licked salt off his upper lip and took courage in that Floyt and Heart were watching him with something a lot like compassion. *It's not every day you throw away your life's work . . .*

"Alert appropriate governmental agencies for rendezvous," he finished.

"Cancellation noted," the Ship spoke in the clear, exalted she-voice. "Deviation from Spican entry course no longer possible."

Alacrity's head snapped up toward the displays. If the White Ship had passed the point of no return, there was no way rescue could reach them and no way lifeboats or other small craft could ever get free of Spica's pull. The White Ship was the most powerful machine humans had ever built.

Alacrity sat himself down at the foot of the captain's chair and buried his face in his hands.

CHAPTER 20

UNEASY LIES THE HEAD

"MAYBE THERE'S SOMETHING WE CAN DO." FLOYT MADE a half step but didn't know which way to turn, surrounded by systemry he didn't understand and realizing that the Ship herself was doing everything there was to be done, which wasn't enough. Heart and the others rushed to control pozzes anyway, even Sibyl Higgins and those who, like her, knew little or nothing of starships.

"I didn't mean for this—" Alacrity started, then realized he was talking to everybody's back. He shut up and got up to go see if he could do something useful.

In the next three minutes they tried every operational command and dodge any of them could think of, and none of those was of any use. The Ship's interior was still cool, but that was an anomaly that would change in a nanosecond when the Ship's power and protection failed.

Alacrity went to Heart. She was there along with Floyt, who'd thrown his tail coat over her father, and held her even though she stood a head taller than Floyt and hadn't quite let herself cry. Floyt's Inheritor's belt gleamed against his Terran wondersuit.

Heart looked to Alacrity dispiritedly. "If you've got any of those famous ideas, this is the time for one."

"Wish I did."

Heart let go of Floyt and she and Alacrity put their

329

arms around each other. Alacrity looked up at a pickup. *At least we can pass along what we know.* "Attention! Open commo link to Nirvana, or nearest relay station." They could transfer some of the Ship's knowledge, for those who would take up the Precursor quest.

"No relay station within range in photospheric turbulence," the meticulous, maddening Ship's voice said. "Shall I attempt to hail nearest vessel once again?"

Floyt looked up suddenly. If a ship was within range when no relay station was, it must be close—which was impossible. "Query: *what* vessel?"

The White Ship answered, "Type unknown nonhuman vessel designation 'Heavyset,' which has been paralleling our course at distance approximately five thousand kilometers for thirteen point two five minutes Standard."

Floyt and Alacrity looked at each other, eyebrows trying to crawl up into their hairlines. It wasn't a fair contest because Floyt's had so much farther to go. Then both launched themselves at a commo terminal.

Wulf, Higgins, and the others were all trying to talk at once until the Nonpareil got them to shut up. "How d'you say 'SOS!' in Heavyset?" Alacrity was yelling at the Ship, ready to put his foot through something. He ordered, "Signal 'SOS,' signal 'MAYDAY,' and signal 'Fireman, Save My Child!'"

"No symbologies with those meanings appear to be available," the Ship said.

Alacrity gnashed his teeth. "Well, what symbologies *are*? How'd you get the Heavies here? How can we get them to save us?"

"Insufficient data," the Ship assured him. "Preliminary runs by subordinate communications and analysis AI's on Precursor/Heavyset symbology correlations resulted in the appearance of the Heavyset starship. All combinations have failed to elicit any further response. Heavyset starship still parallels our course."

"Um, so, what do we—" Alacrity was saying as he

almost got hit in the mouth by Floyt's Inheritor's belt. Floyt was swinging it under an optical pickup.

"You know *these* symbols?" He was thinking of the systemry in Hecate's Precursor site, and how it had saved Paloma and Alacrity and himself when it detected the belt.

"Some are recognizable, some not," the Ship allowed.

"Well, transmit the ones you recognize and try to transmit the ones you don't!" Floyt hollered. He looked to Alacrity. "Link up your proteus there, and send that Precursor music that got us in all that trouble with Hecate! *Snap to it!*"

Alacrity did. "Just what d'you think's gonna happen?"

Everyone was watching them. "I don't know," Floyt said. "Wouldn't anything be an improvement?"

"Maybe the Heavies are just curious to see us go *poof*!" somebody said.

"Then they're going to be rather well entertained, my dear."

"Or perhaps they don't even realize we're in danger," Wulf interjected. "Certainly, *they're* in none."

It was apparent that the Heavysets had some tricks the human race lacked, because one second the White Ship was falling into Spica and the next, she was falling *away* from it, without so much as a hiccup from the intertia-shedding fields or a squeak from the hull or internal structure.

"They're pulling us back up and out," Alacrity said, "or shoving or hoodooing or *something*."

The instruments registered the motion, but no detector or scrutinizer could offer any hows or wherefores.

"I wonder if they'll claim salvage rights on the ship," Floyt pondered, fingering his beard. "Or for that matter, on *us*?"

"As long as they didn't take it as a mating call." Alacrity frowned.

The Heavysets manifestly did not take it as anything of the sort; the White Ship was shifted to her Nirvana orbit, precisely where she'd been. The Heavyset vessel/worldlet returned to its station down near Spica, and no transmissions could coax any further response from it.

There were all manner of transmissions to the White Ship from Nirvana, the White Ship Company, the cops, Uncensored Network, and others. Among this new information were arrest warrants for Alacrity and Floyt, to be carried out immediately on adjournment of the board meeting. Piracy, credit fraud, attempted murder, inciting to riot, vandalism of a public accommodation, and much more were listed on the charge sheet.

Dincrist's body and the restraint-bound, incoherent Constance had been removed by Spican peace officers. The Spican government was about out of patience, sanctity of the board meeting or no. Alacrity and Floyt were in total accord as to their next area of endeavor: headlong flight.

"I'm sure we can have you both cleared in short order," Sibyl Higgins told them as they were about to duck out of the airlock and fire up the *Tramp-Royal*'s gig, and get moving. "If you'll stay, I'll stand by you in this matter."

"In the meantime, somebody'll kill us," Alacrity said sourly. "And we'll be innocent but dead. We prefer being live fugitives."

"We have more experience at that," Floyt explained. He and Alacrity were already dressed in nondescript working-breakabout shipsuits. With the White Ship inner hatch secure, the Ship amiably opened the airlock storage bin so they could retrieve their guns.

"Anyway, I'm not sure what's going to happen about Dincrist's shares and the others', or what the company'll do," Alacrity went on. "But what really counts is what the Ship figures she should do, and it looks like she's going to listen to this New Faction consensus. You sure couldn't do much worse than I did."

"I don't entirely agree," Higgins said. "And some day in the not-too-distant future now, this Ship will be ready to set forth. We shall need trained and seasoned personnel."

"Besides, Alacrity, you already have that pretty captain's suit," Heart added, running pale fingers through his hair, laughing.

It was nearly two full days since the Ship had been yanked back from the flames. Alacrity and Heart had spent as much of that time together in her quarters as they could steal away from crisis management and the other demands upon them. Those included his yearning to see more of the Ship, no matter how painful that was, and a few other matters he had to take care of when no one was watching, not even Heart. Alacrity had, as a matter of fact, just come from a transactions terminal.

The interlude had healed up what had gone wrong between them, made things dearer and deeper, made it, somehow, at once the same love and yet something new and better.

Now the Nonpareil slipped her arm around his waist, but Alacrity shook his head. "No, no; I'm not the captain of this ship."

Higgins looked vexed. "Come, come now! Just because you cannot make the rules you refuse to play the game? That is *infantile*!"

Alacrity sucked his thumb, nodding, then said, "There's more to it than that, Doc. Let's just say I'm finally convinced that I'm not—that it's not in the cards." He exchanged looks with Floyt.

"I hate to be the one to point this out, but time is pressing upon us," Wulf said. "The government is demanding cooperation and we really cannot refuse them much longer."

"All right, you both know how to get in touch with me," Heart told the two sidekicks for the third time. "And *please* use your heads and go to Bankroll and sign aboard the *Slocum*?"

The *Captain Joshua Slocum* was one of the biggest

ships in the Dincrist empire. She was being overhauled on Bankroll, outside Spican authority, for a voyage that would take her to the frontiers and beyond. Heart had given them letters of introduction guaranteed to get them comfortable berths under aliases.

"We'll think about it," Alacrity promised. But he wasn't so happy about the idea. For one thing, it could leave them terribly vulnerable to any enemies they might still have in the Dincrist organization who might get wind of the arrangement.

Heart almost punched him. She'd thought about joining them in their escape, but there was simply no way she could abandon the White Ship at this critical juncture. But the Spican writ, weighty as it was, didn't run far in terms of known space. The galaxy was big, and she knew Alacrity meant to be with her in it, whatever that took—as much as she meant to be with him.

Alacrity and Heart had a last kiss—a thousand wouldn't have been enough—and he and Floyt boarded the gig, Alacrity carrying his warbag and umbrella. He looked into the Nonpareil's eyes, and she into his, until the hatch closed completely.

Floyt let out a long yawn as Alacrity cast loose from the White Ship. Alacrity glanced aside at him. "You tired, too? What's *your* excuse?"

Floyt stretched, joints cracking. "With all those data terminals and info files? Guess."

"So you've been accessing. What for?"

"Well, there's all that Heavyset/Precursor stuff, and more Precursor data than at any other source: field reports, archeological tapes, military intel files—"

Floyt held up his new proteus. "All the really unique material is now duplicated in here."

Alacrity's brows flickered. "Go back, now; what do *we* care about Precursors? No more White Ship, at least not for me, remember?"

Floyt looked distinctly uncomfortable. "Yes, well—you know, I've been thinking, and the mere fact that you aren't Master of the White Ship doesn't mean that you can't unlock Precursor secrets. If you care to. Look here, you know more about them firsthand than perhaps anyone. Certainly it looks as though we're going to be doing a good deal of moving about for some time to come.

"Who's to say the White Ship is necessarily the key to it all? Who's to say the answers couldn't come from a couple of chaps like us, who get around a lot even if we do tend to travel bilgeclass? If we were diligent and perhaps a spot of luck came our way from time to time, as it's been known to?"

Alacrity had the gig moving at very low speed. "Hobart, just what is it you're getting at, here, please?"

Floyt gazed back through the cockpit dome at the White Ship. "I suppose you could say I have my own Grail now. Alacrity, remember in Hecate's Precursor lair? That genealogy, that incredible family tree of humankind? Linking every person who ever lived with every other!"

Alacrity answered slowly, "But Ho—I mean, I saw just a little of what was going on, but I guess Hecate didn't show Paloma or me what she showed you."

Floyt heaved a sigh. "It was miraculous; it was the most compelling Precursor thing I've ever seen. And somehow I'm going to recreate it."

"Why?"

"For what it *is*, I suppose. Besides, wouldn't it be a little harder to cheat someone or starve them or start a war with them if you could see how you were related to them? Just a *little* harder, at least? In some cases?"

"Hobart Floyt, you'll be burned in effigy and shot and stabbed and crucified and clapped in irons and strangled and spat upon and similarly inconvenienced the very first time you demonstrate this impossible thing you're proposing."

"Oh." Floyt's enthusiasm ebbed. "I . . . guess you're—"

"Where d'you think we should start?"

Floyt didn't know what to say, so he just nodded to himself, looking out at the stars. "I've got a little list," he sang at last, tapping his proteus.

"Great!" Alacrity said brightly. "First thing we have to do is get out of Spican jurisdiction. Y'know, it's a relief that you have a reason to really *want* to go off after Precursor secrets. Now we both do.

"Besides, I love Heart, but I really don't want to work for some *company* again."

"Perhaps we can start by tracking down the *Astraea Imprimatur*," Floyt suggested. "Janusz and Victoria would give us a hand, don't you think?"

But Alacrity was shaking his head. "Janusz and Victoria made vague arrangement with Heart to get in touch when the heat half-lifes, but word from them may not come for years."

Alacrity added, "They might even be worse off than we are. We'll have to figure out something else, and I think I know what. I can only imagine how very glad and grateful you must be to have a synergenius for a partner!"

"I suppose so, but there's something else you should know, Alacrity. I intend to find Paloma, as well. I love her."

"Good. That'd give me a chance to sort of make things up to the both of you, helping you do that."

Floyt scratched the underside of his chin. "And, um, there's another matter. I did some research on my Inheritor's belt—on the symbols on it."

The Inheritor's belts had been sent forth by the late Director Weir who, the two had come to understand, was privy to his share of Precursor lore, too. The belts had sigils, symbols, or whatever, in common, but many that were unique to the individual Inheritor.

"So?" Alacrity said.

"So the symbols that Hecate's demon-lover systemry found so interesting—that saved us, I guess—appear to mean the same thing as the words she yelled; I retrieved them from your proteus. Hecate, it turns out, was talking in her native tongue."

"Will you just *tell* me, so I can get back to flying this creampuff?"

Floyt settled back into the seat and looked at the stars. "The words and the sigils on my belt mean both, 'Strange Attractor, and *Attractor* of Strange Attractors.'"

Heart had helped the investigators as much as she could.

"Honest!" as she put it.

Somehow, those two fugitives from justice, Floyt and Fitzhugh, seemed to have either completely disappeared from the universe or temporarily evaded apprehension, depending upon whether the official talking was a law officer of low rank or high.

The investigators didn't push things too hard inboard the White Ship; the board and the White Ship Company still swung tremendous weight in the Spican system.

The Old Guard was being very meek and close-mouthed. Their voting status was returned to them, but Captain Dincrist's stock would remain inactive until Probate had sorted things out and the will was executed. It seemed likely Heart would inherit. The Old Guard wasn't in any frame of mind to offend her.

"There's still the matter of a final vote on some procedural questions," the Ship said to Heart at a certain point.

Heart looked around her at the bridge, striking a faint chime from one duraglaze slipper. "Why are you telling *me*?" Her father's shares might make her First Shareholder, eventually, but not yet. Up until a few seconds before, the Ship had been addressing Sibyl Higgins as First Shareholder, as the Ship had since Dincrist's death.

"In the absence of an elected chairman, First Shareholder shall function in that capacity," the aloof woman-voice cited. Heart suddenly thought that she could get to like that voice if it kept on saying things of good omen.

"As of twenty-two thirty this date, Ship time, with the activation of the transaction-of-record of Shareholder Alacrity Fitzhugh, also known as Shareholder Jordan Bowie," the Ship told her, "you are now First Shareholder."

The bridge dome came alive in displays. It took a few moments to put together what Alacrity had done. Wulf flashed his smile and patted the Nonpareil's hand. "He's transferred all Hecate's shares over to you. And it seems he's given you that one other share, his parents', too."

Higgins was taking it all in. "Heart, you'll have your father's shares as well, but I would say this makes things definite. You're the leader of the New Faction. You're the First Shareholder, but I warn you: I'll always speak my mind and vote my conscience!"

Yester was beaming up at the displays. "Whoever heard of such a gift before? Heart, he's given you the White Ship!"

Heart turned away so that they wouldn't see the tears brim up in her eyes. The tears weren't for the three hundred forty thousand shares but rather for the three hundred forty thousand and first.

The Nonpareil put most of the commo surveillance resources of the White Ship to work, doubly eager for word of Alacrity after she found his note—YOU'RE MINE AND I'M YOURS!—under her pillow. Ten hours into the search, when Spican authorities had been ejected from the Ship and most of the major problems were under control—when it had really come to her that this greatest and most advanced product of human genius and handiwork was hers to control and hers to answer for, with its implications of what the human race would be and should be—the Ship toned for her attention again.

Some subroutine had turned up a feature on the Uncensored Network.

Circe Minx stood outside her yacht, the *Tramp-Royal*, with her arm around the very wide shoulders of a fascinatingly ugly, tremendously powerful looking man a half meter and more shorter than she but far taller than the crowd that pressed round. The man had a blank look, but gazed up at Circe adoringly.

A rumorghoul named Salome Price, in plaid dermal frosting, was conducting the interview, standing on a lift platform.

"Mah plan, Salome, is to retell, as an artist, in song and dance and drama and even comedy, th' story of the long search: *The Circe Minx Chronicles: Lookin' fer th' Precursors!* We'll be showin' our audience many of the most famous sites and finds, along with the very latest ones and even some that've never been studied before!"

Salome was so thrilled with this second exclusive in mere days that her nipples grew prominent under the tartan frosting. "Circe, your trillions upon trillions of fans were overjoyed to hear that, in the wake of becoming your own woman again and jettisoning those two vomit bags, Floyt and Fitzhugh, you've found such fulfillment, as you've put it, in the arms of Gentry Standing Bear! But what gave you the inspiration for this *monumental* undertaking, which, I remind our Uncensored audience, has been underwritten by the Ministry for Educational Media?"

Circe shot the pickups a look with an EMP strong enough to overload unshielded components. "Well, darlin', ah've always wanted to tackle sumpthin' on what you call your higher intellectual plane. An' now ah have the time, resources, and expert advisors.

"Now, we'll be startin' off on this faraway planet called Lebensraum, where there's rumors of some *amazin'* finds!"

Circe shook a finger at the pickup, mock scolding. "An' y'all better believe me, ah'll work harder on this than ah evah worked on anything! An' when mah show debuts, Salome, hon, ah hope people'll see me in a different light. D'you think they will?"

The question was so straightforward that Salome almost dropped her veneer. "Wh—uh, yeah! That is, why not? That's right! Viewers, you heard it here first!"

The crowd was applauding. Heart couldn't see what the search AI was getting at. Then somebody yelled, "Kiss 'im, Circe!" and people whooped and whistled.

As Circe obliged them, a monumental buss with Gentry Standing Bear, the huge and lovely Minx shoulder disappeared out of focus, the pickup automatically ranging in across empty space to focus on two figures lounging around the main hatch of the *Tramp-Royal*.

Alacrity and Floyt leaned against the ship, watching the press conference with expressions that made Heart clap her hands together and mimic Alacrity's voice: "Let's get movin'! We know what we're doin'! Uh, Ho, what *are* we doin'?"

The Nonpareil dropped her hands to her sides. *Alacrity, what* are *you doing?* She dug out the note he'd left under her pillow and *thought* it at the image in the holo.

You're mine and I'm yours!

ABOUT THE AUTHOR

Brian Daley is the author of numerous novels of science fiction and fantasy, the most recent being *Jinx on a Terran Inheritance*. He also scripted the National Public Radio serial adaptations of *Star Wars* and *The Empire Strikes Back*. His whereabouts are subject to change without notice, but he favors Manhattan.